HIT AND RUN

HIT AND RUN

A Main Street Murder Mystery

Sandra Balzo

This first world edition published 2014
in Great Britain and the USA by
SEVERN HOUSE PUBLISHERS LTD of
19 Cedar Road, Sutton, Surrey, England, SM2 5DA

British Library Cataloguing in Publication Data

Balzo, Sandra.
  Hit and run. – (The Main Street mystery series)
  1. Griggs, AnnaLise (Fictitious character)–Fiction.
  2. Birthfathers–Fiction. 3. Heirs–Fiction. 4. Murder–
  Investigation–Fiction. 5. North Carolina–Social
  conditions–Fiction. 6. Detective and mystery stories.
  I. Title II. Series
  813.6-dc23

ISBN-13: 978-0-7278-8394-0 (cased)

All Severn House titles are printed on acid-free paper.

Severn House Publishers support the Forest Stewardship Council™ [FSC™],
the leading international forest certification organisation. All our titles that
are printed on FSC certified paper carry the FSC logo.

Typeset by Palimpsest Book Production Ltd.,
Falkirk, Stirlingshire, Scotland.
Printed and bound in Great Britain by
TJ International, Padstow, Cornwall

For Jerry, my soul
and Hart's inspiration

ONE

AnnaLise Griggs couldn't believe her ears. '*Who* did you say you intend to invite?'

Seated on the opposite side of his massive antique desk, Dickens Hart grinned. 'You're the wordsmith, my dear, but I do believe the proper pronoun in that question would be "whom."'

AnnaLise clenched her teeth. 'OK, *whom* did—'

Hart nodded toward a stack of papers between them. 'By now, you've probably already made a functional guest list yourself.'

Of course, AnnaLise thought, a mite dazed. After all, didn't every bastard child keep track of her philandering father's conquests? Notwithstanding, of course, her own mother, Lorraine 'Daisy' Kuchenbacher Griggs, who had raised AnnaLise with absolutely no help from the indisputable bastard across the desk.

AnnaLise raised an eyebrow. 'I'm sorry, Dickens. Did you say . . . "guest list"?'

'Yes.' Hart raked a hand through his wavy white hair, a perfected gesture combining impatience, arrogance and – mainly – vanity.

Dickens Hart had regularly penned 'Dear Diary' journals for his private amusement. And AnnaLise, under contract to compile them into a publishable memoir, had begun slogging, then just skimming, her way volume-by-volume. According to her birth father's many enthusiastic entries, he'd been quite the happening guy back in the seventies, especially after he'd opened White Tail Lodge, a North Carolina High Country rip-off of the Playboy Club concept.

Situated on Sutherton Lake like the current palatial mansion where they sat, the lodge had been a 'gentlemen's club,' featuring 'fawns' – essentially scantily-clad pseudo-Bunnies – supposedly to serve and entertain the clientele. Clipping after curled-corner clipping from local newspapers and glossy regional magazines showed Hart smiling down the lens as some young female's manicured fingers toyed with his shaggy and darker hair.

'You went through my journals,' Hart was now saying. 'You must have found my big black book.'

'You've given me at least a dozen boxes of journals, diaries and memorabilia,' AnnaLise protested. 'Not to mention digital files on computer disks from back when they still were floppy. How could I possibly—' She interrupted herself. 'Your *big* black book? Don't you mean *little* black book?'

Hart shook his head and held his palms about six inches apart. 'Big' – sliding his hands out another six inches – 'as in bigger, and even . . . biggest.'

What a pig, thought AnnaLise.

But said 'pig' *had* hired her for his memoir project, though admittedly before she knew he was her biological father. On an indefinite leave of absence from a reporter's job in Wisconsin while she tried to sort out her Sutherton mother's ongoing memory problems, AnnaLise was in no position to turn down a paying job.

Especially a *well*-paying job. One hundred thousand dollars as an advance, with a fifty/fifty split of royalties, should there be any. As the saying goes, money can't buy love. Or even respect. But, in this case, it could rent days – nay, weeks, if not months – of AnnaLise's professional time.

'I'm afraid I haven't come across this book yet,' she said, making a note. 'You say it's black?'

'I was using a half-truth to make a joke. And probably a bad one at that.' Hart shifted in his chair, at least having the decency to look uncomfortable, as though actually recognizing that he'd stepped over the line in conversation with a blood-child. 'It has a black-and-white speckled cover with my name on the front in a juvenile's handwriting.'

Wait a minute. 'You're talking about a student's composition book? Geez, Dickens, at what age did you start tallying—' AnnaLise waved away her own question. 'Sorry, none of my business.'

'Oh, but it is *exactly* that. You're writing my memoir, and even those early . . .' Hart put out his hands again, this time fingers splayed, '. . . "peccadillos" are a large part of the story. One might even view me as a bit of a hound.'

That struck AnnaLise as beneath the dignity of understatement. Even though she'd only skimmed through most of the handwritten journals so far, it was clear that the man had seen more tail than the proverbial last dog in a sled-team harness.

She said, 'As one progeny of your "hounding," I'm curious about something.' A pause. 'Do I have any litter-mates?'

Hart shifted again, his uncomfortable expression now approaching pained. 'Honest answer? None with your mother, Lorraine – or "Daisy," as I know you call her. But, otherwise, I'm not entirely sure. I was hoping you'd find any, if they exist.'

'And, as I started to ask you, invite them to dinner here in your rustic, waterfront cabin?' Horror at the idea made AnnaLise's tone rise half an octave.

'Actually, I thought a long weekend might be better, even optimum. With, of course, their respective mothers attending as well.'

'You do understand that you're out of your mind?'

'I do. Or at least that my invitation could be seen as evidence of my being such.' Dickens Hart suddenly appeared old. And very serious. 'Listen, my dear. As disingenuous as it might sound, I truly want to do right by any children I may have fathered, even if they are unbeknownst to me.'

'Unbeknownst?' AnnaLise echoed incredulously, not managing to hurdle the *what* to get to the equally curious question of *why* – or, more particularly – *why now?* 'Weren't you *there?*' Did the guy really think he was God, right down to the miracle of Immaculate Conception?

A frown. 'I'm just telling you that not one of the women I've been with ever told me about a pregnancy. Except, of course, for Ema Bradenham.'

Ema Bradenham, mother of one of AnnaLise's oldest friends, Sutherton mayor Bobby Bradenham. Ema was pregnant and needed money, making the rich "hound" an awfully tempting target. 'But wouldn't the other women, who actually became pregnant by you, have come—'

Now an awkward, if theatrical shrug. 'Your mother didn't.'

AnnaLise clenched her teeth again. Lorraine Kuchenbacher Griggs had made that 'one mistake' with her boss at the time, Dickens Hart, but never revealed her condition to him. Instead, she'd married Timothy Griggs, a good man who'd loved her. And loved Daisy's child, as well, despite the fact he knew AnnaLise couldn't have been his own.

Decision time. 'OK, I'll dig out this "black book" of whatever size, but I'll be damned if I track down your . . . girlfriends.'

'That's fine,' Hart said hastily. 'I'll have Patrick Hoag draft the letter of invitation.'

Patrick Hoag, Esquire, represented Dickens Hart and not three weeks earlier AnnaLise had accompanied her birth father to the law firm of Hoag, Christiaansen and Weir. There, Hart had insisted on legally acknowledging AnnaLise as his daughter, though not before a DNA test – at *AnnaLise's* insistence – which had come back as conclusive.

'So, I drop the notebook off with Patrick?'

'Ah, no. Given his law firm's gleeful fee increases every time it sends me an invoice, I see my money better spent by having Boozer track down the leads first. He can then provide Patrick with names and current mailing addresses for the actual letters themselves.'

Boozer Bacchus III was a broad-shouldered man of about sixty-five. AnnaLise had been told that he'd served Dickens Hart in one capacity or another since the opening of White Tail Lodge. Despite his name, or perhaps because of it, AnnaLise had never seen the man take a drink. The propensities of his grandfather and father – Boozers Sr and Jr – were, however, up for grabs.

With a sigh, AnnaLise jotted another note on her pad. 'OK, I'm to find your composition book and then give it to Boozer.'

Hart squirmed, his expression now clearly pained. 'Actually, I'd prefer that you study it first and generate a list of names with the most current, pertinent data for each. There are, I'm sure, certain personal . . . uhm, evaluations of my encounters that I'd just as soon not have come to his attention.'

AnnaLise had a tough time believing that Boozer had missed many of his boss's self-described 'peccadillos.' Maybe if Hart was so concerned about appearances, he should have kept his 'peccer' in his pants. 'But you don't mind that your own *daughter* sees these "performance grades"?'

'As you've just resurrected, AnnaLise, we are, after all, family.' A shadow crossed Hart's face. 'Though you might want to skip over any entries about Lorraine. And certainly don't pass them on to Boozer.'

All of a sudden, Mr Sensitive.

AnnaLise reminded herself of the medical bills stacking up on the Griggs' kitchen table for Daisy's initial battery of neurological tests. And how many actual dollars her daughter might need to pony up toward covering the rapidly accruing twenty percent of those costs that Daisy's insurance wouldn't.

So,' AnnaLise said, 'to sum up, I should give Boozer the "most current pertinent data" on each wom—' AnnaLise looked up. 'I assume they *are* all female?'

'Yes.' Hart's surprise at the question turned to a blush of apparently genuine embarrassment. 'I mean, I did once consider—'

'Sorry I asked,' AnnaLise said, to ward off any remainder of his answer. 'What do you consider to be "pertinent data" so far as Boozer is concerned?' Height? Weight? Bra size?

Her father looked relieved to move onto safer ground. 'My black-and-white notebook entries are, not surprisingly, chronological. You'll find names, dates and, uhm . . . places?'

AnnaLise looked up. 'As in cities, states?'

'Well, both. But more . . . specific details, too, such as rooms.'

'Hotel rooms?'

'Sometimes.'

AnnaLise began to wonder about the 'specific' aspect. Perhaps entries like *Tuesday, October 3, 1974: 6 p.m., linen-topped table in dining area; 9:05, bearskin rug before a roaring fire near*—

Hart cleared his throat. 'I think simply providing Boozer with each woman's name and the date and location of my being with her should be adequate. You'll find a cross reference of sorts in the back of the book.'

'Cross reference?' AnnaLise's sometimes accursed reporter's training made her reflexively ask cringe-inducing questions. Cringe-inducing for the questioner, at least.

'By state and city, as you guessed earlier. Oh, and when necessary, by country also.'

Now AnnaLise cleared her own throat and, not as successfully, her mind. 'Might you also have noted where a given woman was from? And her age, at least approximately?'

'So far as I knew at the time, yes. Which is just the kind of information Boozer should find helpful in searching for each, as opposed to—'

'How good you thought she was in bed?'

'Exactly.' AnnaLise's father, bless his lustfully dark heart, sounded relieved. 'As a journalist, you'll instinctively know what's important.'

Instinctively, AnnaLise thought, she knew the whole scenario stank to High Country heaven. 'You had a vasectomy at some point after I was conceived?'

'Yes, mid-eighties, roughly,' Hart said. 'But how could you – oh, from my journals. Of course.'

It hadn't been, though AnnaLise wasn't going to tell the man that. Her friend Joy Tamarack had the misfortune of being Hart's third – and last – wife more than a decade after his one-nighter with Daisy had resulted in AnnaLise's conception. It was Joy who had been the not-so-confidential source on the operation.

The fiery little blonde was also not the most discreet of people under any circumstance, but she really threw caution to the winds when it came to her ex-husband. Except, of course, for keeping hidden whatever tidbit of information Joy had on Hart that leveraged her high enough to receive pretty much whatever she wanted from him, starting with a handsome divorce settlement.

AnnaLise hoped to find out more about the 'tidbit' via Hart's own journals, though she was less anxious to reach 'My Vasectomy: The Inside Story.' Especially if Hart wrote about it as extensively as he had about every other aspect of his life so far. Even after thoroughly studying the first half-dozen spiral notebooks crammed with boyish scribblings about classroom and playground triumphs, AnnaLise had barely reached the young man in seventh grade. All the chronicling and introspection made her wonder how much validation the thirteen-year-old had received from *out*side his own head. Like, for example, from his parents.

Setting that question aside, as well, AnnaLise said, 'I raise the snip-'n-clip only because, after that procedure, you couldn't have impregnated anyone else. Do you want me to stop there?'

'Why?'

Either Hart was dense as a post or AnnaLise had become so. 'I thought you wanted to find your natural children. Therefore, once—'

'Oh, yes. Yes, I see what you mean.' There was a glint in the man's eyes. 'I have to admit, though, I wouldn't mind seeing *all* my old flames, whether technically baby-mamas or not.'

There was something very wrong about a near-septuagenarian warmly using the expression 'baby-mama.'

'Even your mansion here isn't big enough for that size of a crowd,' AnnaLise said, snapping her notepad closed and standing up. 'So, I'll find the appropriate information, pass it on to Boozer and he'll carry the project from there.'

Hart rose as well, rubbing an apparent crick from his lower back after their long, seated discussion. 'Of course, you and your mother must come. And I'll invite my ex-wives, as well as Bobby Bradenham, if only for old time's sake.'

'Old time's' being when Hart thought the young boy was his son. For his part, Bobby never knew the man living just across the lake thought he was his father. Good thing, given it turned out to be untrue, as confirmed by the paternity test Bobby had taken at the same time AnnaLise had hers. It was a push as to which of them was more disappointed by the results.

'That's very nice of you,' AnnaLise lied, moving toward the office door. 'And just when are you planning this soiree?'

'Actually, I've been thinking about that,' he said, following his acknowledged daughter into the mansion's two-story, marble-floored foyer. 'As I mentioned earlier, a long weekend seems appropriate, since some people will no doubt need to travel. On my tab, naturally. But there's plenty of room here, so most, if not all, can stay under one roof.'

AnnaLise had to admit the idea of being feted – along with any other illegitimate children, their mothers and assorted ex-wives and 'girlfriends' – at Dickens Hart's east-shore estate did have its attractions.

If only for people who loved watching sunsets and train wrecks.

'I do hope you'll come, AnnaLise,' Hart continued. 'Although I have to warn you: I intend to use the opportunity to conclusively identify my heirs and put them in my will.'

She stopped, dead-center on a huge marble tile. 'Meaning I'll be required to share my inheritance? No need to worry, Dickens. I don't want anything from you.'

'Like mother, like daughter,' Hart said, opening the closet across from the sweeping staircase to retrieve AnnaLise's jacket. 'I hope the other attendees aren't burdened by the same scruples, or Boozer may not be able to assure their attendance.'

'Don't worry. Patrick Hoag's invitation letter will tell them upfront that you're searching for heirs, right?'

'Wrong,' Hart said, now holding the coat spread so she could easily slip into it. 'But Boozer probably will. And should.'

'Ah.' AnnaLise turned as she buttoned up against the November wind beyond the main entrance. 'Might he also allow them to assume – mistakenly, of course – that you're in poor health?' As opposed to what appeared to be the real *why* behind the event: the aging, randy scoundrel wanted to revisit his conquests. Or, more accurately, have them revisit him.

Another theatrical shrug. 'Perhaps. I'll leave the optional tools of persuasion to Boozer.'

Shaking her head, AnnaLise reached to open the door before Hart could. A reprehensible bastard in every way save circumstances of birth, the man had the manners of a Sir Walter Raleigh.

She stepped out onto the veranda, flipping up the collar of her jacket. 'You aren't just out of your mind, Dickens. This "reunion" of yours can only stir up trouble.'

'I know that, and rest assured Boozer is of the same opinion. However, we are talking about *my* life. And even if I can't change the way I've lived it, I do intend to provide for my progeny, as I will for you. None of us – not even me – is getting any younger.'

Supressing a smile at the God-like 'not even me,' AnnaLise started down the steps, reaching the circular drive before she turned back. 'Much as I hate to admit it, Dickens, I wouldn't miss your get-together for the world.'

He winked over a sly smile. 'It will be an event, I can promise you that.'

AnnaLise had her hand on the door handle of her mother's old Chrysler before she realized Hart hadn't given her any dates for his soiree. 'So, when might all this take place?'

'I've just decided while we've been talking,' he said. 'It'll be on Thanksgiving weekend. That way people can arrive Wednesday night or even the next morning. We'll have a gourmet feast of turkey and all the trimmings on Thursday, allowing everyone to stay on afterwards and enjoy the grounds here before leaving Sunday to travel home.'

But his mention of the holiday had slammed into AnnaLise Griggs like a sledgehammer – or, better, a meat mallet – to her chest. She managed to croak, 'Thanksgiving?'

'And I'm hoping we'll *all* have a lot to be grateful for.' With the sly smile virtually plastered on his face, Dickens Hart, self-appointed Emperor of the High Country, waved haughtily before disappearing into his hard-won palace.

TWO

'Does your mother know about this, AnnieLeez?' Phyllis 'Mama' Balisteri – Daisy Griggs' best friend and, after Timothy Griggs' death, AnnaLise's second mother – was shaking a crooked finger at the girl. 'Does she know you're gonna spend your first Thanksgiving home in ten years with that rich retrobate you've started calling "Daddy"?'

AnnaLise, sitting red-faced in the 'family' booth of Mama Philomena's restaurant, didn't bother to tell Phyllis the word was 'reprobate.' Nor point out that the calendar had turned just seven, not ten, years since she'd been home in Sutherton for Thanksgiving. To do so would only be splitting hairs, and besides, AnnaLise had long ago given up on correcting Phyllis. Even the older woman's mispronunciation of the younger's first name as 'AnnieLeez' rather than 'Anna-*lease*.'

But the reporter did intend to set one thing straight. 'I don't call him "Daddy," or even "Father." He's just "Dickens" as far as I'm concerned. Besides, Daisy—'

'And that means what, can you tell me?' Phyllis interjected. 'Why, you call your own *mother* by her first name.'

At least that was true, though 'Daisy' itself was actually a nickname. AnnaLise had taken to calling Lorraine Kuchenbacher Griggs that instead of 'mom,' 'mommy' or 'mama' because, according to the then five-year-old, her mother 'looked like a daisy,' the halo of curly yellow hair like petals around the center of a tanned face.

It had been a comforting fiction for the little girl as her father – *real* father still, in her opinion – lie in a hospital bed slowly dying. Even so young, AnnaLise knew she didn't have the power to make Timothy Griggs well, but she could turn her mother into a flower. The nickname stuck and, quite frankly, simplified things, since AnnaLise also had a surrogate 'Mama' in her mother's lifelong friend.

Phyllis Balisteri had inherited the cozy handle from her own mother, Philomena, when the older woman died, leaving Mama Philomena's, a landmark on Sutherton's Main Street, to her daughter. The only complication? Philomena had been so busy cooking for all of Sutherton and its tourist visitors that she'd neglected to pass the craft of traditional Italian cooking on to the next generation, resulting in Phyllis subsisting on convenience food while all sorts of other folk savored Philomena's made-from-scratch delicacies.

After a few unsuccessful attempts at replicating the Italian classics her mother had never reduced to actual, written recipes, Phyllis had resorted to what she knew: down-home dishes featuring the likes of Campbell's mushroom soup and Bisquick baking mix, Philadelphia Cream Cheese and whatever else one might find on a grocery shelf.

In fact, on the booth tabletop next to AnnaLise was Phyllis' trilogy of inspiration: *Best Recipes from the Backs of Boxes, Bottles, Cans and Jars, 1979; The Kraft Cookbook, 1977; and Favorite Brand Name Recipe Cookbook, 1981.*

All of AnnaLise's life, she and Daisy had helped out in the restaurant, just as Phyllis had in Griggs' Market until it closed the prior year. AnnaLise had grown up bouncing between the two of them – the older women as well as the business establishments that provided both a living and a way of life for all three of them.

That explained why AnnaLise was now seated at the 'family booth' amongst the cookbooks, menu boards and dry-erase markers as a line of patrons waited outside for tables. It was also why the twenty-eight-year-old had to convince Phyllis to amend the unconventional family's Thanksgiving plans, as well as her own mother.

Who – or 'whom' – truth to tell, AnnaLise hadn't even informed of Hart's holiday weekend invitation yet.

Silly girl. She'd thought that Mama might be the easier of the two to start with, at least regarding the reunion.

'Dickens is inviting Daisy,' AnnaLise told her. 'And you, too, of course.'

That last sentence was a fib, unless Phyllis Balisteri's name was to be found in Hart's Black Book, which AnnaLise dearly hoped would not prove to be the case. Regardless, though, as the daughter of all three by nature or nurture, AnnaLise had the clout to make the invitation happen, especially given her new assignment as the keeper of the soiree's invitation list, such as it was.

Phyllis visibly softened. After so many years of serving other people Thanksgiving dinner at the restaurant, maybe an invite somewhere else was unexpectedly appealing. 'What's this shindig about again?'

AnnaLise considered soft-peddling, so Phyllis wouldn't make a scene. On the other hand, it was important that AnnaLise get the restaurateur on her side and, as a result, Daisy as well. And that would happen only if Mama's interest was piqued.

Her prurient interest, that is.

'Hart wants to invite all of his former lovers for the weekend.'

Phyllis' eyes went wide, her mouth dropping open. Nothing escaped, though, except a 'No!' which sounded more like a thrilled gasp than a dictionary word.

'Yes.' AnnaLise was nodding. 'But we're shortening the list to just those with any children he may have fathered by them.'

'Oh, dear.' Now Phyllis looked unhappy.

Had AnnaLise lost her or was there yet another Sutherton secret revolving around Dickens Hart and his sex life? 'What?'

'Oh, nothing, but . . . doesn't that mean you'll have to split the retrobate's fortune once he's on the wrong side of the grass?'

AnnaLise sat back. 'Mama, I don't want Hart's money. We've gotten along fine on—'

'Whether you want it or not, you're his only blood, leastways that I know of for sure. What with your mother's memory spells and all, you never know. We may need that money.'

We. The mothers-and-child union had always seemed comforting. Now it carried a faintly conniving thorn. 'I thought you hated Dickens Hart.'

Phyllis shrugged. 'Doesn't mean I can't like his money. Or what turns into yours, eventually.'

This was a new wrinkle. And a fresh side of Phyllis, one AnnaLise could incorporate within her reunion campaign. 'Dickens wants to do right by me and all his heirs.'

'So there *are* others?' Mama asked as a couple passed them on their way to the front counter to pay.

'None confirmed yet. And there won't be for at least a couple of weeks.'

'Thanksgiving.' Phyllis was stroking her chin.

'Exactly. Now, think about it. Don't you want to be there? Don't you think Daisy should be there, too? Meaning the both of you with *me*, protecting my interests?'

The 'ring-for-service' bell next to the cash register sounded. Twice.

Phyllis ignored it, except to raise a palm toward the front counter. ''Course you should be there, AnnieLeez. In your lawful place, by your father's right hand. And Daisy and me, we'll be there, too, aside you.'

Ahh, the sweet smell of success. And tuna noodle casserole, if AnnaLise was any judge of the odor wafting from the kitchen. 'Perfect. Whither thou goest, Daisy will, too.'

The bell sounded a third time.

'Hold your horses,' snapped Mama over her shoulder. 'Now, AnnieLeez, you shouldn't try to get around your mother like—' A thought seemed to strike the older woman. 'You know, I have this restaurant to consider. What time will we be eating on Thanksgiving, do you suppose?'

'It's still up in the air. People should be arriving Wednesday night and Thursday morning, and Hart is inviting everyone to stay the weekend. Or at least, that's his plan.'

'The whole long weekend?' Phyllis' eyes narrowed. 'Up in that big house?'

AnnaLise nodded.

'Bet he has servants, Dickens Hart.' Mama was gazing off into the distance.

'I've only seen Boozer Bacchus, but I assume Dickens has someone else to clean and so on.'

'Oh, I'm sure,' Mama said. 'A big place like that doesn't run itself. I'm seeing a real opportunity for an entry-penner like me to appreciate how everything runs.'

'Entrepre— Oh, never mind. Sounds like you want to stay over.' AnnaLise had been thinking the three of them would attend Thanksgiving dinner, then return home to post-mortem the event. Maybe go back again as visitors on Saturday or Sunday. But Phyllis obviously had more in mind. 'What about the restaurant here?'

The 'entry-penner's' eyes fell, then came back up, shining brightly. 'No problem to close down for the holiday itself. And the whole weekend falls in our quiet time anyway, what with the pretty leaves on the ground from that last hard rain and its wind. No snow for the skiing yet, so our winter tourists—'

The bell interrupted again. One, two, three, a nearly unimaginable *four* times. And hard, like a fist was pounding on it.

Phyllis Balisteri more grunted than sighed as she began sliding out of the family booth. 'That invitation, now – you respond civil-play to it, AnnieLeez. We're entitled to a break – all three of us.'

THREE

'I'm still not sure this is a good idea,' Lorraine 'Daisy' Kuchenbacher Griggs said on the Wednesday before Thanksgiving.

Mother and daughter were in Daisy's bedroom on the second floor of the two-story building she'd lived – and worked – in most of her life. The storefront that had been Griggs' Market took up one-half of the ground floor, its entrance fronting diagonally on the corner of Main Street and Second. That space was now rented to young Tucker Stanton and had been transformed into a coffeehouse/nightclub called Torch.

Around the corner on Second Street, you'd find the entrance to the Griggs' over-and-under apartment. The door led directly into the kitchen of what to others might seem like an unconventional living space, but AnnaLise just called it 'home.' At least, she had until she'd gone away to college in Wisconsin, returning only for short visits.

And even those, as both Daisy and Phyllis liked to remind her, had become sporadic at best.

'I know it's my first Thanksgiving here in years,' AnnaLise said as Daisy picked through her lingerie drawer. 'But look at it this way. You won't have to cook. According to Boozer Bacchus, Dickens Hart has brought in some high-powered chef from Las Vegas for the weekend.'

Her mother snorted, turning from the drawer with what looked like a very expensive – and skimpy – thong in her hand. 'A chef – I can't wait for Phyllis to hear that. Besides, you know full well that I never made a holiday dinner. Thank the Lord, that's always been at the restaurant.'

And, therefore, a supermarket-case turkey with pop-up timer, stuffing from a box, and canned green beans and mushroom soup, topped with crunchy French-fried onions. Also canned.

None of which AnnaLise could ever remember sneering at.

'. . . oyster stuffing,' Daisy was saying, 'which they'll call "dressing," of course. And maybe fancy cranberry-orange relish. I'm sure this chef—'

'Cranberry-orange relish?' AnnaLise interrupted, nearly reconsidering the campaign to shepherd her two mothers to Hart's mansion for the holiday. Even after leaving home, AnnaLise insisted that *her* Thanksgiving berries be jellied and capable of slithering like a short, squat snake from can directly onto plate.

Tradition was, after all, tradition.

'Oh, I'm sure it'll be a fine meal.' Daisy picked out a few more lacy frills and dropped them into her overnight bag. 'But it won't be Thanksgiving.'

'Is that why you think our going is a mistake?' Not for the first time, AnnaLise reflected on the fact that Daisy – at age fifty – had an inventory of lingerie far sexier than AnnaLise did at twenty-eight.

Given they were leaving late that afternoon to spend a long weekend with her mother's one-night stand, along with his other former lovers and assorted ex-wives, it didn't seem to be the time to ask about the origins of the underwear collection.

Either that, or perhaps the perfect time to ask, though AnnaLise was damned if she would. Way too much information was to be had and, on that front, the last two weeks had been tough enough.

She'd finally found Hart's 'Big Black Book' and dutifully – if gaggingly – gone page by page, recording 'pertinent data' on each woman listed.

In total, there were sixty-three possibilities BV – or Before Vasectomy – that she'd passed on to Boozer Bacchus. Amazing, but then AnnaLise had honestly expected worse, or probably 'better,' from Hart's point of view – given the man's self-proclaimed reputation as a 'hound.'

There were further encounters, mentioning even more females, but the descriptions were pretty sketchy. Sketchy, that is, in the completeness of information Hart had provided. AnnaLise resisted judging the character of his conquests, as God knew both Daisy and she harbored their own glass-house problems in that regard.

Hart had been right about Bacchus' investigative abilities, though. Boozer and his 'emissaries' had been successful at tracking down nearly eighty percent of his boss' encounters. How they'd winnowed those down from there to focus on just those who may have the potential heirs, AnnaLise didn't know. But she had been told that at least three of Hart's former lovers would be joining them for Thanksgiving and bringing along their respective flesh-and-blood tickets in the legacy lottery – two boys and a girl.

'. . . powder keg.'

AnnaLise, who'd been sitting on her mother's bed lost in thought, looked up. 'I'm sorry, Daisy. What were you saying?'

The older woman sighed, then zipped up her bag. 'I was just answering your question about why I think this is a bad idea. However, that's neither here nor there. We're committed.'

'No, but we should be,' AnnaLise said. '*Committed*, I mean.' She rolled her eyes and stood, too. 'Come on, let's get this party started.'

FOUR

The plan was for AnnaLise to drive the three of them in Daisy's Chrysler to Dickens Hart's estate. Even if AnnaLise's own Mitsubishi Spyder had been big enough to fit the trio and their luggage, two months earlier that beloved convertible had met an untimely – not to mention violent – end on a mountain road.

'Can't say this place has been boring,' the dual-daughter muttered, moving the gearshift into reverse so she could inch the car out of the old and narrow garage her mother shared with their octogenarian neighbor, Mrs Peebly.

'It was before you came back,' Daisy muttered in reply, alternating glances between her own and AnnaLise's side window. 'When are you going to buy a new car?'

'Getting tired of my using yours?' Safely out of the garage, AnnaLise stepped on the brake before pressing a button on the remote to close the garage door.

'Getting tired of you dinging my side mirrors, that's for sure.'

'Side *mirror*, singular. Besides,' AnnaLise struggled to pay attention as the garage door refused to close, 'I don't know why you need a car this size in the first place. It's too big for the mountain roads and barely fits into the garage.'

'It's only a mid-size,' her mother said. 'You should have seen the land-yachts your grandfather managed to squeeze through these doors.'

Speaking of which, AnnaLise stabbed at the remote again. 'Why isn't this thing working?'

'Sorry, dear, I forgot. I had to pull out the doo-hickey this morning to open it.'

The 'doo-hickey' being the cord that hung above each car's space and allowed a person to disengage the automatic garage door openers that AnnaLise had had installed at some expense and one gigantic helping of aggravation from both Daisy and Mrs Peebly.

'You . . .? Why?' AnnaLise put the Chrysler into drive and pulled forward to the curb.

'The electricity was off, and I needed to go to the store.'

'It was? The power, I mean?' AnnaLise frowned, trying to imagine her tiny mother hitching herself up on the car to reach the cord. 'I didn't notice.'

'The house was fine,' Daisy said, opening the passenger door. 'I'll get the door.'

'Oh, no you won't,' AnnaLise said, swinging the driver's side open as well. 'That thing weighs a ton.'

'I'm fifty, not a hundred and fifty, and you and I are the same height,' her mother said. 'If I can lift the thing I can certainly lower it.'

'But—'

Too late, her mother was pulling on the garage door, which rolled down with a thud, nearly catching Daisy's foot like a guillotine for toes.

'They had to take the springs off when they installed the automatic opener,' AnnaLise explained as Daisy climbed back in.

'More trouble than it's worth. And I recall telling you not to bother in the first place.'

She had indeed, as had Mrs Peebly even more vociferously. In fact, AnnaLise wouldn't put it past the older women to have sabotaged the garage's electricity to unfairly advance their point of view.

When AnnaLise had decided to have the door installed, she'd intended to be safely back in Wisconsin on her reporter beat while the cranky Mrs Peebly came to terms with the technology. But AnnaLise's month-long leave of absence to deal with her mother's troubles – and to *not* deal with her own, up north – had stretched to nearly twelve weeks now.

With Daisy safely back in the car, AnnaLise pulled the hulking Chrysler away from the curb and to the stop sign at the corner. Turning left onto Main Street, she promptly pulled into an angle parking spot on the beach side of the road across from Mama Philomena's.

'Spooky, isn't it?' Daisy said, looking out the car's rear window toward the restaurant.

AnnaLise nodded, taking in the battened-down shades of the restaurant and the hand-drawn 'Closed 'til Monday' sign behind the plate-glass window. The two-foot-high letters overhead that usually spelled out Mama Philomena's in green neon were dark. Three p.m. on a Wednesday and the place was shut up tight. 'Spooky doesn't begin to capture it.'

'In all these years,' Daisy said slowly, 'I can't remember Mama's ever being closed for an entire weekend, much less a five-day one.'

'Well, then she certainly does deserve a vacation.' AnnaLise tapped the horn to signal to Phyllis that they were waiting. While they all had gathered regularly in both the restaurant and Griggs Market when it was open, Mama guarded her privacy to the edge of zealotry. AnnaLise could count on her thumbs the number of times she herself had actually entered the small apartment behind the restaurant.

'Deserves a vacation, yes,' her mother said. 'But that's entirely different than taking one. I don't understand why Phyllis . . . well, she kind of invited herself along, now, didn't she?'

'To be fair, I included her. I figured she'd be able to convince you to come to Hart's shindig.'

'Did you think I'd let you go by yourself?' Daisy asked, crinkling her sun-freckled nose.

'No, I thought you'd guilt me into *not* going.'

'AnnaLise. Of all people, you should know better than to turn a noun into a verb,' her mother scolded as they saw Phyllis step out of the side entrance to her apartment with a piece of luggage and turn to lock her door. 'I would *shame* you, not guilt you.'

As an aid toward keeping her mother's mind sharp, AnnaLise had convinced Daisy to oversee the town's blog. It was a responsibility the older woman was taking exceedingly seriously.

'I've created a monster,' the journalist muttered as she climbed out to open the sedan's driver's-side rear door.

'Might as well have walked clear around the corner to your place,' Mama groused, 'you making me cross traffic like this.'

AnnaLise stepped out into the lane that separated the business side of Main Street from the small public beach. 'What traffic? You said yourself that November is nearly the only time of year we have the town to our—'

'Phyllis, is that a *carpet*bag?' Daisy interrupted as her life-long friend derricked herself into the rear seat.

'I found it buried in my attic,' Mama said, settling the thing on her lap. 'God knows what my ancestors did to the Yankee who'da been carrying it.'

'Wherever they put him, he can't smell as bad as that thing does,' Daisy said, wrinkling her nose. 'AnnaLise, why don't you put it in the trunk?'

Her daughter went to reach for it then backed off. 'With our luggage?'

Daisy's eyes narrowed, probably thinking about her expensive lingerie. After all, what woman wanted her knickers smelling of mothballs and worse?

'Oh, don't make such a fuss, you two,' Phyllis said. 'It's a short ride and I'll be keeping my traveling companion right here next to me, thank you very much.' She reached out and pulled the door shut. Hard.

With a shrug, AnnaLise climbed behind the wheel, rolling down the window as she did. The distance between 'downtown' Sutherton and Hart's estate might be short as the crow flies or boat sails, but approach-by-auto took a bit longer.

'I don't understand why, all these decades after the Scout Camp closed down,' AnnaLise said as she slipped the gearshift into reverse once more, 'we still don't have a road that parallels the east side of the lake, like on the north, south and west.'

'Two words,' Daisy started, and then interrupted her own self this time. 'You're not going to back all the way across the road to turn around, are you?'

'AnnieLeez, this here's angle-parking,' Phyllis chimed in. 'And you're at the wrong angle. You have to go round the block to head the other way.'

Their daughter willed herself not to lift her face toward the sky and let out a primal scream. Picking Mama up on the restaurant's side of the road, AnnaLise would have had to execute the very same maneuver about which she was now being scolded. 'Don't be silly,' she said, continuing to back up. 'There's nobody—'

Eeeeeeeee . . . whoop, whoop, whooooop . . .

'Told you,' the two older women chorused, as though they'd been spending their leisure hours practicing the chant.

The window already being down, AnnaLise didn't have to lower it. 'Afternoon, Chu—'

But it wasn't AnnaLise's high-school flame, Police Chief Chuck Greystone, who swung open the cruiser's driver's-side door and stepped out – it was the mayor. And there was a passenger in the front seat beyond him.

'Bobby Bradenham,' Phyllis piped up from the back, 'whatever are you doing in that police car? The job of mayor isn't enough to keep up that big house of yours now that Ema's not around to put the squeeze on Dickens Hart?'

AnnaLise saw Bobby flush, even as Daisy turned to her childhood friend. 'Shame on you, Phyllis. The boy not only just lost his mother—'

'God rest her soul,' Phyllis interjected as she made the sign of the cross. Even less a papal person than she was a people person, Mama nonetheless enjoyed dusting off the occasional ritual.

'Ema Bradenham's not dead,' AnnaLise reminded her.

'She is to me.' Phyllis settled back into the seat, her arms crossed.

'But Bobby's had to adjust to a whole new family,' Daisy continued, unfazed. 'The Smoaks, of all people.'

The mayor cleared his throat. And uncomfortably, at that. 'Umm, that's just what I was going to—'

'Gotta be uncomfortable, that's true.' Phyllis hadn't stayed quiet long. 'What with the fact that Bobby is having sexual relations with his own father's widow these days.'

AnnaLise felt her eyes go wide. 'Mama!'

'No, Phyllis is right about that, technically speaking,' said Daisy. 'Though it's not anywhere near as bad as it sounds. Nobody knew that Rance was his father when Kathleen and Bobby took up.'

'After Rance's death, thank the Lord.' Another sign of the cross from the hit-and-miss Catholic. 'Kathleen should be thanking her lucky stars that the womanizing drunkard she had the misfortune of marrying is dead and she now has a man like Bobby – stepson or not.'

The mayor didn't look pleased at the awkwardly phrased compliment.

'We're on our way to Dickens Hart's shindig,' AnnaLise said in a weak attempt to change the subject. 'Are you coming?'

Bobby shook his head. 'Can't. Rance's father—'

'The very tree that rotten apple didn't fall far from,' Phyllis opined.

'Now what kind of tail-first sentence is that?' Daisy demanded, twisting around to face her friend. 'I keep telling you: subject, verb, direct object. Rance – the rotten apple – didn't fall far from the tree, meaning his equally shady dad—'

'Roy Smoaks?' AnnaLise was peering past Bobby toward the man in the passenger seat of the squad car.

'That's the one,' Daisy confirmed. 'The most power-hungry chief we've ever had, though Rance was a close se—'

'No.' AnnaLise pointed.

Daisy waved for her daughter to sit back so she could see past her into the marked car. 'Roy Smoaks?'

'That's what I said . . . ouch!' AnnaLise yanked her hair out from under Mama's hand, the older woman having grabbed the driver's headrest to lever herself higher for a closer look.

Roy Smoaks – Rance Smoaks' father and, as a result, Bobby Bradenham's newly discovered grandfather – doffed his Miami Dolphins ball-cap from his seat in the car. 'Afternoon, Phyllis, Lorraine. Good to see you again.'

Bobby seemed surprised by the graciousness of the greeting, especially given the grammar lesson Daisy had just directed to Mama, with Roy as bad-apple illustration. 'Like I started to say, Roy came up from Florida for the holiday.'

'Had to see the new addition to the family,' Smoaks said, leaning forward to see past that new addition at the wheel. 'What with Thanksgiving and all.'

AnnaLise nodded politely, not knowing quite what to say about this development. Until three months ago, Roy Smoaks had simply been Sutherton's retired police chief, and not a very popular one, at that. Now, as it turned out, he was also Bobby's grandfather.

Forced to step down at sixty-five, Roy had groomed his son, Rance, to take over the office. Four years later, though, a shake-up in town government led by Dickens Hart, whose plans to redevelop the prime land where the defunct White Tail Club stood were being blocked, signaled the end of the Smoaks' dynasty and the appointment of a new chief, Chuck Greystone.

Chuck and AnnaLise had dated in high school, before he realized – or admitted to himself – that he was gay. AnnaLise had already moved to Wisconsin by the time Chuck was named chief, but she'd heard the appointment was bitterly opposed by the Smoaks, who'd attempted to oust the new chief. The mud-slinging had had nothing to do with ability and everything to do with Chuck's sexual orientation. And now here was one of the 'slingers' dirtying the chief's car. 'Where's Chuck?'

AnnaLise colored up as Bobby cocked his head at what had to seem like a non sequitur, given that even he, her oldest friend, couldn't read her mind. 'I mean, since you're driving the . . .' she waved vaguely toward the 'Sutherton Police' logo on the side of the cruiser.

'Oh, that,' Bobby said. 'I drove Chuck and his mother to the Charlotte Douglas International. His personal car wasn't big enough for them and their luggage, and neither was mine.'

'As luck would have it, my flight was arriving just as theirs was pulling out, so Bobby here could kill two birds with one stone.' Roy, who had to be in his seventies, winked at AnnaLise. 'And you, pretty lady, are . . .?'

Legend was the Smoaks males came roaring out of the womb with facial hair and a sex drive. Apparently they limped toward the grave the same way.

'You know my daughter, AnnaLise,' Daisy snapped.

'My, my. Sure grew up pretty,' Smoaks said appreciatively.

'You'll do well to keep your hands – and eyes – off her.' Phyllis let go of the headrest abruptly, sending it snapping AnnaLise forward again.

The journalist rubbed the back of her head. 'Where are Chuck and his mother going?'

'Dublin,' Bobby said. 'His—'

'Ireland?' This from Daisy.

'That's the one.' Bobby seemed relieved by the change of subject. 'His mother still has family there, though she'd never visited before now. Given how quiet it is in Sutherton late November into mid-December, I encouraged Chuck to go now. His mom's not getting any younger.'

Chuck was Irish on his mom's side and Cherokee on his deceased dad's, resulting in the blessed combination of green eyes and strong facial features.

'That's wonderful,' AnnaLise said. 'How long will they be gone?'

'Two weeks,' Bobby said.

'Two weeks?' Phyllis echoed.

'Coy Pitchford will be in charge during his absence,' the mayor assured them. 'With the county for backup, of course.'

Coy was a good guy, but it was his wife and fellow officer, Charity Pitchford, who, in AnnaLise's experience, had the real brains in the couple. Still, in the department Coy outranked Charity, so that, as Mama would say, was that.

'Wouldn't have found me out of my town, much less the country, for two weeks,' Roy grumbled. 'Not when I was chief.'

'I'd have paid for him to go myself,' the voice behind AnnaLise piped up.

Bobby, always the diplomat, looked like he'd already debated the subject – perhaps the whole two-and-a-half hours back from the airport in Charlotte. He held up a hand. 'Enough, Roy. You're not in charge here anymore.'

Smoaks sat up straight. 'Well, now, aren't we high-and-mighty? Best remember, boy, that *you're* not Sutherton ar-is-to-cra-cy no more, neither.'

AnnaLise rose to her friend's defense. 'No matter what the gossips said,' she worked at keeping her eyes from flicking back toward Phyllis, 'Bobby never believed he was Dickens Hart's—'

'No matter,' Smoaks interrupted. 'Ema Bradenham put on airs, too, living in that big house she named after herself and acting like she was better than the rest of us. And, as it turns out, she wasn't.' He grinned at Bobby. 'Though that there is water over the dam. Right, boy?'

The mayor didn't respond but stood, jaw clenched, staring at his shoes.

AnnaLise once again opened her own mouth, but Roy Smoaks apparently wasn't done flapping his. 'Now, as for King Dickens Hart, I heard tell of this party for his bastard offspring all the way down to my condo in Florida. If I'da known we were invited—'

'*You're* not invited,' Bobby said between tight lips. 'And I'm not going.'

'I reckon that's up to you, but I'm thinking we'll have a bird's-eye view from across the lake just the same and it sure does sound interesting.' Disappearing momentarily, Roy Smoaks straightened up with a pair of binoculars. 'Even brought my . . . You might call 'em my soap-opera glasses.' He laughed at his own joke.

With an audible groan, Bobby gave AnnaLise an apologetic look and got back into the cruiser. 'We'd best be going.'

'Same. Have a good . . . um, weekend,' she said awkwardly.

Bobby mouthed, *yeah, right*, but said only, 'You, too.'

'My sentiments exactly,' Roy Smoaks said, raising the binoculars as they pulled away. 'We'll be . . . seeing you all.'

FIVE

'Asshole.' The pseudo-Catholic in the backseat had been the first to break the silence as they drove eastward on Main Street.

'God rest his soul,' AnnaLise muttered.

Daisy looked sideways at her daughter and started to giggle. The other two joined in and soon tears were streaming down all three women's faces as AnnaLise tried to keep the car where it belonged on the narrow road.

'Oh, dear,' Daisy finally managed. 'This looks to be quite the holiday on the lake. I'd love to be a fly on the wall during Thanksgiving dinner at Bradenham.'

As Smoaks had alluded to, Bobby's mother had, ever so modestly, named their 'McMansion' on the western shore of Lake Sutherton 'Bradenham.' Now there was just Bobby there.

'I'm not sure that dinner with Bobby and his grandfather could be any worse than what we're going to face,' said AnnaLise.

'Kathleen might not agree with that,' Mama said.

Phyllis Balisteri had a point. Bobby Bradenham had proposed to Kathleen Tullifinny at the age of eighteen, but the honey-haired beauty had turned the mayor-to-be down in favor of the older, already police chief Rance Smoaks. After Rance's body had washed up on the beach, victim of a gunshot wound, the two high-school sweethearts had rekindled their romance, only to discover mere days later that Bobby was Rance's blood-son from a long-ago teenage fling.

And, therefore, Bobby was, as Mama so delicately put it, 'doing his stepmother.'

'"Dysfunctional family holidays" seem to be the theme this year,' AnnaLise said, slowing the car as they approached where Main Street ended and the potholed eastern shore road commenced. Which reminded her: 'What two words, Daisy?'

Her mother cocked her head. 'Whatever are you talking about?'

'When we were parked back at the restaurant, you said that "two words" were the explanation for why Main Street hasn't been continued along the lake and kicks away to the east here past the inn instead.'

'Your friend Sheree is doing a fair business,' Mama observed as they passed the parking lot of the bed and breakfast.

The thirteen-room Sutherton Inn's owner, Sheree Pepper, had gone to school with AnnaLise. And while Mama was right about the half-dozen cars in the parking lot, AnnaLise was disappointed to see that writer James Duende's wasn't among them.

With Chuck off the eligible board and Bobby Bradenham in an apparently happy – if somewhat complex – relationship, the newcomer was the only age-appropriate man with a brain in town.

Not that AnnaLise was looking, at least so soon after a relationship that had ended badly. Very badly. But . . .

'For goodness' sake, AnnaLise.' Daisy broke into her thoughts. 'I'm not sure why you're worrying about *my* memory when you're always off on your own flights of fancy.'

'Sorry,' AnnaLise said, as Main Street turned into Scout Road, which curved like a backward 'C' away from the lake.

'No, you're not.' Phyllis was leaning forward to join the conversation. 'You've always just said that to pronate us.'

'"Placate,"' Daisy corrected before AnnaLise could bring herself to do the same. 'You need to watch those kind of careless mistakes in your blog posts, too. Spell-check doesn't pick them up, Phyllis.'

'You see what you've done, AnnieLeez?' Mama said, twisting

her head. 'Like daughter, like mother. Daisy's becoming you, what with your oh-so-grand grammar and all.'

'Sorry,' AnnaLise said again.

Phyllis sputtered and sat back as the car hit a pothole.

'Whoa,' AnnaLise said, slowing down, 'this cow path needs fixing. I suppose since the Scout Camp closed nobody uses this road much.'

'Dickens Hart,' Daisy said.

'What?'

'Your two words. Dickens Hart owns the land and leased the camp to the scouts.'

AnnaLise whistled. 'That's a lot of land. And some very valuable footage along the lakefront.'

From the backseat came: 'Your daddy's money's not sounding so bad now, I'd wager.'

'He's not my/her daddy,' AnnaLise and Daisy protested in tandem.

'Timothy Griggs was my daddy,' AnnaLise expanded. 'Dickens Hart just happens to be the biological father.'

'Tomato, tomahto,' added the peanut gallery.

AnnaLise slowed and turned left into a driveway leading back toward the lake. 'I came in from the north the last time, but I think this driveway has been resurfaced.'

Daisy said, 'Well, will you look at that?'

AnnaLise did.

The private road led uphill toward the house, which had the feel of a traditional southern plantation structure scooped up from a manicured lawn of the Carolina Low Country and plopped down on a slope of the state's northwestern mountains. Beautiful, concededly, with white brick, tall columns and multiple verandas, but jarringly out of place.

AnnaLise had been to the house a few times since returning to Sutherton, first to pick up her birth father's near endless boxes and boxes of journals, discs and drives, and then to consult with the man himself about his memoir.

But even the last time, just a couple of weeks ago when Hart had told her his family reunion plan, it hadn't looked like this. The concrete paving stones of the circle drive now looped around a stately fountain that would look even statelier but for the marble water nymphs – naked, naturally – frolicking in it.

Could the man actually have had this enormous renovation completed in a mere two weeks? AnnaLise wondered.

She pulled around the new fountain to the front door where two valets – in full livery, no less – awaited, seemingly eager, the soles of their shoes tapping on the concrete as though the pavers were hot coals.

'Welcome!' The driver's side valet had the fresh-scrubbed look of a male student from the nearby University of the Mountain.

'Thank you,' AnnaLise said, turning off the engine as the valet swung open her door and his clone scurried around the car to get Daisy. 'May I take your luggage?'

'Oh, of course.' AnnaLise popped the trunk and retrieved her purse.

As the valets lifted the lid and unloaded the bags, a young woman in a black dress punctuated by a white ruffled apron approached with a tray of fluted glasses, each half-filled.

'Champagne?'

'Why, thank you.' Daisy had joined her daughter on the sidewalk and snagged a glass for AnnaLise before doing the same for herself.

As the trunk slammed, knocking could be heard. Impatient and continuous.

'Oops. Hold this, please?' said AnnaLise, handing the drink back to her mother and reaching in to unlock the Chrysler's rear door. 'Sorry. Must be child safety—'

'AnnieLeez,' Phyllis climbed out with her carpetbag while surveying the scene, 'weren't you the one told me that our Dickens Hart didn't have house servants?'

AnnaLise shrugged. 'I never saw anybody but Boozer Bacchus before today. I'm betting Dickens hired all these people for the occasion. And had that fountain built, too.'

But Mama was already handing the valet her bag and motioning over the champagne lady. AnnaLise looked around for Daisy and her own glass of bubbly, but neither were in sight.

It hadn't exactly taken a full-court press to break down either woman's resistance.

'Incredible,' AnnaLise muttered to herself as she crossed onto the lush side lawn to get away from the spray of the fountain being battered by cold and gusty High Country winds.

If the temperature dropped another twenty degrees, Hart could be seeing snow and his stone nymphs freezing their cute little privates off under a layer of ice. And for the fountain to survive the winter, their host best have its pipes drained first thing Monday morning.

While the slanting afternoon sun gave the illusion of warmth, even here at the foot of Sutherton Mountain they were 4,000 feet above sea level. The first trace of snow had already fallen – and promptly melted – on the first of October, and the ski slopes would be open by Christmas, even if that meant unleashing their arsenal of snow guns, an artillery version of Hart's fountain that combined water and pressurized air to supplement the natural fall of flakes. Or, during an uncooperative winter, just plain 'supply' the slopes with acceptable amounts of the white stuff for visiting skiers.

Buttoning her wool jacket up to the throat, AnnaLise moved far enough away from the house to be able to see the lake and a small sand beach. Beyond the beach a solid, workman-like fishing pier jutted into the water, a knot of trees masking what Hart probably considered an eyesore from view through the expansive windows at the back of the house.

'Crikeys,' a voice said in a godawful cockney accent. 'The Lord of the Manor must be mounting a carnival for the villagers.'

AnnaLise turned to see the former 'lady' of the manor, Joy Tamarack. Fortyish, with short-cropped, white-blonde hair, Joy was an athletic trainer who both smoked and drank. Now she held two oversized wine glasses with broad bowls but stems so slim and delicate AnnaLise thought they would snap under the weight of the rather generous amount of wine above each.

Joy extended one to AnnaLise. 'Methinks you'll like this better than the champagne.'

AnnaLise accepted hers carefully, taking a sip before closing her eyes in sheer, internal bliss. 'This may be the best red wine I've ever had.'

'Should be. It's a twenty-five-year-old cabernet I found squirreled away in Hart's wine cellar.' Borderline criminally, Joy chugged a third of her glass. 'I split the bottle between our two glasses.'

'Dickens doesn't mind you opening the good stuff?' Or the really good stuff. AnnaLise gently swirled hers before lifting it toward the sun to appreciate the nearly opaque, deep ruby color.

A Cheshire cat's grin. 'I didn't ask.'

'Someday you'll have to tell me what dirt you have on him that gives you free run of his house and other treasures.'

A native Midwesterner, Joy had met Dickens Hart circa 1995, when she and a group of college friends came to the High Country for a girls-getaway. The couple had been married for just a year when Joy abruptly left the marriage – and town – with a hefty enough financial settlement to set local tongues wagging.

Not that it took much.

'Are you kidding?' Joy asked. 'If everybody knows, I lose my leverage.'

'I'm writing his biography,' AnnaLise said. 'Are you telling me there's a skeleton in an obscure closet that Dickens didn't chronicle in the thousands of disturbing pages I'm sifting through?'

'You'll have to let me know when you're done sifting.'

'He *is* an interesting man,' AnnaLise said.

'He . . . was.' Joy's tone was tinged with a note of regret, perhaps even genuine sadness.

Although the two women had known each other casually from Joy's annual visits to Sutherton, after her divorce they had struck up a true friendship when the older woman returned in September to open the spa at Hotel Lux on the summit of Sutherton Mountain.

Now AnnaLise touched her friend's arm. 'I'm sure this isn't easy for you, Dickens' other wives and lovers showing up.'

'Actually, I've always been friendly with his two other ex-wives.'

'Do you think they'll both be here?'

'Kate, my direct predecessor, died of breast cancer last year, but Shirley's coming. She was Hart's first wife and a real pistol. You'll like her.'

'I'm sure I will.' But, all of a sudden, AnnaLise's stomach was tied in knots. 'I'm glad you're here.'

'What? You don't want to meet your probably mutant half-brothers and half-sisters all by your lonesome?'

'Believe me, I'm never "by my lonesome" these days and, anyway, both Mama and Daisy are here with me.'

Joy's eyebrows were raised. 'Well done. How did you ever manage that?'

'Played to their curiosity. And, at least on Mama's part, a little of her greed. On my behalf, of course.'

'Of course. I have a hunch we're in for an interesting weekend.'

'I'm glad you're here,' AnnaLise repeated, raising her glass in salute. 'I was hoping that Bobby would come, too, to keep me sane.'

'And what am I, chopped liver?'

'No, but when it comes to the subject of Dickens Hart you're certainly not a role model for mental balance.' She held up her free hand. 'Sorry. I'm a fine one to talk.'

But her friend didn't seem to have taken offense at her characterization. 'Bobby's even-keeled for the most part, I'll grant him that, which would come in handy this Thanksgiving weekend.'

'Don't I know it. We just ran into him, driving Roy Smoaks back from the airport.'

'What? You don't think it's heartwarming?' Joy asked, seeing the look on AnnaLise's face. 'Grandfather and grandson discovering each other after a lifetime apart?'

'And, coincidentally, when said grandson has inherited the second-most impressive house on the lake.' AnnaLise waved across the lake at Bradenham, with its trellised wooden deck cantilevered out over the lake. 'Not that it seems enough for Roy. He was reminding Bobby that he – Bobby, I mean – was no longer part of Sutherton's *ar-is-to-cra-cy*.' She drew the word out like Smoaks had.

'Nice guy. But, as you said, it's only the *second* most impressive, this place being numero uno.'

AnnaLise shrugged. 'Roy has no grounds to grouse about that. If Bobby *had*, indeed, been Dickens' son instead of Rance's, Roy would have no claim on him in the first place. And, I might add, Bobby would be here with us.'

'I'm sure he'll wish he was by the time Grandpa Roy leaves. I can't imagine how they're going to occupy themselves all weekend. From what Kathleen tells me, the only thing the Smoaks men know how to do is drink, shoot and screw. Generally in that order.'

'Lovely,' AnnaLise said with another sigh. 'Poor Kathleen.'

'Hey, Kathleen was stupid enough to marry into the family, but at least she's learned her lesson. She's spending the holiday with her mom.'

'Poor Bobby then,' AnnaLise amended, glancing back toward Hart's circular driveway. 'I guess there are worse places to be than here.' Anywhere with Roy Smoaks being one of them.

'You bet there are, and besides, you need to protect your turf,' Joy said. 'If all goes as my loving ex-husband plans, you stand to lose a shitload of money this weekend.'

'I don't want his money.' AnnaLise was feeling simultaneously anxious and weary and it was only late afternoon on Wednesday. She'd still need to get through tonight and Thanksgiving Day itself before she could even hope to extricate herself.

'Listen.' Joy's free hand clamped on AnnaLise's shoulder and she brought her face close – not all that difficult, since they were bookends at five feet tall. 'I don't know about the other people who are coming, but you *are* Dickens' daughter and you deserve his fortune, whatever's left of it when he turns up his toes. Claim it here and now and stop this whiny "I don't want it" crap before the gravy-train passes you by.'

AnnaLise tried to shrug her friend off without spilling any wine over the rims of their glasses. 'Passes me by?'

The hand dropped. 'There's Boozer. He'll give you an earful on what he thinks of all this.'

'I already know, thank you very much.' AnnaLise waved at Bacchus, who appeared to be coming from the garages on the other side of the main house. In contrast to his usual uniform of khakis, Hart's right-hand man was wearing a pressed, dark suit. Raising his hand in response to AnnaLise's greeting, he hesitated, using the hand to shade his eyes as he peered up into a tall tree.

'What's he—' Even as Joy started to ask the question, there was movement in the tree – a bending almost like a leafy springboard and then a gigantic bird emerged, wings beating, but nearly silent against the air currents.

'Holy shit!' AnnaLise ducked involuntary despite the distance. 'I'd forgotten how big our owls are. That thing must have a six-foot wingspan.'

'Very nearly.' Joy tipped her head to watch as the bird gained altitude. 'Amazing how quiet they are for their size, too, isn't it?'

'I'm sure it comes in handy for sneaking up on a snack,' AnnaLise said dryly.

'They have to eat, you know. And I bet the out buildings here are Mickey and Minnie-free.'

'Mice don't bother me so much. It's more the squirrels and cats.' She shivered and returned to their earlier subject. 'Boozer is the one who had to track down Dickens' tootsies.' She looked at Joy. 'Present company excepted.'

'"Tootsies"?' Joy repeated. 'God, you *are* a throwback.'

'What do you want me to call you all?'

'Wait a second.' Joy devolved into mulling mode. 'We need to define our terms more specifically for this lollapalooza of a weekend. The women he fooled around with can be Bimbettes; the ones, like me, who married him, Fools.'

AnnaLise's jaw was set. 'My mother's not a Bimbette.'

'Relax,' Joy said, punching her in the shoulder. 'Daisy is, and always will be, just Daisy – a one-hundred-percent original. But we should get back. It looks like the curtain is about to be raised on Act One.'

AnnaLise followed her gaze toward the stretch limousine that was slowly making its way up the long drive. The valets and servers were lining up to greet the new arrivals like something out of an episode of *Downton Abbey*. 'Do you know who they are?'

'Your "tootsies"? Nope.' Joy started toward the front door, then stopped and swiveled, her still significant volume of wine wildly sloshing enough to make AnnaLise feel seasick. 'Do you?'

'Of course. My dear father,' she felt her lip curl at the word, 'had me come up with the list of former lovers that Boozer then vetted as to whether they had children who might be his and thus be invited. Dickens approved the final list.'

Joy actually sighed. 'I wish I could say that surprises me, but it doesn't. So dish, girl. Or do you want me to guess?'

AnnaLise handed her glass to Joy and dug through her purse, coming up with the list she'd jotted down when Bacchus had called her with the results of his efforts.

'Is that a unicorn?' Joy asked, blinking at the brightly colored artwork at the top of the paper.

'And a rainbow,' AnnaLise said, shaking out the list. 'Daisy kept all of my old Lisa Frank pencils and notebooks and such. Bottom drawer, right next to the Beany Babies and Hello Kitty backpack purse.'

'The nineties have a lot to answer for,' Joy said.

'I can't argue with you there.' AnnaLise reclaimed her glass. 'Now, can I assume you just care about the ones who are actually attending?'

'Versus the ones he simply shtupped? Yes, please. Life is too short for a recitation of the entire *dis*honor roll.'

'It's not as many as you might expect, particularly given the carrot he dangled.'

'So to speak.'

AnnaLise felt herself blush, but continued. 'The only ones coming are Rose Boccaccio and her son Eddie, Lucinda Puckett and *her* son Tyler, and Sugar Capri and *her* daughter—'

'Sugar?'

'Yup, and her daughter is called Lacey.' AnnaLise shook her head. 'Lacey Capri. Honestly, who would do that to a kid? Though I suppose if your own parents had named you something like Su—'

But Joy seemed more concerned about the mother than the daughter. 'But Sugar herself is coming? Why?'

AnnaLise canted her head. 'Presumably because she and Hart did the dirty, with Lacey the product. Remember? It's the theme of the party.'

'But that's impossible. Not them doing the dirty part, of course. That's a given. But Hart met Sugar a full decade after he had his vasectomy.'

'Huh?' AnnaLise, looking again at her list, frowned. 'If so, I shouldn't have put her on here as a "possible."' She re-scanned the names. 'I hope I didn't make a mistake.'

But Joy Tamarack was already striding away from her across the green lawn: the long white limo was gliding to a stop at the mansion's main entrance.

SIX

AnnaLise Griggs followed her friend, trying not to lose any of the fabulous wine still nearly filling her glass. When she reached the front of the house, though, Joy Tamarack had disappeared.

AnnaLise didn't quite know what to do or where to go. If Dickens Hart hadn't yet appeared to greet his guests, his acknowledged bastard-daughter certainly wasn't interested in playing hostess.

'Psst.'

Joy and Boozer Bacchus were perched above her on the rail of the upper-floor veranda. Dodging the conga line of valets and drink-bearers, AnnaLise slipped in through the front door. Other than Hart's office, to the right of the vaulted-ceilinged and marble-floored foyer, she had seen very little of the house.

Safe to assume, though, that the sweeping staircase would bring her to the second-floor bedrooms. And that the first one to the right – directly above Hart's office – would provide access to the occupied balcony.

Climbing the steps, AnnaLise found herself on an unwalled, balustraded catwalk running the length of the house from north to south. The walkway overlooked the foyer to the east, or front of the house, and a lofty room with a view of the lake to the west. The latter featured, on the near wall, a fieldstone fireplace and cozy seating area with moss-green sofa and armchairs.

But that was pretty much where the 'cozy' ended.

The center of the massive room had been cleared for a long buffet table, its top dotted with silver chafing dishes that would soon hold pre-dinner canapés. The wall opposite the fireplace – and probably forty feet away from it – was all glass and opened onto the patio and the lakeshore beyond.

'Well, la-dee-dah,' AnnaLise said, and then turned her attention to the upper floor.

The open walkway where she stood morphed into a traditional walled hallway in both directions once away from the vaulted core of the house. Choosing north, AnnaLise opened the first door on the right and stepped into a lovely room with a four-poster bed. The polished rosewood table by the door held, appropriately, a vase of pink roses and beside that was a piece of parchment, folded into the shape of a pup tent and printed in ornate script: 'Welcome to Hart's Head?' AnnaLise said, reading the legend on the paper as she stepped through the open French door to join Joy and Boozer Bacchus on the balcony. 'I never knew this place had a name.'

'Didn't till yesterday,' Bacchus said. 'The boss had those things express-printed overnight.'

Joy shrugged. 'I voted for "Dick Head" myself, but Caesar Disgustus overruled me.'

Bacchus smiled and turned to AnnaLise. 'Good to see you, AnnaLise. Did Lorraine drive with you?'

AnnaLise had forgotten he knew Daisy from the days she'd worked in the White Tail Club's kitchen. Lorraine Kuchenbacher had never been a 'fawn,' or at least so she'd assured her daughter. 'She did. And Mama – Phyllis Balisteri – came with us, too.'

Bacchus seemed less happy to hear that last sentence, but before AnnaLise could wonder why, the threesome's attention was drawn to the limousine.

'Holy shit,' Joy observed, as guests piled out. 'Looks like the stretch version of a clown car at the circus.'

'Should only be six of them,' said Bacchus, pulling at this grizzled mustache. 'Less'n they brought friends.'

'Six . . . seven,' AnnaLise said, counting. 'Could one of them be Shirley, the other surviving ex?'

Joy gestured with her wine glass. 'The age-appropriate one with the blonde helmet hair streaked by gray.'

'Actually,' AnnaLise said, 'most of them are surprisingly

age-appropriate. Or at least closer to Dickens' age than I would have expected.'

'I tried for a nice cross-section,' said Bacchus. He'd taken a silver flask out of his suit coat's inside lapel pocket.

AnnaLise ignored the flask. Who was she, with most of a half bottle of wine in her glass, to ask Boozer if he'd started – or resumed – well, boozing? 'What do you mean? Didn't you or Patrick Hoag just send them all a letter?'

'He did,' Bacchus said, unscrewing the attached lid and tipping the container to his lips. 'But you know yourself there were sixty-plus women on that list. And the sad fact is, out of that whole group not one person responded.'

'Imagine that,' Joy said, eyes wide and her tone sarcastic.

'What did you do, Boozer?' AnnaLise asked.

'Well, now, I took matters into my own hands, but seeing as I only have the two of them, I needed to be particular. Couldn't just knock on every woman's door and explain the situation. So I chose one or two a decade – ones who'd had youngsters that qualified time-wise, starting in—'

'Will you look at that?' Joy was pointing to a tiny woman with pure white hair being helped into a wheelchair. A cloud of musky-scented perfume wafted up to their balcony. 'Did Hart have a cougar? Or, maybe back in the day, they were still called saber-toothed tigers.'

AnnaLise quashed a laugh, thinking her friend might be smarting from Bacchus' 'generational' approach.

'Rose Boccaccio, age seventy,' said Bacchus, sealing and replacing his flask. 'And the man with her is her son, Eddie, fifty-one and a dentist.'

Joy's head tick-tocked like she was juggling numbers in it. 'So Rose is two years older than Hart, and her son's seventeen years younger. That means that Hart couldn't have been more than sixteen or seventeen when they danced the horizontal mambo.'

But AnnaLise was looking at Eddie, a handsome if thinning tow-head, who was probably about five-nine. A dentist, Boozer had said, and the right height and age for . . .

She mentally shook herself, taking a mouthful of the lovely wine. The last thing Daisy needed right now – sexy underwear aside – was a boyfriend. Especially one who might prove to be AnnaLise's half-brother.

'Yup,' Bacchus was saying. 'Most boys appreciate a skilled and steady hand on the tiller that first time and I'm sure the lieutenant was no different.'

'Lieutenant?' AnnaLise managed around the cabernet, still unswallowed.

'You forget me and your daddy went way back to the service?'

AnnaLise, nearly choking on her wine at the word 'daddy,' also managed to shake her head.

'Yeah, yeah, yeah,' Joy interrupted. 'They were in the army together. Loyalty, honor and so on. But can we get back to the cast of our current play?'

AnnaLise shrugged apologetically, but Bacchus seemed fine with the somewhat cutting remark. 'Joy's right. It's water over the dam, that's for sure. Now those two over there—'

They followed his pointing finger to a woman in her mid-fifties with carefully coiffed strawberry-blonde hair and a glass of champagne in her hand. 'Lucinda Puckett,' Bacchus shifted his compass needle, 'and her son, Tyler, age thirty-five.' The latter was smiling as he accepted a flute of champagne from a pretty server. 'Lucinda is from the early days of Mr Hart's lodge.'

'Like a stroll down the memory lane of Dickens' sex life,' Joy said dryly. 'I assume Lucinda was a fawn?'

'She was,' Bacchus said, nodding. 'Going to the university back then. Mighty pretty girl, but she knew it, if you get my drift.'

'You didn't like her?' AnnaLise asked.

Bacchus shrugged. 'Had nothing against her personally, except that she broke up the boss' marriage to Shirley.'

'Were they married long?' The journalist in AnnaLise wanted to get her timelines right.

'Five years, maybe? The lieutenant met Shirley just after he got out of the service. And from the beginning they were good together. She was the one and only for him. Uh, no offense.' He bobbed his head at Joy.

'None taken,' she said. 'In fact, I wish you'd persuaded Hart of that way back then. Might have saved us all – me, especially – a lot of trouble.'

'Oh, I tried, but you couldn't tell the boss anything and I'm starting to think nothing ever changed. It's like he just plain can't let himself stay happy.'

'At least he's reaching out to make amends, however late.' AnnaLise couldn't believe she was defending the man.

'Well, now, there can be a fine line between making amends and stirring things up,' Bacchus said, shaking his head. He landed his palm lightly on her shoulder. 'He's got you in his life now, AnnaLise, and I know he's grateful for that. But—'

'There she is!' Joy hissed urgently. 'Sugar.'

Bacchus sighed. 'She's the one I asked Mr Hart *not* to invite. Strictly speaking, she shouldn't be here – or her daughter.'

AnnaLise leaned over the railing to get a gander at Sugar and Lacey Capri.

'Will you look at that?' Joy said, obvious envy in her voice. 'She literally hasn't changed a bit, right down to the wardrobe.'

The two women below – both petite with lustrous blonde hair – could easily have been taken for sisters rather than mother and daughter. The elder had a vintage vibe in boots and denim jacket over a short baby-doll dress, while the younger wore simple jeans and a sweater.

'Wow,' AnnaLise said. 'This Sugar's certainly aged well.'

Joy's eyes narrowed. 'What do you mean by that?'

'You, yourself, said she hadn't changed,' AnnaLise protested. 'And from what you said earlier, she was at White Tail in the mid-nineties. That—'

'Would have been right around when Hart and I were married,' Joy finished for her. 'You're absolutely correct. Turns out that Sugar and I were "overlapping" – so to speak – right in this very house.'

A gust of wind blew water from the fountain toward the group below. Sugar squealed.

'You mean she and Dickens were doing—'

'Each other? Yes. And in my bed. Or *our* bed, as Dickens' reminded me. Which apparently gave him the right to have sleep-overs when I was away. He'd sneak her in so the staff couldn't tell me. The man was obsessed with her.'

'And blind to boot,' Bacchus added, seeming to want to make up for his earlier comment.

'Obviously,' AnnaLise contributed staunchly. 'And it cost him his marriage to Joy.'

But Hart wife number three was squinting down at the duo. 'Boozer, how old's the daughter?'

'Lacey? Fifteen.'

AnnaLise looked back and forth at the females below. 'But Dickens had his vasectomy in the mid-eighties, not too long after

I was born. Lacey can't possibly be his daughter.' The journalist had a thought. 'Unless he had the operation reversed?'

Joy was shaking her head. 'No way. But don't worry. You won't need to share your fortune with this one, at least—'

AnnaLise interrupted. 'I keep telling you, I don't *want*—'

This time Joy got her back up. 'I know, I know. The oh-so-independent bastard daughter doesn't want Hart's money. But like I said before, you deserve it. Right, Boozer?'

'She's right, AnnaLise,' Bacchus weighed in. 'Your mother never told anybody about you, never asked the boss for so much as a dime. But given the uncertain future you've come home to, you need to take what the boss intends to give you. For Lorraine, if not for yourself.'

AnnaLise didn't try to argue the point. 'Yes, sir.'

'Good.' Bacchus turned back to Joy. 'Now, you were saying to AnnaLise about Sugar?'

Joy had an I-told-you-so grin on her face. 'I was just speculating on Lacey's age, because to my eye she looks just like her mother did then.'

'When she broke up your marriage?' asked the reporter reflexively.

'I broke up my marriage,' Joy said flatly, 'when I found out.'

'About Sugar?'

'About Sugar's age.'

'Which was?'

'Fifteen.' Joy grinned with glee. 'Exactly the same age as Boozer's telling us her own daughter is right now.'

SEVEN

Well, thought AnnaLise. I guess that answers the question of what Joy Tamarack 'had' on Dickens Hart at the time of their divorce. Not to mention how well Sugar Capri had 'aged.' If she had been fifteen at Lacey's conception and mostly likely sixteen by the time her now fifteen-year-old daughter was born nine months later, that meant Sugar could be no older than thirty-one. Just three years older than AnnaLise herself.

The journalist gave an involuntary shudder. A gap approaching four decades between consenting adults was creepy enough, but fifteen and fifty-something? 'Wasn't the age of consent in North Carolina at least sixteen then?'

Boozer Bacchus hesitated, then nodded his head just once. 'I told the boss he was in for it if anybody found out.'

'What about Sugar's parents?'

'They'd decided she was no good a while before Mr Hart ever met her.'

'"A while before"?' AnnaLise was astounded. 'The girl was just fifteen years old, for God's sake!'

Joy waved her down. 'I've been through all this, AnnaLise. I was married to the man at the time and, believe me, if I could have thrown him to the dogs I would have. But no one else – not Sugar, nor her parents – wanted to accuse Hart of anything.'

'Do you think he paid them off?' AnnaLise was hanging over the railing herself now, trying to get a better look at the twosome below.

'The parents? I'd put money on it,' Dickens Hart's ex-wife said, but his right-hand man's face stayed blank.

'So, did Dickens know at the time, Boozer?' AnnaLise pressed.

'How young Sugar was?' Bacchus was shaking his head. 'Hell, no. The boss always had trouble keeping it in his pants, but there's no way he was looking for *that* kind of trouble. She wouldn't have been working at White Tail in the first place, except that Sugar lied about her age.'

Bacchus took one look at the women's faces and held up a hand, palm out like a crossing-guard's stop sign. 'Now, I don't mean to go blaming the victim. Sugar probably had her own reasons for lying, probably starting with needing to support herself, what with her parents no longer interested. I'm just saying . . .'

'. . . that there were mitigating circumstances,' Joy finished for him, her expression bordering on dangerous. 'The poor, *poor* boy was duped. Not only did Sugar fib about her age, but Hart also was struck by selective amnesia and forgot he was married.'

Before Bacchus could defend his boss, if he were so inclined, an announcement boomed up from below.

'Everyone's to go in,' Bacchus explained, stepping back through the doorway to the bedroom. 'Mr Hart plans to make his grand entrance in the Lake Room.'

'The Lake Room?' AnnaLise asked as she and Joy followed him in.

'At the rear of the house between the kitchen and movie theater,' Bacchus supplied, seeming happy to be on safer conversational ground. 'The one with the wall of windows facing west toward the lake?'

Of course. The enormous room downstairs that was already set up for the party. AnnaLise tried to re-tent the welcome letter on the table where she'd found it, but it kept slipping off the highly buffed surface.

'Don't bother,' Joy said, passing into the corridor before pivoting to point at a small sign on the wall next to the door. 'This is your room, see?'

Sure enough, the card read 'AnnaLise Griggs' in the same meticulous script used to letter the welcome card.

'I had name badges printed, too,' beamed Boozer proudly. 'So everybody'll get to know each other.'

'That's . . . nice,' said AnnaLise, not really knowing what else to say.

'I'm just the next door down the hall,' Joy said, reaching back to pat her friend's arm. 'In case you need someone to talk you down.'

As Joy descended the stairs, a valet squeezed by going the other way.

'I think that's mine,' AnnaLise said, reaching for the blue suitcase dangling from one hand of the young man who had greeted them when they'd arrived.

'The boy'll take care of that,' Bacchus told AnnaLise. Then, to the valet: 'Clothes hung up and in the dresser, suitcase in that closet in the corner. Understand?'

'Yes, sir.' The kid practically saluted. 'Do you know where this . . .' He held out Phyllis Balisteri's carpet bag.

AnnaLise reflexively backed up a step, her hand covering her nose. 'That belongs to Mama,' she said, muffled, 'and that last one is Daisy's.'

'Lorraine and Phyllis will be sharing this room,' Bacchus said, opening the door across from AnnaLise's to reveal another beautiful room – this one with two queen-sized beds and a view of the lake. Like AnnaLise's, the table by the door held a vase of roses, but these were red rather than pink. 'You might want to put that carpet bag on the balcony after you empty it, just to air it out a bit.'

'I'm sure Mama would appreciate it,' AnnaLise said.

'And your mother, I reckon, even more so.' Bacchus' brow was furrowed as he watched the young valet follow orders. 'I told Dickens that Lorraine, of all the people invited besides you, deserved a room to herself.'

'My fault, I'm afraid,' AnnaLise said as voices filled the space below. 'I invited Mama along and even Hart's Head has only so many bedrooms.'

'Don't be thinking Phyllis was the straw on the camel's back. That was our Sugar.'

Bacchus started toward the stairs, but AnnaLise held back, tugging on his sleeve to stay outside the door as the valet finished unpacking Mama's carpet bag. 'I didn't *think* Sugar was on the list I gave you.'

'No, she surely wasn't. Not that I would have invited her even if you wrote her name a foot high. But the boss saw it differently.'

'So *Dickens* invited her?' AnnaLise asked, admittedly a little miffed that in addition to the so-called 'baby-mamas' he'd bid her to find, the man had acted independently on his desire to see 'old flames' beyond the ones – like Shirley and Joy – he'd managed to extinguish by marrying. 'Why would he do that?'

Unnecessarily, Bacchus straightened the placard identifying the room as that of 'Lorraine Kuchenbacher Griggs and Phyllis Balisteri.'

'Like you said, it might be that Mr Hart's making amends. Maybe to a wider circle than just the mothers of his blood-children.'

AnnaLise heard something in Bacchus' tone. 'But you don't think so.'

'What I think is the boss does believe that.' As the valet crossed to AnnaLise's room with the final bag, Boozer stepped into Daisy and Phyllis' suite and surveyed it, pausing to pluck a petal from one of the roses that was apparently not up to snuff. 'But I do admit some wonder that he's still . . .'

'. . . sweet on Sugar?'

An embarrassed grin as Bacchus glanced around for a waste basket before settling for stuffing the petal in his pocket. 'More like . . . intrigued?'

'By the underaged one who got away?' AnnaLise shivered and moved into the hallway. 'Boozer, that's sick.'

Bacchus closed the bedroom door behind them. 'Sure would be, and, hear me now, I'm not saying that it's true.'

As Bacchus started down, AnnaLise hesitated on the catwalk. The new arrivals had filtered through beneath to enter the big room facing the lake. The magnificent water view of less than an hour ago was losing definition in the dusk, while, across the water, Bradenham's flickering lights served as a reminder of Bobby's own family reunion.

Smaller, perhaps, but AnnaLise was betting it was every bit as uncomfortable as the one at Hart's Head. If, hopefully for Bobby, a tad less pretentious.

On a level with AnnaLise's nose, an enormous crystal chandelier had sprung to life, illuminating the scene below. Joy was already at the buffet, while a smiling Daisy left Sugar and Lacey Capri to move toward Rose Boccaccio. Rose's son Eddie was crossing the room from the bar to the window wall, offering drinks in old-fashioned glasses from a tray theatrically, if imprudently, center-balanced on his left palm. He seemed to be introducing guests to each other as he went, like he'd already been crowned the golden child.

Or, more accurately, middle-aged man.

'It's just that I've known the boss for a long time.' Bacchus had stopped on the second step down the huge staircase. 'And he's given me a good sense for who's his type and . . . well, Sugar's it. And she's . . .'

As Bacchus continued to descend, AnnaLise lost his voice in the babbling of the assembly below, though with each step she was still thinking about her birth father's 'type.'

And that's when it struck her. Every woman visible below – Daisy, Joy, Rose, Lucinda, Shirley, Sugar, and even Lacey – was petite. And other than Rose, who had let her hair go white, all were various shades of blonde, too. AnnaLise was willing to bet, once she got down there to meet them face-to-face, she'd find the female guests were also blue-eyed, like Daisy and Joy.

All of which just made Boozer Bacchus right: Dickens Hart had a preferred, even exclusive 'type,' one he'd chosen as a randy young male. So much so that, if you squinted, all the invited women could be just one, caught freeze-framed during each decade of his rutting life.

And then, surprisingly unaccompanied by signature music or spotlight, the man himself appeared in front of the fireplace. He scanned the crowd while absently settling his champagne flute on the rustic mantle beside him.

'That's not going to stay!' AnnaLise called down as the base of the crystal teetered on the uneven barnwood.

Before she could yell a more urgent warning, a thud punctuated by 'Shit!' drew her attention toward the floor-to-ceiling windows, where Eddie Boccaccio was struggling to control the drink tray. A *ping* from the vicinity of the fireplace confirmed the demise of Dickens Hart's own crystal flute, even as AnnaLise watched its sturdier brethren slide off Eddie's tray to smash on the tile floor. Beyond Boccaccio, the window appeared to shimmer of its own volition, independent of the sunset it framed.

The trick of light must have distracted the show-off, AnnaLise thought, or— 'The window!' she screamed. 'Get away from—'

At the sound of her voice, Eddie dove for the floor as the rest of the guests pivoted to look up at her. The gigantic pane behind them seemed to distort, roiling like an angry sea once, then twice, before it finally crumbled from the top down like a glass tsunami shattering on the beach.

EIGHT

AnnaLise ran down the steps, wine splashing out of her glass. 'Ohmigod!' a voice was saying while the journalist rounded the newel post and exploded into the Lake Room. Lacey Capri was at the now non-existent window, pointing at the receding silhouette of a winged creature over the lake. Having probably knocked itself senseless by running into the window, it was gaining altitude, albeit unsteadily. 'Did you see the size of that bird?'

'Our resident Great Horned Owl, my dear. I'm afraid it's tried to . . . crash our party.' Smiling at his joke, Dickens Hart crossed the room to help up Eddie Boccaccio. 'Are you all right, son?'

Boccaccio was examining the back of his hand, but brightened at the word 'son.' 'Of course, but what—'

AnnaLise had trailed in her birth father's wake. 'A bird must have hit the window just right.' She nodded at Boccaccio's hand, which was bleeding. 'You're cut.'

'Hell of a bird, but this is nothing,' Eddie said with a glance at Hart. 'Barely a scratch.'

'That's the spirit,' their host said, throwing his arm over the younger man's shoulder. 'Let's get you a Band-Aid and a drink.'

As the two went off toward the bar, a male intoned behind AnnaLise, 'Seems I've missed the opening act. What happened?'

She turned to see Dickens Hart's lawyer, Patrick Hoag, approach with Daisy. 'Probably not a good omen for this weekend, but a great horned owl took a wrong turn and smashed into the window.'

'I'm so glad it wasn't hurt, poor thing.' Daisy seemed more concerned about the bird than any damage done.

Though only in his early thirties, Hoag had prematurely graying hair above old-school black-framed eyeglasses. Now he pushed the frames up on his nose. 'I'm sure the owl will be fine. But we have a more immediate problem. It's November, and even with a practically balmy day by our High Country standards, that respite's not going to last.'

As Hoag stepped sideways to survey the massive, gaping hole to the left of the French doors, his shoe sent a shard of old-fashioned glass from Eddie Boccaccio's tray skittering across the floor.

Boozer Bacchus bent over, carefully picked it up between thumb and forefinger and joined their threesome. 'Watch yourselves. We don't want anybody else cut, though that's not likely, given the tempered glass in these big windows.'

'Sure made a mess,' Daisy said. 'Thousands – maybe millions – of fragments came raining down.' She shuddered. 'That Eddie got off lightly.'

'Mostly dull pellets and less than thumb-size, thank the Lord, rather than jagged shards like this one that could have sliced somebody open or even blinded them,' Bacchus said. 'I'll get those college kids in to sweep up the glass and help me cover the hole before they leave.'

'Good idea,' Hoag said. 'I'll make sure they're compensated for the overtime.'

AnnaLise noticed he didn't offer to help. 'Is there anything we can do?'

'Just keep everybody,' Boozer nodded toward the rest of the group, 'on the far end of the room by the fireplace.'

Daisy touched his shoulder. 'Thank you, Boozer. Truly.'

'No need to thank me,' he said, seeming embarrassed. 'It's my job.'

'I know, but—'

AnnaLise didn't hear anymore because Hoag began drawing her away. 'Where did you get that wine?'

Surprised, she looked down at the still-intact glass in her hand. 'Huh? I forgot I had it.'

Apparently the broken window had shaken AnnaLise more than she'd realized. Looking off in the direction Hart's owl had flown, she saw the lights of Bradenham and wondered how Bobby was faring with Roy Smoaks. Imagining the old man's 'soap opera glasses' focused on them from across the lake, she shivered, thinking how pleased Smoaks would be that Hart's 'party for his bastard offspring' had already taken a dramatic turn.

'See what I mean?' Hoag started to shrug out of his suit jacket. 'Temperature's already dropping. Why don't you take this?'

'No, thanks. I'm fine,' AnnaLise said, lifting her goblet. 'And as for the red wine, Joy's the one who found it. You may want to ask her.'

But the lawyer shook his head, apparently preferring not to deal with his client's bristly ex-wife. 'That's OK.' Hoag was distracted, scanning the crowd. When the attorney's gaze reached Sugar and her daughter, he added, 'My-oh-my.'

'Notice anything?' AnnaLise asked him.

'Like what?'

'Like Dickens is a High-Country John Derek.'

'Who?'

'John Derek – the actor. And director. He was married four times. I don't know about the first wife, but the last three were beautiful, statuesque blondes with impossibly high cheekbones. In sequence, Ursula Andress, Linda Evans and Bo Derek. Practically identical, except for their ages, of course, which descended in inverse proportion to said cheekbones.'

'Always trading up. That's Dickens for you, too.'

AnnaLise elbowed him in the ribs. 'Jerk.'

'Hey, don't kill the messenger, AnnaLise. Or, in this case, the receiver of *your* message.' He plucked a flute of champagne from one of the silver trays now passing around the room again.

'You do see what I mean,' she continued. 'Dickens obviously likes blue-eyed blondes but, in his case, petite over statuesque since he's short himself.'

'It just happens the gentleman prefers—'

The lawyer's unpromising defense was interrupted by the accused himself, Dickens Hart.

Their host had re-positioned himself in front of the stone hearth facing the guests and, beyond them, the now largely open-air view of the lake.

Hart passed a hand through his unruffled hair before clearing his throat and raising his voice. 'May I have your attention, please?'

Across the way, AnnaLise saw that Daisy had joined Mama. The restaurateur had a drink in one hand and a plate piled with hors d'oeuvres in the other. But who could fault her for taking advantage of other people's cooking for once?

What astonished AnnaLise, though, was that the walls had, literally, come tumbling down and nobody seemed to care. Apparently they all figured there were bigger fish to fry.

And AnnaLise turned her attention to the catch of the day.

'Well, let's give this another try,' Hart said with a self-deprecating smile. 'I apologize for our *au naturale* air-conditioning.'

The attendees laughed appreciatively as Hart gestured toward the window wall, where the former valets were already scurrying to sweep up the glass and tote in sheets of plywood to cover the twenty-foot wide expanse. 'We're going to pump up the heat so we don't freeze as Mr Bacchus' helpers go about their work. In the meantime, I'd like to welcome all of you to Hart's Head.'

'Dick Head,' came as a stage whisper from behind AnnaLise. She turned to catch Joy and the woman she'd identified as Shirley, Hart's first wife, smirking. AnnaLise cut them a dark look, thinking there had already been enough drama for one afternoon into evening.

'Believe me,' Hart continued with a smile, almost as though he welcomed the heckling as a segue. 'I'm well aware that this is an unusual situation. Some of you may know each other and others may not, so I've asked Mr Bacchus,' Hart indicated the man who, having set the valets to work, was moving amongst the clumps of attendees handing out cords of some kind, 'to provide each of you with a name badge.'

As he spoke, Hart slipped a lanyard over his own head, straightening the badge at the end of it so they could see the Hart's Head logo as well as his name. 'They'll come in handy for now, but I'm hoping, by the end of this weekend, we'll all be friends and, for some of us, family.'

Gagging noises.

AnnaLise launched into a theatrical coughing jag to cover the juvenile antics of the ex-wives, earning her a proffered glass of champagne from one of the white-aproned servers to go with the wine she still held in the other hand. She pointed the server to Hoag, whose glass was empty.

Switching the two out, Hart's lawyer said, 'You realize you can't be held responsible for the ex-wives club's behavior, right?'

AnnaLise put her finger to her lips as Hart continued: '. . . luggage has been taken to your assigned rooms. And Mr Bacchus,' a nod toward his harried right-hand man who, having practically tossed AnnaLise her lanyard, picked up a stack of folded papers from the table next to her, 'will distribute a floor plan of Hart's Head, noting your room. You'll also find a placard next to each door, should you get turned around on the second floor. It is,' a markedly *im*modest shrug, 'a very large abode, and we'd hate for anybody to accidentally stumble into the wrong room. Though, take it from me, it *is* a good way to make new friends.' Hart chuckled, but nobody joined in.

It may be decades later, Dickens, AnnaLise thought, *but it's still too early.*

Apparently Hart realized that, too. 'I do want to apologize for any hurt I may have caused. And to right things as thoroughly as humanly possible.'

Someone started to applaud – AnnaLise's money was on a shill, maybe one of the valets hidden away somewhere – and the rest of the group joined in more enthusiastically than she would have expected, given the circumstances and the number of palms already occupied with champagne flutes, name badges and, now, floor plans.

But then the 'circumstances' included people hoping to gain – immensely – from this weekend.

Setting her wine glass on the end table to accept a sheet of paper from Bacchus, AnnaLise unfolded it. A drawing of the ground floor filled the first side of the legal-size sheet, with the second floor on the reverse. 'Geez, this *is* a big house.'

Patrick tapped the logo at the top of the sheet with his finger. 'Indeed it is. Eleven bedrooms, each with its own en suite bathroom.'

'Not that I should quibble with your numbers, but I see ten. Six on the south end of the catwalk.' She pointed at the parallel lines that represented the second floor open walkway where she'd stood earlier, looking down. 'And four – or, wait, is it five? – larger rooms on the north end where I'm staying.'

'Four in the north wing. That,' he indicated the door at the end of the north hallway, 'is just a big storage closet. I know, because I'm staying in the corresponding room in the south wing.'

'Your room is a closet?'

Hoag laughed. 'No, though I got turned around and went north instead of south and one of the valets had to assure me I wasn't to be stashed with the cardboard boxes. My room is one of the smaller ones by this place's standards, but luxurious by any other's.'

AnnaLise found the lawyer's suite at the end of the floor plan's south hallway. Rose's name was on the room to the right, Lucinda's to the left. Eddie was next to his mother on the other side, and Tyler, the other side of *his* mother. Sugar and Lacey were sharing a room next to Tyler's. 'I still don't see the eleventh bedroom.'

Patrick took the map and flipped it. 'Here. On the ground floor.'

She saw where he was indicating. 'The entire north wing, as you put it, of this floor is the master suite?'

'Pretty much, except for the media room and office.'

Sheesh. 'Excess, thy name is Hart.' AnnaLise looked more carefully at the logo for the house. 'Are the "a"s in "Hart's Head" stylized hearts?'

'Yup,' Patrick said. 'Apparently the font dates back to his White Tail Club days. Did you notice the "d"?'

AnnaLise squinted. 'Is that something sprouting off the top of it?' Now she closed both eyes. 'Dear God, please don't tell me that's a—'

'Relax.' the lawyer said, 'No human body parts involved. It's a tail. You know, of a white-tailed deer?'

Opening her eyes, AnnaLise still didn't see it. Nonetheless, she was relieved. 'I'll take your word for it. And I have to admit the hearts are kind of cute.'

'Cute or not, we don't know they're "Hart's."' Daisy had come up behind them.

AnnaLise was confused. 'What?'

'Eddie and Tyler. We don't know they are Dickens' issue, but I will agree with you that they're cute.'

AnnaLise put an arm around her mother and gave her a squeeze, managing to crumple the floor plan in the process. 'You're the one who's cute, Daisy. But I meant "hearts" – you know, like Valentine hearts?'

'It's only Thanksgiving.' Daisy was scowling at AnnaLise. 'You can stop testing me, you know. My mind is fine.'

From confused to flabbergasted. 'I'm not testing anything,' AnnaLise said. 'I just . . .'

But her mother waved her off. 'Let's return to the subject at hand. Do you know if any paternity testing has been done?'

AnnaLise looked at Patrick, who merely shrugged. Typical lawyer. Why were they called mouthpieces if they never *said* anything? 'I think the plan is for everyone to get to know each other,' she said. 'And then maybe the testing will come later.'

Another voice chimed in. 'Probably using the DNA from their saliva when each of them kisses his ring.'

Joy Tamarack had joined them, along with her fellow heckler, Shirley Hart.

'I'm AnnaLise Griggs,' she said to Dickens Hart's first wife, putting her hand out.

'Ah, the one known-to-be rightful heir of our mutual host,' Shirley said, shaking it. Then: 'Hello, Patrick. I guess I should have expected you to be here.'

'You two know each other?' AnnaLise asked.

'Sure do,' Shirley said. 'I was county clerk, back before Patrick's papa retired and Junior here took over the first name in "Hoag, Christiaansen and Weir."'

The woman had a pleasant smile and a no-nonsense manner that reminded AnnaLise of her fourth-grade teacher. As Joy had predicted, the journalist liked her immediately.

'Shirley's the one who suggested these.' Hoag tilted his eye glasses.

'And don't forget the coif,' she said, reaching up to pat his head. 'That was, in my humble opinion, a stroke of genius.'

'Wait a second,' AnnaLise said, cocking her own head. 'Is Shirley saying you intentionally dye your hair gray?'

The lawyer shared a smile with the first Mrs Hart. 'Just here and there to achieve the salt-and-pepper effect. With a concentration of salt, of course, nearer the temples where—'

'And the glasses?' Joy snatched the spectacles off his face and held them up to the light. 'These aren't corrective lenses, either. Just plain glass.'

'Polycarbonate,' Patrick corrected, more defiant than friendly as he reclaimed them. 'Lightweight, but they do make me look more authoritative, don't they?' He slipped the black frames on and struck a grave, counseling pose.

'So you're trying to play older?' AnnaLise shook her head. 'What happened to earning your clients' respect because of your ability at lawyering?'

'I'd have been happy to take the high road,' Patrick said, now defensively, 'if only nature had given me that chance.'

'Patrick's right, if semi-pathetic,' Shirley said, nearly joining arms with the man. 'Despite graduating from Harvard Law School, our newly minted attorney here looked about eleven.'

'Like Doogie Howser,' Daisy agreed. 'Only a little younger.'

'Clients didn't trust me to handle their affairs,' Patrick lamented. 'They insisted that my father—'

'Who by then was a brick or two shy of a full load—' Shirley interjected.

'Represent them, even though he was, sad to say, beginning to falter.'

AnnaLise glanced at Daisy, who had thankfully been drawn aside by Joy. Feeling guilty for having judged Hoag the Younger, given her own parent's cognitive problems, she said, 'I'm so sorry. How's your father doing now?'

Hoag used his middle finger to push the faux glasses higher on his nose. 'He died last year.'

Now AnnaLise felt doubly sorry, even while wondering if Hoag had just subtly flipped her off. She willingly followed as the lawyer changed the subject back to the gathering at hand. 'I've seen the list of invitees, of course, and I know the locals, but not the, uh . . .'

'Best we leave it at "others," dear,' Shirley said, patting his arm. 'So much better than pretenders to the throne and hangers-on.'

'Do you know everybody, Shirley?' AnnaLise asked.

Wife number one turned toward the rest of the crowd. 'I've heard of Rose,' she said, pointing to the white-haired lady. 'Dickens loved to nettle me with how he'd been deflowered, so to speak, by her. Then there was Lucinda, of course, who marked the end of my own marriage.'

'I'm sorry,' AnnaLise said quickly. 'I didn't mean to resurrect bad memories.'

'Hey, I came here, as we all did, knowing full well what we were getting into. You shouldn't feel like any of us need protection, my dear.'

Patrick threw AnnaLise a 'told-you-so' look and she felt the surface of her face flame. Apparently peacemakers weren't going to be involved, much less blessed, this weekend. 'So I've been told. I guess it's just my way, trying to get people to play well with others.'

Joy had returned to the conversation, and proved it by pinching her hard.

'Ouch!' AnnaLise rubbed her stinging upper arm. 'Why'd you do that?'

'Somebody's got to toughen you up.'

'Not a bad course,' Shirley said. 'You have a lot to lose this weekend.'

Before AnnaLise could state, again, that she didn't want Hart's money, another voice rang out.

'That bastard!'

NINE

'**D**on't shush me, Tyler. Dickens Hart is a thief.'

The strawberry blonde that Boozer Bacchus had identified as Lucinda Puckett was standing near the bar with her son, Tyler. She grabbed the cord dangling from her offspring's neck and yanked sharply. 'Do you see this?'

'Mother, please.' Tyler Puckett was leaning back like a recalcitrant Great Dane being tugged by its leash. 'It's just a name badge, so . . .'

'Not the badge,' she snapped. 'The font on the fucking—'

'Mother!'

Startled, Lucinda dropped her pup's leash.

Rubbing his neck where the cord must have bitten in, Tyler said, 'Now will you *explain*? And calmly, please?'

Lucinda lowered her voice and turned away, forcing AnnaLise to move a bit closer to the pair. Patrick, Daisy, Joy and Shirley followed like a rugby scrum.

'. . . studying graphic arts at the university,' Lucinda was saying. 'Hart hired me to design a custom typeface and logo for the White Tail Club.'

Tyler looked confused. 'But I thought you were already working for Hart. As a Doe.'

'*Fawn*,' his mother corrected. 'And I was, but this more . . . well, professional association meant we could spend time together without his wife complaining.'

AnnaLise felt, rather than saw, Shirley Hart rear up, but the ex-wife seemed to contain herself.

Tyler cocked his head. 'And which wife would this have been?'

'Shirley.' Lucinda's hand gestured vaguely toward the buffet crowd. 'The really old one.'

Now Joy clapped a pre-emptive hand over Shirley's mouth.

'In the wheelchair?' Tyler asked.

'Heaven's, no.' Lucinda seemed to be losing patience. 'That's Rose and she was *well* before my time, I'll have you know. Besides, Rose and Dickens never married. Shirley is . . .' She was scanning the crowd for the woman who stood not ten feet behind her.

'Never mind,' Tyler said. 'I'm sure I'll run into her. But go on. You said you designed what?'

'The whole corporate identity campaign for the White Tail Club, right down to a custom font with lower case "a"s that look like hearts.' This time she lifted her own badge. 'See?'

Tyler was looking puzzled. 'There are no "a"s in your name.'

'No!' his mother exploded. 'In the logo for the house, Hart's Head!'

'Oh, yeah.' Tyler stared. 'Is that a penis on the "d"?'

'It's the plume of a white-tailed deer,' his mother said between clenched teeth.

Tyler shook his head. 'Maybe that's what you designed, but it sure looks like somebody took liberties with your . . . tail.' A glance at his mother. 'So to speak.'

AnnaLise laughed. And then slapped her own hand over her own mouth before Joy could do it for her.

Lucinda, though, had heard and pivoted on her pumps to face them. 'You have a problem?'

'Of course she does,' Joy dove in for her friend. 'Dickens Hart – just like everybody else here.'

'Amen to that,' Shirley said. 'By the way, Tyler, I'm the "really" old one.'

He turned bright red. 'I'm sorry about that.'

'Hey, don't be sorry. She's,' Shirley tilted her head toward Lucinda, 'the one who said it.'

'Well, then, I'm sorry,' the strawberry blonde said, looking genuinely embarrassed. 'It's just such an odd situation.'

'Certainly makes for strange bedfellows,' Patrick Hoag said, earning him an eye roll from AnnaLise. Seeing it, he asked, 'What?'

AnnaLise just turned to Lucinda. 'We couldn't help but overhear.

You were responsible for the White Tail . . . what did you call it? Corporate identity?'

Lucinda was nodding. 'The logo, permissible color palate and, last but not least, a custom-designed typeface.'

'Which he's still using?'

'And, of course, never paid me for. Except in semen. I just assumed he wasn't going to use it.'

'Resulting in *me*,' Tyler said a little bitterly. 'Now if you'll all excuse me, I'm going to talk to "Dad."'

'Handsome boy,' Daisy said, watching him walk away.

Lucinda glanced down at Daisy's name badge, obviously wondering who she was.

Joy leaned in toward AnnaLise and whispered, 'Dickens really should have included a flow chart on the badges. You know, so we could see how everybody . . . fit in?'

AnnaLise ignored her. 'Lucinda, I'm AnnaLise Griggs, and this is my mother, Daisy. Or Lorraine, back then.'

At that news, Lucinda's eyes grew speculative. 'The only confirmed heir and her mother.' She put out her hand to Daisy. 'It's a pleasure to meet you.'

'You can just see the wheels turning, can't you?' Shirley said in a low voice as Daisy and Lucinda strolled away, chatting.

'What?' AnnaLise asked.

'She's usually quicker on the uptake,' Joy apologized to Shirley and Patrick. Then, to AnnaLise: 'What my fellow ex-wife means is that if Lucinda can pair Tyler and you up, then the Puckett family is assured of "payment" for Lucinda's services, whether Tyler proves to be fruit of Hart's loins or not.'

Joy cupped her ear. 'Hark!'

AnnaLise hadn't heard anything surprising beyond the nattering of the ex-wife. 'What?'

'It's . . . why it's,' Joy's head was now swiveling, 'yes! I doth believe a giant sucking-up noise has engulfed the room.'

AnnaLise turned her attention to where her friend's gaze had finally landed. Dickens Hart was surrounded by Boccaccios and Pucketts, the youngest of each pair intent on making a good impression. But their target's attention was drawn to an even younger pair.

Sugar Capri and her daughter, Lacey.

'Daisy, I happened to notice you talking to the Capris earlier.'

AnnaLise and her mother were standing to the side of where Boozer and his minions were, thankfully, finishing their work. 'Are they,' the wordsmith daughter was desperately searching her mental thesaurus for any 'soft' adjective, settling lamely on, '. . . nice?'

Daisy's eyebrows rose. 'Nice? Well, I suppose so. At least, for gold-diggers.'

AnnaLise, ever the contrarian, jumped to the gold-diggers' defense. 'Now that's not fair. From everything I've heard, this is all on Dickens Hart. First the original incident – crime, really – and now, inviting them over Boozer's objection.'

Daisy scrunched up her nose. 'What original incident?'

AnnaLise felt her eyes go wide. There was nothing to be gained by sharing Sugar's chronological age at the time Hart 'had' her. And with few exceptions, everything that went into Daisy's ear eventually came out of Mama's mouth.

'Nothing, nothing,' the journalist said.

'What do you mean, "nothing"?' her mom said, hands in a what's-up-with-this posture. 'You're obviously privy to something I'm not, and it feels like you're trying to spare a poor, failing parent something that might hurt me.'

'Privy?' AnnaLise squeaked, trying to buy time to come up with something plausible. 'Good word, but I'm not privy to anything. I thought you were and that if you thought I knew, you'd tell me.' Convoluted, but not entirely ridiculous. She hoped. 'Besides, you're the one who just called them gold-diggers.'

'I did not.'

AnnaLise's stomach dropped, like it always did when her mother forgot a short-term memory these days. At first she had played along or laughed it off, even pretended it hadn't happened at all. Now she tried to spark her mother's recall. 'Yes, you did. Barely two minutes ago.'

Daisy rolled her eyes. 'Please wipe that '"Daisy's-gone-nuts" expression off your face, AnnaLise. What I meant was that Sugar's the one who said they're gold-diggers. Along with everyone else here, of course. We even had a good laugh over it.'

That just didn't compute for AnnaLise. 'Did Sugar also say why they'd been invited in the first place? Dickens had a vasectomy twenty-eight years ago, so Lacey can't be his daughter.'

'Goodness.' Daisy seemed taken aback. 'You seem to know more about your father than I do.'

'I'm writing his memoirs. At your urging, I might add. Information – the good, the bad *and* the ugly – kind of comes with the territory.'

'True,' Daisy seemed to sink inside herself, and AnnaLise fervently hoped that 'Daisy's-gone-nuts' expression hadn't returned to her *own* features.

Then her mother seemed to come up for rational air. 'If you're right about the timing of Dickens' operation, then Lacey *is* far too young to be Dickens daughter. But . . .'

'But what?'

Daisy actually smiled. 'Sugar isn't.'

TEN

'Well, I just heard a sickening possibility.'

'What's that?' Joy pulled a candidate wine bottle from the rack, read the label and shoved it back. She was trying to snag another bottle of the glorious cabernet from Hart's wine cellar before dinner was announced, which would likely be done by a butler with a bell, given the tenor of the event so far. Or, maybe, a giant gong. 'Sugar couldn't be Dickens' daughter, could she?'

'*God*, no!' Another bottle didn't make Joy's grade. 'There's a limit to even *his* perversity. But, tell me, where did you get that idea?'

'Daisy.'

Bent over to peruse the lower shelves, Joy swiveled her head sideways toward AnnaLise, her eyes narrow. 'Your mother?'

'Oh, she doesn't know anything about Dickens and Sugar – or, more specifically, her exact age at the time.' Happily the cellar was dim, or Joy would have seen AnnaLise color up at the thought of how close she'd come to telling Daisy.

'Good. Keep it that way.' Joy slid another bottle out and, straightening, blew dust off the label so she could read it.

'But Daisy – wrong though you say she is, thank the Lord – did make me think. Someone like Dickens who doesn't stick, sexually speaking, to his own age group—'

'No, he's always stuck it to pretty much any woman who's gotten too close for too long.' The latest bottle went back in, too.

'Damn. I could have sworn there was a case of the cab we were drinking.'

'I know I was raised in an all-female household so maybe I'm naïve about this stuff,' AnnaLise continued, undeterred, 'but isn't there some kind of male parallel to maternal instinct? You know, a protective predisposition that would deter somebody like Dickens from . . . umm . . .'

'Doing?' Joy supplied, inspecting another bottle.

Good a word as any. 'OK, "doing" somebody young enough to be his daughter, if he had one?'

'Which he does. *You*, should a reminder be needed.'

'Believe me, I'd love to forget,' AnnaLise muttered.

'Listen, kid,' Joy said, 'I'm sure some would say the only instinct males have is to propagate the species via whatever "innies" accommodates their "outies," but you're not going to get that crap from me. As far as I'm concerned your birth father – and my ex-husband – is a pig. The trick is to figure out how to make bacon out of him.'

AnnaLise wrinkled her nose, a brunette echo of her blonde mother earlier that evening. 'Like you did?'

'Exactly. Ahh, here it is.' She held up a bottle cruddy enough to have been found in a shipwreck. 'And now I'm heading upstairs, where a corkscrew and our glasses await.'

AnnaLise and Joy had the wine open and were sharing it with Shirley when Dickens Hart got around to them on his grand working of the room.

He took a look at the wine in the glasses, then lifted the bottle on the cocktail table next to them, evidently reading the label.

'Anything wrong?' Joy inquired sweetly.

'Not at all.' Hart set it down. 'In fact, I hope you're enjoying it, because we're having the same wine with dinner.'

Even Joy looked surprised and, to AnnaLise, a little disappointed that she hadn't succeeded in aggravating Hart. 'You really *are* going all out—'

'Dinner is served!'

It was neither butler nor gong, but a curvy platinum blonde of about forty. She was wearing a short skirt, five-inch heels and a white coat with 'Chef Debbie' embroidered on the pocket. 'Could everyone please move into the dining room?'

They obeyed, only Hart hanging back to have a word with the chef.

AnnaLise stepped aside to let Shirley precede her. 'Leave it to Dickens to find the best-looking chef in the hemisphere,' the older woman said.

Following her into the dining room – which, thanks to Hart's 'pumping up' of the heat – was a tad too toasty, AnnaLise saw a gigantic cornucopia overflowing with apples, pears and other autumn bounty serving as the centerpiece of a wide, linen-covered table. It had been set for thirteen – six on each side and one place at the head of the table. That chair had a red cushion on it – for Hart, himself, naturally.

'Nice little touch, eh?' Joy said in her ear.

'What is?' There was nothing 'little' about anything in the room.

'The Horny Plenty.' Joy nodded to the centerpiece. 'Kind of strikes the vibe for the weekend.'

'I thought it was a "horn of" plenty,' said a young voice.

AnnaLise turned to see Lacey Capri. To support the girl, AnnaLise whispered, 'Ignore her,' indicating Joy, who was moving to the other side of the table. 'It *is* a horn of plenty. Or a cornucopia.'

'Ohmigod, that's just the word I was trying to think of.' Lacey blushed. 'I'm kind of a word nerd.'

AnnaLise smiled. 'Me, too. Good eyes, by the way, catching sight of that owl flying away.'

Said eyes grew big. 'Ohmigod! I've never seen anything that big. At least flying.'

'Agreed. I can even remember the first time I saw a wild turkey take off. Seemed like something out of a cartoon.'

The blue eyes got even larger. 'Turkeys . . . fly?'

AnnaLise smiled. 'Not the ones like we'll feast on tomorrow. Those are raised for their meat and are too fat to get off the ground. But, yes, wild turkeys can fly. At least, in short bursts.'

'Wow.' Her young face changed as she twisted her badge name-out so AnnaLise could see it. 'Oh, I'm sorry. My name's Lacey. My mother is over there.'

Dropping the lanyard, she pointed to where Sugar Capri sat talking with Phyllis Balisteri over the vacant chair that separated them. Across the table, Daisy was being chatted up by Lucinda and Tyler Puckett.

'I'm AnnaLise, and my mother is across from yours,' AnnaLise said to Lacey. Close-up, the girl was even prettier than she looked from the second floor, with milky white skin and piercing blue, verging on violet, eyes.

'AnnieLeez!' Phyllis was waving at them. 'I saved a seat for you.'

A little embarrassed that, at age twenty-eight, she still had seats 'saved' for her, AnnaLise said, 'Maybe Lacey would like to sit next to her mother.'

'No, I'm good,' Lacey said, continuing on down the table's line of chairs to the end.

Surrendering, AnnaLise slipped into the chair and put out her hand to Sugar. 'AnnaLise Griggs.'

'I've heard all about you,' Sugar said, shaking. 'Impressive.'

'Mama and Daisy exaggerate,' AnnaLise said, unsure which had been singing her praises.

'No, actually it was your *father*.' Sugar nodded toward Dickens Hart, who had just entered the room.

'Oh, that's nice,' the journalist said, albeit weakly. 'I didn't know that he and you were still in touch. I mean after, umm . . .'

'. . . all these years,' Mama supplied, leaning across her.

'Oh, we haven't been, really,' Sugar said. 'At least not up until a few days ago. When I found him online?' A conspiratorial look at AnnaLise. 'You know how it is, Googling old beaus.'

AnnaLise nodded, knowing that the only thing that would come out of her mouth – should she trust herself to open it – would be an astonished 'old *beaus*?'

Speaking of the devil, himself, Hart was approaching the head of the table, seeming pleased to find Lacey Capri seated to his right. Mistake, perhaps, because the contrast with the coltish girl made the self-styled lothario look both aged and rickety as he settled into his chair.

'. . . and so we just started emailing and texting,' Sugar was saying, 'and Dickens told me about this get-together. I couldn't resist seeing the place again. And him, too, of course.'

'You've been here before, then?' AnnaLise asked, regretting it immediately. Joy was diagonally across the table – a mere distance of five or six feet, easily breached if she wanted to get her hands around Sugar's throat.

'Oh, yes. When we were dating, I spent a lot of time here. Now, though, I couldn't pass up the invitation, especially since Lacey and I were in the area.'

Considering that the 'dating' had taken place when Hart was still married to Joy and the 'time spent' included sneaking into the marital bed, AnnaLise felt more at ease responding to Sugar's last comment.

'You live nearby?' she asked lightly. 'Since you arrived in the limousine from the airport with the others, I assumed you must have just flown in.'

'Oh, we left the car at Charlotte Douglas. So much easier than finding our way here on the mountain roads. Besides, Lacey had never ridden in a limo before.' Sugar giggled.

As mature as Sugar might have appeared at fifteen, she sure didn't seem to have progressed much since, right down to her choice of clothing and makeup. In fact, the few words her daughter had advanced seemed more articulate to AnnaLise's ear than Sugar's contributions.

Mama pulled at AnnaLise's sleeve to get her attention. 'What are you going to do?' she whispered.

'Do?'

'That girl is in your seat.' Phyllis was chin-gesturing toward Lacey Capri, talking to Hart. 'We're all wearing tags saying who we are. Why not cards telling folks where their rightful place is?'

'I think Dickens wants us to mingle,' AnnaLise replied. 'Besides, you're the one who wanted me *here*.'

'But you're the legitimate heir,' Mama maintained stubbornly. 'You belong at his right hand.'

'I'm *il*legitimate, remember? Besides, there are other people here who may have as much claim as I do.'

'No, no,' Phyllis was saying. 'I looked into this and you can ask Patrick Hoag if you want. Dickens Hart recognized you as his heir and put you in his will. He definitely hasn't done that for nobody else.'

Phyllis had put some thought – and research – into this, and while AnnaLise did appreciate all that effort on her own behalf, the 'golden child's' mantra hadn't changed. 'I told you, Mama. I don't care—'

'You'd better care!' Phyllis thundered as a waitress stopped to fill her wine glass, decanter hovering in one hand, white wine bottle in the other.

Everyone at the table looked at them and then, embarrassed, away.

'Umm, red or white?'

'Nicole?'

The waitress was Nicole Goldstein, college student and

granddaughter of Sal Goldstein, who owned Sal's Tap on the lake's beach across from Mama's.

'Hi, AnnaLise,' Nicole said. 'Wine, Mama? I have a full-bodied cabernet,' she held up a decanter, 'or a crisp Sauvignon blanc.'

'Go red,' AnnaLise advised.

'I'll take the sovey-young,' Phyllis said obstinately. 'Only the heavens know what this "chef" of Dickens will be putting in front of us.'

AnnaLise looked skyward and Nicole, trying to stay in role, carefully poured Phyllis her wine. 'Will you also be having red or would you like me to take the glass away?'

'Better *pour* away, instead,' AnnaLise muttered. 'I may need some backup.'

A laugh gurgling in Nicole's throat, she filled Phyllis' red wine glass with the cabernet and then AnnaLise's as well.

'So, Mama,' AnnaLise said after Nicole had moved on and the acknowledged daughter took a blessed sip. 'Is it nice having a weekend off?'

'Don't you be changing subject on me, you hear?' This time Phyllis at least kept her voice down.

'The subject being Dickens Hart's money and that I should want it? Well, I don't. Case closed.'

'That's all fine and well.' Phyllis' eyes narrowed and AnnaLise thought another tirade was coming, but instead, tears started to trickle down the older woman's cheeks.

AnnaLise had never seen Phyllis Balisteri cry. Ever.

'Please, don't,' she said, holding out her napkin. 'I'm sorry for . . . whatever.'

'I'll tell you whatever.' Phyllis snatched the napkin perfunctorily rather than gracefully. 'For thinkin' just of yourself. Daisy's got stacks of doctor's bills for her tests and she may well have stacks more if it's the Alls-whiners. Even worse, maybe all this forgetting is on account of a tumor in her brain.'

AnnaLise felt like she'd been stabbed through the heart. The tests, so far, hadn't shown a tumor, but . . . 'Then we'll find the best neurosurgeon out there.'

'And who's going to pay this "best" head-cutter? You?' Phyllis demanded.

'Insurance, of course.'

'Your insurance?'

'I'm on unpaid leave from the newspaper. But even if I wasn't, my insurance wouldn't cover Daisy.'

'So, you *do* see what I'm saying?'

The daughter just flat-out didn't.

And then she did.

Taking back her napkin, AnnaLise said, 'Mama, please don't tell me Daisy doesn't have health insurance.'

'That's exactly what I'm telling you. Neither of us in our lives.'

'You've *never* had insurance? But what do you do when you get sick?'

'We pay the doctor ourselves, of course. Since we don't work for big companies, individual insurance is sky-high. Doctor Stanton – and Doc Williams, God rest, before him – is fine with being paid on time.'

'But that's *crazy*.' Daisy's head turned their way and AnnaLise lowered her voice. 'What if something catastrophic happened to one or both of you? A car accident or—'

'AnnieLeez, you can't pay what you ain't got.' Mama's face was stern now. 'That's the long and the short of it. And as for "catty-strophic," which you seem to enjoy the sound of, we just took our chances.'

'A bet you lost.'

A sigh. 'I can't deny that.'

AnnaLise closed her eyes, trying to come to terms with needing to come up with not just the twenty percent she assumed they'd owe beyond what insurance covered, but the entire hundred percent. Dickens Hart was paying her a hundred thousand dollars for writing his memoirs. She'd gotten fifty already, and would get another fifty on satisfactory – to Hart – completion of the manuscript.

AnnaLise opened her eyes. 'Mama, has Daisy told you the total of her bills to date?'

'She has, but she don't want you to know.'

'Give, Mama. How much?'

'She said something came from the lab people just before we all left this morning, but up 'til then it was around eighty-three.'

'Eighty-three *hundred*?' AnnaLise brow furrowed.

But Mama was shaking her head. 'Thousand.'

Lacey Capri's laughter rang out in reaction to something Dickens Hart said, as AnnaLise let the idea of $83,000 in unpaid medical expenses – and counting – take center stage in her brain.

ELEVEN

'I told you so,' Joy said to AnnaLise. After dinner had broken up, they'd taken their wine out onto the patio so Joy could satisfy her nicotine jones.

While Joy's cancer stick might be keeping her warm, neither the nearby space heater nor AnnaLise's revisiting of recent conversations were doing the same for her.

Their backs were to the newly-applied plywood wall, providing privacy that the glass windows couldn't have. Not that it was necessary. The rest of the reunion had moved into the media room to watch a movie. Appropriately – or perversely *not* – *When Harry Met Sally*. It was a favorite of AnnaLise's and would probably prove a good choice for cutting across the generations and tastes of the small but diverse audience, only the journalist hadn't been in the mood for a love story. Especially one overlaid upon the real-time less-than-romantic farce.

Noticing herself being somewhat slow on the uptake, AnnaLise had just registered Joy's first foray. 'Told me what?'

Joy grunted. 'That you shouldn't turn your nose up at your inheritance. I just hope it isn't too late for you, what with all these hyenas sniffing around.'

'They were invited to "sniff,"' AnnaLise said wearily. 'And besides, whatever Hart might leave to me down the line isn't going to help much now.'

'We could do him in.' Joy took a drag and blew out its residue as the door from the house opened. 'Or, being the squeamish type, you could just ask him for a loan.'

'There you are.' The words came from Dickens Hart himself. 'Who needs a loan?'

Joy gave AnnaLise a significant look, which she promptly ignored. '"Loaner," actually. We were talking about my wrecked, and therefore *no*-car, situation.'

'You're welcome to borrow the Porsche, if you'd like.' Hart started to settle his butt on the corner of a massive wooden planter before standing up with a grimace to brush glass pellets off the seat of his pants. 'Though I'd have to caution you against driving it in the mountains once the snow starts falling.'

Which could be any day now. 'Thanks, but I'll be fine,' AnnaLise said simply, then changed the subject. 'How are you enjoying catching up with everyone?'

A snort from Joy.

Hart ignored her. 'Very much, AnnaLise, and thank you for asking. It's been like . . . well, a bit like *This Is Your Life*, what with Rose from my much younger days, Lucinda from early in the White Tail years, then your mother. And, of course, Shirley and Joy.'

'If I'd have known "Sweet Jail-bait" was going to be here,' Joy retorted, 'you can bet I wouldn't be.'

At the phrase 'jail-bait,' Hart threw a startled look toward AnnaLise before saying, 'Joy, I don't know what you mean.'

'Amazing that you don't want AnnaLise to be aware of your little misstep,' Joy said. 'Yet you invited the only one who really knows what happened – Sugar, herself.'

Hart said, running a practiced hand through his hair, 'I happened to mention the weekend to her in passing, and it seemed rude not to include both Sugar and her lovely daughter.'

'Pig,' Joy snapped.

'*Who*,' Hart continued icily, 'at least so far, aren't repaying my hospitality by helping themselves to my wine or making crude jokes at my expense.'

Joy dropped her cigarette and ground it into the patio block with a toe, seeming ready for a fight.

'Well, I'm going to head in,' AnnaLise said, having had enough theatrics for one day.

'I'll go with you,' Hart said hastily. Her biological father was many things, but stupid wasn't one of them.

As AnnaLise opened the French doors and stepped into the Lake Room, she almost collided with Nicole Goldstein, who was carrying a glass of wine in one hand and the bottle in another.

'Excuse me, AnnaLise,' Nicole said, steadying the goblet. 'Mr Hart asked me to open another bottle of wine, but we've run out of the one we were serving. I thought he might like to try this.'

Hart reached for the cabernet, apparently checking its pedigree. A lot of that was going on in general. 'I'm afraid your choice is a very big red and could do with another four of five years of cellaring.'

'Oh, I'm so sorry,' Nicole said, seeming mortified. 'I should have asked you before I opened it.'

'Not to worry, my dear,' Hart said. 'With a little time to breathe, the glass you've already poured should be passably drinkable, if not optimum. Could you just leave it on my bedside table?'

Nicole nodded. 'I'm glad to, but I'm not sure which room upstairs is yours.'

'The master bedroom is on this floor,' Hart said. 'It has the double doors at the end of the hall, just past the media room. Since it's barely ten-thirty, I'm going to catch some of the movie with our guests before I turn in.'

'Shall I throw out the rest of the bottle?' Nicole held it up.

'Heavens, no!' Hart commanded, and then lowered his voice as the girl cringed. 'Just put the cork in loosely and leave the bottle on the bar. The wine should mellow nicely by tomorrow. And for the rest of our guests, why not open that nice merlot I use as an everyday wine. You'll find three or four bottles in the rack to the right when you enter my wine cellar.'

'I can take the glass,' AnnaLise said to Nicole as Hart disappeared into the media room. There was no way she wanted the girl to visit Hart's bedroom, however innocently. Only God could know what she might find in the aging lion's love lair. Besides, after seeing the depiction on the floor plan, AnnaLise was curious.

'Thanks,' Nicole said, gratefully handing over the wine. 'I need to stash this bottle and open a new one. These folks drink like fish, so it's a good thing they don't have to drive anywhere. The road on this side of the lake is treacherous enough at night without having a snoot-full.'

AnnaLise looked at her own nearly empty glass. She'd thought about trailing Nicole to the kitchen for a refill, but given the girl's opinion of 'these folks,' decided to set a better example. Besides, both Joy and AnnaLise had already done considerable damage to Hart's supply of 'good stuff.' Not to mention their own respective livers. 'Very true. And you be careful on the way home yourself.'

'No worries,' Nicole said. 'My granddad is coming to pick me up. He doesn't like my driving at night.'

AnnaLise wasn't sure that Sal's driving – especially after his taproom closed – would be an improvement. 'That's very nice of him, but won't that be quite late?'

'It will, but I'll need to clean up the media room after the movie anyway.'

'Nicole? Got a sec?' Chef Debbie was at the doorway to the kitchen, sans the white coat. Though she and AnnaLise had to be about the same size, the über-high heels made Debbie tower over the reporter. The chef stuck her hand out. 'You're Dickens' daughter, right?'

AnnaLise held up the two glasses awkwardly. 'Sorry, I can't shake, but yes. I'm AnnaLise Griggs.'

'Anything special you'd like to have tomorrow? I'm missing a couple of items, so need to stop at the store in the morning.'

'I'm not sure you'll find a grocery open tomorrow.'

Debbie's brow wrinkled. Or tried to. 'Why not?'

'Thanksgiving,' Nicole said, trying to be helpful.

'Well, sure, but don't the supermarkets open, at least for a few hours in the morning?'

AnnaLise shook her head. 'My experience, which could be out-of-date, says no. Not around here.'

Debbie grimaced. 'Well, *that's* not good. And I assume no all-night convenience stores.'

'Sorry.'

The chef sighed. 'Not your fault. But I'll do my best. That's why your father's paying me the big bucks.'

'I just need to set this down,' Nicole held up the bottle of wine toward Debbie, 'and I'll be right with you.'

'Great. Just want to go over the menu with you before I leave. Good to meet you, AnnaLise.'

'Same here.'

Nicole made a beeline for the bar, while AnnaLise went the other direction, past the media room to the massive double doors. Opening one of them, though, was problematic with a goblet in each hand. With a glance over her shoulder to confirm that Nicole was already out of sight and couldn't come to her aid, AnnaLise finished off the wine in her glass and tucked it awkwardly under one arm to turn the knob.

In contrast to the marble hallway outside the door, Hart's room was lushly carpeted. The oversized platform bed was already turned down for the evening, the lamps on the flanking ornate nightstands casting a soft glow. AnnaLise looked up, but there was no mirror overhead, as she'd smarmily expected. But then the man was nearly seventy. He'd probably had the mirrors removed with the velvet trapeze.

To her left, the lake-facing wall of the room was floor-to-ceiling glass, opening onto a moonlit private patio. On the opposite wall was a low dresser built of the same exotic wood as the nightstands and even the small waste basket that stood next to it.

Wanting to set the two wine glasses on the dresser, AnnaLise rescued a crumpled scrap of what looked like the Hart's Head floor plan from the trash and flattened it with the palm of one hand to serve as a make-shift coaster.

Placing the glasses on the paper, AnnaLise noticed a number scratched onto it in blue ink. 'Seven-oh-two area code,' she read. 'Chef Debbie's Las Vegas cellphone, perhaps?'

Unsurprised that the old leopard hadn't changed his age spots, AnnaLise turned to survey the rest of the room. An armless, high-backed slipper chair was positioned in the shallow corner formed by a bump-out – probably a closet – next to the entryway into the suite. Simple and sleek, the chair was much more to AnnaLise's taste than the heavier, carved furniture in the room.

But it was the wide hallway beyond the chair that caught her attention. Assuming it led to a spa-like bathroom, AnnaLise passed between mirror-image walk-in closets (one, alone, the size of her bedroom in Daisy's house) and stepped into the en suite.

The twin centerpieces of the room were a deep soaking tub/ whirlpool and a bow-front shower. The tub looked big enough to allow for swimming laps, and the shower like it had been designed to decontaminate Hart after he teleported in from another planet. Each side of the room had its own granite-topped vanity and a separate room with toilet and bidet.

Trying hard to tamp down thoughts of *my mother can't afford health insurance, while my father is living like this*, AnnaLise returned to the bedroom.

She'd assumed the wall behind the chair she'd admired was yet another big closet, but returning to the double-door entrance AnnaLise realized it actually hid a small switchback staircase. Hand on doorknob, she could just make out the film voices of Billy Crystal and Meg Ryan punctuated by laughter, including – she thought – some from Dickens Hart.

Figuring she had time to take a quick peek upstairs before Hart said good night to his guests and turned in, AnnaLise climbed the carpeted steps to find herself in a personal library. To the right of the stairs was a door.

Opening it, AnnaLise found a wall of books. Boxes upon boxes of them, apparently not deemed worthy of being displayed on the floor-to-ceiling shelves of the impressive library. There were so many boxes she couldn't even step into the storage room.

Shutting that door, AnnaLise approached the bookshelves. She'd expected to find leather-bound volumes, bought for show, not for reading. But these books – hardcover and paperback, fiction and non-fiction – had been read, and many not just the once. The only furniture in the room was an overstuffed leather recliner so huge she couldn't imagine anyone short of cyclopsed ogres wrestling the thing up the narrow stairs.

'OK,' AnnaLise said softly. 'This setup I *do* covet.' She'd never have taken Hart for a reader, but maybe a love of the written word was the one thing, other than dark hair and brown eyes, that she'd inherited from the man. She slipped a copy of Jeremiah Healy's *Blunt Darts* off the bookshelf.

A door opened below. AnnaLise returned the novel to its shelf and tiptoed to the top of the stairs, trying to ascertain whether the sound had come from out in the foyer or inside the master bedroom itself.

To avoid further awkwardness, the proper thing would have been to call out immediately, beg forgiveness for nosing around and hightail it out of there. Unfortunately, by the time AnnaLise realized the noise had, indeed, been one of the double doors to the room opening and decided what she *should* do, the time to take the high road gracefully had, unfortunately and irretrievably, passed.

The sound of something being set down. Then the creak of bed springs and . . . had that been a whimper? Or a groan?

Fearful that she'd find her father out of his clothes and perhaps into . . . well, something – or somebody – else, AnnaLise debated staying upstairs.

Eventually Hart would have to use the bathroom. Or fall asleep. The steps were right around the corner from the door, so she wouldn't need more than five seconds to be down and, quite literally, out.

In the meantime, AnnaLise would be comfortable enough up there, maybe even pass the time by reading a book.

But luck was with her, and it wasn't five minutes later that AnnaLise thought she heard a door close from the direction of the bathroom. Not hesitating and risk losing her chance again, AnnaLise crept down the steps.

Near the bottom, she could just make out the sound of water running. Continuing down, AnnaLise snuck her head around the corner and, seeing no one, stepped out past the slipper chair to look down the bathroom hallway. Sure enough, the door was closed, a sliver of light showing beneath it.

Turning to leave, AnnaLise nearly collided with the chair. She steadied herself on its high back and did a double take. A small, brightly flowered nylon bag with a black handle and shoulder strap had appeared on the seat.

Just large enough to hold a change of clothes. And a toothbrush. Either daddy's become a cross-dresser or he's at it again, AnnaLise thought. *And I'm betting Chef Debbie from Vegas is the unlucky woman.*

Not wanting to push her own luck, AnnaLise Griggs tiptoed to the door and, as silently as possible, let herself out.

TWELVE

Now standing outside the media room, AnnaLise debated going in.

Much as she loved *When Harry Met Sally*, the best scenes were probably already history. Besides, given the chattering going on in the room, AnnaLise wouldn't be able to watch the film in peace as she'd prefer, but rather be expected to make small talk.

And, God knew, enough of that would be clogging the balance of the weekend.

The door opened with a bump, and Shirley Hart came out.

'Movie over?' AnnaLise asked.

'No, but the deli scene just concluded, and it's been a long day.'

'Amen to that,' AnnaLise said, falling into step with her as they climbed the stairs.

Shirley took her hand off the railing to settle an errant hank of gray-streaked hair. 'As much as I convinced myself that this would be a lark, it *is* a tad irritating watching the two boys – Lucinda's Tyler and Rose's Eddie – try to out-audition each other. And that Sugar seems determined to rekindle something that shouldn't have happened in the first place. I'm surprised Joy hasn't knocked her block off yet.'

'I think Joy's still reeling from not having the whole sordid thing to hold over Dickens' head any longer.' As they reached the top of the staircase, AnnaLise said, 'Have you spoken anymore with Lucinda?'

'Meaning *my* "other woman"?' Hart's first wife asked. 'A little – my trying to fan the flames of her anger over this "logo" work she feels Dickens stole.'

'You and Joy are determined to be troublemakers, aren't you?'

'Do I detect a hint of surprise?' Shirley asked. 'We didn't come this weekend to give Dickens Hart the "Ex-wives Seal of Approval," you know. The two of us made a pact. That we'd enjoy ourselves.'

For her part, AnnaLise was just hoping to survive. 'Did you manage to rile Lucinda up even more than she already was?'

A sigh. 'Sadly, no. Apparently Mama Bear has decided not to jeopardize Baby Bear's chances during this treasure-hunt weekend. She may well be steaming internally, but outwardly she's as boring as ever. I remember thinking, at the time Dickens took up with her, that he must be going through a dead-fish period.'

Shirley interrupted herself, hooking a thumb north. 'I'm at the end of this hallway.'

'And I'm the same, but this first door on the right.' AnnaLise nodded at it.

'Across from your mother and Phyllis, while I'm opposite Joy farther down. I'm sure you noticed from the floor plan that all of the non-locals are in the south wing.'

'I did.' AnnaLise realized she'd left her diagram downstairs somewhere. 'Do you think that's significant?'

A lift of an eyebrow from Shirley. 'Only in that Dickens seems to have his game pieces positioned right where he wants them.'

AnnaLise laughed. 'I do like your attitude.'

Shirley patted the younger woman's shoulder. 'And I, your fortitude. I divorced Hart and can choose to be done with the bastard. You're stuck watching him play Lord of the Manor, as Joy says, for life.'

'True, but at least he does it well,' AnnaLise said. 'And it *is* quite the manor.'

'Without a doubt, on both counts. My only regret divorcing the cad is that I didn't get a chance to live here.' Shirley Hart shook her head. 'And I was naïve enough to think I'd taken the bastard for everything he had.'

* * *

When AnnaLise turned over the next morning, the sun was already slanting through the windows. She checked the clock on her bedside table: eight forty-six.

After leaving Shirley Hart, AnnaLise had gotten to bed at about eleven and was just dropping off when the movie must have ended. While the vaulted foyer and Lake Room looked magnificent, noise from people heading up the stairs to their rooms echoed from the marble foyer right through the walls.

Things had gradually quieted down, with the last straggler – Joy, since Shirley was already in her room – passing through the north wing's hallway at about eleven-thirty. AnnaLise knew this because she'd lain watching the bedside clock's digital numbers change for another half hour after that. Finally, approaching midnight, she'd crawled out of bed and dug through her purse for aspirin, hoping the drug would ward off the – admittedly fine – wine-induced hangover she already felt coming on.

Coming up with two tablets, AnnaLise was padding back to bed when an engine roared out front. She'd parted the French door curtains to see a green land yacht pull up on the circle drive and hear the front door below open and close. A figure trotted down the porch steps – Nicole, almost certainly, being picked up by her grandfather.

AnnaLise had finally fallen asleep after that, but somehow the eight hours hadn't refreshed her. In fact, her stomach was queasy and her head ached. So much for the healing qualities of aspirin.

But then, there was always caffeine.

Pulling on sweats, she padded down the steps toward the dining room. With luck, everyone else would be long done with breakfast and AnnaLise could have her coffee in relative peace without seeing anybody or being seen, given the way she feared she might look.

Alas, the one man even close to her age, Tyler Puckett, and Rose Boccaccio's son, Eddie, were still at the breakfast table. AnnaLise couldn't help but notice that Tyler was wearing his lanyard name badge, while Eddie wasn't.

She pasted a bright smile on her face. 'Good morning!'

'Happy Thanksgiving!' Tyler said, looking up from what he was reading. 'Like part of my paper?'

'I'd love it,' said AnnaLise, grateful that no chit-chat seemed required. 'Just as soon as I get my coffee.'

'Nicole just brought it in fresh.' Eddie waved toward the

sideboard. 'I think there's some toast and eggs, too, though I'm sure she'll bring you something else if you'd like.'

'Nicole's great,' AnnaLise said, returning to the table with her coffee. Even dry toast seemed too much to handle at this point. 'She goes to the University of the Mountain here in Sutherton.'

'Like my mom,' Tyler said. His hair was more auburn than strawberry blonde like Lucinda's, but he had her fine spray of freckles across the nose and cheeks and a friendly smile. 'Did you go there, too?'

'Too expensive for my "towny" blood, I'm afraid,' AnnaLise said, tipping cream into her cup. 'Besides, I wanted to go away to school, so I studied journalism at Wisconsin.'

'The flagship campus in Madison?' Tyler asked, passing her the Sports section. 'They've got a good pre-law curriculum, not to mention a great football program.'

But Eddie looked confused. 'I don't mean to pry, but why would tuition have been a problem? You are Hart's daughter, correct?'

'I am.' AnnaLise thought she knew where this was leading. 'Though for most of my life, I didn't know that. Nor, in fairness, did Dickens.'

'Then not so much different than Tyler or me,' Eddie said, raking his bandaged hand from the window blow-out through thinning blond hair. 'Assuming, of course, that the results of our DNA tests – when we have them – come out the same.'

AnnaLise took a tentative sip of her coffee, wondering if Eddie's gesture was natural or an attempt to mimic Dickens Hart. 'Were you cut badly last night?'

'A mere flesh wound,' Eddie said shortly, putting the hand in his lap.

'Just because Dickens didn't want his party interrupted doesn't mean you have to be a hero if you're hurt,' AnnaLise said. 'If you need stitches or something for pain—'

Tyler interrupted, like a ten-year-old eager to redirect the conversation to himself. 'I can certainly understand Dickens' desire for the weekend to go off perfectly. This is an important weekend for him. And for the three of us.'

'The three of *us*?' AnnaLise repeated. 'I—'

Tyler grinned. 'Sorry, I meant Eddie, Lacey and me. Though now that I think about it, you're the one who has the most to lose, while we only stand to gain.'

'Potentially,' Eddie reminded him pointedly.

'But Lacey . . .' AnnaLise started to say, then let her voice drift off, realizing that Hart's vasectomy was none of their business, for now. In fact, AnnaLise wouldn't know about it, either, if she wasn't privy to his journals – and Joy, of course.

Happily, Tyler took up where he thought she'd left off. 'I know. Gotta give the old guy credit, maybe having a daughter that age.'

'Hey,' Eddie said, taking off his reading glasses. 'Lacey's fifteen and Hart's sixty-eight, so he wouldn't have been much older than I am when she was conceived.'

'But, don't you see, my—'

'You think sex ends at forty?' Eddied demanded, the pupils in his eyes getting bigger. 'Men far older have fathered children.'

'No, I mean that it's an amazing . . .'

AnnaLise jumped in. 'Age-span between Dickens' potential children? I agree. Between you, Eddie, and Lacey would be . . . thirty-six years?'

'Exactly,' Tyler said, gratefully. 'Have to admire that kind of . . . of . . .'

'Libido?' AnnaLise suggested, her head starting to pound again. If she was to serve as both thesaurus and referee, this was shaping up to be a very long weekend.

Happily, the conversation was interrupted by the arrival of yet another late riser – the girl they'd just been talking about.

'Morning,' Lacey said, rubbing her eyes like a sleepy toddler. 'Am I too late for breakfast?'

'Nope. And you're only a few minutes behind me,' AnnaLise said.

'I'm not much of an early riser,' Lacey said. 'Ooh, toast!'

'Eggs, too,' Eddie said, as he had when AnnaLise arrived. 'Though I'm not sure how hot they are anymore.'

'That's OK,' Lacey said. 'Toast and juice is fine.'

She stacked two pieces of toast on a plate and added marble-sized balls of butter. 'Do we have jam?'

'In there,' Tyler said, pointing toward what looked like a Waterford crystal jelly jar.

'Oh,' Lacey said, picking up the tiny spoon. 'This is so cute. But I was just looking for those little jam packets to take back to our room.'

'You're not going to join us?' AnnaLise was disappointed. The presence of the teenager might save the reporter from further discussion of her biological father's profile, biologically speaking, anyway.

'I'm not really presentable,' Lacey said, looking down at her pajama pants and baggy T-shirt.

'That's OK,' AnnaLise said. 'I'm in sweats.'

'Oh, let the kid go,' Tyler said, with a wink at Lacey. 'She obviously doesn't want to sit here with us geezers.'

Lacey looked sheepish. 'It's not that, really. I just—'

'Go run along, tadpole,' Eddie said, waving his hand. 'Your mother went for a walk on the lake with the rest of the group.'

'You all didn't want to join them?' Lacey asked, spooning jam on the edge of her plate and then getting a juice glass.

'My mother came knocking at my door, waking me out of a sound sleep.' Tyler yawned. 'But I prefer to ease into my mornings.'

'Same,' Eddie said. 'I woke just in time to see the hikers heading out across the back lawn.'

'I even missed that,' AnnaLise admitted. 'Your mother must be an early riser, Lacey.'

'She is. Though, like I said, I'm just the opposite.' The girl picked up her juice and plate, seeming uncertain how to make a graceful exit.

'You're excused,' AnnaLise said with a smile. 'Enjoy your breakfast.'

'Nice kid.' Tyler was watching her leave. 'Bet she's wishing she brought a friend along for the weekend.'

'She did – her mother.' AnnaLise felt herself redden. 'Sorry, that was catty. It's just that Sugar doesn't look much older than Lacey.'

'She doesn't act it, either.' Eddie slipped his reading glasses back on. 'The mother went off hiking this morning in a short plaid skirt and thigh-high knee socks.'

'*Clueless*,' AnnaLise said. 'The movie, I mean. Nineteen ninety-five, Alicia Silverstone?'

'I'll take your word for it,' Eddie said, lifting the newspaper section he'd been reading. 'Smacked more of naughty schoolgirl to me.'

Determined not to further criticize Sugar, AnnaLise got up to get a piece of dry toast. 'So,' she said, re-taking her chair, 'how was *When Harry Met Sally*?'

'Good,' Tyler said. 'There was probably more talking than watching, but I have to hand it to Hart: it's a good choice as a generational ice-breaker. I'm kind of surprised you weren't there.'

'I'd had a long day.' And too much wine.

'It wasn't a late night,' Tyler said. 'The movie was over by about a quarter past eleven, I think, and then Dickens left, more or less bringing the party to a close.'

'Nobody to impress,' Eddie said a little sourly from behind the newspaper.

My, my, somebody seemed to have gotten up on the wrong side of the bed.

Not that AnnaLise would let that stop her from making nice, now that her own head was feeling a little better. She picked up her coffee cup. 'What do you do for a living, Eddie?'

'Why?' His voice was sharp as he set aside his reading material.

'Jesus, take a pill,' Tyler said, tossing his napkin on the table. 'She's just making conversation.'

'Sorry, sorry.' Eddie held up his hands. 'I'm just a little touchy. As . . . well, as interesting and potentially life-changing as this whole situation is, it also feels like a competition.'

'I get that,' AnnaLise said. 'And I'm sorry. But Tyler's right, I was just making conversation.'

'No, I'm the one who should be sorry,' Eddie said, looking sheepish. 'To answer your question, I'm a dentist.'

'Oh,' AnnaLise said, perking up. They'd never had a dentist in the family. Actually, they'd never had anybody in their family besides her, Daisy and Mama. 'And what about you, Tyler?'

'Broker.'

'Real estate has—'

At that moment, Boozer Bacchus came in. Hair disheveled and eyes red, he looked worse than AnnaLise, making her wonder if he'd hit his flask as hard as she had the cabernet. 'AnnaLise? Can I talk to you in the other room?'

'Sure.' AnnaLise scooted back her chair. 'Excuse me for just a second?'

She followed Bacchus through the hallway and into the Lake Room. 'Is there something wrong? I mean, besides the obvious?' She crossed the room to the twenty-foot-wide plywood non-window.

'I'm afraid I had to run out at dawn to see my dad.' He seemed apologetic.

'Heavens, it's Thanksgiving,' AnnaLise said. 'I think you're entitled. Why? Is Dickens upset you left?'

'No, in fact, he's still sleeping, which is why I wanted to show you.'

'OK . . .' AnnaLise wasn't sure what he was getting at.

'When I got back a few minutes ago, I decided to go back over the floor in here again. You know, make sure no broken glass was still on it.' He nodded toward a broom propped next to the fireplace, along with a dustpan and plastic waste basket.

'I wouldn't be surprised, given that it was dusk and that monstrosity,' she pointed at the chandelier above them, 'can only illuminate so much of the room.' She picked up the waste basket and shook it, getting a faint rattle for her efforts. 'Not bad.'

'Oh, the boys did a fine job last night. Just found a couple small fragments all the way over by the fireplace.' He reached into his jacket pocket. 'But this, too.'

Taking her hand and turning it over, he dropped a deadly piece of heavy metal into her open palm.

THIRTEEN

'**A** *bullet* broke the window?' Even as AnnaLise said it, she glanced reflexively toward the lake, only to be defeated by the plywood blocking the view.

'I don't see how else that slug got in here,' Bacchus said, retrieving a glass from the fireplace mantle and crossing to the bar with it. 'You?'

'So it wasn't the owl.' AnnaLise was examining the misshapen metal.

Bacchus set the champagne flute down and turned. 'I never did get a glimpse of it, myself, but from what people said, it was flying away?'

AnnaLise nodded. 'Unsteadily. I assumed it had been stunned.'

'Probably scared by the shot, or maybe just caught his dinner,' Bacchus said, returning to her. 'A rodent that's fighting for its life can throw off a fellow's flight trajectory.'

'I'll take your word for that.' AnnaLise held up the slug. 'You said you found this by the fireplace?'

'Maybe five feet this way, just barely under the edge of the couch there. Like it might've hit off the fieldstone and bounced.'

'It could have killed somebody.'

A nod. 'It being rifle season, it might've been a deer hunter, I suppose.' Bacchus took the bullet from her. 'Or maybe some yahoo jus—'

'Excuse me?' Nicole Goldstein was at the hall doorway. 'Have either of you seen Chef Debbie?'

'Not this morning – yet,' AnnaLise said, cocking her head at a sound from outside. 'But I've been up for less than an hour.' It just *seemed* longer. 'You, Boozer?'

'Can't say that I have, though like AnnaLise here, I haven't been looking.'

Nicole was nervously plucking at the strings of the apron she'd wrapped around her slim waist and then tied in front. 'She told me she'd be here by six-thirty to get things started. I've done what I can, but . . .'

Bacchus slipped the slug back into his coat pocket and winked at AnnaLise, before turning to Nicole. 'Don't you worry; you and me'll track her down.'

Taking Bacchus' gesture to mean they'd keep the shooting between them for now, AnnaLise followed his verbal lead, even as she walked the other way, toward the French doors. 'You might want to ask Mama and Daisy to pitch in.'

'Oh, they're already in the kitchen.' Nicole said, coloring up. 'I told them I could handle things, but—'

'They didn't listen,' AnnaLise finished as she cracked open the door. 'Do yourself a favor and let those two help for now. Debbie can fight them for her kitchen when she gets here.'

A relieved smile crossed the girl's face before she scurried after Bacchus.

Stepping out onto the patio, AnnaLise had a sunlit view of the deck of Bradenham. A figure moved across it, leaned down to adjust something, then retreated to the other end of the structure.

The sound of a gunshot rang out across the water.

'Roy Smoaks!'

The 'yahoo' in question turned to face AnnaLise.

'Morning, missy,' Smoaks said as she crossed the wooden bridge that connected the house to the cantilevered deck while still allowing the lake trail to pass under it.

The man was carefully placing empty bottles of various sizes

– and proofs – atop a table at the far end of the deck. 'You folks sure are early risers across the bay. Was that you I saw playing "kerplunk" at the fishing pier this fine Thanksgiving morn'?'

'A group is hiking the lake trail,' AnnaLise said, not having time for whatever version of skipping stones 'kerplunk' might be. A deer rifle was propped up against the deck railing and she reached out to touch the barrel. It felt warm. 'And I'm hoping you're not going to shoot them. Accidentally, of course.'

The man turned. 'Me? Now whyever would I do that? I don't have nothing against *those* people.'

'The "bastard off-spring," as you put it?'

'Potentially, yes. That would be them, all right.' Smoaks held the whiskey bottle up to the light, then tipped it to his lips. Wiping off his mouth with the back of his hand, he continued: 'What with my grandson out of the running, it's no skin off my grassy ass who gets what when that sonovabitch finally goes to his maker.'

Apparently Smoaks hadn't forgiven the 'sonovabitch' for insti-gating the campaign that gave the town a mixed-use condominium development where the White Tail Club had stood, as well as a new police chief – one that wasn't a Smoaks. Though on the plus side of the ledger, the old man should be grateful that it had also resulted in his 'new' grandson, Bobby Bradenham, being elected mayor.

'A big window was shot out at the house,' AnnaLise said, wondering how Ema Bradenham would feel about this charmer as a guest.

'Is that so?' Smoaks shielded his eyes to look east across the lake. 'Well, sure enough, 'less Hart's boarding up the place for the winter.' He laughed, showing a gold-capped canine tooth.

AnnaLise found it hard to believe the man was just now noticing the plywood patch, especially if he'd had his binoculars leveled on Hart's Head as she'd suspected the night before. Still, she had no intention of letting Smoaks know what she was thinking. 'Listen, it's going to be a very long weekend, as it is, with a lot of low-landers wandering around cluelessly. We're certain it was an acci-dent, but if you could just be care—'

'You are, now?' The man leaned in close to retrieve the deer rifle from the railing and took the opportunity to run his eyes up and down her body in the process. 'I mean, "certain" it was an accident?'

The reporter willed herself not to gag on the sweet, stale smell that wafted off him. She'd been too young to have dealings with the older Smoaks, but his son Rance had ruled the town through intimidation – bullying, really. As Mama had said, the rotten apple hadn't fallen far from the tree, though it apparently stopped short of Bobby, thank the Lord. Nurture versus nature, but it boggled AnnaLise's mind that her friend was related to this . . . person.

'Whether it was you or some hunter who broke the window, I sincerely hope it wasn't on purpose.' She backed up a half step before turning away. 'But I'm going to mention it to Bobby, nonetheless.'

'Tattlin' to the mayor, huh?' he said to her back. 'Too bad that fag of a police chief is out of town, or you—'

AnnaLise pivoted and slapped him hard, her weight moving forward and through, like a tennis stroke.

Smoaks staggered back, still holding onto the rifle.

AnnaLise started forward, hoping to grab it, but Smoaks took his hand away from his cheek and raised the rifle. 'You little bitch! Who—'

'What the *hell* is going on?'

Bobby was standing by the open door to the house. AnnaLise backed away from Smoaks, one step at a time, until she was safely standing next to her friend.

'He shot out Dickens window last night.'

'She hit me!' Smoaks said, rifle dangling now. The left side of his face was aglow, like he'd suffered wind-burn.

'He called Chuck a "fag."'

'For God's sake, Roy.' Bobby rubbed at his forehead. 'Rance lost, Chuck won, and it was years ago. Leave it be.'

'Who are *you* to tell—' The old man broke off, the obstinance that had been on his face replaced by a more calculating expression. 'You're right. Water over the dam.'

'Good.' Bobby turned to AnnaLise. 'Now what's this about a window?'

'A huge one, facing the lake.' She pointed to the Hart's Head across the way. 'At first we thought an owl had hit it just right – or wrong – but this morning we found a bullet.'

Bobby's forehead wrinkled and he flinched like it hurt. 'Where?'

'In front of the fireplace.' She peered at him. 'Are you hungover?' AnnaLise was a fine one to talk, given her wine consumption of the night before. But the fact was that Bobby had gone through a tough patch and AnnaLise dearly hoped he wasn't self-medicating.

Her friend ignored the question and addressed Smoaks. 'Did you have anything to do with this?'

'Nope.' The old man crossed his heart with his non-gun-toting hand. 'Scout's honor.'

Bobby didn't seem to quite buy his new grandfather's denial, but turned back to her. 'It *is* deer season, AnnaLise.'

'But this is private land,' she protested.

'Like that stops 'em.' Smoaks hawked up a loogie and spat it out over the railing with enough loft to send it into the lake. 'Probably somebody's last ammo when the sun went down.'

Deer *were* most active after sundown, AnnaLise knew, supposedly because of their acute night vision. Though maybe the animals were just smart enough to know that darkness meant safety, hunting being illegal from a half hour after sunset to thirty minutes before sunrise.

But then, so was poaching on private land.

'Weren't you here?' she asked Bobby. 'Don't you know what your guest was doing?'

'Sure. We had an early dinner—'

Smoaks interrupted. 'Being from the "land of the early-bird special" now, a man gets hungry.'

'—and a few drinks,' Bobby continued. 'I must have fallen asleep on the couch.'

Sounded more like passing out than sleeping, but AnnaLise realized she was getting nowhere. 'Listen, I need to get back, it being Thankgiving and all.' She sniffed at the warm air escaping from the open door from the house. 'Your turkey isn't in the oven yet?'

'We're just doing burgers on the grill.' Bobby nodded at the sleek stainless steel mini-kitchen across the way from them.

'Not much of a Thanksgiving dinner,' AnnaLise said, but stopped short of inviting the two to their own feast across the lake. Talk about a recipe for disaster.

'You know how we mens are,' Smoaks said with a grin and a shrug. 'Ease trumps tradition every time.'

To be honest, as the product of a female household, AnnaLise didn't know how 'mens' were. Especially one like Smoaks. 'Will you both,' she risked a quick glance at the elder, 'promise me, no shooting across the lake?'

'Scout's honor,' again from Smoaks, this time accompanied by a toothy – if, to AnnaLise's eye, insincere – grin.

She shrugged and started down the stairs. 'OK, I'm leaving. You two behave.'

'Scout's—'

'Enough!'

Unlike Bradenham, Hart's Head smelled like Thanksgiving turkey when AnnaLise stepped into the foyer.

Why come all the way from Florida for the holiday, AnnaLise wondered, if Smoaks and Bobby weren't even going to observe it? Hamburgers for Thanksgiving dinner? It was near sacrilegious.

Closing the door behind her, she hesitated, her hand still on the knob. Might there be another reason Smoaks had chosen this particular long weekend to visit? He'd said himself that he'd heard about Dickens' get-together for his 'bastard offspring' down in Florida. Could the former chief's resentment be so deep that he'd made the trip to Sutherton just to disrupt the gathering?

'Thank God, you're—' Boozer Baccus had entered the foyer at a gallop, probably in response to the sound of the front door opening and now he slid to a stop. 'I'm sorry – I thought you were that chef.' The bullet found in the Lake Room was seemingly lost in Bacchus' more immediate gastronomical concerns.

'Debbie's still not here?' The turkey roasting must be Nicole's work, bless her. And her two mothers helpers.

But AnnaLise was thinking about the overnight bag she'd seen in Dickens' bedroom the night before.

'Not unless the woman is invisible. Don't suppose you have a phone number for her?'

AnnaLise thought she knew where to find one – and, perhaps, the chef, herself. But hoping to avoid having to personally crash Dickens' pajama party, she said, 'No, but how about Patrick? Might he have hired her?'

'The lawyer? No. He's not much use except for writing letters and checks.' Bacchus was rubbing his chin. 'Well, that leaves just the one person.'

'Dickens.'

'I hated to wake him until now, but the boss is the one who found Chef Debbie, so he'll have her number.'

One way, if not the other, AnnaLise thought. As Boozer started toward the master bedroom, she grabbed his arm. 'I'd knock first.'

Boozer stopped. 'I always do, but is there a special reason this time?'

'It's just that I saw a woman's overnight bag last night when Dickens asked me – or Nicole, really – to put a glass of wine in his room. I thought it might be Debbie's.'

'Well, then,' Boozer said, continuing his trajectory, 'she should be easy to find.'

He knocked on the door as AnnaLise shrank back. Then he turned the knob.

'Wait,' she whispered. 'Should you burst in on them?'

Now Bacchus looked confused. 'For sure, it wouldn't be the first time.'

'That Dickens did the chef?'

'That the lieutenant did *some*body.' Bacchus entered the room.

*Any*body. 'Point taken,' AnnaLise said to his back with a nervous giggle as a tap-tap of footsteps approached from the direction of the kitchen.

Dickens Hart's biological daughter was trying very hard to grow a thick skin. Her father was – as Joy put it and AnnaLise had already concluded – a pig. Need to get used to that.

'AnnaLise? It's about time you got up.'

Recognizing the voice, AnnaLise turned, hoping to deflect her mother as Bacchus dealt with Dickens Hart. And . . . whomever. 'Morning, Daisy. You're wearing an apron.'

'Because I'm cooking, of course. Or helping Phyllis to do so. Poor Nicole was running herself ragged trying to keep up. We offered to get the turkey started while Boozer tracked down Hart's chef.'

She was trying to look past AnnaLise into the room. 'Is she in there?'

AnnaLise didn't envy a chef who tried to take back control of a kitchen once Mama had gotten her convenience-food claws into it. But then she didn't envy a chef who was 'in there' with Dickens Hart, either.

'It's fine, if not,' Daisy continued. 'To tell you the truth, we're all better off with Phyllis cooking rather than all the time bitching—' She slapped her hand over her mouth. 'Sorry.'

Sweet Daisy wasn't always quite so sweet anymore. Whether that shift was simply a function of getting older and feeling entitled to say what she thought, or some sort of side effect of the memory problems, AnnaLise hadn't decided.

Bacchus re-emerged into the hallway.

'No sign of the chef?' Relieved when he wordlessly shook his head, AnnaLise turned back to Daisy. 'So maybe you should go back to the kitchen and tell—'

'Boozer,' Daisy said, concern in her voice. 'Are you all right?'

Boozer Bacchus was holding on to the door jamb, looking ashen-faced.

Sensibilities forgotten, AnnaLise pushed past him.

Dickens Hart was lying face down on his bed.

A gasp came from behind her and AnnaLise turned to see Boozer Bacchus enveloping Daisy in a scene-of-the-accident way, trying to hold her back.

Dickens Hart was naked, but that wasn't the most shocking thing. The back of the man's head was caved in, and the overnight bag on the chair had been replaced by a champagne bottle, a smear of blood obscuring the fancy crest of the label.

FOURTEEN

Apparently, Dickens Hart had died in his sleep.

Or, at the very least, in his bed.

As the deceased's daughter – hell, even as his employee – AnnaLise Griggs knew she should feel . . . something. But *feeling* you should feel and actually doing it were two entirely different things. For now, AnnaLise set reflection aside in favor of dealing with the realities of what had happened to the owner of the house in which they were all staying.

Boozer Bacchus had called 9-1-1 but, once he'd shown the first responders to the master suite, AnnaLise had offered to take over with the police. Unlike her, Hart's longtime employee and friend was visibly shaken and, if he didn't at least sit down, AnnaLise feared he might fall down.

Officer Coy Pitchford and AnnaLise now occupied Dickens Hart's office, where AnnaLise had first heard about plans for the weekend's grand gesture. They were seated respectively in the two guest chairs that fronted the desk.

Outside the window a white panel truck with 'Medical Examiner' on its side had joined the ambulance. There'd been no hope of intervention in Hart's passing.

'Sure wish you'd been nosy enough to look into that night bag,' Coy said, writing on a note pad he'd taken from the chest pocket of his uniform. 'That way, maybe we'd know for sure who it belonged to.'

'You and me both,' the journalist said. 'At the time I was just trying to get out of there without being seen or embarrassing anyone, including myself. I do think, though, that the fact Chef Debbie has disappeared along with the bag suggests a connection.'

'It does, though it'd be nice to have more than her profession and first name to go on.' Only in his mid-twenties, Coy's round face made him look even younger. 'Like that phone number you said you saw, for example. I can't find it.'

'It was written on a scrap of the floor plan Dickens handed out. Did you check the waste basket? That's where I found it in the first place.'

'I did.' Coy pulled on an earlobe. 'Surely wish Chuck would've picked a different time to go out of town.'

'Me, too,' AnnaLise said, and then quickly added, 'not that you can't handle the situation, Coy. But,' she was remembering what the mayor had said about the sheriff's department acting as backup, 'are you going to call the county in?'

Acting Chief Pitchford looked a little hurt. 'I expect so. Though I'd like to see what Doc Kilgore has to say first.'

Doctor Kilgore was the area's longtime and, unfortunately, aptly named medical examiner, though most of the times the man had been called out over the last forty years were more accidental drownings in the lake or lost hikers freezing to death on the mountain.

But even if that weren't the case, AnnaLise didn't quite see what Doc could say that would change the facts. It was beyond belief that Dickens Hart had smashed *himself* in the back of his head with a champagne bottle.

A knock at the door and Doc Kilgore entered, nodding to AnnaLise before saying, 'A word with you, Coy? In private.'

Pitchford joined the M.E. in the hallway, closing the office door behind them. AnnaLise could hear voices, but not specific words, much less sentences. When the acting chief returned, he was slipping a phone into his chest pocket and looking, if possible, even more forlorn.

'No surprise. The doc has confirmed that we have a homicide on our hands.'

Not a surprise, maybe, but hearing it aloud was shocking, none-theless. *My father has been killed*, AnnaLise said to herself, trying it out. Still, she felt no emotional—

'Coy Pitchford, are you telling us that Dickens Hart was murdered?' The words came from Phyllis Balisteri's mouth, across the threshold of the now open door.

Pitchford turned toward her. 'Now, Mama, don't be starting no rumors, especially from what you hear that wasn't directed toward you. I said "homicide," not "murder."'

Phyllis took affront. 'Well, you and the doc were standing there in the hallway, plain as day. I can't help it if Daisy and me heard you two while we were setting the dining room table for Thanksgiving.'

It seemed that if the medical examiner and acting police chief had wanted privacy, they would have been better off in the office with AnnaLise than in the hallway within earshot of Mama, Daisy and the other dozen or so people who might be roaming about.

Which reminded AnnaLise that the house was full of guests, and was likely to stay that way. Given that Hart's bedroom suite had become a crime scene, she was certain nobody would be going anywhere soon. 'Mama, I saw Eddie and Tyler in the dining room earlier, but that's about it. Where's everybody else?'

'Still out on their walk, most of them. But back to this murder—'

'Homicide,' corrected Pitchford.

Having covered the crime beat in Wisconsin, AnnaLise explained to Phyllis, 'The act of killing another human being is "homicide," but it's not "murder" unless some other factors are also involved.'

'AnnaLise Griggs,' Daisy joined them, 'that makes no sense at all.'

'Yes, ma'am, it does,' Pitchford said. 'Murder means that some-body had to be possessed of a malicious intent to kill.'

'"Malicious"?' Mama repeated. 'You been up at the university taking fancy crime courses?'

'Criminal justice,' Coy corrected. 'And it's true I did study—'

But Daisy was not to be diverted from her personal curiosity's sense of the main track: 'Seems like hitting somebody with a cham-pagne bottle would be malicious, by definition of that word.'

'It does,' AnnaLise concurred, 'but we don't know what the circum-stances are, Daisy. For example, it could have been self-defense.'

'That sure would make some sense,' Mama said. 'About time

somebody stood up for themselves and made that man pay for his bad intents and acts.'

This last bit seemed to be directed at Daisy, though AnnaLise's mother just looked puzzled. 'But Dickens—'

'Enough conjecture!' Acting Chief Pitchford exploded. 'And, yes, Mama, that's another fancy crime word.'

Phyllis Balisteri's eyes narrowed, but before her claws could be fully extended, AnnaLise said, 'Do I smell something burning?'

Mama sniffed the air. 'The bird should have at least another hour in the oven so's it's done nice and dry, the way we like it.'

'I think I smell it, too, Phyllis. We'd better check.' As Daisy tugged Mama toward the kitchen, she threw Coy a 'you owe me one' look.

'I'm going to pay for that,' Coy muttered.

'Could be,' said AnnaLise, with the experience of one who'd ante'd up that price plenty throughout her young life, or at least the earlier years of it. 'But, Coy, you have a job to do.'

'That is the truth.' Coy Pitchford seemed more resolute now that his authority had been challenged, even if by a turkey-burning restaurant owner. He pulled the phone out of his pocket and checked a message. 'Crime Scene is just pulling off the main road into the drive here.'

AnnaLise followed Pitchford into the foyer. 'Is there anything you want me to do?'

'Maybe just keep them,' he hooked a finger in the direction of the kitchen, where Phyllis' dark head and Daisy's blonde locks had just disappeared, 'out of the way?'

'I'll do my best,' AnnaLise said. 'What about the guests?'

'You said they're mostly from out of town?' Pitchford swung open the front door.

'Five flew in yesterday and drove up with two others from Charlotte for the holiday weekend.' AnnaLise hadn't gone into detail on the purpose of the gathering. 'Then there's Mama, Daisy and me, of course, plus Joy and Patrick Hoag. We—' .

'I'll want to interview each of you,' Pitchford interrupted, straightening the parade hat on his head. 'And since everybody planned on staying the weekend, anyway, it's fine to go about your business here, so long as nobody leaves the grounds.'

'Excuse me,' Daisy interrupted from the dining room, 'but we'd be happy for you,' her eyes grew wide as the crime-scene van had just pulled up outside, 'to join us for Thanksgiving dinner.'

'Thank you, ma'am. But you folks go ahead and have your feast, and please tell everyone I'm real sorry it has to be one person short.' Pitchford touched his brim.

'Thank you, Coy,' Daisy said, tears glistening in her eyes. 'That's kind of you.'

As the door closed behind the acting chief, AnnaLise slipped an arm around her mother's shoulder. 'Dickens Hart might have been an asshole, but he was *our* asshole, right, Daisy?'

Her mother laughed and gave AnnaLise's encircling arm a little slap before snagging a tissue from the apron's pocket to blow her nose. 'Your language aside, AnnaLise, I just find it so awfully sad.'

'You mean Dickens being dead?'

'I mean that even after sixty-eight years on this earth, nobody's likely to mourn him.'

FIFTEEN

When AnnaLise accompanied Daisy into the kitchen, she expected Phyllis Balisteri to start firing questions. The restaurateur, though, was too busy answering them.

'. . . setting the table for dinner and heard Doc plain as day in the front hall,' Phyllis was telling Nicole. 'Murder.'

Knowing when she was beat, AnnaLise didn't bother to argue the homicide/murder point.

'Murder,' Nicole breathed. She touched AnnaLise's arm. 'It could have been one of us instead.'

'Us? How?'

'Mr Hart asked me to put the wine by his bed, but you offered to do it instead. What if one of us had stumbled upon the killer in his suite?'

AnnaLise thought Nicole's concern was a bit of a stretch, but it quickly became obvious that the journalist was distinctly in the minority on that issue.

'Oh, my Lord!' Mama's hand flew to her mouth. 'This girl is exactly right.'

'You were in that man's bedroom?' Daisy demanded of her daughter.

Oh, for God's sake, AnnaLise thought. Dickens Hart was her father, and through no fault of her own. 'Not to worry, Daisy. I merely took the opportunity to case the master suite, for when it became mine.'

'That's the spirit,' Mama said. The other two women, though, looked scandalized.

AnnaLise held up both hands. 'Down, Daisy. Like Nicole said, Dickens wanted wine in his room and since Nicole had her hands full with the other guests, I ended up taking it there.'

'He was alive then?' Phyllis asked.

'And fully dressed?' Daisy followed.

AnnaLise blinked. She and Nicole exchanged puzzled looks before the youngest woman tipped to it. 'Ohh, I see why you're confused. Mr Hart wasn't *in* the bedroom.'

The light dawned for AnnaLise, too. 'Right, right. Dickens wanted the wine for later. He was on his way to the media room to watch the movie. I assume you two were in there, too.'

'I was,' Daisy said. 'Phyllis didn't care for the movie.'

'Who doesn't like *When Harry Met Sally*?' AnnaLise asked. 'It's a classic.'

'It's a lot of romantic pap.' Mama sniffed. 'Real life isn't like that.'

'Which is why we watch movies,' her lifelong friend countered, as if she'd made the argument a hundred times before.

'Why *you* watch movies,' Phyllis snapped in reply.

'Shouldn't our hikers be back soon?' AnnaLise asked, ever the peacemaker. Or at least a deflector.

Nicole, smart girl, circled around the granite-topped peninsula that held a shallow bar sink and overhead stemware rack to make her escape into the hallway, carrying a stack of napkins for cover.

'Sooner than we know.' Mama picked up a bag of frozen corn. 'Assuming nobody gets shot for trespassing.'

Or by Roy Smoaks, AnnaLise thought.

'. . . trail is a public right-of-way,' Daisy was saying. 'They're much more likely to break an ankle than get shot.'

'That *is* true.' Phyllis dumped the corn into a casserole dish and added two giant cans of creamed corn. 'The rules just say you have to provide a path, not that it can't be made of banana peels or have exposed tree roots to trip people up.'

For as long as AnnaLise could remember, property owners abutting Sutherton Lake were required to maintain a public right-of-way for hikers. Just what constituted that right-of-way – or maintenance, for that matter – was a subject of perpetual debate.

'It's gun season for the deer hunters,' AnnaLise reminded the other two women. 'Maybe going out for a hike wasn't the best idea.'

'They had their minds set,' Daisy said, straightening up from peering in at the turkey. 'And we were just as happy to have the lot of them out from underfoot.'

''Sides,' Mama was stirring the two types of corn together, 'if they stay along the lake they should be just fine. Most hunters head on up the mountain.'

'True,' AnnaLise said, thinking about her conversation with Bobby and Smoaks. 'Which is the argument I should have used.'

'Argument?' Phyllis looked up. 'When?'

The journalist quickly weighed the pros and cons of adding the bullet Boozer had found – and her subsequent visit to Bradenham – to the stew of intrigue Mama and her mother already had simmering. AnnaLise came down firmly on the side of cons.

'Joy and I were just talking earlier about what people might want to see while they're here,' she fibbed. 'Less argument than discussion.'

Daisy looked confused. 'Must have been before she ran over to the restaurant.'

'Oh,' AnnaLise said, wishing she'd been even vaguer, lest she get caught in a lie. Fact was she hadn't even seen Joy yet that morning. 'Why'd she do that?'

'Well, we sure couldn't make Thanksgiving dinner with what was here.' Phyllis waved her hand in dismissal of the array of fresh ingredients – asparagus and shallots, whole cranberries and fennel, etc. – that had been shoved aside on the big table to make room for the likes of boxed stuffing mix and miniature marshmallows, cream of mushroom soup and, joy of joys, jellied cranberry sauce.

'Shouldn't the can be chilled?' AnnaLise asked, pointing. The only thing worse than room-temperature jellied cranberry sauce was no jellied cranberry sauce at all.

'You do that,' said Phyllis. 'And while you're in the refrigerator, can you get me an egg and some milk?'

AnnaLise obliged, then watched Mama add a dash of milk and the beaten egg to the corn, along with a soupçon of sugar.

Daisy was surveying the array of cans and boxes on the table.

'Aren't we making green bean casserole? I see cream of mushroom soup, but no beans.'

'Freezer,' Phyllis said.

Daisy slid open the lower drawer and retrieved the prescribed bag. 'Do you want to cook the beans first or just stir them frozen into the mushroom soup?'

But Phyllis had other things on her mind. 'Damnation! Didn't we tell Joy to bring the Ritz Crackers?'

'Over there.' AnnaLise's birth mother pointed to a red box next to the stove. 'I needed a snack to keep me going through all this.'

'Well, it's a good thing you left me enough to top off the creamed corn,' said Phyllis, pulling out a sleeve of the crackers and whacking it with a rolling pin before dumping the resultant crumbs on top of the corn mixture.

'Thanksgiving wouldn't be a holiday without your scalloped corn,' Daisy agreed. 'Here's some butter.' She handed over two sticks, which Phyllis cut up and used to dot the cracker crust.

'And *that* is that.' She slid the casserole dish into the oven and straightened up, listening. 'Is that the hikers?'

Daisy pursed her lips. 'They'll likely be entering the house from the lake side, AnnaLise, and not see the commotion out front. What are you going to tell them?'

'The truth, I guess,' said her daughter, 'though I'm not sure it should come from me. Maybe Boozer?'

'You . . . rang?' The man in question appropriately lurched into the kitchen. AnnaLise didn't have to see the flask in his hand to know he was drunk.

And, God help her, her first thought was to join him, as the people outside sounded to be coming ever closer. This had been Dickens Hart's soiree, yet here they were with only his acknowledged daughter to explain what—

'Looks like you could use some food in you,' Daisy said, guiding Bacchus to a chair.

Phyllis shook her head side to side before addressing AnnaLise. 'I don't know whether Boozer's up to joining us at the table, but we were thinking that we'd eat family-style, maybe asking Nicole and him to join us. Is that all right?'

'Great idea,' AnnaLise said. 'Though I'm not sure you need my approval.'

'Don't be dense, girl,' said Phyllis. 'You didn't just replace Dickens as the host. You damned well *own* this place now.'

'Whoa,' AnnaLise held up her hands like double stop signs. 'Dickens isn't even cold—'

'Coy tells me the king is dead.' Joy Tamarack entered the kitchen from the dining room and did a sweeping bow. 'Long live the princess.'

'Please tell me you're not drunk, too,' AnnaLise said.

'I'm not . . . drunk . . . too,' Joy said, spacing out her words. 'After I got back from my trip to Mama's, Rose invited me in for a chat. She had some dynamite Mary Jane to share.' Joy snitched one of the French-fried onion rings from the can Daisy had just opened to top the beans.

Daisy slapped gently but firmly at Joy's hand. 'You were smoking weed with the old lady in the wheelchair?'

Joy chuckled. 'Cool broad – went to Woodstock, even.'

And, given the wheelchair, unlikely to have gone on the walk, even if the group could have stayed on only the more level surfaces.

'At least the two of you will be hungry for dinner,' Daisy said.

'True. Rose's having a little nap this second.'

AnnaLise frowned. 'Where is her room? I thought there was just the master suite on the ground floor.'

'Righty-oh, but if you're asking me how Grandma Ironsides is getting up and down between floors, well, the elevator of course.' Now Joy opened the refrigerator.

Phyllis slammed it closed, almost catching the younger woman's fingers, but also managing to knock the receiver off the wall phone in the process. 'Hear that, AnnieLeez? You got an elevator in your new house.'

The new 'heiress' retrieved the dangling receiver. 'It's not mine. Besides, why does a two-story house need an elevator?'

'Would you want to haul furniture up the staircase in the foyer?' Joy was inspecting her nearly-mangled fingers. 'Hart had a freight elevator installed.'

AnnaLise frowned again. 'But where? I—' The sound of the patio doors opening and a burst of conversation interrupted her.

'Hellooo . . .' Patrick Hoag's voice called. 'We're back.'

'Perfect timing,' Mama said, opening the oven to check her turkey. 'We'll give this bird another twenty minutes or so and then let it set before the carving. That'll give the casseroles time to brown up and everybody to have a much-needed drink before our feast.'

Feeling, if regretting, the mantle of being in charge descend upon her shoulders, AnnaLise said, 'I guess I'd best go in and explain to them what's happened to Dickens.'

Joy followed her friend into the Lake Room which, given the patch job to one side of the French doors, was half sunlit, half wood-shaded. 'What's wrong? Is the good girl a little stressed?'

'The good girl, if you mean me, is a lot stressed,' AnnaLise said. 'My father's just been "homicided," remember?'

'Oh sure. *Now* he's your father.'

'Joy, cut me a break, OK? Apparently he's always been my father, just nobody chose to tell me. Including those two,' she instinctively lowered her voice, 'smart-asses in the kitchen.'

'Steady, girl,' Joy said. 'You update the assembly and I'll staff the bar.'

A stoned bartender – just what they needed. 'Given the situation, I'd prefer that those few of us who still have our wits about us stay that way,' AnnaLise said, leading the way into the big room.

'Ah, lighten up,' Joy said, slipping behind the drinks station on the shady side of the room. 'And *catch* up. The twenty-four hours before Thanksgiving dinner is one of the heaviest drinking periods of the year and you're running behind.'

AnnaLise stopped. 'Is it really?'

'Even has a name: "Blackout Wednesday." Everybody – except you, apparently – goes back to their home towns for Thanksgiving and gets shit-faced.'

'In order to tolerate their relatives at the big dinner?' AnnaLise watched her crowd of at least potential family, piling their coats onto Nicole's outstretched arms.

'That, and they don't have to get up the next morning.' Joy raised a bottle of vodka over her head. 'Who wants a Bloody Mary?'

A collective roar of approval went up.

AnnaLise glanced behind the bar, expecting to see the re-corked bottle of the cabernet Nicole had nearly served the prior night. No sign of it, but maybe the young woman had mistakenly put it in the wine cooler. The handling of fine wine was not something Nicole would have necessarily learned from her grandfather at Sal's Taproom. But she probably drew a hell of a pint of draft Hickory Stick Stout or Honey Badger Ale, not to mention all the local micro-brews.

As people gathered around the bar, AnnaLise raised her hand. 'Everybody?'

Nobody paid her any attention, so she raised her voice. 'Excuse me?'

Tyler Puckett, who'd just entered the room with Eddie, caught her eye and smiled.

'You watch that boy, AnnieLeez.' Mama had arrived from the kitchen with Daisy. 'He's just sidling up because he wants your money.'

AnnaLise ignored her and tried again. 'Please?'

Seeming to realize something was wrong, Tyler put the pinkies of both hands to his lips and emitted a nerve-curdling whistle.

This time everybody shut up, except for his mother, Lucinda. 'Goodness, Tyler. Do I still have to tell you it's not polite to make that awful sound in someone else's—'

'Listen up, folks!' Joy yelled. 'AnnaLise wants to tell you why the *gendarmes* are here.'

'The police?' Patrick Hoag – apparently both an attorney *and* bilingual – pushed to the front of the group. 'This is Dickens' house and obviously it's his call, but there's no need to involve the police in a simple homeowner's claim.'

'Homeowner's . . .?' AnnaLise repeated blankly, before she registered that he was talking about the broken window. 'No, it's not that. There's been a . . .' She swallowed and tried again, 'I'm afraid that Dickens Hart was found dead this morning.'

'In his bed,' Mama contributed.

'Alone?' Shirley Hart asked, and a couple of nervous giggles were stifled.

'What happened?' Eddie Boccaccio asked. 'Was he on medication? Was it an overdose?'

AnnaLise frowned. 'Overdose? Why would you—'

'Don't be silly,' Joy contributed from the bar. 'Dickens didn't take sleeping pills.'

'Not when I knew him,' Lucinda Puckett agreed.

'Same here,' Shirley agreed.

Sugar Capri, who was wearing a beret to go with her skirt and thigh-high socks, looked shell-shocked. 'I don't know. I mean, neither of us slept—'

'Can it, honey.' Rose Boccaccio had wheeled in silently from wherever she'd been napping. 'Anything Dickie taught you he learned from me.'

AnnaLise tried to keep her eyes from rolling up into her head. 'Could we all just—'

But it was a lost cause. Everybody was talking as Lacey Capri entered the room, looking bewildered. 'Is something—'

'I *told* you we shouldn't have come.'

'What do we do now?'

'Maybe we should just—'

'Your attention, please!' a voice thundered from the hallway and, unlike AnnaLise's similar bid for attention, everybody actually shut up.

Coy Pitchford stood in the doorway, seemingly transformed. Maybe it was the booming voice he'd found or that his wife and fellow officer Charity was now standing beside him, but the acting chief seemed to have gained confidence and purpose.

Pitchford glanced curiously at the boarded-up window before he cleared his throat. 'As AnnaLise has no doubt told you, Dickens Hart is dead, the victim of a definite homicide.'

A gasp from the crowd.

'I hadn't quite gotten to that part,' AnnaLise said apologetically.

'Let me just say,' Pitchford continued, 'that this is still a fluid situation. *And* an active crime scene. Our technicians will be working in the master bedroom and that entire suite will be off limits with a guard posted. The county sheriff's department has also been contacted for their backup and assistance.'

Even though AnnaLise had anticipated the move, the words brought home the seriousness of the situation. Once the county came in, they'd likely take over the case from the town's meager force.

Not only was the chief of police out of the country – something AnnaLise hoped wouldn't bite Chuck Greystone in the butt – but Dickens Hart was well known in the state and even the region. The county, with its laboratory and experienced detective squad, would be better equipped than Sutherton to handle a high-profile investigation.

Still, Coy Pitchford was in charge for now and he seemed determined to make that clear.

'Do you know how Dickens died?' Sugar Capri asked, her daughter next to her now. The older of the two was visibly shaking and Lacey slipped a protective arm around her mother's waist.

AnnaLise glanced over at her own mother, still standing side-by-side with Mama. One had the feeling that, together, the pair was indestructible. AnnaLise hoped that was true, given Daisy's recent medical problems. And bills.

'There's apparent blunt-force trauma to the head,' Pitchford was saying. 'Though it will take an autopsy to confirm that was the cause of death. In the meantime, we'll need to get your names, addresses and connection – or connections, plural – to the decedent.'

Eddie Boccaccio raised his hand. 'Officer, some of us may not know your last part for sure as yet.'

'And why is that?'

'Let me explain.' AnnaLise was dreading her next words before she clearly formed them. 'Dickens invited his ex-wives to this weekend as well as ex- . . . umm, girlfriends. He was hoping to find out whether more heirs to his fortune might exist.'

Pitchford scratched his head. 'You mean in addition to yourself?'

AnnaLise nodded.

'Well, that's interesting, I have to say.' Now Coy Pitchford rubbed his chin. 'Mighty interesting, indeed.'

SIXTEEN

'Welcome to Thanksgiving with the Hatfields and the McCoys,' said attorney Patrick Hoag.

He was seated on one side of AnnaLise, with Joy on the other. Across from them were Mama, Daisy and Shirley.

On the opposite end of the table, just past the massive cornucopia centerpiece, were the Boccaccios, Pucketts and Capris. Sugar was sobbing quietly as Nicole Goldstein, elevated to the only empty seat – that of Dickens Hart – handed her tissues. Lacey was looking on with wide eyes, probably wishing she'd stayed in their room or, better yet, home. As for Boozer, he was hopefully sleeping it off somewhere.

What with the police needing to talk to everyone before dinner, it had been mid-afternoon when they'd finally sat down to eat. That meant the turkey had cooked longer than even Phyllis Balisteri liked. Her scalloped corn and green bean casseroles had formed congealed, crusty brown tops, and part of the marshmallow topping on the sweet potatoes had turned to ash and been scraped off, leaving only a cake-like icing of white goo.

The brown-and-serve rolls had been spared, but only because they still rested, forgotten, in all their plastic-bagged, gummy goodness on the kitchen table.

'I didn't realize Sugar was so . . . attached to Dickens,' AnnaLise said, leaning out to see past the sprawling centerpiece. 'Nicole's going through that whole box of Kleenex.'

Patrick Hoag lifted a wine glass halfway to his lips. 'Truth be told, the whole lot of them look considerably more stricken than those of us occupying this end of the table.'

'That's just because we experienced Hart more recently and frequently,' Joy said, displaying the amazingly precise diction of the recently stoned. 'Pass the sweet potatoes, please?'

AnnaLise obliged, managing to get some marshmallow topping on two fingers. She licked it off.

'Table manners,' her mother counseled. 'Use your napkin.'

Her daughter shook her head and held up the monogrammed square of starched linen. 'I'd hate to get this dirty.'

'You'll get over that once you've lived here for a while,' Shirley said, helping herself to another serving of stuffing. 'Just pretend the "D.H." stands for "dickhead."'

'Ha! That's what *I* used to do, too,' Joy said and the two former wives knuckle-bumped each other over the platter of desiccated turkey.

'Who says I'm going to live here?' AnnaLise dropped the napkin back into her lap.

'AnnaLise, honey,' Daisy said, leaning across the table with an opened palm, 'you really should consider it.'

'You want to move?' AnnaLise asked, surprised that her mother would even consider leaving their family home.

'No, dear.' Daisy reached for the sweet potatoes Joy had just set down. 'I want *you* to move.'

AnnaLise's mouth dropped open.

'Grown-ups need their privacy,' Phyllis intoned solemnly. 'You can't live with your mother forever.'

'But I moved back to Sutherton, just so I would be—'

Patrick Hoag, oblivious to the recent turn in the conversation, broke in. 'It *is* odd, now that I think of it.' He was still focused on the opposite end of the table. 'From what you all have said, neither

Sugar nor her daughter had any legitimate hope to inherit anything from Hart.'

'I'm thinking that the mother had her heart set on getting Dickens back,' Daisy said.

'Cute as pie with him, that's true,' Mama agreed. 'And Daisy here says Sugar same as admitted being a gold-digger.'

'I thought she said *every*one who came here this weekend was a gold-digger.' AnnaLise reached across Joy to score a slab of white meat turkey. 'Speaking of which, does anybody know when Chef Debbie was last seen before she went missing?'

'The chef's gone?' Patrick looked down at his plate of food. 'I should have guessed.'

'You shut up now, do you hear, Patrick Hoag?' Phyllis said. 'You oughta be grateful you're not eating oysters or some such foreign thing on this all-American holiday.'

AnnaLise didn't want to be the one who informed the domestic oyster industry that it was no longer part of the United States.

'Oh, we are,' Patrick Hoag covered gracefully. 'It was just that she looked like a . . . nice person.'

'She *looked*,' Joy said, 'like another one of Hart's Bimbettes.'

'Patrick,' AnnaLise whispered to the lawyer next to her. 'Did Coy tell you anything more when you spoke with him?'

'He can't tell you that,' Daisy said. The woman had the attuned senses of a foraging fruit bat. 'Attorney/client privilege.'

'Thank you, Judge Daisy,' AnnaLise said, smiling. 'But I didn't mean anything that Patrick told Coy, rather the other way around.'

'Either way,' Patrick said, 'the answer is no. I just wanted to let him know that I was here if I could help.'

AnnaLise glanced around, making sure that neither Coy nor Charity was lurking. 'I'm not sure if I should be telling you all this, but I've already told the police . . . There was a woman's overnight bag in Dickens' bedroom last night.'

'Whose?' The question came from Shirley. Apparently good hearing was another thing Hart's former wives and other lovers had in common.

'I don't know,' AnnaLise said, leaning forward. 'But it wasn't there when I entered the room, so I'm thinking that the person I heard come in – who I thought was Dickens – was this woman, instead.'

'Wait a second,' Patrick said, pushing his pseudo-spectacles up on his nose. 'If it wasn't there when you entered, when did you see it?'

'When I left, of course. That's why I know whoever brought it must still have been there.'

'And where were you?' Patrick asked. 'Hiding under the bed?'

'Not a chance,' Daisy said, in a down-home, matter-of-fact tone. 'It's a platform bed.'

'I bet she hid upstairs,' Shirley chimed in.

'Of course, the library,' Joy said. 'Smart girl.'

Phyllis Balisteri was looking around at her tablemates. 'For goodness' sake. Am I the only woman here who *hasn't* spent time in that man's bedroom?'

'Don't be silly,' Daisy said to her. 'We've all just been nosing around. Are you telling me you weren't curious?'

'I certainly am,' Phyllis huffed. 'Curious as to what everybody saw in him.'

'I ask myself that same question, Mama,' Joy said. 'But he must still have it, given Chef Bimbette.'

'Chef Debbie,' AnnaLise said automatically. 'And we can't be certain the bag belonged to her.'

'Hopefully Coy will be able to narrow it down by going through the contents,' Patrick said.

'But that's just it,' AnnaLise said. 'It wasn't there this morning when Boozer, Daisy and I found the body.'

'I sure didn't see it,' her mother said, 'but then Boozer was doing his darndest to keep me away from seeing anything. Where was it, AnnaLise?'

'On the slipper chair by the stairs.'

Daisy frowned. 'But that's where you said the champagne bottle was.'

'Exactly,' AnnaLise said. 'She must have taken the bag and dropped the murder weapon there.'

'Talk about your poetic justice.' Joy whistled. 'Killed by his own shtick.'

'Joy, please?' AnnaLise had heard enough penis jokes from the weekend's assemblage to last her a lifetime.

'Not "stick," *shtick*,' Shirley clarified. 'As in the champagne.'

'He'd pop its cork before he popped his own,' Joy expanded.

They all looked at Daisy for an additional contribution, but she just pressed her lips into narrow bands. 'No help here. I didn't drink back then.'

'A champagne bottle *would* make an excellent weapon,' Patrick said. 'Weighted on one end like a juggler's club or bowling pin, and the glass itself has to be thick to withstand the internal pressure of the carbonation.'

'I wondered about that,' AnnaLise said. 'I mean, why it didn't break when Dickens—'

'God rest his soul,' Phyllis interjected. When the others looked at her, she shrugged. 'Deserving or not.'

AnnaLise glanced toward Daisy, who was tearing up again. 'As bizarre an idea as this gathering seemed when Dickens raised it, I think in his own way he did want to make amends.'

'Or,' Joy offered in her stoner tone, 'get an accurate body count of his personal effect on our planet's exploding population.'

Raised voices drew their attention to the other end of the table.

'What do you suppose that's all about?' Shirley asked in a low voice.

'No idea, I'm sure,' Phyllis said. 'But I do know they're not doing justice to my meal.' The duplicate set of food-laden serving dishes on the opposite end of the table were nearly untouched. The restaurateur didn't take kindly to picky eaters.

'Poor Nicole looks miserable, sitting there in the midst of them,' AnnaLise said. 'Maybe I should tell her to—'

Mama cut her off. 'Don't be foolish. Once dinner is over, I plan on getting hold of that child and pumping her for information on what they're plotting.'

'Plotting?' Shirley asked. 'What makes you think that? They barely know each other.'

'Divided by age, but united in a common purpose,' Joy observed. 'Getting their greedy fingers on money they don't have now.'

'I don't think either Eddie or Tyler are hurting financially,' AnnaLise said. 'Tyler's a broker, though I'm not sure whether real estate or stock, and—'

'Stock,' Shirley supplied. 'And from what Lucinda said, the current market volatility hasn't been kind.'

'Sounds like many of us might be members of the same busted club,' Patrick said, chiseling a piece of congealed Ritz topping away from the corn and nibbling on it like a cracker. 'What about Eddie?'

'Dentist,' AnnaLise said. 'And I must say he's a little touchy about it.'

'I'm not surprised,' Joy said. 'His pupils are barely pinpoints.'

'But what—'

'Opiate addiction, dear,' Daisy said, reaching across to pat her hand. 'Remember Ethel Allan up at the top of the mountain? *Her* dentist prescribed Percocet after an extraction and wanted her to come by with the pills, just to make sure they were right.'

Phyllis was nodding. 'Turns out, he was having all his patients do that. Would take the pill bottle for a closer look and swap the Percocet out for sugar pills. Ethel was left hurting and the dentist was higher than a kite, selling what he didn't swallow himself.'

'Now that's unfair,' AnnaLise protested. 'Just because Eddie's a dentist doesn't mean he's hooked on Percocet.' Though it might explain why Eddie's first thought on hearing about Dickens' death was that he'd overdosed.

'Of course not,' Joy said. 'Besides, if Eddie wants to get high, all he has to do is talk to his mom.'

'That's right,' Shirley said. 'I hear Rose was at Woodstock.'

AnnaLise's headache was creeping back. She used the pads of her index and middle fingers on both hands to massage her temples in forward-and-back concentric circles.

Mama noticed. 'Now don't you worry. We're not going to let these vultures get ahold of your fortune.'

'She doesn't have—' Hart's attorney started before slapping his mouth shut.

Not that Phyllis noticed. She was busy stabbing a turkey leg with her knife and dragging it off the serving plate and onto her own. 'If I were them, I'd be looking to get some of that paternity testing done. And double quick, too.'

Joy seemed to have been thinking about that. 'They'll need DNA from Hart, and I'm not quite sure how they'd get that at this point.'

Patrick Hoag put a finger up. And then down again, as if he'd reconsidered.

'A comb or a toothbrush, probably,' Phyllis said, around the turkey leg. 'That's what they'd do on TV. Once the police are done in that bedroom and they cart him away, we'd best lock that door, keep out pilferers.'

AnnaLise shook her head. 'As far as I'm concerned, if they want DNA, they're welcome to it.'

The other five all stopped eating and looked at her.

Mama lowered her turkey leg. 'Honestly, if you weren't practically my own kin, I'd slap some sense into you. You gotta protect yourself here.'

'Maybe she should hire an attorney,' said Shirley. 'Like Patrick here.'

'Now that, I think, would be a conflict of interest,' AnnaLise said.

'Well, whether it's Patrick or not,' Daisy said, 'Shirley's right.'

'Think of it like you won the Powerball jackpot, AnnieLeez,' Mama said, raising her drumstick again. 'The first thing those lottery winners do before even claiming their prize is get themselves a lawyer.'

'I don't want a lawyer, and I don't intend to stop the Boccaccios and Pucketts – or even the Capris – from trying to prove they're related to Dickens.'

Phyllis looked like she was going to throw the turkey leg at her.

AnnaLise held up her hands. 'And don't you be giving me the evil eye, Mama. The inheritance would be timely, granted, but not at the expense of acing someone else out of what Dickens intended them to have. Case closed.'

She stood up just as the dining room door opened. Boozer Bacchus, neatly dressed in a suit but looking a little worse for wear around the gills, cleared his throat. 'Excuse me.'

'Boozer,' AnnaLise said. 'I've finished eating, so why don't you take my seat and have some dinner?'

'You sit back down, AnnieLeez,' said Mama, waving at her. 'Boozer can pull up a chair here on the end.'

'They want me to lock Dickens' room,' AnnaLise explained.

'*And* hire a lawyer,' added Daisy.

Bacchus looked confused. 'Well, now, I can't speak about the first, at least until the police are done, but as for the second, you might want to ask Patrick there.'

'Why's that?' AnnaLise had actually been hoping for a little clearer backing from this quarter.

Bacchus hooked his finger for her to come closer and lowered his voice. 'Coy Pitchford sent me. He wants to have a word with you.'

SEVENTEEN

'They probably just want to tell me they're done for tonight,' AnnaLise told Joy, who had insisted on accompanying her to help carry plates of food that Mama, in turn, had insisted they take with them. 'Or maybe they want to know what to do with Dickens' body. I have no idea which funeral home – or even whether he'd prefer burial or cremation. Do you?'

'Nope. But then, I always just assumed he'd spontaneously combust, like an oily rag in hell,' Hart's ex-wife said. Plates of turkey and its fixings in both hands, she tapped on the door to the master bedroom with the toe of her foot.

Charity Pitchford opened the door.

'We figured you might be getting hungry,' AnnaLise said.

'Thanks,' Charity said, 'but can you just leave them on the hall table out there? We need to preserve the crime scene as best we can.'

As AnnaLise and Joy deposited the plates on the round foyer table, the reporter was feeling uneasy. 'Doesn't look to me like they're wrapping things up. You?'

'Not really, though—' Joy was interrupted by the front door opening. Two men came through with a gurney. 'I could be wrong.'

'I'm such an idiot,' AnnaLise said, smacking a palm against her forehead. 'Of course they'll need to take him to the county morgue and do an autopsy.'

'Of course.' Joy was looking a little green around her own gills.

'I'm sorry,' AnnaLise said, lightly resting the smacking palm on her friend's shoulder. 'I don't mean to upset you, but . . . well, as a police reporter, I learned how some of this stuff has to play out.'

Joy burped. 'The only thing that's upset about me is my stomach. That second helping of yams wasn't a good idea.'

'My opinion, the first helping was a mistake.' This from Tyler Puckett, who had just entered the foyer with his coat on. 'I thought I'd go walk it off before it gets dark. You two want to join me?'

'Afraid we need to deal with all this.' AnnaLise gestured toward the bedroom where Dickens Hart's body still lay, if not for long. 'Rain check?'

'Certainly,' Tyler said. 'And I'm sorry about your father, AnnaLise.'

'And maybe yours?' Joy seemed to be probing.

Tyler shrugged, his freckled face grim. 'We may never know now. Mom is in there with the Boccaccios talking about paternity tests and all, but . . . well, sometimes it's best to let sleeping dogs lie.'

'Or lying dogs sleep,' Joy muttered as Tyler exited.

'Are you dissing Dickens again?' AnnaLise said, tucking the cloth napkins around the plates to keep them warm. 'After all, the man *is* dead.'

'Actually, I was talking about Tyler-boy there and his professed disinterest in what has to look like tens of millions of dollars from what they've seen here in the last twenty-four hours.'

'You think it's an act?'

'Are you kidding? Only *you* could act so indifferent to that kind of money and actually mean it.'

'Now that you mention it,' AnnaLise said, 'I did notice that Tyler has taken off his name badge now that he knows that Dickens is dead.'

'What more proof do you need?'

'You say that facetiously, but—' AnnaLise had her hand on the knob when the master suite door swung open abruptly.

They jumped back to allow the gurney, now laden with what was probably Dickens Hart's covered body, to be rolled out through the main entrance.

Coy Pitchford looked up as Charity ushered AnnaLise in and closed the door behind them. 'AnnaLise – good. Did you happen to notice that last night?' He was pointing to the dresser, where a crime-scene technician was carefully pouring the contents of a wine glass into a jar.

'Morris, is that you?' asked AnnaLise.

Morris Seifert had been AnnaLise's partner in biology class at Sutherton High School. He looked up from what he was doing. 'Hey, AnnaLise. Welcome home.'

'Thanks,' she said to the technician. 'Good to see you're still in—'

Coy cut them off. 'If you all don't mind me interrupting this reunion, would you mind answering the question, AnnaLise?'

AnnaLise stopped, thinking that Coy had a way to go before he understood how things were done in Sutherton. The thought made her realize how quickly she, herself, had re-acclimated to the mountains.

She and Morris exchanged looks that said, *Flatlander*, before the technician returned to bagging the now empty wine glass, and AnnaLise to the acting chief. 'Just being polite, Coy. Now what was your question again?'

'I asked if that wine was here last night.'

'Yes, it was,' AnnaLise said. 'Remember? I told you I brought it in here for Dickens.'

Coy frowned and pulled a notebook out of his pocket and flipped it open. 'No, I don't think you did. Just that you were snooping around and saw the overnight bag before you left.'

She'd actually said 'nosing around' but the sentiment was the same, so why quibble? 'And that was true, as far as it went. But the original reason I came in was to leave the wine for Dickens. I'm sorry if I didn't tell you about it in the first place, but the bag seemed more significant at the time. Especially given it had disappeared.'

'I'm sure.' Coy made a note. 'Nobody else seems to be able to tell us anything about this "Chef Debbie," nor the Las Vegas phone number you said was on the dresser.'

'Including Boozer?' AnnaLise asked.

'He says the decedent met her once in Las Vegas, so that fits, but Bacchus didn't have any particulars.'

'We'll be looking into the phone records and such,' Charity said, only to earn a perturbed look from her husband.

'Now, AnnaLise,' Coy continued, 'does anything else here look different than it did when you left this room last night?'

AnnaLise scanned the room before closing her eyes. 'The bed was already turned down, as it is now. Though, of course, there wasn't the umm, rumpling, and . . . and . . . blood.' AnnaLise was trying not to look at the impression – and stains – Hart's body had left on the plushy duvet.

'Of course,' Charity said, ignoring the daggers her husband was again tossing her way. 'Coy said that you were upstairs when you thought Mr Hart came into the room – is that right?'

'It is. I was embarrassed to come down, given that I was . . . snooping,' a nod toward Pitchford, 'so I waited and left while he was in the bathroom.'

'How do you know it was Mr Hart, then, rather than this Chef Debbie? Or anybody else, for that matter?'

Both Coy and Charity were set to full alert, like two separate pointer dogs suddenly picking up the same interesting scent in the woods.

'I don't, honestly,' AnnaLise said, a little unnerved. 'In fact, I was just saying—'

'To whom? And when?' Coy interrupted, sounding like Mama and Daisy earlier.

AnnaLise felt her face flush. 'People in the dining room, before Boozer came to get me.'

'And you were telling them?' Charity prompted.

'Oh, sorry. Just that thinking about it after the fact, since the overnight bag wasn't there when I entered the room, I realize it's very possible it was her, rather than him, that I heard.' She wasn't even convincing herself. 'Meaning the bag-owner, rather than Dickens.'

AnnaLise instinctively folded her arms.

Coy frowned. 'No need to get defensive, AnnaLise. We're just friends, here, asking a few questions.'

AnnaLise was astonished. 'I'm not being defensive. I—'

'Ignore him, AnnaLise,' Charity said. 'He's been reading one of those books on how to tell if somebody's lying.'

'I'm not lying!' AnnaLise said, probably a little hoarsely. 'Why—'

'Non-verbal protective gesture,' Coy said. 'You crossed your arms.'

'Sorry, I didn't know.' She dropped them to her sides.

'Not a problem,' Charity said. 'Returning to this unseen person, though. You had no indication whether it was a man or woman? He or she didn't cough, for example?'

'Nor speak, which I assumed meant it was just one person, not two. The room is carpeted, as you can see, so I couldn't even tell you whether the person was wearing shoes or, beyond that, heels or flats.'

'Not important,' Coy said irritably. 'We know Hart came into this room because he died here.'

Charity sighed. 'I'm just trying to establish the facts, Coy. You don't have to get your boxers in a bundle.'

His face reddened this time. 'And *you* don't have to . . .' He interrupted himself before they got into a real row. Or further into what would likely develop into one tonight at home. 'Now back to the wine. AnnaLise, you brought it in, but did you also pour it?'

Now both Coy and Charity were watching her closely again. Even Morris, who was stashing both the glass and the jar he'd transferred the wine to in a paper bag, looked up.

'No,' AnnaLise said carefully. 'Nicole did.'

Coy had the notebook out again. 'And Nicole is?'

'Nicole Goldstein. You know, Sal's granddaughter?'

'Oh, sure.' Coy wrote it down, despite seeming to lose interest in Nicole in particular, if not the wine itself. 'Who told Nicole to pour the wine?'

'Apparently Dickens. We'd run out of the cabernet that was served at dinner, so she had to choose a new wine to open and it was a bit young for his taste.'

Charity muttered, 'First time for everything, I hear.'

Coy shot his wife another look and AnnaLise tried to pick up where she'd left off. 'Nicole felt terrible, but Dickens said the wine in the glass would open up and be drinkable by the time he went to bed, so would she put it in his room? She had her hands full, so I offered to help.'

'Then where did Mr Hart go?' Coy asked as the crime-scene technician packed up.

'Into the media room, where the others were watching a movie.'

'And you came into this room straightaway,' Coy said.

'Correct.'

But Charity's eyes narrowed. 'AnnaLise, you said Nicole had her hands full. Of what?'

'Dickens told her to cork the opened bottle and put it on the bar in the Lake Room, then open a different bottle for the guests.'

'Hear that, Morris?' Coy asked the technician.

'Yes, sir.' Seifert was on his way up the steps. 'There next.'

'For the wine bottle?' AnnaLise asked. 'It's not on the bar. But why—'

'You just said that's where Mr Hart told Nicole to put it,' Charity pointed out.

'I know, but I looked this morning and there was no bottle on the bar. Maybe she stashed it in the wine fridge or cupboard instead. You'll have to ask her.'

'So,' Coy pursed his lips, 'not only has the overnight bag gone missing, but so has the wine bottle?'

More than a little weary, AnnaLise put a hand to her forehead. 'I can't speak for the whereabouts of the wine, but the bag – flowered with a black handle – was there.' She pointed at the slipper chair. 'I'm just sorry I can't tell you who the owner was and make things easier.'

Coy bristled. 'We don't need you to make things easier for us.'

'I didn't say "for you,"' AnnaLise protested. 'I meant for everybody.'

'Here we go,' Morris said, coming down the stairs. He held up a bagged glass. 'I'll just see what I can pull up in the way of fingerprints on this, and that should help . . . "everybody."' He winked at AnnaLise.

AnnaLise squinted at the glass. There were grains of sediment in the bottom of it. 'Where did that come from?'

'Upstairs,' Morris said. 'Right on the top step, like somebody was maybe sitting there with it.'

'Seems like you would have practically kicked it when you were up there,' Coy said. 'Another thing you forgot to tell us, maybe?'

AnnaLise tried to think back though her fatigue. 'I'm certain there was no glass on the stairs. But—'

'Could this mysterious woman have brought it with her?' Charity suggested. 'So they'd each have a glass.'

The journalist glanced toward the paper bag where Morris had put the wine glass and its contents and then toward the dresser. 'Was there yet another glass? A third one, on the dresser?'

Coy, now. 'You mean on top of the phone-number note you also told us was there?'

'Yes.' Now AnnaLise was trying to control her temper. And her nerves.

''Fraid not,' said Coy.

The bottom dropped out of AnnaLise's stomach and she raised her hand, staring at Seifert as if asking permission to speak in that long-ago biology classroom.

But it was Coy who called on her. 'Yes?'

'It's possible I know whose fingerprints might be on Morris' upstairs glass.'

'Whose?' the three others raggedly chorused.

AnnaLise looked down at her feet. 'Mine.'

EIGHTEEN

'**M**aybe it's not so much Daisy's memory that's tanking, but thine own.'

Joy Tamarack and AnnaLise Griggs were out on the patio, bundled in jackets as the sun went down on Thanksgiving Day. Seated at a round, wrought-iron table, Joy had a cigarette, AnnaLise a margarita – sans lime, Cointreau or salt. 'Hair of the Chihuahua,' Joy had called it when she poured the tequila for her friend.

AnnaLise took a tentative sip and shook her head. 'Honest to God, Joy. It does make me wonder.'

'Like that old movie, *Gaslight*, except you don't realize that you're the one who's crazy, even as you're making your mother think she's crazy.'

'My mother is *not* crazy,' AnnaLise snapped and then lowered her voice, 'and neither am I. Just . . . forgetful.'

'So did you "forget" you took the glass upstairs with you?'

'Absolutely not,' the journalist said. 'I forgot that I'd taken my empty glass in with me and left it on the dresser. I know *I* didn't take it up to the library, but that doesn't mean Morris won't find my prints on it. I thought it best they hear it from me.'

'And what about this sediment?'

'I'd drunk every cubic centimeter of that cab – no sediment.'

'Then maybe the glass Crime-Scene Morris found upstairs was Hart's from the new bottle and he'd finished it.'

'Possibly, but I saw Morris pouring wine into a jar when I went to the master suite, meaning *that* was the full glass I'd brought in for Dickens.'

'Still full?'

'I can't be sure. Morris had already started to pour before I took notice. Besides, the glass of wine – the one Dickens deemed too young to drink – wouldn't have had sediment. Anything in the bottle should have settled to the bottom and stayed there when that first glass was poured.'

'Unless Nicole shook the bottle or turned it upside down, which I grant you is unlikely. But if it wasn't sediment, what was it?'

AnnaLise closed her eyes, then opened them before answering. 'I hate to say it, but . . . could it be Rohypnol?'

'Somebody put a date rape drug in Hart's wine? Why? The man would drop trou if a woman so much as looked his way.'

'Thanks for the visual.' Another sip of tequila. 'However, maybe the roofie wasn't intended for Dickens, but for his guest.'

'Hmm. Not bad. You're suggesting Hart split the wine into the two glasses – yours and his – and slipped the roofie into the drink of the woman who owned the overnight bag.'

'Presumably Chef Debbie,' AnnaLise said, and then had another thought. 'When you and Boozer – and then all three of us – watched people arrive yesterday, did you happen to notice a brightly colored bag amongst the luggage?'

'Uh-unh.' Joy seemed confused. 'But why do you ask? Chef Bimbette would already have been here.'

'Just trying to eliminate any other possibilities.' AnnaLise was chewing on her lip. 'Though the bag I saw was pretty small, so it could easily fit inside a suitcase. I always stick an extra tote in my bag when I travel, just in case I want to shop or—'

'Shack up?' Joy asked. 'Which brings us back to our missing cook. If this Debbie planned to stay with Hart, why would he have to drug her?'

'She thought she'd have her own room, only to find out differently?'

'You did see Debbie, right?' Joy asked. 'Great looking, and definitely his type, but not exactly born yesterday.'

AnnaLise didn't cite the fact that Joy and the Las Vegas woman were both around forty. 'Age doesn't necessarily equate to wisdom, especially around a charismatic philanderer like Dickens Hart,' AnnaLise said, feeling considerably older than her own wisdom level might indicate. 'I'm just thinking that if he tried to slip her a mickey, Debbie might have whacked him with the champagne bottle and bolted, taking her bag with her.'

Joy was thinking. 'But why not use the champagne? In my experience with the Hound of Hart's Head, it was more Hart's style.'

'Maybe he couldn't hide the Rohypnol as easily in a clear, bubbly liquid as he could in red wine. Or Debbie – like us – doesn't like champagne.'

'Hey, she's probably "swallowed worse," as my gramma used to say. Besides, when somebody offers you Dom Perignon, you drink it. If only to be able to say – haughtily – that it's not to your taste.'

'Dom Perignon.' AnnaLise's jaw dropped on the last two syllables. 'Is that what Dickens was serving yesterday?'

'Why? Because you would have tried it?'

'Well, I . . .'

'So, I've made my point.'

'You've made your point *to* a point,' AnnaLise said. 'But Debbie is from Las Vegas and, as you say, not a kid. Maybe Dom Perignon was old school to her. Maybe she would have preferred – I don't know, Cristal?'

'Cristal? My, my,' Joy said, lighting another cigarette. 'Aren't *we* the hip girl from down on the farm who's up-and-seen Par*eee*?'

'Not really,' AnnaLise said. 'It's just the brand I hear bandied about in celebrity news. In fact, I'm surprised Dickens didn't serve that instead of Dom Perignon, if his purpose was to impress the gathering of young folk.'

'Hart was a traditionalist,' Joy said, and AnnaLise thought she detected a whiff of nostalgia, along with the tobacco and whatever dried leafy substance Rose Boccaccio was smoking inside. 'Which raises the question of champagne flutes.'

'Champagne flutes?' AnnaLise frowned. 'I didn't see any. Why?'

'Because *I* don't see Hart inviting some woman to his room for champagne and debauchery and re-using the red wine glasses you'd left there.'

'He intended to rinse them out?' AnnaLise suggested. 'Too bad he didn't get to it.'

'Meaning your fingerprints might have been washed off?' Joy asked. 'But wouldn't that be all the more suspicious in Coy's mind? Especially after you already told him to his face that the glass they found on the stairs was, in fact, yours.'

'True.' But AnnaLise's thinking had already begun moving on to the bloody champagne bottle she'd seen on the slipper chair. It had been removed – probably already bagged and tagged – when she'd returned to the room to be questioned by Coy and Charity. 'What does a Dom Perignon bottle look like?'

'To my eye? Pretty much like any other champagne bottle, though aficionados might differ. The label is distinctive, though. A shield with fancy script lettering.' Joy paused. 'Why do you ask?'

'That matches the champagne bottle in Dickens' bedroom,' AnnaLise said. 'Though I saw it as more a coat of arms or crest than a shield, at the time.'

Joy was frowning. 'If the bag you saw belonged to the killer, why not just shove the bloody champagne bottle into it and get rid of both?'

'Good question. Though the flowered bag wasn't big, as I said. I'm not sure the bottle would have fit.'

But Joy had already moved on to another question. 'So, assuming Monsieur Dom Perignon is our murder weapon, where – or how – does the red wine fit in?'

'Got me. We don't know what was blended into it, if anything, after the stuff left the barrel or bottle. Nor, for that matter, who drank it. Or, at least, who it was intended for.' AnnaLise was feeling muddled. 'We can't even be absolutely sure that the mysterious visitor was Debbie. Maybe it was one of the other guests.'

'Sure, why not?' Joy blew out a stream of smoke, but whether it was from her cigarette or just the cold, AnnaLise couldn't tell. 'Sugar or Lucinda could have stashed a bag with a toothbrush and a change of clothes in Hart's room, so our slut-of-the-evening doesn't have to do the walk of shame the next morning wearing the same outfit.'

'You're leaving out Rose? I'm surprised.'

'That would be the "roll of shame," given the wheelchair. And you'll notice I also didn't mention Daisy.'

'Thank you for that. But if it wasn't Chef Debbie, why did she disappear?'

'Can we just call her the chef? Or Debbie? I'm starting to feel like the woman should have her own line of snack cakes.'

'That's Little Debbie,' AnnaLise said. 'But have it your way: so why did the chef take off?'

'Maybe becoming Hart's latest little bonbon didn't sit too well with her, given this weekend's theme, and he reacted out of piggish pride. Or the chef witnessed something and Hart's attacker killed them both.'

'Cheery thought.' AnnaLise looked out across the lake. It would be mostly frozen over in a month, the only holes those from ice fishermen and snowmobilers who failed to remember the 'mostly' part.

'It wouldn't be hard to dispose of a body out there,' Joy said, following her friend's gaze.

'They wash up eventually.'

Joy looked at her sideways. 'And you know this how?'

'Experience,' AnnaLise said. 'Or more precisely, long-term anecdotal evidence from a number of sources – some reliable, some not so much.'

'Listen, I know I only visited occasionally over the nearly two decades between my divorce and moving back to Sutherton this year, but you're telling me this happens a lot?'

'Let's just say I wrote an essay in ninth grade entitled, "They Always Come Home to Mama's."'

Joy's eyes bugged out. 'The bodies turn up at her restaurant?'

'On the beach across the street.' AnnaLise shrugged. 'I considered it dramatic license. Thing is, though, why would somebody kill Debbie and dump her body, but leave Dickens in the master suite?'

'The bad guy got interrupted by Chef Debbie, who bolted, only to be run down out here some place? As for Hart . . .' Joy paused, mid-puff, this one definitely from the cigarette, '. . . maybe they needed proof of death to inherit.'

The door cracked open and Charity stuck her head out. 'Coy and I will be back in the morning. We've stationed Officer Fearon as guard in the foyer and sealed off the master bedroom.'

AnnaLise got up to join her inside the considerably warmer, if not currently cozy, Lake Room. She wanted to ask about the residue in the wine glass, but didn't quite know how.

Happily, Morris was at the bar. 'Did you find the wine bottle you were looking for?' AnnaLise asked.

'We did.' Morris lifted a paper bag, presumably containing said wine bottle.

'Nicole told us she put it in the cabinet under the sink so nobody would think to drink it,' Charity said.

'Smart girl,' AnnaLise said. 'Especially if it's possible,' she slewed her eyes over to Morris, 'there's something in the bottle.'

As she expected, Charity didn't react, but the technician nodded. 'We'll test the contents to see.'

Deadpan, Charity asked, 'Why do you think there was something in the wine?'

'Because I saw particles in the bottom of the glass Morris held up in the bedroom,' AnnaLise said, hoping she sounded as matter-of-fact as she was trying to be.

'You mean your empty wine glass?'

'Possibly.' AnnaLise was trying to stay cool. 'But that glass was completely empty; there were no particles.'

'You're sure?'

'I'm sure. It was really good wine, and that was the last of it. I didn't leave anything, not even dregs.'

Charity looked like she could believe that, at least. 'Then how did the particles get there?'

'I don't know. Maybe it was Hart's glass and the leavings did come from that bottle somehow.' AnnaLise pointed at Morris' brown bag. 'Or somebody used my glass to split what was in Hart's.'

'Maybe,' was all Charity said.

'I'll get this over to the county lab tonight,' Seifert said cheerfully. 'I assume the report should go to both the sheriff's department and Coy?'

'Please,' Charity said.

With a wave, Morris Seifert headed out of the Lake Room. They heard the front door close behind him.

'When do you expect the sheriff's department?' AnnaLise asked.

'Not certain, given the craziness of this particular Thanksgiving. But as stretched as we are with Chuck gone, there's no choice but to hunker down and wait.'

'We're not the only ones having a . . . trying day?' AnnaLise asked as they moved into the hall that paralleled the gangway on the floor above. On the ground floor, to the south, the corridor led to the kitchen. To the north it led to the media room and Dickens Hart's bedroom.

Charity nodded to the man – presumably Officer Fearon – who sat with his back against doors now festooned with yellow crime-scene tape. 'Drinking and domestic disputes, of course. And when they're not fighting over who insulted Uncle Jeb and what football game to watch on the television, the morons are dropping twenty-pound turkeys into six-gallon deep fryers that are *already* filled with five gallons of hot oil.'

'I've never tried that, myself. Deep-frying a turkey, I mean.'

Charity shook her head. 'Neither have I. But one would think torching your wooden deck and setting your guests on fire teaches even our dimmest citizens a lesson in volume and capacity damned quick.'

The sound of a cork popping in the media room was followed by laughter. Daisy was right. As rich as Dickens Hart had been, few would spend much time mourning his passing.

'That's just wrong,' AnnaLise said.

Charity eyebrows went up. 'Are you surprised at the celebration? From what I've seen and heard most, if not all of these people came here hoping to inherit upon his death. Which reminds me . . .' She stopped.

Against her better judgment, AnnaLise took the bait. 'Reminds you of what?'

'I couldn't help but notice that Hart did some home improvements . . . or, rather, enhancements for this shindig. The fountain out front, for one thing.' Charity hooked a finger to the expanse of wood where glass had once been. 'Only why in the world did he leave this eyesore?'

'He didn't. The window was broken early last evening as we were having drinks. At the time we thought an owl had gotten disoriented and flown into the glass, but Boozer found a bullet this morning.'

'And didn't think to tell us.' Charity glanced around the room. 'Where?'

'Under the corner of the sofa there.' AnnaLise nodded toward the moss-green couch. 'The slug was pretty badly deformed, so he figured it probably bounced off the fireplace. His thought was that it was some "yahoo" target-shooting. Or maybe a deer hunter.'

'Same thing, sometimes.' Charity had followed AnnaLise's gaze toward the mantle. 'Do you have it?'

'The bullet?' AnnaLise thought about her conversation with Bacchus, trying to remember. 'I believe Boozer took it back.'

Charity pulled a notebook from her chest pocket and wrote something.

'Do you think the bullet's significant?' AnnaLise asked.

'You mean in connection to Hart's death? I don't see how. A shot-out window is fairly commonplace in these parts,' she gestured at the west wall, 'if not usually of that size. Still, it's something that bears documenting and you may need a police report in order to file an insurance claim.'

Good point, given the vandalism was now human rather than avian. 'For what it's worth, Roy Smoaks is in town,' AnnaLise volunteered. 'He's staying with Bobby across the lake.'

Charity crinkled her nose. 'Roy Smoaks?'

AnnaLise realized that Charity hadn't been in Sutherton long enough to have known the man, much less share the rest of the town's jaundiced view of him and his son. 'Roy was police chief at one time and—'

'On the job, huh?' Charity looked up from her notes. 'Are you thinking he might give us a hand?'

That was the *last* thing on AnnaLise's mind. 'God, no . . . I mean, he's just here for Thanksgiving. You know, with family.'

'I suppose that's just as well. I'm not sure how Coy would feel about it, anyway, given he's already had to call in the county.' Charity slipped the notepad back into her pocket. 'For what it's worth, they should be here sometime Saturday. In the meantime, we're to secure the situation.'

'And, presumably us, too?' AnnaLise said. The next morning was Friday and, even if the county sheriff's department did arrive to take over the case on Saturday, there was no guarantee they'd wrap things up by the following afternoon. In fact, the opposite was likely.

'Charity, the out-of-towners probably have flight reservations out of Charlotte on Sunday. Should I tell them they may need to reschedule?'

'You can tell them whatever you want,' Charity said, following Morris to the door. 'But from what I've seen, none of these people are in much of a hurry to leave their new-found lap of luxury. You may have to pry them out of your new home, AnnaLise.'

Then Charity Pitchford glanced up and seemed to look past AnnaLise. 'Assuming you get to keep it, of course.'

NINETEEN

'I didn't like how she said that,' AnnaLise muttered to the empty foyer.

'Hey, the great man died under – at best – mysterious circumstances and you're the heir apparent.'

AnnaLise turned to see Patrick Hoag, who had apparently come from the media room. 'You're saying I'm a suspect in Dickens death?'

Dickens Hart's lawyer grinned. 'You're certainly the one most likely to benefit. Police One-oh-One: The "heir apparent" becomes, by definition, the "suspect apparent" as well.'

'I thought the spouse – or ex-spouse – always drew the most attention.' AnnaLise waved her hand toward the party on the other side of the door. 'And, God knows, we've got enough of those.'

'Enough of what?' Rose Boccaccio had motored up noiselessly behind them.

'Exes,' AnnaLise explained.

'Hexes?' Rose was fiddling with a wire behind her ear. 'How exciting. I've heard there's still an active Wiccan community up here. In fact, I used to belong to a coven back in the day.'

AnnaLise and Patrick exchanged looks, before he cracked a grin and ducked back into the media room.

AnnaLise said, 'I didn't know that, Rose, but I said "exes," as in ex-wives and ex-lovers. Not "hexes," as in spells.'

'Ahh, that makes much more sense. I'm afraid I lost a bit of my hearing during my rock 'n roll phase.' Rose reversed the chair as she spoke then pushed the lever full forward, making the thing almost leap toward the kitchen. 'Fucking woofers.'

AnnaLise laughed and trailed after her, grateful for the distraction. 'Anything I can get for you, Rose?'

'No. No, but thank you, dear. I was just going up to my room.'

'Are you taking the elevat—?' AnnaLise paused, silently cursing at herself. 'I'm so sorry. That was a stupid question.'

'Not so stupid,' Rose said. 'I have been known to hoist myself out of this mini-tank for special occasions.' Then a sigh. 'Although I doubt I'd have the stamina anymore to climb Mt. Everest there.' She inclined her head toward the staircase.

'Was it a stroke?' AnnaLise asked as she accompanied the woman into the kitchen.

'That put me in this chair?' Rose maneuvered herself close enough to the counter next to the stove to reach a pan of Rice Krispy Treats. 'Stroke of luck, maybe. I fell from a third-story window and lived to tell the tale, though my spine's a little worse for wear.'

AnnaLise levered out a hunk of the Krispy Treat, putting it on a napkin and extending the sticky bar to Rose. 'I'm so sorry.'

'Don't be,' the older woman waved off the younger one with her non-engaged hand. 'It sure wasn't your fault.'

'If I may ask, how did you fall?'

'"Fall" is the way I candy-coat it for public consumption, but since we're nearly back-door family, I can level with you.' A wicked grin. 'I jumped.'

'You tried to commit suicide?'

'Ineptly, as it turns out. At the time I couldn't seem to do anything right. I was pregnant and jobless – though in those days just being knocked-up was enough to make you unemployable. When my druggie boyfriend dropped out of the scene, too, I swallowed what few pretty pills he'd left behind and took a swan dive.'

AnnaLise searched for something vaguely reassuring to say, but could come up with only, 'How old were you?'

'Twenty, then. And, very nearly, forever.' Rose maneuvered her wheelchair to the doorway opposite of that they'd just entered through. 'If you're going upstairs, the elevator is this way.'

AnnaLise followed her along to a back hallway. Straight ahead were the stairs to the basement and a door that would lead to the garages on the side of the house. To the right was a powder room and opposite that . . .

'The elevator,' AnnaLise said. 'Joy and I walked through here on our way down to the wine cellar and I never even noticed. The door blends into the cabinetry nearly seamlessly.'

'I'm sure no expense was spared, given what I've seen of this place. It's also the quietest elevator I've ever been on and, I'll tell you, I've ridden more than my share.'

'I guess you have.' AnnaLise had been thinking about what Rose had told her. 'You mentioned the druggie who left you. He wasn't Eddie's father?'

'I'm impressed,' Rose said, adjusting her chair to push the button. 'You actually listen to this nattering old bag. However, no, he wasn't.'

'So that leaves Dickens. Why didn't you approach him for help when you got pregnant?'

'First of all, like I said before, my being twenty made Dickie just eighteen. I didn't hold out much hope that he could support him*self*, much less me and a child, too.'

'But what about his family?'

Rose cocked her head as the elevator door slid open. 'Do you know much about your paternal grandparents?'

'No,' AnnaLise admitted. 'I do have Dickens' journals for writing his memoirs and—'

'Memoirs?' Rose repeated. 'He was having *you* write them?'

'I think it may have been an innocuous ploy by him, toward getting to know me before I knew he was my birth father.'

'Innocuous. If I understand the word, Dickens was never that, nor even innocent. Not unlike this little gathering, before any paternity testing – to my knowledge – has even been done.' The wheels in Rose's head seemed to be rolling as smoothly as those on her chair. 'Did *he* know?'

'That I was his daughter, you mean?'

She nodded.

'I think he suspected. Or maybe he just had a soft spot for Daisy over the years.'

Rose smiled in a kind way. 'And decided to recognize you formally, however late in the process. Though it seems like there's a lot of that going on around here.' The older woman appeared to be chewing on something. 'Related matter – no pun intended. Have you seen how that Bacchus man looks at your mother?'

'Boozer?' AnnaLise was momentarily surprised, though she realized she shouldn't have been. The grizzled, tattooed ex-soldier always seemed to soften when Daisy was in the vicinity. Or even mentioned.

'But back to Dickens' parents.' AnnaLise redirected the conversation. 'I don't recall him mentioning them in his journals, even the very early ones.'

'Not surprising, since from what he told me they weren't around much. By the time I met Dickie, he was at a college preparatory school in upstate New York. He reminded me of young Ebenezer Scrooge in *A Christmas Carol*, always left behind on holidays.'

Another kind smile as the second-floor door opened. The movement of the car had been so slick and silent, as Rose had predicted, that it had been barely noticeable.

The older woman leaned forward in her chair to hold the door. 'I was living with a bunch of other kids – hippies to look at us, but never very dedicated to peace or harmony. Still, I felt kind of sorry for the little wretch, so I invited him for Christmas. We had turkey TV dinners, as I recall.' Now appearing embarrassed, Rose gestured AnnaLise into the hallway.

The reporter stepped out. 'It's sad – almost a self-fulfilling prophesy – that the child named Dickens became a real-life version of his character in the novel by his namesake, Charles Dickens.'

'Sad, maybe,' Rose said. 'But not a coincidence.'

'Because his given name is what spurred your thought of Scrooge in the first place?'

'I'm afraid you have the cart before the horse, dear. Dickens named *himself* after the author. His birth name was "Richard."' Rose rolled out of the elevator and stopped her chair. 'You didn't know that?'

'Honestly? I had no idea.' AnnaLise felt even worse for the man who'd died alone, even in his crowded mansion, and who had apparently lived much the same way, despite all surface appearances to the contrary.

'Don't feel sorry for him,' Rose said, as if she could read AnnaLise's mind. 'He chose his path, just like we all do.'

The elevator door glided back to its closed position.

AnnaLise stepped away from the wheelchair, so that Rose didn't have to crick her neck to maintain eye contact. 'Then again, maybe this weekend was his "aha" moment – like Scrooge the morning after the visits from the Ghosts of Christmas Past, Present and Future.'

'So Dickie flings open the window and calls for Bacchus to run and buy the "prize turkey" in the butcher's window? That would make the rest of us the Cratchit family.'

'Exactly. Though one holiday early.'

'Well, then. God bless us every one, Tiny Tim,' Rose said, rolling farther down the hall. 'Especially your writer's imagination.'

AnnaLise frowned. 'Believe me, my imagination's not good enough to make up this situation. The gathering of the heirs—'

'Or not.' Rose pushed the joystick on her chair. 'This is my room here, closest to the elevator.'

'That's convenient.' AnnaLise had expected Rose to enter her own bedroom, but the woman kept right on rolling toward the end of the hall.

'C'mon,' she said. 'I'll show you the "South Wing" of the house that dick built.'

AnnaLise tried to decide if Rose had capitalized the next-to-last word.

Rose slowed and reached back to pat her hand. 'No smarmy reply? You're such a nice girl. Are you sure you're related?'

'To Dickens? So I'm told.'

'Well, lucky you. You've had the best of all possible worlds. Inherit the big man's money, but raised by genuine human beings.'

'I certainly don't have any regrets about my childhood, that's true. Though I'm sure a little of that money early on would have smoothed our way considerably.'

'Yet, like Dickens, it was your mother's path to choose, bumpy as it might have been. You have to respect that.'

'I do. Believe me.'

'Now *this* door,' Rose said, starting the tour at the end of the hall, 'is that lawyer's.' She winked. 'Just in case you want to know.'

AnnaLise didn't pursue it. 'And, from what I've been told, corresponding to a closet on the north wing, where I am.'

Rose was nodding. 'The layout *is* considerably different on that side of the floor, but the room assignments are thoughtful, at least in their own perverse logic.'

'How so?'

'Come now, you must have noticed: ex-wives and recognized heirs and her mothers in the larger rooms of the north wing; lawyer, affairees, mistresses and other bastard children, the south.'

'Affairees differentiated from mistresses?' The conversation harkened back to AnnaLise's 'Bimbette' discussion with Joy.

'I – and your mother, for that matter – were "affairees." Dickens Hart was not married during either her time or mine. I've been many things in my life, but not a home-wrecker.'

AnnaLise felt herself flush at the memory of a less-than-honorable segment in her own last few years. 'You've never lived here?'

'Heaven's no, even if we'd been more than a fling, this place wasn't built until the early nineties. I believe Joy and Dickens were married in that big room by the lake.'

'How lovely,' AnnaLise said, meaning it. Joy had never mentioned the venue for her wedding.

'I do admit it's damn impressive,' Rose said, positioning her chair to see the full length of the corridor. 'I took a buzz around last night when everybody was having drinks before dinner. Don't care much for alcohol. I prefer—' She pressed her thumb and forefinger together and put them to her mouth like she was taking a hit.

Ah, yes. 'Joy said you and she were smoking pot this morning.'

'Everybody went out for a walk and left me behind. I had to find something to occupy myself.'

This time AnnaLise knew better than to offer sympathy. 'So you brought your stash for just those kind of moments?'

'Nah.' An impish grin. 'I found it in Dickie's bedroom when I was taking my grand tour, pre-dinner.'

AnnaLise stopped. 'You *stole* the pot?'

'It's an illegal drug in this state. Isn't your indignation a bit misplaced? Though . . .' Rose, who had been about to thumb her throttle again, hesitated. 'Is it possible that it's medical marijuana and Dickens was being treated for something?'

'No.' But even as she said the word, AnnaLise began to wonder. She'd asked Dickens whether Boozer's possible 'tools of persuasion' toward inviting guests might include an implication that their host-to-be was in poor health. Maybe it *was* true. 'I mean, I don't think so.'

'Hmm.' Rose turned the chair to face AnnaLise full on. 'It was in his nightstand, for what that might be worth to your theory.'

'It's *your* theory and, besides, what would I know about it? I've never even tried the stuff.' She ignored Rose's skeptical expression. 'Is pot an aphrodisiac?'

Rose shrugged. 'It relaxes you, so in that way, yes. Though I've known guys that it . . .' She dangled a finger loosely.

Now where did one go conversationally from there? AnnaLise wondered. Especially with the septuagenarian hippie mother of the man who seemed increasingly likely to be your half-brother.

'But as to the weekend at hand,' AnnaLise proffered, pretending not to see the knowing grin on Rose's face as the woman started the wheelchair rolling slowly and still northward. 'It's a shame Eddie never had more time around Dickens.'

Rose responded over her shoulder with, 'You're assuming they're father and son?'

'Well, yes,' said AnnaLise, who came to a sudden halt. 'You did say your boyfriend, the "druggie," wasn't.'

'True, but that leaves any one of five or six men. Or more "boys," as I then thought of them.' Rose laughed, but kept rolling forward. 'I don't even have to see your face to tell that I've shocked you, but it's the truth. 'Twas the sixties, and I believed in loud music and free love.'

Shaking her head, AnnaLise caught up but didn't comment.

'Now, let's see.' Rose was craning her neck to see the high placard next to the door. 'Yes, this is Tyler's room next to Lucinda's. That puts Sugar and Lacey in the room closest to the stairs, with Eddie across the hall from them.'

'What do you think about Tyler?' AnnaLise asked.

The older woman frowned as she moved the chair forward again. 'I don't see the resemblance, quite honestly. The boy's too tall, for one thing, and his mother is a shrimp, as is – was – Dickie.'

'For what it's worth, Joy doesn't trust him. She thinks he's a little too disarming.'

Rose was nodding. 'I noticed that. All this, "Gosh, whatever happens, happens" crap. Who *doesn't* need money? Or, at the very least, want it?'

AnnaLise couldn't argue with that. Even if she hadn't thought she wanted her birth father's money, Daisy needed it.

Rose coasted to a stop on the gangway just short of where the sweeping staircase from the floor below met it. 'If I were you, I'd settle into this place, happy as pie.'

'It *is* lovely,' AnnaLise said, taking in the view of the water through the two-story windows – minus one – of the Lake Room below. 'If a little . . . lonely.'

'Doesn't have to be, though I saw the look on your face when I suggested a booty call with that lawyer. I take it he's not the man in your life?'

'Patrick Hoag? Good Lord, no.' AnnaLise honestly hadn't even imagined him in that context.

'A little too clean-cut, I'll agree with you there. Like Clark Kent

in those glasses, though who knows? Maybe he's Superman where
it counts.' She elbowed AnnaLise mid-thigh, which is where the
two lined up given Rose's stature in the wheelchair.

AnnaLise backed safely out of reach. 'Maybe, but I'm not in the
market for a man, I'm afraid. Not even if he was super.'

'Lesbian?'

AnnaLise smiled. 'Not so far as I know. Just chose badly regarding
my last lover – male, before you ask.'

'Sworn off men for the time being, eh? Well, there's nothing
wrong with that. In fact, you might want to seek out a coven for
support. Great networking, not to mention they've got some kick-ass
vibrators in the catalogs.'

Wait a minute. Witches had . . . catalogs?

'Well, it's been real,' Rose continued, doing a 180 degree turn
with her chair and trundling back toward her room before AnnaLise
could ask.

Probably for the best. Nothing good could come of delving further
into Rose's past life. Or lives.

''Night,' AnnaLise called after her, getting a wave and 'sweet
dreams' in return.

On the floor below, the party was still going strong in the media
room. The polite – or at least social – thing to do was to join the rest
of the guests, but AnnaLise just didn't feel like celebrating anything.

A man was dead and even if she couldn't say she'd loved him,
Dickens Hart had been her father. Richard 'Dickens' Hart, as it
turned out. AnnaLise hadn't known even that about him and, thanks
to the killer, anything else she learned was likely to be second hand
or, at best, posthumously from his journals.

Rose's door closed down the hall and the upstairs went quiet.

AnnaLise hesitated, but just for a moment.

TWENTY

Returning to her room, AnnaLise tossed the shoes she'd been
wearing onto the floor of the closet in favor of padding
around in her stocking feet. Pushing the door closed, she
paused to consider.

She was going 'snooping,' as Coy Pitchford had called it.

The logical place to start was the south wing, since that's where the potential heirs were staying. They were, after all, the people who might benefit from Hart's death.

She honestly didn't expect to find the flowered bag. In fact, AnnaLise much preferred not to. If the thing belonged to Chef Debbie and the woman had taken it with her, she had probably killed Dickens Hart for some reason yet unknown. Case closed, if not exactly cleared.

But what if the bag wasn't Debbie's? Or any woman's for that matter?

While it screamed 'female,' AnnaLise supposed that could have been calculated to throw off the police, or even Hart. If Dickens entered his suite and saw the thing, he'd have assumed a woman was showering in his bathroom, with a strong chance that he'd strip down naked and join her. Or maybe lie expectantly on the bed for whichever one to lavish her charms upon him.

In AnnaLise's generation and world, that would have been down-right crazy and not a little creepy. But for an aging swinger like Dickens Hart, maybe it wasn't just business as usual, but exciting: genuine emotional stimuli in scoring another trophy.

But instead of a one-night stand slipping into bed with him, a murderer had struck him hard enough to bash in his skull.

It *was* possible, AnnaLise thought. At least possible *enough* to make searching for the bag reasonable before the thing ended up filled with rocks, heaved into the water and thus anchored on the bottom of Lake Sutherton. If the police weren't going to take what she'd seen seriously—

AnnaLise froze, with one hand hovering over the knob to leave her room. It was true that Coy and Charity Pitchford hadn't done a search. In fact, they hadn't so much as questioned the other guests about the bag. Was that because they didn't believe her? Or, given Chuck's absence, mere oversight?

Either way, it didn't bode well. If the bag wasn't here or with Debbie – meaning if it was never recovered – then the logical conclusion was that AnnaLise was lying. And the obvious follow-up question was why? To frame somebody else for a crime she'd committed?

Enough. Get a grip on yourself.

AnnaLise stepped out into the hallway and listened. The upstairs remained quiet, with muffled conversation and music drifting from the media room.

The one person AnnaLise knew to currently be on the second floor was Rose Boccaccio. Accordingly, the snooper decided to start with the south-wing room farthest from the older woman.

Sugar and Lacey's.

AnnaLise crept across the gangway, grateful there was nobody below to spot her. Then she tapped on the door, trying to formulate a reason should somebody answer. Happily, when there was no response, she cracked open the door and slipped in.

The suite was nearly identical to the one Mama and Daisy shared. The two queen-sized beds might as well have been twins for the proportional amount of space they occupied. There was a sitting area with a sofa and a desk. The floor was carpeted, thank God, so nobody below would be able to hear her moving around, even without shoes.

Nonetheless, she tiptoed to the bed. It had been made by somebody, but clothes were strewn across it, like somebody – or two somebodies – had been having trouble deciding what to wear.

Moving to the closet, AnnaLise had just opened the door when she heard the sound of footsteps outside the room.

'Hello?'

AnnaLise turned to see Lacey Capri. 'I'm sorry,' she said, pulling a spare pillow off the top shelf. 'I'm turning down the beds. I thought everybody would be downstairs for a while.'

'They decided to watch *The Big Chill*.' Lacey's tone conveyed how she felt about yet another baby-boomer fave.

'Daisy probably had something to do with the movie selection. She loves the music.' AnnaLise folded down the blanket and set the pillow at the head of the bed. 'There you go. Would you like me to do the other bed?'

'I can do it,' Lacey said. 'I made the beds this morning. I didn't realize there was . . . maid service.'

'Oh, yes,' AnnaLise said. Then: 'Though with Dickens death they seem to have abandoned us. I'm filling in.'

'That's so nice of you,' Lacey said, moving aside a dress to sit down. 'What do you think happened? To Mr Hart, I mean. Nobody's telling me much.'

'I wish I knew,' AnnaLise said honestly. 'He was hit in the head, but how and why?'

'People are saying the police asked about Chef Debbie, like she had something to do with it.'

'It's anybody's guess at this point,' AnnaLise said, not wanting to add speculative fuel to the fire. 'But enough about sad things. Your mother says you live near Charlotte. Where do you go to school?'

'Online. We've moved quite a bit since Daddy died, and it's easier than switching schools and trying to make friends all over again.'

AnnaLise, who'd never been out of the High Country until she moved away for college, couldn't imagine that. 'So it's just you and your mom?'

Lacey nodded, and AnnaLise thought she saw the tell-tale glint of tears.

'I'm sorry about your father,' AnnaLise said. 'Mine died, too. When I was five.'

A look of confusion. 'But I thought Dickens Hart was your daddy.'

'As it turns out,' AnnaLise said, not sure how much more to tell the girl. 'But I had no inkling of that until just a couple months ago.'

'So . . . um, your mom and Mr Hart, were . . . umm . . . like my mom and him?'

AnnaLise nodded, thinking that Rose Boccaccio – despite her advanced age – would be a whole lot more comfortable with this conversation than AnnaLise Griggs would. Ever.

But Lacey seemed fine with the simple affirmation. Relieved, even. 'Well, that's good. That you know finally, I mean.'

'It is,' AnnaLise said. 'Just feels a little . . . odd.'

Lacey's turn to nod. 'You mean knowing that your mother had sex and all? *Tell* me about it. I mean, you're older and know more about the world than I do, but doesn't it kind of weird you out, too?'

Now the girl sounded like a true teenager. AnnaLise laughed, thinking that Lacey's mother was not so much older than AnnaLise herself. This must be the way Daisy felt when AnnaLise treated her like a dinosaur. And a sexless one, at that.

'So you take classes online,' AnnaLise said. 'That's interesting. Back in my day— Yikes, I sound old, even to me.'

'Not as old as the people downstairs,' Lacey said with a little smile. 'Or the movies they watch.'

'You weren't a fan of *When Harry Met Sally* either?'

'I bailed. It was kind of fun seeing Meg Ryan and Billy Crystal when they were young, but . . .' Lacey shrugged.

'I take it you're a little bored?'

'A *lot* bored,' the girl admitted.

AnnaLise smiled. 'I have my iPad with me. There are some books loaded on it, and a bunch of apps. Would you like to borrow it?'

Lacey's face lit up like a firecracker. 'That would be awesome. Do you have any mysteries?'

'I do, in fact,' the journalist said, pleased the girl chose ebooks over video games. 'Let me go grab it now.'

AnnaLise retrieved the iPad from the desk in her bedroom. When she came back, Lacey was waiting at the door, hands bobbing eagerly. 'Thank you *so* much.'

'Have you used one of these before?'

Lacey shook her head, looking a little embarrassed.

'Not to worry, there's nothing you can do that I can't undo,' AnnaLise said, handing the tablet over. 'Just play around with it.'

'Ohmigod, thank you *so* much,' Lacey Capri said again, clutching the iPad to her heart. 'I'll return it to you tomorrow, first thing.'

'Any time before you leave is fine,' AnnaLise said. And then, after the door closed, added in a whisper, 'Whenever that is for any of us.'

Uncertain whether she had time to continue her snooping under the guise of turning down beds, AnnaLise slipped over to the gangway to look down. Nobody in the Lake Room and most of the noise still seemed to be coming from the ever – if not universally – popular media room.

A door opened below and AnnaLise crossed to the other side of the gangway to peer down into the front foyer. Boozer Bacchus shut the front door behind him and, locking the deadbolt, turned left into the dining room.

AnnaLise padded down the steps and found him in the kitchen. 'Hey, Boozer.'

Bacchus' head had been in the refrigerator and now he yanked it out, startled. 'You scared the daylights out of me, AnnaLise.'

'Sorry. I was upstairs and saw you come in. I wanted to ask how you were. We haven't really had a chance to talk since . . . well, since we found Dickens.'

If AnnaLise felt weary, Bacchus looked sucked utterly dry of energy. 'I'd be lying if I said it hasn't been a tough day.'

AnnaLise pulled out a chair. 'Why don't you sit down and I'll heat up some leftovers.'

He let out a sigh. 'That would be mighty nice. Thank you.'

Collapsing into the seat, he said, 'I want to apologize for my state yesterday. And this morning.'

AnnaLise turned with a foil-wrapped turkey leg in her hand. 'Your state?'

'My drunken state.' His head had been down, but now he lifted it and met her eyes. 'I gave up the bottle a lot of years ago, knowing it was always poison for the men in my family. But these last few weeks have been taxing, and . . .'

AnnaLise took out white turkey meat sliced off the breast, added the leg and some thigh meat to it and brought the platter to the table. 'Want dressing and mashed potatoes?'

'Maybe just the dressing, cold, and some cranberries and bread. I'll make me a sandwich.'

'A turkey, dressing and cranberry sandwich,' AnnaLise said, bringing the components. 'One of my favorites. Mayonnaise?'

'Don't mind if I do.' Bacchus accepted it from her and slipped a couple of slices of bread from the loaf. 'Can I make you one?'

'Don't mind if *you* do.' AnnaLise smiled warmly and snagged another plate. 'Probably the last kind of meal I need this late, but it sounds good.'

'A turkey's not the only thing that needs stuffing sometimes,' Bacchus said.

'You told me the last few weeks have been tough,' AnnaLise said. 'And I'm guessing that's because of all the preparations for this weekend.'

'It wasn't all that bad and the boss did all he could. He even hired those young people from the university to play valet, so I wouldn't have to do all the heavy lifting. Very kind of him, I thought.'

Not to mention that a fleet of uniformed valets and waiters and waitresses were more impressive than one aging veteran meeting guests. 'Are the kids still here somewhere, Boozer? I haven't seen anybody but Nicole Goldstein since the valets helped clean up the broken glass in the Lake Room.'

Boozer snapped his fingers. 'I knew I was forgetting something. The insurance company. They'll likely need to send somebody out before they authorize a repair this size.'

'It's Thanksgiving,' AnnaLise reminded him. 'You wouldn't have reached anybody anyway.'

'That's true now, isn't it? So much has happened today, it feels more like a week.' He shook his head. 'Not what you were asking, though?'

She had to think for a moment. 'Oh, about the kids from the college. Whether they're still around?'

'Nah, that was a one-day hire. That way they could all travel home to their own families for the holiday itself.'

Made sense. Nicole was probably the only full-time local amongst the group. 'Still, I hate that so much fell on you. I should have taken over more.'

'Oh, no. No, that was just fine as it 'twas. It's more,' Bacchus looked at his fingers, 'my pa's been real bad.'

'Daisy said you'd moved him here to be close by?'

'I did. But he's been failing steadily ever since.'

'I'm so sorry. How old is your dad, Boozer?'

'Ninety-three, but he's been fighting the cancer now for more than two years.'

'What type?' AnnaLise's earliest memories were of a hospital waiting room, while Timothy Griggs – the man she'd always think of as 'Daddy' – was taken inch-by-inch by his cancer in a hospital room she never entered.

'Esophageal, they say most likely from his smoking. And drinking. One more reason I should know better.'

'I'm sorry,' AnnaLise said again, taking the bread away from him and spreading mayonnaise on a slice. Then she piled on turkey, a spoonful of cold dressing and, finally, a slice of jellied cranberry sauce before adding another piece of bread and cutting the sandwich diagonally. She slid the plate over.

Bacchus hefted his triangle, then nodded for her to sit and take the other. 'If we're still hungry, I can make another fresh when we finish off this one here.'

'Good idea,' AnnaLise said, helping herself.

Bacchus took a bite, chewing, swallowing and wiping his mouth before he continued. 'My pa, he can't do this anymore.'

'Eat, you mean?'

Bacchus nodded. 'Started out having some trouble swallowing, but we barely took note of it. "Just getting old," he said.'

'But it was the cancer.'

'Problem is, most people don't even know they have this esophageal kind until it's too late. Every day seems like his last, but the next one I go and there he is, suffering bad but hanging on.'

Bacchus picked up his half-sandwich only to put it down again. 'My dad was a veterinarian for years – no, *decades*. Couldn't stand to see an animal suffer. He'd say to people – the owners, mainly – "You'll know when it's time, when she's gone away inside and there's nothing left but a shell." Well, my pa's brain's been gone for a long, long time.'

AnnaLise put her hand on his. 'And now . . . well, I know how close you were to Dickens.'

Bacchus' eyes welled up. 'When you and me went in there this morning, I . . . I couldn't believe it. The man who should be taken is still here, and the lieutenant, he, he—'

The kitchen's overhead light went off.

'Hello,' AnnaLise called, as Lacey had earlier.

'Oops.' Daisy's voice came from the doorway. 'I didn't know anybody was in here.'

The light went back on and she peered at the table. 'Is that a turkey, dressing and cranberry sandwich?'

'It is,' Boozer said, his face lighting up. 'Would you like me to make you one?'

'Well, it *is* awfully late,' Daisy said, without much conviction behind the words.

AnnaLise stood up and swept a hand, inviting her mother to take her place. 'If your movie's over, Daisy, sit down and keep Boozer company. I—'

But her mother had already appropriated her chair, and Boozer Bacchus, tired as he had been, seemed happy to be constructing a meal for her.

Neither of them seemed to hear AnnaLise say good night.

TWENTY-ONE

AnnaLise Griggs took coffee to Officer Fearon before going to bed and, again, the next morning.

'How long is your shift?' she asked, setting the cup and

saucer on the end table she'd brought into the hallway outside the master suite the night before.

'Long as I'm needed, ma'am. The night shift is my usual, so I'm not bothered by the hours.'

AnnaLise admired Fearon's dedication as well as, presumably, his bladder control. 'I'll bring you breakfast when it's ready. Do you know when Coy and Charity will be back?'

'Mid-morning, I'd guess,' Fearon said. 'They're waiting for the preliminary autopsy results.'

'Today already? I'm surprised they were able to do it so quickly on a holiday weekend.'

'Seems like the pathologist doesn't get many dinner invitations.' The officer said it straight-faced.

'Well, that's too bad,' AnnaLise said, placing a small cream pitcher next to the cup. 'Probably carves a heck of a turkey.'

Fearon cracked a smile. 'I'd allow that's likely true, ma'am.'

Leaving the officer to his coffee, AnnaLise entered the kitchen to find Phyllis Balisteri scrambling eggs and young Nicole Goldstein making more coffee.

'I smell bacon. But,' AnnaLise did a quick three-sixty scan. 'Where is it?'

'In there.' Nicole indicated the wall oven. 'Mama just laid a whole pound out on a couple of sheet pans and we're baking it at four hundred degrees for ten minutes.'

'Give or take,' Phyllis said, nodding. 'We'll check it then and maybe pull some out for the wiggly crowd and leave the rest for the crispy critters.'

'Very slick,' said AnnaLise, looking around.

'Old caterer's trick.'

'Where's Daisy?'

Phyllis turned. 'As for your mother, I was hoping maybe you might know where she took to bed last night.'

Uh-oh. AnnaLise glanced toward Nicole's back. 'I . . . umm, take it she didn't sleep in your shared room last night?'

'She did not,' said Phyllis. 'And now I'm thinking you and her didn't have a mother-daughter sleepover neither.'

Nicole seemed *very* focused on her coffee-making.

AnnaLise didn't quite know what to say – or how to feel. If Boozer Bacchus and Daisy had a 'sleepover,' more power to her. Or, AnnaLise figured that's the way she *should* feel. As it was, she was . . . well, as Lacey Capri would probably say, 'kind of weirded out.'

'Mama, I saw her late last night.' At least that part was truthful. As for the rest, 'Daisy said she was going to run home for something. She probably stayed there. You know, to sleep in her own bed?'

Phyllis set down the fork she was using to abuse the eggs and put her hands on her hips. 'Now what are you talking about, AnnieLeez? We all came here together, the three of us. You saying she just drove herself home last night, out of the blue?'

'Well, I don't know, but—'

'Daisy's car is here,' Nicole said, opening the oven to check the bacon. 'I saw it when I took the garbage out this morning.'

'Well, that's . . . *good*,' AnnaLise improvised. 'It means she's back.'

Phyllis didn't seem to be buying it, but her attention was drawn to Nicole and the bacon. 'That needs another minute or two, even the wiggly pieces. Close that door and you watch it, you hear?'

'Yes, ma'am.' Nicole obeyed.

'Morning!' Daisy danced – yes, danced – into the kitchen.

Or at least that was the way AnnaLise interpreted it. Her mother did have sex last night. And with a very nice man, Boozer Bacchus. Not, perhaps, the most fortunate choice of names, but . . . Oh, what the hell. AnnaLise knew her problem wasn't with Boozer or his name. It was with her mother having sex with *any*body. Probably wearing – God, so much worse, *not* wearing – her lacy lingerie.

AnnaLise shivered.

'I hope you're not catching a cold, dear.' Daisy gave her a kiss on the cheek.

'No, I'm . . . I'm just ducky. I was telling Mama,' AnnaLise jerked her head toward Phyllis, who was spooning eggs out of the pan. Their joint daughter tried to send 'go-along-with-me' signals with her eyes, 'that you ran home last night and probably slept there. Returning here very early since Nicole,' she slewed her eyes meaningful toward the bacon-watcher's back, 'saw your car here this morning.'

'Oh, for God's sake. You'd put fables to shame.' Daisy got a cup out of the cabinet and poured herself some freshly brewed coffee. 'I spent the night – quite enjoyably, I might add – in Boozer's room here above the garage.'

AnnaLise's mouth dropped open and both Phyllis and Nicole whirled toward Daisy; Mama with a spoon of eggs in her hand, and Nicole holding the pan she'd just removed from the oven.

'Oh,' Phyllis said. Then: 'Well, next time let me know. I was worried.'

Nicole beamed and held out the sheet pan. 'Bacon?'

Fortified with caffeine, AnnaLise helped Phyllis and Nicole set out a buffet on the sideboard in the dining room. In the kitchen her mother downed a breakfast more suited to a burly farmhand than a five-foot-nothing woman.

It was just past 8 a.m. and none of the other guests were down yet. Probably not surprising, given the holiday weekend and the fact most of them were still up and probably 'cavorting' after she'd gone to bed.

Before AnnaLise sat down for breakfast herself, she prepared a solid, on-duty plate of scrambled eggs, bacon (two wiggly, two crisp) and toast for Officer Fearon.

Getting closer to him, she realized the man was on his cellphone. 'The Sutherton Inn? Did she . . . yes, sir. I'll see you then.'

'Are you finally getting relief?' AnnaLise asked.

'Yes, ma'am, but not for another couple hours, so I'm truly grateful for this.' Fearon gestured toward the plate as he slipped the phone back into his pocket.

'It's the least we can do, given the circumstances we've dragged you into out here.' AnnaLise handed him the napkin-wrapped silverware and waited until he'd set it on the table next to him before passing him the plate.

'Mama's in the kitchen?' Fearon asked, surveying it.

'She is,' AnnaLise said. 'But how could you tell?'

He pointed. 'Cream cheese in the eggs. The woman does know how to cook.'

Not to mention add fat and calories, AnnaLise thought. But that was the least of her worries right now. 'It was very good of Mama to pitch in,' she said, calculatingly, 'what with Dickens Hart's chef going missing and all.'

'Oh, you can rest easy on that front, ma'am,' Fearon said, spreading butter on his toast. 'Your chef's not missing.'

'She's not?' AnnaLise felt like her head was a pressure cooker lid without a safety valve.

'No, ma'am. Chef Debbie, as I believe y'all call her, was staying at—' He took a bite of the toast mid-sentence and, as a well-reared child of the South, chewed it with his mouth closed. And, therefore, silently.

'The inn, right?' AnnaLise prompted, taking an educated, eavesdropping-driven guess.

Fearon swallowed. 'As I said, I fear the answer to that line of inquiry is that she *was*.' He impaled a piece of bacon – wiggly – on his fork. 'Got on the road early yesterday. More's the pity, but we've got an alert out for her.'

AnnaLise felt her facial features head due south. Yesterday was Thanksgiving, with Dickens killed some time the night before. How 'early' could Debbie have departed? 'You mentioned an "alert," meaning she's a suspect?'

Fearon stopped chewing, seeming to realize he shouldn't be talking – with or without food in his mouth – about the case. 'More a person of interest, ma'am. But that's the final thing I can say. Coy will be here in a couple of hours and I'm sure he'll tell you what he sees fit.'

AnnaLise was sure of that, too. Unfortunately, what Coy 'saw fit' was unlikely to match up with what AnnaLise wanted to know.

Returning to the dining room, AnnaLise found Joy at the table. A volcanic mountain of eggs formed an island on her plate, with bacon and toast lining the near shores. 'If loving you is wrong, I don't want to be right,' she sang to the cream-cheesy scramble.

'Thank you, Barbara Mandrell.'

'Only one of many singers to cover it and probably not the most notable, the latter crown belonging to the incomparable Luther Ingram. But Barbara and Luther do stand on the shoulders of everybody from Rod Stewart to Tom Jones. Interestingly,' Joy finally looked up from her plate, 'Al Green is the one who didn't record the song, though it's often attributed to him.'

'We have to call Sheree.'

A confused, out-of-context of the conversation look. '*Sheree* thinks Al Green sang it?'

'No. Apparently she was renting a room to Chef Debbie.'

'I thought we agreed we weren't going to call her that.' Joy put down her fork. 'But as a development, it *is* interesting.'

'I thought so, too.' AnnaLise cherry-picked a piece of bacon off her friend's plate. 'Officer Fearon said Debbie left the inn early yesterday, but he wouldn't say any more. That's why—'

'Gary Fearon?'

'I don't know his first name, but—'

'It's Gary and he's a good guy.'

AnnaLise cocked her head. 'You've had dealings with Sutherton's finest since moving back?'

Joy drained her orange juice glass. 'Gary and I have gone out a couple times. Want me to ask about the chef?'

'Tempting, but I'd hate to get him in trouble with Coy.' AnnaLise had her phone out. 'That's why I thought we could call Sheree at the inn.'

'Call?' Joy said, standing up. 'Let's just go over there.'

'I haven't had my breakfast yet,' AnnaLise protested. 'Besides, is it all right to leave?'

Joy was pulling a leather jacket off the back of her chair. 'Have you been arrested?'

'Of course not.'

'Then don't be such a weenie in a free country. Let's go.' Shrugging into her coat, she was already at the door.

AnnaLise Griggs snagged a triangle of toast from Joy Tamarack's now abandoned plate before retrieving her own jacket from the foyer closet and trailing after her.

TWENTY-TWO

'For God's sake,' Joy said, 'what are you worried about? Gary Fearon hopping into his cruiser to chase us down?'

They were in Joy's car – a silver BMW – driving to the Sutherton Inn. AnnaLise twisted back around in her seat to face forward again. 'I guess not, but Coy said he wanted everybody to stay put.'

'Always the good girl.' Joy got a look at AnnaLise's face. 'OK, not always. But I assume Coy was referring to the out-of-towners. He certainly knows where to find the rest of us if he needs to.'

'True.'

They turned right off the road onto a gravel brick-lined driveway. Dating back to 1916, the Sutherton Inn had been built by a wealthy cotton broker from Charlotte as a mountain retreat so he and his family could escape the sauna of city summers.

The inn was one of the few structures at the south end of the lake that was actually on the water. Other than Sal's Taproom, the rest of Main Street's businesses were on the opposite side, in order to preserve the view of the lake and the beach itself.

'Looks like Sheree's here,' AnnaLise said as they pulled up behind the white pick-up truck belonging to the inn's current owner.

Check-out time was 11 a.m. and check-in not until 4 p.m. Given that it was barely nine, Sheree would likely be supervising the morning part of the bed-and-breakfast experience.

Getting out of Joy's car, both women climbed the steps to the front porch. When AnnaLise tapped on the door, Joy rolled her eyes and inserted an old-fashioned key into the matching period's lock above the knob. 'I live here, remember?'

Joy's annual girls-getaway had always taken place at the inn and now, despite owning the hotel spa at the top of the mountain, she continued to keep a room here at its base.

'Doesn't it get expensive?' AnnaLise asked as they stepped into the lobby. 'I mean, you've been back in Sutherton full time for three months now; don't you think it's time you found a place of your own?'

'Says the woman who's sponging off her mother.'

Trying to maintain at least a shred of dignity, AnnaLise said, 'I noticed James' car wasn't outside.'

Joy grinned. 'Wondering if the chef as a Bimbette pulled a coup and took off with that handsome author under Sheree's jilted nose?'

Besides being handsome, James Duende was also a legendary biographer, one so successful AnnaLise had been astonished when Dickens Hart chose her to write his memoirs over the more experienced author. That was, of course, before she found out she was Dickens Hart's daughter. Nepotism begins at home.

'It hadn't occurred to me,' AnnaLise said quite honestly. 'Though if Debbie tried, it might explain her sudden disappearance.' Sheree Pepper had set her sights on James the moment the man had registered at the inn, and she didn't take kindly to competition.

Joy laughed. 'I'm going to run up to my room. You find our friend the femme fatale.'

'Will do,' AnnaLise said as Joy, not waiting for an answer, took the steps up to the second floor, two at a time.

The physical trainer smoked and drank. Not to mention she was pushing forty and therefore a dozen years older than AnnaLise. Yet Joy made the younger woman feel like a lump of protoplasm that so far hadn't evolved limbs.

To the left of the lobby was a parlor. To the right, the dining room where the clatter of dishes and murmured conversations signaled breakfast was indeed still in progress, though perhaps winding down for the day.

AnnaLise went to the arched entrance of the dining room and looked in. A long table was set with white linen, breakfast served family-style at 8 a.m. for social types. Before or after that, guests could wander in and help themselves to a continental menu at the sideboard or simply have a tray delivered to their rooms.

A man and women were seated at one end of the table, evidently the last of the morning's guests to eat. Both had newspapers blocking their faces.

'Why, AnnaLise Griggs, as I live and breathe,' said Sheree Pepper, appearing from the kitchen with a pot of coffee. 'Whenever did they let you out?'

Sheree was a tall, buxom redhead. Today she was wearing pencil jeans and a V-neck sweater, a fact not lost on the male guest. As Sheree refilled the cup in front of him, he lowered the paper to improve his vector of leer.

'Mmm. Thank you,' he said, but didn't reach for the coffee.

'AnnaLise, why don't you step into the parlor?' Sheree said. 'Let me just finish with these good folks and I'll be right with you.'

AnnaLise crossed the foyer into her favorite room in the inn. The parlor walls were clear yellow, the main furnishings a floral sofa and cherry-red armchairs. In the corner was a maple secretary with writing implements, stationery and a black wire rotary tower of postcards.

AnnaLise sank into one of the chairs. Joy was right. Getting away from Hart's Head had been a good idea. AnnaLise only hoped she wouldn't feel the same when – or if – it became hers.

'So,' Sheree said, sweeping in and taking possession of both the room and the sofa, tucking her legs underneath her. 'Did you hear that Roy Smoaks is back?'

'I did,' AnnaLise said. 'In fact, we ran into Bobby driving him home from the airport.'

'I don't know what our friend Bobby is thinking having him

there,' Sheree said, wagging her head back and forth. 'At least Kathleen has the good sense to be conveniently "away" during his stay.'

'You talking about Chief Roy?' Joy barged in, still wearing jeans but having exchanged her shirt for a tunic-length sweater. 'You can add Chuck to the list of the lucky.'

AnnaLise cocked her head. 'Why?'

'That's right,' Joy said, taking the other red chair like it was a deer blind and she was the hunter in waiting. 'You were living in Wisconsin when Chuck had the audacity to take over the post of chief from Roy's son Rance.'

'I did hear the Smoaks didn't take it well.'

'That's putting it rather mildly, to my way of thinking,' said Sheree. 'I was honestly worried for Chuck.'

AnnaLise felt her eyes go round. 'Afraid that they'd hurt him?'

Sheree shrugged. 'It was the only thing they *didn't* try in order to oust him from office.'

'But things blew over?'

'Eventually. Chuck took office, Roy retired to Florida and Rance became a drunk. Or more of a drunk.' Sheree seemed to have lost interest in the subject. 'Now, for the *real* dirt. What's going on at the big house?'

'We wanted to ask you about this chef,' Joy said. 'She was staying here?'

Sheree nodded, tucking her leg again. 'Arrived on Tuesday, was going to depart on Monday.'

'What happened?' AnnaLise asked.

'I was hoping you might be able to tell me,' Sheree said. 'Yesterday morning about seven, I'm starting breakfast and Ms Dobyns pops into the kitchen just spitting mad. She—'

'Her last name is Dobyns?' AnnaLise was glancing around for something to write on. She hopped up and filched a piece of stationery and pen from the writing table. 'How do you spell that?'

'D-O-B-Y-N-S, I think,' Sheree said.

Joy was looking impatient. 'What was Debbie Dobyns pissed about?'

'My guest told me she'd gotten a call saying her services were no longer needed.'

'Did you believe her?' AnnaLise asked.

'To be honest?' Sheree leaned forward. 'I didn't give a rat's behind why she was leaving. My rooms are booked for a minimum of three nights, guaranteed. Your chef could stay or not, but either way, the room would be paid for. And since the fault was hers, I could – and perfectly legally – rent it back out.'

'Did you tell her that?' Joy asked.

'I did.' Sheree raised her right hand, palm out. 'And before you go asking me what Debbie said, I'll tell you.'

They waited, if not patiently.

'She reminded me that the room was on Dickens Hart's credit card so that was just fine with her. Then, off she went.'

AnnaLise felt her own forehead wrinkle. 'But wasn't Debbie from Las Vegas? How'd she get a short-notice flight on a holiday weekend? And from what airport?'

'You'd have to ask her that,' Sheree said. 'She might have driven to Winston-Salem, or Charlotte. Hell, as mad as she was, I wouldn't be surprised if your Debbie drove herself all the way home to the *other* city that never sleeps.'

Joy cut AnnaLise a pointed look. 'Could have been an act – the anger, I mean.'

AnnaLise nodded. 'Sheree, did Debbie say who called her?'

'She surely did not. I assumed it was Hart, given the crack about him being stuck with the room bill.'

'And the call – from whomever – was to her cellphone?' AnnaLise was trying to conjure up the number on the slip of paper she'd briefly seen on Hart's dresser, but to no avail.

'Had to be. We didn't receive any calls on the landlines here last night.'

'Did the police ask you for Debbie's cellphone number?'

'They asked, certainly, for all the good it did them. The reservation was in her name but, like I said, the charge card and contact information were Hart's.'

A bell jangled, Sheree popping up immediately. 'Sorry, but duty calls. Come over for margaritas this week, assuming they don't just clap the lot of ya'll in jail.'

'I'll come if she can't,' Joy, getting up, called after her while glancing at AnnaLise.

'Thank you, friend,' AnnaLise said, following Joy into the front hall.

Joy opened the door. 'No *problema*.'

AnnaLise stepped out first. 'How are the police going to track down this woman? No address, no phone number, no credit information.'

'Do you remember the phone number you saw?'

AnnaLise shook her head. 'Just the seven-oh-two area code, and Las Vegas is a big place.'

'Then it seems that Debbie Dobyns done disappeared.' Joy started down the porch steps.

'Cute,' AnnaLise said, following her. 'The alliteration, I mean.'

Reaching the BMW, AnnaLise got in the passenger side. As Joy slid onto the driver's seat, AnnaLise saw her slip something into the side pocket of the door.

'What was that?' AnnaLise asked.

'Protection,' Joy said, starting the car.

Geez, was *everybody* planning on getting lucky this weekend? So much so that her friend had to get condoms or similar from her room at the inn? 'What kind of protection?'

Joy hefted a snub-nosed revolver. 'The Smith and Wesson kind.'

TWENTY-THREE

'A re you going to carry that gun into the *house*?' AnnaLise Griggs whispered harshly as she and Joy Tamarack exited the car at Hart's Head. 'Isn't it bad enough that somebody shot out the window? We have to have guns *in*side, too?'

Joy stopped and frowned. 'To your first point: no, I planned to leave the revolver in the car, so my BMW can cover the other vehicles' asses. Hell, *yes*, I'm taking it in the house.' Joy now engaged her friend's eyes directly. 'As to your second point, though, I thought that big ol' owl broke the glass.'

Too late, AnnaLise realized only she and Boozer knew about the bullet he'd found. And, as of last night, Charity. 'I'll tell you later,' she said, noting a second marked cruiser parked beside Fearon's. 'But for now, get rid of that gun before Coy sees it.'

'I have a permit to carry a concealed weapon.'

'Well, then, "conceal" it somewhere, OK?' AnnaLise was holding up her hands, like she was warding off a demon.

'Sure,' Joy reached around and tucked it into a holster under her long sweater. 'Why do you think I changed clothes?'

'I'm surprised you even had that much sense. I don't know why you—'

Joy turned. 'For God's sake, AnnaLise. You were a police reporter. You know bad things happen. Your father and my ex-husband was murdered in there two nights ago. You should be glad my snubbie and I will be in the next bedroom down the hall from yours.'

'Just so you don't shoot me through the wall accidentally.'

'Glaser safety slugs. They're frangible, meaning no penetration of walls and such.'

'But they will "penetrate" people.'

Big smile. 'And devastatingly.'

Lovely.

The front door cracked open and Officer Fearon stepped out onto the porch.

'Hey, Gary,' Joy called cheerfully.

AnnaLise scowled at her armed-and-dangerous friend before gesturing to the second cruiser. 'Your relief has arrived, I see. I imagine you'll be glad to go home and get some sleep.'

'I will that,' Fearon said, blinking in the bright sunlight. 'Though with us shorthanded, there's no rest for the weary.'

'Hopefully that'll be true of the wicked as well.' Coy Pitchford had emerged right after him.

'Our temporary chief is looking at you,' Joy whispered to AnnaLise.

'He is not.' AnnaLise elbowed her friend.

Joy sidestepped, nearly knocking into Fearon as he trotted down the steps and flashed her a quick smile before continuing to his car.

'Who's not?' Coy asked. The officer's eyes narrowed, but whether that was because of the bright sun or suspicion, AnnaLise couldn't decide.

She *did* decide, however, to put her cards on the table. Better AnnaLise know now where she stood with the Sutherton police. 'Joy felt you were referring to me when you said "wicked."'

'Stoolie,' Joy Tamarack muttered under her breath.

AnnaLise ignored her. 'Coy, straight up and straight out. Am I a suspect in Dickens' death?'

Coy, who seemed to have picked up a bit more swagger during the prior twenty-four hours, pulled at his shirt collar thoughtfully. 'Well, now, I wouldn't say exactly that. We're investigating all sorts of possibilities. And the county, when they get here, will be—'

'Any update on when they're expected?' AnnaLise asked. She wasn't sure if the arrival of the sheriff's department would improve matters or not, but they would certainly move things along. Despite the fact that it had been only a single day since the discovery of Dickens Hart's body, it felt like she'd been sinking in quicksand ever since.

'. . . what with the holiday,' Coy was saying. 'To make matters worse, there was a twenty-car pile-up on the highway this morning.'

'Where at?' AnnaLise asked, unconsciously echoing rhythms of speech that had faded during her time away.

'Down by Tuckerville, where the fog sits some mornings,' Coy said. 'And a bad one it was, too.'

'Coy?' Charity was in the doorway with a cellphone in one hand and her notebook in the other. 'Still nothing on the chef.'

'But Sheree told us Debbie left the inn yesterday morning,' said AnnaLise. 'Shouldn't somebody have—'

Now Coy interrupted her. 'You've been down to the inn, AnnaLise?'

'Yes, Joy needed to get . . . something from her room there.'

Mercifully, Joy didn't pull out that 'something' for display.

'As to the chef,' Charity said, consulting her notebook as she stepped out to join them. 'I don't suppose you remember the rest of that phone number you saw?'

'Afraid not,' AnnaLise said.

'What good would it do anyway?' Joy asked. 'If this Debbie's a killer, she's certainly not going to answer her cellphone.'

'You'd be surprised,' Coy said. 'Most criminals don't have lots of smarts. Especially ones who act in haste and then react in panic.'

'Is that what you assume happened?' AnnaLise asked.

'I don't assume anything,' Coy said, hooking a thumb in the leather super-structure of his holster rig.

'Seems like a crime of opportunity,' Joy said. 'Dickens pissed somebody off and they took that opportunity to smack him one.'

'At least one,' Coy said with a poker face.

'So you got the autopsy results?' AnnaLise asked.

She expected him to prevaricate with technical terms or outright refuse to answer, but he nodded. 'Just the preliminary, but no surprises. Cause of death was blunt-force trauma.'

'No drugs involved?' AnnaLise was thinking about both the kind you smoked and the kind you dissolved in some unsuspecting person's drink.

Coy cocked his head. 'Now why would you ask that?'

AnnaLise didn't bring up the weed, lest Coy wanted to know where it had gone. 'As I told Charity last night, I saw something granular in the bottom of the wine glass Morris bagged upstairs.'

'The glass AnnaLise said was hers,' Charity added for Coy's benefit, putting away her cellphone and taking out a pen.

'The one I *assumed* was mine, since it was empty. But as I told you, Charity, and Joy can corroborate,' the police reporter hooked a finger toward her friend, 'there was no sediment in the wine either of us was drinking.'

Seeming to be confused, Joy cleared her throat. 'No. I mean, yes, there was no sediment. And given the way AnnaLise was guzzling, I'm sure there wasn't a drop left.'

Not exactly a ringing endorsement, but AnnaLise would take it. 'If that *was* my glass, somebody added something to it. The other option is that it was the full glass I'd brought in for Hart, and there was something already in it.'

Charity was shaking her head. 'Nothing in that wine, or the bottle either. As for the victim, the preliminary labs are clean of everything but alcohol and the prescription drugs we've accounted for.'

'Do you think you've given our suspects enough information?' Coy snapped.

'Oh, for God's sake,' Charity said, turning on him. 'We need information, which means interviewing instead of you walking around as the cock of the roost, buffing your own badge until the county gets here.'

But Joy had gasped. 'We're *both* suspects?'

Coy grinned. 'Not so much you.'

'Hey, Joy's the ex-wife,' AnnaLise protested, her misery yearning for a little company. 'And we have another one of them around here, too, someplace. Not to mention a chronologically tiered array of gold-diggers-cum-potential heirs.'

'Fine way to talk about your houseguests,' Patrick Hoag said with a smile as he rounded the corner from the side of the house. 'Can I be of help in any way?'

'Please,' AnnaLise said, honestly glad to see an attorney, *any* attorney. 'Patrick, tell Coy that other people were here Wednesday night who could gain from Hart's death.'

'Did you draft Mr Hart's will?' Charity asked the lawyer.

'Estate plan, actually.'

'Wait a minute. You can't ask him about that,' Joy said.

'Will you let the man speak,' AnnaLise hissed to Joy. 'Whose side are you on, anyway?'

'His client is dead,' Coy said. 'Besides, we can get—'

Patrick Hoag held up his hands. 'I'm happy to tell you what's in the plan. I don't have a copy with me, obviously, but Bacchus may know where Dickens had one that's conveniently accessible. If not, Bacchus will certainly have his own as Dickens Hart's executor.'

AnnaLise felt a seismic shift ripple from her feet through the ground beneath them. '*Boozer* is Dickens' executor?'

'See?' Joy glared at Coy. 'Another suspect.'

'Dickens' estate plan is exceptionally straight forward,' Patrick said. 'Other than an annual stipend to Bacchus, everything goes to AnnaLise as Hart's acknowledged daughter.'

Everybody looked at her.

'What about the *other* heirs?' AnnaLise asked between gritted teeth.

'Ach, that's true, isn't it?' Coy said, scratching his head. 'That's why everybody's here in the first place.'

'Yes,' said AnnaLise. 'Tell them, Patrick.'

'They aren't "heirs," as such. At least, not yet. No recognition in the will. Nor were they legitimatized by Hart before—'

'Neither am *I*,' AnnaLise exploded. Honest to God, the welcomed 'mouthpiece' was becoming absolutely obtuse. 'Eddie, Tyler and me – all illegitimate.'

'If you'd let me explain what I mean by "legitimatized—" Patrick tried, but Charity interrupted.

'Do these other – call them "potential heirs" – have proof?' she asked.

'Not yet.' AnnaLise knew she was throwing her potential half-brothers under the bus to join Joy, but at this point she didn't care.

Twelve weeks ago, she'd been a fatherless child minding her own business, scratching out a living by covering the crime beat for a Wisconsin newspaper. Now she was a purported heiress and perhaps the central suspect in a homicide. Three guesses on which she'd have preferred.

'But,' AnnaLise continued, 'all they'll need is Hart's DNA. Seems like they could get that from the coroner.' She was looking toward Charity for support.

The officer shrugged. 'I suppose. Probably need a court order.'

'Even if they can't get that,' Joy said, 'there's plenty of DNA around this place. Starting with the mirror above his bed.'

An involuntary 'Eeeuw,' from Charity, but Coy and Patrick seemed rather impressed.

AnnaLise, for her part, turned to Joy. 'There's *no* mirror above the bed. I was wondering about that, because it sure seemed in character.'

'It was up there in my day,' Joy said. 'The old man must have redecorated.'

Well, that was a kick in the DNA, AnnaLise thought, then rallied. 'Just a hair or toothbrush would probably suffice, right, Patrick?'

But the lawyer was holding up his hands again. 'Let's step back and take this one issue at a time. First of all, in North Carolina, an illegitimate child has the same rights to inherit property from his or her *mother* and the mother's family as any other child.'

'Only seems fair,' Charity said, nodding.

'On the other hand,' Patrick went on, 'an illegitimate child does *not* have a right to inherit from his or her putative birth *father*—'

Joy interrupted with, '"Putative," like we're going to jail the guy?'

'No.' It was obvious that Patrick Hoag was not lightly suffering the intrusion on his mini-lesson about the law. 'The word here is "putative," as in alleged or supposed birth father, not "punitive," as in punishing someone.'

'Too bad,' said Joy, disappointment the major tone in her voice. 'The "putative birth father" should probably have at least one nut cut—'

'Joy?' AnnaLise said, sensing her friend knew full well what 'putative' meant, but couldn't resist sniping anywhere that Dickens Hart was concerned, even now. 'Please?'

Her friend shrugged unhappily, but didn't continue.

'As I was saying,' Patrick said, his eyes brooking no further comments, 'the illegitimate child has no right of inheritance from a putative father who dies intestate, unless . . .'

AnnaLise said a little prayer that Joy wouldn't pun 'intestate' with the testicle she evidently wanted as her ounce – or two – of flesh.

'. . . at least one of the following pertains.' Hoag cleared his throat and wiggled his fingers as though warming up for a piano recital. '*First*,' raising his index finger in the air, 'the putative father has legally been declared the child's actual father – which includes, by the way, the mother and putative father marrying after the birth of the child.'

Joy seemed like she just couldn't help herself. 'But that never happened here with any of them.'

'Correct.' Patrick drove on. 'Or, *second*—' His middle finger rose at its natural angle to near his index one.

AnnaLise shot a glance at Joy, who seemed ready to burst with some allusion to the middle finger's other meaning. But Joy managed to restrain herself, and AnnaLise mouthed a silent *thank you*.

'The putative father has acknowledged the child as his own in a written document, signed before the proper official and filed in the proper court, at the proper time.'

'And Hart did neither your "first" *nor* "second"?' asked Charity.

'Except the second for AnnaLise,' Patrick said, obviously pleased to have a parrot-apprentice to balance out the heckling crow.

'And now never can,' said Coy. 'Given the man's dead.'

Eyes turned again toward AnnaLise, who was thinking furiously before saying, 'But Hart didn't die intestate.'

Coy blinked. 'What?'

'Patrick said that an illegitimate child doesn't have the right to inherit from his or her intestate father. Dickens didn't die intestate. He had a will.' She turned to the lawyer. 'Or, as you called it, an estate plan.'

'Oh, very good,' Patrick said, pantomiming applause toward AnnaLise. 'A man can, indeed, put an illegitimate child in his will. In fact, Dickens did exactly that with you, AnnaLise, as well as acknowledging you legally – thereby legitimatizing you – as in my second option.' He wiggled his middle finger.

'But AnnaLise's status aside,' Charity said, 'you're still saying Dickens Hart did *none* of these things to recognize the other potential heirs, correct?'

'Yes. But only as far as it goes,' Patrick said.

'Why didn't you explain all this at Thanksgiving dinner yesterday?' Joy demanded. 'When everybody was up in arms about DNA and all.'

'AnnaLise was so adamant about recognizing the other heirs, I thought it had become a moot point.'

'What do you mean?' Coy looked like he was trying to follow, if lagging a bit.

Hoag drew in a deep, oratorical breath. 'AnnaLise said at dinner yesterday that she didn't want the fact that Dickens had died to prevent Eddie Boccaccio and Tyler Puckett from inheriting, should they be able to prove their parentage.'

'See?' AnnaLise brightened.

'Generous,' Charity said approvingly.

'Or sly diversion,' Coy growled. 'Dickens Hart had already been killed, and she had to know she'd be the obvious suspect.'

'Hey,' AnnaLise said, waving her hands. '"*She*" is standing right here. And, besides, didn't you say just a few minutes ago that I wasn't necessarily—'

'Regardless,' Patrick continued smoothly, 'I didn't bother going into all this at the time, because we were all drinking *and* it's complex and really had no bearing.'

'Moot.' Coy was nodding.

'Or, at least, not applicable. You see, if AnnaLise wanted to split her inheritance, she certainly remains free to do so.'

'Thank you,' said the woman in question.

'But on Wednesday night when Hart was killed, the others,' Charity checked her notes again, 'this Eddie Boccaccio and Tyler Puckett, would have no way of knowing whether she intended to do that?'

Coy, head cocked at a different angle as though he had an infinite number of default settings on the cervical beltway of his spinal column, said, 'That's right. Meaning those two boys, at least, had no obvious motive to kill Dickens Hart.'

'Wait a second,' from AnnaLise, waving a hand, but nobody paid her any attention.

'Coy has a point,' Charity was saying.

'So what if they didn't know that AnnaLise intended to share?' Joy interrupted. 'They still would have thought they could inherit by proving paternity.'

'It's easy to go online and get a quick – if not as complete – answer to the question,' Patrick pointed out.

'Leading us to the same conclusion,' Charity said. 'If Boccaccio and Puckett *did* know they couldn't be legitimized, as you say, once Hart was dead, they had no reason to kill him. Just the opposite, in fact.'

'He was Dickens Hart, for God's sake,' Joy said. 'There was *always* a reason to—'

'Charity's right,' Coy said. 'Smart money would be on killing the man *after* you were in the will.'

AnnaLise stopped waving.

'Like Coy was saying,' Joy tried, 'Criminals are stupid. Maybe—'

'If I might?' Patrick said it softly, which may have been why people shut up and paid attention to their newfound fount of wisdom.

'Yes?' AnnaLise said politely.

'I wasn't done with my explanation of the North Carolina General Statutes, concerning succession by, through and from illegitimate children.'

'By, through and . . . from?' Coy quoted back.

'For our current purposes,' Patrick continued smoothly, 'I think it's best we just stick with "by."'

'Good idea, Patrick,' Charity said. 'Assuming, that is, it has a bearing on all this. None of us standing here is getting any younger, you know.'

'I think you'll agree it does have a bearing, if not a material difference.'

AnnaLise felt her eyes cross and, more like a judge than a suspect, intoned, 'Proceed. Please.'

'Now, I've already covered the ways a child can be legitimatized prior to the death of the putative father. Shall I recap?'

'No!' the assembly chorused.

'Good. Then I'll move on to my final point. A section of the statutes stipulates that no action shall be commenced nor judgment entered after the death of the putative father, unless the action is commenced either, *one*,' the index finger went up again, 'prior to the death of the father.'

'We've already gone through this,' Joy said in an agonized voice.

'Or *two*,' Patrick waggled the middle finger meaningfully, 'within one year after the death of the putative father.'

AnnaLise, perhaps listening more closely to the lawyer's analysis, thought she saw where he was headed. 'So Eddie and Tyler have one year from yesterday to prove they have a right to part of Dickens Hart's estate?'

'They do. Of course, there are other considerations, such as when a proceeding for administration of the estate of the putative—'

Charity mercifully interrupted. 'Is it safe to say, Patrick, that Boccaccio and Puckett can still get *some*thing from Hart's estate, assuming they prove paternity within a year?'

'And with DNA proof, even longer, beyond three years.'

'You wanted a reason to kill Hart?' Joy said, nodding toward Charity. 'There it is. And it's every bit as strong as AnnaLise's.'

'Well, maybe not quite, but I see your point,' Charity said, as her smartphone dinged a text message.

AnnaLise was studying Patrick Hoag, not knowing whether to thank him or not. While misery might love company, a little clarity wouldn't hurt either. 'Given the woman's overnight bag and Debbie Dobyns—'

'Debbie Dobyns?' It was Hoag's turn to ask a question.

'The chef,' Joy explained.

'Ah, yes,' Patrick said with a smile on his face. 'The Monroe-esque platinum blonde.'

Joy's eyes narrowed. 'Did Dickens' smarmy soul move on to you at his passing?'

'Me?' Patrick said. 'No, but I am male.'

AnnaLise sighed. '*Anyway*, the "Monroe-esque platinum blonde" has disappeared. Why are we even talking about other suspects until she turns up?'

'Funny you should say that,' Charity said, holding up the phone. 'Guess who's just turned up?'

TWENTY-FOUR

'Debbie Dobyns is . . . dead?'

Charity Pitchford's brow wrinkled at Joy Tamarack's question. 'I didn't say that.'

'You told us just now that she's turned up. I thought maybe that was a euphemism, like she turned up her toes or,' Joy slid a glance AnnaLise's way, 'washed up on shore.'

'Noooo,' Charity said slowly, catching the interplay. 'Ms Dobyns just landed at McCarran International.'

'Has Las Vegas Metro picked her up?' Coy asked.

'They have.'

'Where's she been all this time?' AnnaLise asked. 'According to Sheree, Debbie left the inn early yesterday morning.'

'Apparently, instead of returning her rental car to Charlotte, she drove all the way to Atlanta and flew from there.'

'Makes sense, actually,' Patrick Hoag said. 'Atlanta's Hartsfield-Jackson is the busiest passenger airport in the world. There'd be plenty of nonstop flights to Vegas, versus only connections from Charlotte. Especially given her change in itinerary.'

AnnaLise asked, 'Did Debbie have the brightly colored overnight bag with her?'

Charity shook her head. 'Metro said she had a purple carry-on. A roller-bag.' The officer slid the phone back into her breast pocket and gestured for Coy to follow her inside, signaling the end of conversation on both fronts. The lawyer followed them into the house.

Joy turned to AnnaLise. 'The smaller overnight bag is probably inside the wheelie, like you said. Besides, if she's willing to pull a purple bag through an airport, a flowered tote for overnight would seem right up her alley.'

AnnaLise mounted the last couple of steps and took a seat on the black, wrought-iron bench right of the door. 'If you say so.'

'Hey, cheer up,' Joy said, settling down next to her. 'Even if it's not in her luggage, she could have disposed of it on the way to the airport in Atlanta.'

'I guess so.' AnnaLise shifted. 'This bench looks nice, but it sure is uncomfortable.'

'Hart chose his furniture the way he chose his women.'

The reporter didn't feel a need to respond. After all, as one of those women, Joy was the expert. 'The thing is that Debbie has no way of knowing that I saw the bag in Dickens' room.'

'You're sure she didn't hear you?'

'I can't see how. The bathroom door was closed and the shower was running.'

'Well, if she isn't worried that somebody saw the bag and could therefore use it to connect her to Hart's death, there's no reason that she'd get rid of it.'

'Exactly.'

'Good.' Joy patted AnnaLise's knee. 'Then the police should find it in her suitcase. You can have only one carry-on in addition to your purse, you know.'

'OK, I'll hang on to that thought.' AnnaLise stood up and drew in a familiar aroma. 'Must be lunchtime.'

'Can't even be eleven yet.'

'I didn't have breakfast. If there's food in the kitchen, I'm eating it.'

'Good to know you're not letting a murder rap hurt your appetite.'

'Homicide rap,' AnnaLise emphasized, swinging open the front door. 'Let's not convict me of something before I'm even charged.'

'Who's been charged?' Phyllis Balisteri's face was anxious as she came out of the dining room.

'Nobody,' AnnaLise said. And then, because she knew her surrogate mother wouldn't be satisfied with that: 'But they have found Chef Debbie, so that's good news.'

Only Phyllis looked less than pleased. 'Damnation. Did she wash up across from the restaurant?'

'She was found—'

'I *knew* I should have kept the place open this weekend,' Phyllis lamented.

AnnaLise turned to Joy. 'Contrary to what one might think, corpses seem to be good for business.'

'Why doesn't that surprise me?' came from the fitness trainer.

'Chef Debbie isn't dead,' AnnaLise told Phyllis.

'Then I suppose she'll want her kitchen back.' Mama was already untying her apron.

'Afraid not,' AnnaLise said. 'She's in Las Vegas.'

Joy nodded. 'Though with any luck, she'll be back here soon.' A pause. 'But not necessarily to cook.'

'Speaking of cooking, something smells wonderful,' AnnaLise said.

'Chicken spaghetti.' Mama still looked grumpy. 'Though I made it with turkey, given those out-of-towners barely touched theirs yesterday.'

'More for us,' AnnaLise said. 'Is this the one with cream of chicken soup in it?'

'And mushroom, since we had an extra can from the green bean casserole. And it's all just coming out of the oven. If you want to go in the dining room I'll have Nicole bring plates to you.'

'Not for me, I just ate breakfast,' Joy said as Phyllis bustled off.

'Come and sit with me anyway,' AnnaLise said. 'I don't want to subject myself to more of Mama's questions and it'll be lonely in that big dining room.'

'Better get used to it,' Joy said, following her, 'unless you end up sharing it with your two evil stepbrothers.'

'I don't think either of them is evil,' AnnaLise said, pulling a high-backed chair away from the table. 'No matter what Daisy says about Eddie's eyes.'

'Eddie's eyes?' Joy was rounding the table to sit on the other side.

'Tiny pupils, remember? You brought it up and Daisy suggested Eddie might be abusing some drug like Percocet.'

'Speaking of our sunny little drug czar, where *is* your mother this morning?'

'I'm afraid to ask.' AnnaLise leaned forward and whispered, 'Apparently she spent the night with Boozer Bacchus.'

'Good for her.' Joy shook out a napkin. ''Bout time she got some. Boozer, too, for that matter.'

'I thought you weren't hungry.'

The swinging door from the kitchen bumped open. 'Two cheesy turkey spaghettis,' Nicole said brightly. 'Coming up.'

'Thanks,' AnnaLise said as the girl placed one in front of her. 'Smells like home. Or Mama Philomena's family booth at the restaurant.'

'I've learned so much from Mama and Daisy.' Nicole was circling the long table to serve Joy. 'I had no idea that cooking was this easy.'

'A package of this, a can of that,' Joy contributed.

'It's like a miracle,' Nicole agreed. 'Now, what can I get you to drink?'

AnnaLise and Joy looked at each other across the table.

'I think a white, no?' said the fitness trainer.

'Joy, it's eleven o'clock in the morning.'

'You're right.' She lifted her chin. 'Nicole, do you know how to make mimosas?'

'I do, but I'm afraid we're out of champagne.'

Joy glanced at AnnaLise. 'Between the celebrating and interim homicide, I'm not surprised.'

'It is odd, though, isn't it?' Nicole said. 'Nobody seems sad that poor Mr Hart is gone.'

'To know him was to hate him,' Joy offered.

'That's not nice,' AnnaLise scolded. 'The man did what he could.'

'The man did *every*thing he could,' Joy corrected. 'Or everybody, assuming it had a—'

'Joy!' from AnnaLise.

But Nicole giggled, then put her hand to her mouth. 'Sorry, AnnaLise.'

'Don't be, Nicole. In fact, sit down. I'd like to ask you something.'

'Sure.' She pulled out a chair as Joy shot a puzzled expression toward AnnaLise. 'What can I tell you?'

AnnaLise had been thinking about this. 'Wednesday night—'

'The night Mr Hart died?'

'Yes. I saw both you and Chef Debbie about . . . what, ten-thirty?'

'Maybe just after, because I remember Mr Hart saying that it was only ten-thirty and he was going to watch some of the movie before turning in himself.'

'Right, right.' AnnaLise was chewing her lip. 'Which is when I said I'd deliver the wine to his room for you. But immediately after that, we ran into Chef Debbie.'

'And you broke the bad news that the grocery stores wouldn't be open on Thanksgiving morning.'

AnnaLise turned to Joy. 'Apparently there were some things she needed.'

'So we know Debbie was making plans for Thanksgiving dinner?'

'And, seemingly,' AnnaLise said, '*not* staying at Hart's Head that night.'

'No,' Nicole said. 'Mr Hart had reserved a room for her at the inn.'

It made sense that Nicole would know that. What didn't was that AnnaLise hadn't thought to ask her.

'That jibes with what Sheree told us,' AnnaLise said to Joy. 'Though it's not consistent with the theory that Debbie is the one who was in Hart's room.'

'Sure it is,' Joy said. 'Hart would have booked the room at the inn for cover. You know, so everybody wouldn't know he was hooking up with our family-holiday chef.'

'Why would he care?' AnnaLise asked. 'He "hooked up" with pretty much every other female who's here this weekend.' She paused. 'With the relieved exception of those of us who are or might be the product of said hooking up.'

'Exactly my point,' Joy said. 'He wouldn't want to sully the weekend by rubbing the noses of past conquests in his current . . .'

'Inamorata?' Nicole suggested.

'Oh, good one,' Joy said. 'Much better than—'

'Back to Wednesday night,' AnnaLise interrupted wisely. 'What time did your granddad pick you up, Nicole?'

'Earlier than I expected,' the girl said. 'The movie ended at about eleven-fifteen. When I realized I'd have the media room cleaned up by quarter to twelve, I texted him and he snuck out during a band break to pick me up.'

The 'band' at Sal's was Sal and his iPod. 'So he arrived here at around midnight?' That would tally with the car AnnaLise saw leaving.

'Yes, and good thing, too. The taproom was open past one, what with it being Black Wednesday.'

Apparently everybody but AnnaLise was familiar with the term. 'Was Debbie still here when you left?'

'Uh-unh.' Nicole was shaking her head. 'She was out of here maybe ten minutes after you and I talked to her.'

'Did you see her leave?'

'Actually walk out the front door?' Nicole closed her eyes for a second. 'No, I can't say that I did for sure. But when I returned to the kitchen after putting away the wine, she was pulling on her coat. We went over the menu quickly and then I ran to the cellar to get the merlot that Mr Hart suggested I open for the other guests.'

'Any sense of whether she went out the back door or the front?'

'Front, I think. She used the kitchen door to the hallway and foyer.'

'Which leads to the front door, but also the media room or master bedroom.' AnnaLise turned to Joy. 'It had to have been Debbie I heard entering Dickens' suite while I was there.'

'Timing sounds right,' Joy said. 'Though I suppose it still could have been Hart himself.'

'Oh, no,' Nicole said. 'He was at the corridor door to the media room, looking for the wine when I rushed back with it. Mr Hart took the bottle, thanked me and went in to the movie.'

'And about time, as I recall,' said Joy. 'The natives were getting restless without their refreshments.'

AnnaLise wrinkled her nose. 'I didn't know you watched the film, Joy.'

'Of course you didn't. You left me cooling my heels out on the patio when Hart and I started mixing it up.'

'Ahh, that's right. You'd just called him a pig.'

'If the cloven hoof fits.' Joy twirled some spaghetti onto a fork with a tablespoon.

AnnaLise nodded. 'And I, on the other hand, decided to make a graceful exit. That's when I very nearly ran into Nicole with the wine. Eddie told me that Dickens retired when the movie ended, and the rest of the party had broken up soon after. Is that the way you both remember it?'

Nicole was nodding herself now. 'I saw Mr Hart go to his room. In fact, he said good night to me.'

'What about the rest of the group?'

Joy had one eye closed, thinking. 'I poured myself one more glass of merlot for the road. By the time I turned around, everybody was already out of the media room.'

'And up the stairs?'

Nicole took this one. 'Yes. Well, except for Ms Boccaccio, of course. She took the elevator.'

'Neither of you saw anybody head the opposite direction toward Dickens' bedroom?' AnnaLise asked.

'Like I said, everybody was out of the media room and going up the steps when I came out into the hallway,' Joy said. 'I suppose somebody could have slipped in before that.'

But Nicole looked dubious. 'Not after Mr Hart went into his room, unless it was after I left for the night. I stood outside his door as everybody filed out and then went into the media room to tidy up.'

'So somebody could have snuck into the master suite when you were cleaning?'

'AnnaLise, I don't think so,' said Nicole. 'Once the group was upstairs, the ground floor was very quiet. I think I would have heard footsteps on its marble tile.'

'What did you do after you finished in the media room?'

'Took the glasses into the kitchen to wash and called Granddad.'

Joy looked at AnnaLise. 'Somebody for sure could have snuck in then.'

'Uh-unh,' Nicole said. 'Sorry, but I used the *second* sink where all the wine glasses hang, facing the hallway. I didn't close the door because it was spooky down here all alone.'

'So you could see the full length of the hallway to the master suite doors from there?'

Nicole nodded. 'I rinsed the glasses and slid them into the rack above to dry. Then I went to the foyer and waited for Granddad to pick me up.'

AnnaLise was arranging it all in her head. 'So that leaves us with Debbie – who could have *said* she was going to the inn, but snuck in while you were in the wine cellar – or pretty much anybody else, assuming they waited until you were gone.'

'Correct,' Nicole said. 'What happened after I left, like I told Charity, I can't say.'

'Charity knows all this?' AnnaLise asked. 'The timeline, I mean?'

'Oh, yes. She seemed very interested.' Nicole lowered her voice. 'You know what she asked me?'

Joy and AnnaLise shook their heads.

'If Chef Debbie ever mentioned roofies.'

The sediment in the glass. Charity had said that preliminary testing showed no nonprescription drugs in Dickens' system. Also, nothing in the full wine glass, nor the bottle. Neither she nor her husband, though, had said anything about the empty glass.

And AnnaLise, now kicking herself, hadn't asked that specific question. '*Did* Debbie mention—'

'Are you kidding? *Not* the kind of thing that comes up when you're peeling potatoes and all.'

'Suppose not,' Joy said. 'But you do know what they are?'

'Of course,' Nicole said. 'You're asking for trouble if you're my age and don't. When I go out with my friends, we guard each other's glasses when one of us dances or goes to the restroom.'

That was sad, AnnaLise thought. Things hadn't been quite that hazardous when she was Nicole's age. 'Did Charity say why she was asking?'

'Just that some had shown up in "preliminary test results."'

Joy looked at AnnaLise. 'Maybe you were right. Hart tried to drug Debbie and she hit him in self-defense.'

But AnnaLise had just had a thought, one that could confirm that Debbie had stayed over. Or, conversely, prove just the opposite. 'Nicole, do you remember if Debbie's car was still here when Sal picked you up at midnight?'

The girl scrunched up her face as she thought about it. 'No. But then I wouldn't have, anyway. Granddad pulled into the circle drive and picked me up square in front of the door. The cars were all parked around the side, next to the garage.'

'True.' AnnaLise was wondering whether she should be glad Nicole's reply had been inconclusive or not, when the kitchen door swung open.

'AnnieLeez!' Phyllis Balisteri thundered. 'You planning on eating that turkey spaghetti or just talking it to death?'

TWENTY-FIVE

Despite her scolding, Phyllis Balisteri had insisted on reheating the turkey spaghetti, resulting in AnnaLise and Joy still being at the table when the assemblage trouped in for their noon meal.

Since the Thanksgiving feast, the group had fallen into taking the same chairs at each communal meal. Outsiders on the south end and locals on the north, much like their sleeping arrangements on the floor above. Or warring factions in a middle-school lunchroom.

Unfortunately, AnnaLise and Joy had planted themselves square in enemy territory. 'Do you think we should shift?' AnnaLise hissed across the table.

'Hell, no,' Joy said. 'It's your house – at least for now – and besides, don't you want to find out what they're saying up here?'

AnnaLise did, of course. But the fact was nobody on the south end was saying anything. Or eating anything.

'Pretty soon we'll *have* to redistribute ourselves,' Joy continued, digging into the crisp cheese crust of her turkey spaghetti. 'We're going to outweigh them two-to-one. Tip the table like a teeter-totter.'

It was true that the visitors didn't seem as fond of Mama's cooking as the locals were. AnnaLise watched Lacey Capri, sitting next to her, pick at her plate. 'Having fun yet?' AnnaLise whispered.

Lacey started. 'Oh, sorry. Yes, of course I am.' She tried to smile. 'And thank you again for letting me use your iPad. I'm really enjoying it.'

Lacey sure looked like she was.

'You keep it as long as you're here, like I said,' AnnaLise reminded her. 'And don't lose heart. There may have been a break in the case.' She hoped.

'Really?' The girl's eyes widened. 'What—'

'Did I hear you say there's been a break in the case?' Lucinda, sitting next to Joy across the table, might not talk much, but Tyler's mother also didn't miss much.

'I'm sure that the police will tell—'AnnaLise started.

'Police?' Lucinda waved her be-ringed hand. 'They've come and gone already. Poof! And told us nothing. Left another poor man to sit in front of that bedroom door for hours on end.'

'Now, mother,' Tyler said, flashing a smile at AnnaLise. 'You were asking questions that I'm not sure the town police can answer. Better to wait for the county sheriff's department.'

Joy was watching suspiciously. 'What kind of questions were you asking? How you can get DNA before Hart is planted in his grave?'

Lucinda's eyes narrowed – dead fish turned mama tiger. 'Tyler has a right. Dickens Hart may be his father and invited us here for just that—'

'Wait, wait,' AnnaLise said wearily. 'No need to get into a tussle about this. When the sheriff's department arrives, I'll ask them to provide you with anything you need to do your testing.'

'Not at AnnieLeez's expense.' Phyllis' hearing – four people down – wasn't bad either.

'Please—'

But Patrick Hoag weighed in. 'The parties trying to prove paternity would be responsible for any costs, of course.'

'And well worth it,' Lucinda muttered. 'Once the results are in.'

'If Tyler and Eddie are Dickens' heirs,' AnnaLise said, 'then, of course, the three of us will share equally.'

Sugar Capri, next to Lacey, looked a little down in the dumps not to be included in the named participants. 'But you were saying we might get out of here soon?'

AnnaLise figured that filling them in on Debbie's whereabouts would do no harm. And it sure beat picturing DNA samples from a corpse being divvied up like proceeds from a Christmas grab bag. 'The police have found Chef Debbie who, as you've likely noticed, disappeared Wednesday night or early Thursday.'

The south end nodded en masse.

'Well, Debbie was picked up by the Las Vegas police when she stepped off her plane there.'

'They've arrested her?' Lacey asked.

Having grabbed their attention with the tabloid headline, AnnaLise qualified the story behind it. 'Not yet. Debbie's just a person of interest for now.'

'She has to have done it.' This came from Eddie, who was sitting between Daisy and Rose. 'Why else disappear?'

AnnaLise said, 'Apparently, Debbie was told her services were no longer needed.'

'A lie, obviously,' Tyler said, supporting his potential half-siblings' premise. 'This Debbie must have gone to Hart's room—'

'But why?' Lacey asked.

Tyler looked at Sugar, who just squirmed in her chair, while the rest of the group exchanged glances that said, *What moron among us wants to answer that one?*

Joy, apparently. 'Here's the thing, kid. Hart was a sleaze.'

'Joy, please,' AnnaLise said, a note of protection in her voice this time. Her friend might enjoy shocking people, but—

'Hey, he was *your* father, not hers. And my ex. Besides, the girl asked a question – she deserves an answer.' Joy sat back and folded her arms.

AnnaLise tried for understated paraphrase. 'Dickens liked women.'

'Oh, I know that,' Lacey said. 'It's the reason everybody's here, right? What I meant was why would Debbie go to Mr Hart's room and then kill him?'

'Excellent question,' Patrick Hoag said.

'From what we heard,' AnnaLise said, 'there may have been Rohypnol involved.'

Now Lacey looked puzzled.

'You may have heard them called roofies.'

'Ohmigod, the date-rape thing.' The doorbell sounded and Nicole's quick footsteps crossed the foyer floor outside the dining room.

'That's the one,' Daisy said. 'I heard that maybe Dickens tried to slip roofies into our Debbie's champagne and she got wise to him.'

'And smacked him one with his own bottle.' Phyllis made the

appropriate hand chop, just missing clocking Eddie in the ear. 'Served him right.'

The dining room door opened and Coy Pitchford stepped in. 'Excuse me, folks, hate to interrupt your—' He looked at the plates. 'Is that Mama Philomena's chicken spaghetti?'

'Turkey,' Phyllis said, standing up. 'Would you like me to get you a plate?'

'I sure—' Appearing to remember he was acting chief, he cut himself off. 'I just need to see AnnaLise.'

'But she's eating,' Phyllis protested. 'Coy, why don't you just sit down and—'

'I'm done, Mama,' AnnaLise said, folding her napkin on her plate and rising.

Coy beckoned her out to the foyer. 'Let's sit in Mr Hart's office.'

Now AnnaLise was getting worried. The police wanted to see her in a chair away from everybody else. That seemed more serious than a simple chance encounter while standing. 'Well, sure,' she said, with a glance back toward the dining room, from which normal – or at least semi-normal – sounds were still emanating.

AnnaLise led the way into Dickens' office. Charity was already there, but still leaning a shoulder into the wall herself. 'Why don't you sit behind the desk, AnnaLise? Coy and I can take the guest chairs here.'

So they'd both be facing her. Was that significant? AnnaLise wasn't sure, but in the police interrogations she'd been privy to see, the officers certainly wanted to be facing a suspect, not sitting side-by-side with him.

Or her.

AnnaLise took Dickens Hart's leather desk chair. 'Have you found out more about Debbie?'

Coy took off his hat and hung it on the back of his chair before he sat in it. 'We have, that's for sure.'

There was a tap at the door, which opened just wide enough for Patrick Hoag, Esq., to stick his head into the room. 'Excuse me, but I thought that perhaps AnnaLise would want me here.'

She felt herself nodding. Vigorously. 'That would be nice. Thank you.'

'You're thinking you need a lawyer?' Coy raised his eyebrows.

AnnaLise frowned. 'Patrick is here as my friend, who happens to be a lawyer.'

'It's true that AnnaLise hasn't retained me,' said Hoag, hovering over the last empty chair. 'But as her deceased father's attorney, I'd like to be present.'

Charity looked at AnnaLise. 'Up to you.'

The journalist was confused. Was she being questioned? If so, wouldn't they need to recite her Miranda rights? Or was that only after they made an arrest? And would having Patrick stay or not affect her right to have a specialist in criminal law be present later?

As a police reporter – and someone who'd 'dated' a district attorney – AnnaLise knew she should have such maneuverings down pat. But she didn't. In fact, at this particular second, she wouldn't trust herself to spell her own name correctly.

So she decided to rely on any available support. 'I want Patrick to stay. Now please, tell me what's going on?'

Hoag settled into the chair next to the mahogany filing cabinet as Charity produced her ever-present notebook. 'I just got off the telephone with LVMPD.'

For Las Vegas Metro Police Department, thought AnnaLise. 'Have they questioned Debbie?'

'They've asked Ms Dobyns a few things at our suggestion.'

'So then they'll send her back here.' AnnaLise felt her teeth begin to chatter despite the air temperature not being especially cold.

'We're not altogether sure that's necessary,' Coy said. 'At least, not right now.'

AnnaLise began to feel that the Pitchfords' cryptic answers were an intentional ploy to keep her asking questions and, maybe, slip up in the process. 'You mean until the county takes charge?'

'There's that, too,' said Charity. 'But what impresses us most is that Ms Dobyns is sticking to her cellphone story.'

'That she got a call telling her she was no longer needed?'

'That's interesting,' Charity said. 'You heard that, too?'

'Sheree told us – Joy and me. I thought I'd relayed that on to you.'

'AnnaLise, seems you thought you told us a lot of things,' Coy said, crossing an ankle over his knee and settling back in the guest chair.

'Regardless,' AnnaLise drove on, 'Sheree said Debbie told her that she'd gotten a call indicating she was no longer needed.'

'Did Sheree tell you the call came in on Ms Dobyns' cellphone?'

'Sheree assumed it did, since the inn's landline didn't register a ring. To be honest,' AnnaLise leaned forward, 'I don't think Sheree was a hundred percent sure that Debbie was telling her the truth.'

'Well, Ms Dobyns was, as it turns out.' Charity flipped back a page in her notebook. 'The call came in at five fifty-seven a.m. early on Thanksgiving morning, according to the cellphone company's records.'

AnnaLise felt her brow furrow. 'From where? Can you tell?'

'That's the interesting part,' Coy said, now unhooking his foot. 'The call came from the landline right here in this house.'

AnnaLise was thinking furiously. 'But was Dickens still alive then?'

'Not according to the M.E. Time of death was more like midnight, give or take a couple hours.'

'Then who could it have been?' Now AnnaLise was nearly freezing. She crossed her arms and involuntarily hugged herself.

'That's what we wanted to know,' Charity said. 'So as you might imagine, we had Las Vegas Metro ask Ms Dobyns.'

'Had Ms Dobyns answered the call that early?' Patrick asked, standing up. AnnaLise couldn't help but notice that his face had turned worried. 'Or did it go to voicemail?'

'No, she answered it, all right,' Coy said.

'Well, who was it?' AnnaLise thought she was going to scream.

'Who?' Charity Pitchford made like she had to consult her notebook for the information, then looked up from it. 'Why, *you*, Ms AnnaLise Griggs.'

TWENTY-SIX

'Honest to God, it was like one of those slasher movies.'

AnnaLise and Joy were outside on the patio again, seated in low chairs, their only warmth provided by blankets and stiff drinks, both courtesy of the thoughtful Patrick Hoag.

'Slasher movies?' Joy was swirling her drink so the cubes clinked melodically against the sides of a cut-crystal glass.

To AnnaLise's ears though, it was the sound of the *Titanic* hitting the iceberg. And she was onboard. 'You know, where they trace the call from the psycho killer and find out it's coming from inside the house. Except this time,' she allowed herself a sigh before a sip, 'I'm the psycho killer.'

She glanced at the closed door to the house and lowered her voice. 'Or supposed to be. They even printed me.' She held up smudged finger pads.

'Hey, we all got printed.' Joy wiggled her matching digits. 'As for your supposed "slasher" movie, you're talking about *When a Stranger Calls*. Carol Kane and Charles Durning. Not a *great* flick, but certainly a cult classic for that one scene with Kane babysitting. She's been terrorized by threatening phone calls and dials the police, who tell her all they can do is try to trace the next one if he calls again. Well, he does, asking her if she's checked the children. Then the phone rings yet again and she picks up, screaming, "Leave me alone!" But this time it's the voice of the police sergeant telling her, "We've traced the call – it's coming from *inside* the house!"'

Joy indulged herself in a full-body shiver. 'That was one of the most chilling moments in the entire history of cinema as far as I'm concerned.' She tugged her blanket a little closer.

'Huh,' AnnaLise said dully, staring out across the frigid lake. 'I was thinking it was one of the *Scream* films. Or maybe even *Scary Movie*?'

'Nope. Nineteen seventy-nine. I was a kid and you weren't even born yet. Since the original, I'm sure the idea's been poached – and spoofed – any number of times. There was even a remake.'

'Yeah?'

'Yeah. It sucked even more than the original.'

They were quiet for a moment, squinting out into the sun's chilly reflection off Lake Sutherton's surface.

Then: 'So you get my current point.'

Joy nodded. 'Charity and Coy think you're the serial killer who called Debbie. From inside this house.'

'I'm not . . . oh, never mind. Bad analogy.'

'Where is Patrick?' Joy asked, looking down at the ice in her glass.

'He wanted to talk to Charity and Coy. Hopefully he's trying to persuade them not to arrest me.'

'You know, it does kind of make sense.'

'What?' In AnnaLise's view absolutely nothing made sense. And she was wondering how she was going to tell her mother – mothers, plural – that apparently she was the prime suspect in a homicide.

'That you'd call Debbie,' Joy said, taking another sip of amber liquid. 'I mean, who else but Hart would have the authority – hell, even the *idea* – to fire her?'

'First of all, I wasn't the one who telephoned the woman,' AnnaLise said, trying to rally herself, if only as a dress rehearsal. 'Secondly, with Dickens Hart still alive, I *didn't* have the authority.'

'You're Hart's daughter and Debbie knew that. Didn't you say you two had talked before she left?'

'Yes, but I certainly didn't act like I was running the house.' AnnaLise realized her front teeth were gnawing on her lower lip again. 'At least, I don't think I did.'

'All this Debbie knew was what she was told by Hart, I assume, maybe with some filling in by Boozer Bacchus.'

'Boozer would be more likely to give orders in Dickens' absence than me.' AnnaLise heard a door open, seemingly from the garage side of the house.

'Only Boozer's been a bit out of the loop, what with his being busy doing your mom and all. But, that aside, you said the voice Debbie heard on the phone was a woman's.'

'But it wasn't mine!'

'I know, I know.' Joy reached over and gently clinked glasses. 'Drink more. It'll calm you down.'

AnnaLise did, then stifled a gag. 'Ugh. I *hate* bourbon.'

'That's OK, because this is Scotch. And like all of Hart's self-indulgences, really top-notch.' Joy hunched forward like a Girl Scout sharing secrets around a campfire. 'Hey, what do you think of "Top-notch Scotch," marketing-wise?'

'What I think is you've had enough, drinking-wise.'

Joy settled back, tugging her own blanket more around her shoulders. 'You're not even fun when you're scared to death.'

'Can we please return to the subject of—'

'"The Landline Call"? Fine.' Her tone said it was clearly *not* fine, yet she'd slog onward for her friend. 'I honestly don't think you have anything to worry about. Once the police lab guys compare the voice on the message to yours, they'll realize they don't match.'

'But there *was* no message,' AnnaLise said, taking another vile sip in spite of herself. 'Despite the pre-dawn hour, Debbie actually answered the phone.'

'Has it occurred to you that she could be lying?'

'Who?'

'AnnaLise, who have we been talking about, Snow White? Little Debbie Dobyns, the Bimbette Chef.'

Brightening a bit, AnnaLise said, 'You're right. If Debbie did kill Dickens, of course she'd have to cover her butt.'

Only now Joy was frowning. 'However, am I remembering right? As we arrived back here with my snubbie earlier today, didn't you tell me a bullet broke Hart's window on Wednesday night?'

'I did.' AnnaLise was surprised her friend remembered, given all the water – and now Scotch – under their bridges since this morning. 'Boozer found the slug in the Lake Room and showed it to me.'

'Interesting. Could you tell what kind of gun it was fired from?'

'Me? No chance. Boozer seemed to think it might have been a deer rifle, though, so I paid a visit to Roy Smoaks at Bradenham.'

'Bradenham?' Joy repeated, looking across the lake toward the mini-estate in question.

'Yes. Smoaks was on the deck target shooting Thanksgiving morning.' AnnaLise shaded her eyes. 'Did you see that just now?'

'What?' Her friend took a belt of her Scotch.

'A glint of light from over there. Like a mirror or—'

'Laser sight!' Joy snapped, gesturing at AnnaLise's forehead. 'The red dot – duck!'

The journalist did, only to be rewarded by the other woman's raucous laughter. 'Oh, that's just hilarious.'

Straightening back up, AnnaLise started, thinking she'd caught movement again, this time on the near side of the lake in the trees masking the pier.

Watching her, Joy said, 'Jesus, AnnaLise. Are you OK?'

'I'm a nervous wreck, thank you. And you're part of the problem.'

Looking ashamed, Joy knocked a cigarette from her pack on the table. 'I'm sorry. I didn't think you'd honestly believe old Roy Smoaks was about to shoot you.'

'Says the woman carrying a concealed weapon.' AnnaLise re-arranged the blankets that had slipped to the floor when she'd reacted to Joy's warning. 'But it does seem strange that he chose Thanksgiving to visit Bobby. They didn't even have turkey.'

'And this . . . offends you somehow?'

'Roy Smoaks offends me. He seems to hate everybody in Sutherton, including Dickens for having had a hand in Rance's losing his job. In fact, I wouldn't be surprised if the old man chose a time when he knew Chuck – Rance's successor – was going to be gone just to fly up and cause trouble.'

'Seems like you're giving this Roy Smoaks an awful lot of credit for being Machiavellian. Besides, Chuck's been in office for more than two years now *and* Rance is dead. Why,' finger quotes, 'take revenge,' finger-quotes closed, 'now?'

AnnaLise ignored the sarcasm in Joy's digits and in her voice itself. 'Maybe *because* Rance is dead. Roy just snapped.'

But Joy still looked skeptical. 'What does Bobby say about all this?'

'Not much,' AnnaLise admitted. 'He seems to be self-medicating with alcohol to get through the weekend.'

'Can't say I blame him.' Joy finally lit her cigarette, drew in, and then let out a stream of smoke before continuing. 'Did you share your theory with the police?'

'I told Charity about Smoaks being here, as well as how the window was broken. She doesn't think there's any connection, though she did make a note of it.'

'Charity makes a "note" of everything, in case you hadn't "noted it."' Joy was thinking. 'I will give you that Hart wandering among his guests in that well-lighted room would be an inviting target. But from across the lake it'd be one hell of a shot.'

'And one that he missed. Dickens *wasn't* shot and the only person hurt was Eddie Boccaccio, who was cut by flying glass.' Then AnnaLise frowned. 'Though, as Boozer said, that's unusual in itself, given that it was tempered.'

'Kind of like cutting yourself with a spoon – you'd really have to work at it. Are you sure Boccaccio wasn't faking to get "Daddy's" attention?'

'No, this was genuine. Eddie was circulating drinks and greeting people—'

'You mean like a . . . host?' Joy asked.

'More a waiter. But what are you thinking?'

Joy knocked an ash off her cigarette and onto the patio. 'Just that maybe Eddie wasn't cut from glass, but grazed by a bullet meant for—'

'Dickens?' AnnaLise absently picked up her Scotch and sipped. 'They do have similar builds.' Setting her drink back down jogged a memory of Dickens Hart going to place his own champagne flute on the fireplace mantle. AnnaLise had assumed the flute fell, but it had still been there when Boozer showed her the bullet the next morning. In fact, she'd watched him carry it to the bar. 'The richochet.'

'What?' Joy was understandably looking puzzled.

AnnaLise was trying to get the sequence straight in her own head. 'Just as Dickens was putting down his champagne glass to speak, there was a thud and Eddie called out. As I turned toward him, I thought I heard Dickens' glass fall.'

'So the bullet hit it.'

'No, the glass was still there and intact the next morning. The "ping" I thought was fine crystal hitting the floor might, though, have been the bullet richocheting off the fieldstone.'

'I suppose in the confusion it could have sounded like that.' Her expression added: *To somebody who didn't know any better.*

'It all happened very fast,' AnnaLise said in her own defense. 'The thudding sound at the window and Eddie's exclamation—'

'When he was shot—'

'The pinging of the richochet from the same bullet as it hit the fireplace and Eddie's tray falling to the floor. Then—'

'The waterfall of tempered glass.'

'Exactly.' AnnaLise was thinking furiously. 'The problem is how does this tie into Dickens being beaten with a champagne bottle? Besides, how would Smoaks even know—' She stopped, remembering her shiver at the thought of the man watching them from across the lake.

'Know . . .?' pressed Joy.

'That he missed Dickens, I was going to say, but I just answered my own question.'

'Not aloud, you didn't. Dish, my friend.'

'Binoculars. Smoaks showed them to me on Wednesday and said he would enjoy watching the "soap opera" over here.'

'Well, he had that right, I guess. But like you just asked, what then? Smoaks shows up here in the dead of the night to finish the job like a caveman with a mammoth club? How would he even get in?'

AnnaLise felt the adrenaline that her theory had sent through her veins start to wane. And any hope along with it. 'I don't know.'

'For God's sake, don't give up so easily,' Joy chided. 'Think.'

OK. 'Maybe Smoaks . . .' AnnaLise was searching for something, anything, '. . . has an accomplice?'

'Good girl.' Joy sounded like a first-grade teacher encouraging the class slacker. 'And who . . .?'

'Debbie Dobyns? In cahoots with Roy Smoaks?' AnnaLise perked up, given she didn't like the latter and scarcely knew the former. 'But why?'

'That I don't know.' Joy let loose a column of smoke that would have shamed the chimney of a coal-burning power plant. 'But even if they're not working together, you say Smoaks is keeping an eye on this house. Maybe he saw something that could help you.'

AnnaLise sat forward in the chair, her blanket forgotten. 'I bet that was the glint coming from over there – sunlight off the lenses of his binoculars. He's probably watching us right now.'

'Who?' Patrick Hoag had come out behind them, holding a drink of his own.

'A nosey neighbor,' AnnaLise said, not having the energy to lay out her not-yet-fully-formed theory only to have the lawyer poke holes in it. She waved Hoag into the seat next to her. 'So, Patrick, what did you find out? Did Charity and Coy tell you why they believe Debbie? It's my word against hers and they *know* me.' Even to herself, AnnaLise sounded pathetic.

'They're not saying much but, then again, that's not surprising.' Hoag settled into the cushioned seat, before leaning to set his own sampling of 'top-notch' Scotch on the table. 'They already have you right where they want you.'

'Scared shitless?' AnnaLise covered her mouth. 'Uh, sorry.'

Joy rolled her eyes. 'Your "mamas" aren't here. Besides, you're suspected of committing patricide. That kind of entitles you to have a potty-mouth.'

'Surprisingly, it doesn't make me feel any better, though I am impressed by your vocabulary.'

'Potty-mouth?'

AnnaLise shook her head. 'Patricide. And you, pretending you didn't know what "putative" meant. Shame on you.'

'Oh, lighten up,' Joy said. 'What do you say we take a spin around the lake and see Bobby this afternoon? It'll do you good.'

'Didn't you hear what Patrick just said?' AnnaLise asked. 'I'm going to be formally accused of *murder*.'

'Umm.' Patrick lifted his glass. 'I didn't mean to convey that, exactly. In fact, I have a feeling Coy is keeping both you and Debbie

– through the Las Vegas police – on ice until the county gets here and decides who it wants to charge.'

'What'll they do – flip a coin?' AnnaLise caught her own grousing tone, then looked up at Patrick. 'By the way, thanks for your support in Hart's office just now. Does that mean you're my lawyer now?'

'Sorry, but no can do. As you said yesterday, it'd be a conflict of interest, given I'm the victim's attorney. Besides, I don't do criminal law. I can refer you to someone who does, though.'

'A referral, how professional of you,' Joy said. 'But in the meantime, why the hell are you parading around acting like you *are* her lawyer?'

Patrick shrugged. 'Can't hurt to let the police know that *some* professional's watching after AnnaLise's interests.'

'And, like I said, I'm truly grateful,' AnnaLise assured him. 'I'd also appreciate that referral to a . . . defense attorney.' The last two words were barely audible.

'If you want,' Patrick said gently, 'I can give her a call first and explain the situation in legalese.'

'That would be even better.' AnnaLise thought she'd even managed to summon up a smile. 'Thank you. Again.'

Then she closed her eyes, took a deep breath and let it out slowly. She should be relieved that Patrick would make sure she was properly defended. But instead AnnaLise felt like a passive target. Weak, even.

And that's not the way to win. Hell, that's not even the way to fight.

AnnaLise opened her eyes and gave Hoag a flinty look. 'OK, enough self-pity. Patrick, is it your impression that the Pitchfords don't necessarily believe Debbie any more than they do me?'

'Well, yes.' Patrick had been holding his drink but now put it back on the table without AnnaLise seeing him take a drop. 'The problem, though, is the call from here to her cellphone on Thanksgiving morning.'

'There's no getting around that?' Joy asked. 'Nothing Chef Debbie could have done to the phone to make it just *appear* that way?'

'I don't see how,' Patrick said. 'The cell company records registered a call from this landline at five fifty-seven a.m. to Debbie Dobyns' cellphone at the Sutherton Inn.'

'Before dawn, even.' Then AnnaLise Griggs sat up straight. 'But . . . are we sure that she – and her cellphone – were *at* the Sutherton Inn?'

TWENTY-SEVEN

Joy Tamarack's eyes were big and round. 'You're saying Chef Debbie was still here in this house?'

'Maybe even still in Dickens' master suite,' said AnnaLise. 'Is there any way of knowing which room the landline call was made from?'

'There's just the one line,' Joy offered. 'When I lived here we had a dedicated number for the fax machine and another for dial-up internet. But I'm sure not anymore.'

'How sure?' Patrick Hoag asked.

'Hey, your client might have been rich, but he was also cheap. Hart told me he was even thinking of doing away with the one landline remaining, given there was only Boozer and him here, both with cellphones.'

'So,' AnnaLise was picturing the layout of each floor, 'Debbie could have made the call to her own cell from any room with a landline extension.'

Joy frowned. 'Can't the police tell where the cellphone was at the time the call came into it?'

'But that's just what I mean,' AnnaLise said. 'They should check the GPS records. Right, Patrick?'

The lawyer was rubbing his chin. 'I presume the Pitchfords – or the county sheriff or prosecutor, more likely – will do just that, but only eventually. They'll need a court order first.'

'Another complication,' Joy said, hand in the air, 'is that GPS isn't very accurate in the mountains.'

'True,' the lawyer concurred. 'My map app leads me astray more often than not.'

'But there are cell-towers, too,' the prime murder suspect said. 'You know, that the call has to pass through.'

Joy still looked skeptical. 'Given the short distance between the inn and here – or here and here, if you're right – would the towers even—'

'Problem is,' Patrick cut in, 'we're theorizing without the most basic of knowledge. Either about cell and GPS technology, in general, or Debbie Dobyns' phone in particular.'

Nonetheless, AnnaLise was starting to feel better. 'The point is that the authorities need to get a court order and check, not just *assume* Debbie's telling the truth when she says she received the call at the inn.' She turned to Joy. 'Do you remember what time she told Sheree she was checking out?'

'Sevenish?' The fitness trainer scrunched her eyes closed. 'Sheree said she was in the kitchen making breakfast when Debbie popped in and told her she was popping out.'

'So,' AnnaLise said, 'if Debbie made the call from here at five fifty-seven a.m., then—'

Joy took it up, 'She could drive to the inn, sneak in, pack up and be saying goodbye to Sheree by seven, no traffic and no problem.'

AnnaLise stood and took a self-satisfied gulp of her Scotch. It still tasted awful, but the budding warrior princess resolved not to show it. 'I'm going to tell Coy and Charity.'

'It's a great theory,' Patrick said into his own drink.

AnnaLise waited. 'But?'

He looked up. 'I'm sorry. No, your version hangs together pretty well, so far as I can see. Only . . . maybe you've already "told" the police more than enough before consulting with a criminal defense attorney.'

Joy nodded. 'I agree. Why give the Pitchfords time to pick apart your theory?'

'When do you want to spring it on them?' AnnaLise asked. 'The penalty phase of my trial?'

Joy frowned again. 'Girl, I liked you better when you were wallowing in self-pity.'

The master suite was still taped off, but there was no sign of any uniforms. AnnaLise checked the media room next, only to find it deserted, too. In the Lake Room, though, she saw Sugar Capri lounging in an overstuffed chair near the fireplace, newspaper in her lap and pen in her hand.

It took a moment for AnnaLise to realize that the other woman – in so many meanings of that phrase – was working on a crossword puzzle. 'Have you seen Charity or Coy?' AnnaLise asked.

Sugar looked up, looking bewildered. 'I'm sorry. Who?'

'Of course. I should be the one apologizing. You'd have no way of knowing the first names of the Pitchford officers are Coy and Charity. They're husband and wife.'

'The two police officers who've been here? I did think it was weird they had the same last name on their uniforms, but I didn't give it much thought, given the . . . circumstances.' Tears threatened, but she seemed to try to rally. 'Must be nice having a spouse in the same business. Or . . . any spouse at all.'

The rally hadn't lasted long. AnnaLise settled on the arm of an adjacent chair as tears brimmed in Sugar's eyes. 'Lacey told me that her dad was dead. I'm so—'

'Oh, we weren't married.' A flush of color actually rose in Sugar's cheeks, and AnnaLise had to remind herself that this 'elder' Capri was only a little older than she was. 'Suppose I shouldn't admit it so freely in nice company like this.'

'I don't know how "nice" it is,' AnnaLise said. 'After all, some-body did kill our host.'

Sugar's face dropped again. 'I'm so sorry about Dickens. I . . . well, kind of hoped we could maybe get together again.'

AnnaLise studied her face. 'You didn't hold what he did against him?'

'You mean me being so young? No, that wasn't his fault. I flat out lied to him. To everybody. He wasn't even my first, you know.'

AnnaLise hoped her internal shock didn't show. 'Still—'

'There is no "still." Nor "ifs," "ands" and "buts," neither. Dickens Hart never treated me with anything but kindness. Bought me clothes and—'

'How did Dickens find out you were underage?' AnnaLise inter-rupted back, not wanting to hear where the 'schoolgirl' skirt and thigh-highs might have come from.

'Boozer Bacchus saw that my driver's license wasn't . . . well, it wasn't mine,' Sugar said. 'That man never did like me much. Or Joy, though with her I could understand it.'

'Dickens and she being married and all.' AnnaLise was trying for deadpan.

Sugar plucked at the paper in her lap. 'You know, that's the thing I *do* regret, looking back. It's not right sleeping with a married man, especially in his and his wife's own bed. But Dickens was just so handsome and I was a teenager, head-over-heels in love with him. Nothing else seemed to matter.'

'Mom?' Lacey Capri's head snuck around the corner. 'Oh, hi, AnnaLise.'

'Did you need your mother?' the journalist asked, hoping the girl hadn't overheard. 'I was just leaving.'

'No, don't do that,' Lacey's smile was nearly maternal, like she was happy her mom was making new friends. 'I just wanted to say I was back from my walk and going up to take a bath.' She shivered. 'It's getting cold out there!'

Sugar nodded. 'Just be out before I need to get ready for dinner, you hear? No two-hour soak.'

'I hear.' A giggle and the head disappeared.

Her mother smiled. 'You should have heard Lacey when we got here. "Mom – he's *ancient.*"' Sugar did a credible imitation of her daughter. 'But . . . there was always something about Dickens Hart. It'll sound silly, you knowing all you do, but the man made me feel safe. Lacey and I, we haven't had a lot of that lately.'

A tear escaped from one eye and slid down Sugar Capri's cheek.

Leaving the Lake Room, AnnaLise nearly collided with Joy.

'Let's go.' Joy held an oversized yellow slicker that matched the one she was wearing.

'Go where?'

'Don't be dense. To Bradenham to talk to Roy Smoaks and find out what he might have seen.'

'I want to catch Coy or Charity first.'

'You can spring your theory on them when we get back. Maybe you'll have more to tell.' She held out the jacket.

AnnaLise took it, but let it dangle from one finger. 'This is damp. And it isn't mine.'

'And this lovely number isn't mine, either.' She did a pirouette, rubberized fabric billowing around her. 'I grabbed these from the rack at the back door to save us time.'

'But I have a jacket.' AnnaLise tried to hand the slicker back. 'I'll just get it.' She paused. 'Or did I leave it in the car?'

Joy looked skyward. 'Will you put the damn thing on so we can get started?'

'What are you in such a hurry for?' AnnaLise protested as she slipped on the coat and followed the diminutive force of nature through the deserted kitchen and into the back hallway. Then AnnaLise put on the brakes. 'Wait. You think they're going to *arrest* me.'

Joy opened the back door and tugged her through. 'So what? Even *you* think they're going to arrest you.'

AnnaLise raised the hood of her slicker against the wind. Lacey was right about the temperature. Late November in the High Country was always quirky and now there was definite moisture in the frigid mountain air. 'Are we walking?'

Over her shoulder, her friend responded, 'You kidding?' Then Joy strode to her BMW and unlocked it. 'It's miles.'

'And miles,' AnnaLise echoed as she got into the passenger seat. 'But then why did we have to don these?' She plucked at the slicker.

'Just how long did you live in these mountains?' Joy asked, starting the car. 'The weather changes in an instant so you go nowhere – not even the grocery store – without the proper layers. If you don't want to wear it, put the thing in the back seat.'

'No, it's fine.' AnnaLise stayed silent as Joy backed the BMW out from between a pair of SUVs. When they were gliding down the newly re-surfaced driveway, she finally said, 'We should think about how we're going to do this.'

'I already have.' Joy stopped at the end of the long drive, then turned left. 'You hold him down and I'll beat him with a rubber hose.'

Rubber hose? And Joy called AnnaLise a throwback. 'Why are you going counterclockwise instead of clockwise around the lake?'

'Same distance and these roads are better. Besides, we don't have to go through town where somebody could see us.'

AnnaLise stared at her. 'Honest to God, you're scaring me.'

Joy shrugged. 'Just being cautious. Now, what's your plan?'

'I guess we'll have to play it by ear.' The journalist didn't remind her friend that this little excursion had been her idea. It was like talking to a rock.

A yellow, rubber-covered rock.

'My, my – these days it's against the law to own binoculars?' Roy Smoaks asked mildly.

'If it were we'd have sicked the Pitchfords on you,' said Joy.

The four of them – Smoaks, Bobby, Joy and AnnaLise – were in the living room of Bradenham. Its windows, not nearly as large as those of Hart's across the way, still provided a magnificent view of the lake.

Bobby Bradenham had taken their damp slickers and hung them on a rustic hat rack. Then he moved a pizza box from a couch cushion so the two women could sit. The coffee table in front of them was littered with chip bags and beer cans.

Now Bobby held up his hands. 'Let's not snipe at each other, all right?' He turned to AnnaLise. 'What exactly is it that you're asking?'

She shifted uncomfortably. 'Honestly, I'm not sure. As you're both certainly aware by now, Dickens Hart was found dead yesterday morning.'

Bobby nodded. 'I'm very sorry about that, AnnaLise. I should have called you.'

'That's OK,' she said. 'I'm sure you've been' – a glance at Smoaks, as the man dropped his sorry butt aggressively into a delicate armchair – 'busy.'

'Not quite as busy as you folks.' This from Smoaks, who lifted his muddy boots to the corner of the coffee table, dislodging one of the chip sacks onto the floor.

The comment reminded AnnaLise of something Smoaks had said the day before. Actually, two things. 'I know you shot out Dickens' window.'

'Now how would you know that? It could have been anybody.'

'I "know that" because of what *you* knew that I didn't tell you. You said it was likely a hunter getting in his "last hurrah" before the sun went down.'

'So?'

'So, how did you know the window was shot out at dusk?'

For the first time, Smoaks looked uncomfortable. 'Maybe I saw it. I do have those binoculars *you* keep harping about.'

OK, time to move on to item two: 'What's "kerplunk"?'

Bobby looked surprised. 'Kerplunk? I've never heard of it.'

But AnnaLise's attention was on Smoaks. 'You also said yesterday that "we folks" were early risers and asked if I'd been playing "kerplunk" at the pier. I assumed it was a game like skipping rocks. But it's not, is it?'

'Well, now, I was just making polite conversation.' Smoaks grin was wide enough to expose his gold tooth. 'You know, *kerplunk*. Like "splash"?'

'The sound of somebody tossing something into—' Then it struck AnnaLise. Maybe the bottom of the lake was, indeed, where the missing overnight bag lay.

'Who was the somebody?' Joy contributed. 'And the something?'

Smoaks linked his hands in the air above his head and stretched, letting out a crisp fart in the process. 'Now *that* I reckon I can't answer.'

'What's wrong?' Joy waved vigorously at the air in front of her nose. 'Aren't your spy-glasses strong enough?'

'Oh, no, they're high-powered all right.' A lecher's smile. 'Just like me. Problem is, though, I heard the kerplunk, but she was turned away from me by the time I got the lenses focused.'

AnnaLise felt hopeful. 'So, it was a—'

Smoaks lowered his feet to the floor. 'Broad? Think so, less'n it was a shrimp of a swinging dick.'

AnnaLise considered both the answer and the source before asking simply, 'Notice anything else? Build? What she was wearing?'

'Now, much as I appreciate giving a comely woman the once-over,' Smoaks said, leering at both of them and getting to his feet, 'I can't say much about this particular one.'

'Can't or won't?' Joy looked like she wanted a reason to deck the man.

'Can't.'

'Why not?' Bobby looked puzzled.

'Not that I don't want to, Grandson of Mine.' Smoaks picked up one of the beer cans with his right hand and shook it. Finding the thing empty, he crumpled it with one impressive squeeze. 'Cuz'n she was wearing one of those.'

He tossed the can at the hat rack and it bounced off a yellow rubber slicker. 'Score!'

TWENTY-EIGHT

'I don't see it.'

Joy put her hand out to steady AnnaLise, who was hanging off the ladder of Hart's Head's fishing pier, scrutinizing the water below. 'You're sure this is where Smoaks meant?'

'He said a figure in a slicker dropped something – "kerplunk" – into the water at the end of the pier. Given our clear, spring-fed lake here, I can see all the way to the bottom. And there's nothing.' Despair was rising in her voice. 'Certainly not a bright floral bag.'

'Maybe Smoaks is lying.'

'There is that.' AnnaLise scaled the top two rungs of the ladder before swinging herself up and onto the pier. 'This would be so much easier if we could pin the whole thing on him.'

'We'd also have to tie him to Debbie or somebody else in the house,' Joy reminded her, still staring down at the water. 'Maybe the person didn't weigh the bag down and the waves took it away.'

AnnaLise brightened. 'That means it'll eventually show up on the beach across from Mama's restaurant.'

'That's the spirit,' Joy said. 'Or . . . maybe the woman did weigh it down but heaved it as far as she could, and we'll need a scuba diver to find it.'

Back to bleak. 'In near-December water temperatures?'

'They must have suits for that, right? I mean, they go after stupid ice fishermen who "kerplunk" themselves during the season.'

'Yes, but if the diver scours the lake bottom within "heaving" range and comes up empty?'

Joy said, 'OK, voice of gloom and doom, let's go back inside. I'm getting the creepy-crawlies.'

'From being here?' AnnaLise asked.

'Hell, no.' Joy gave a shiver. 'From having been in the same room as Roy Smoaks.'

Once through the front door, AnnaLise resumed her hunt for the authorities, while Joy opted for a nap.

Given that AnnaLise hadn't spotted the overnight bag at the bottom of the lake, she planned to relate only her first theory – that the call to Debbie Dobyns' cellphone was not only made from the house, but received in it. No need to bombard Coy and Charity with too many theories at once and look desperate.

Which, of course, was how she increasingly felt.

Charity Pitchford was sitting behind Dickens Hart's desk when AnnaLise stuck her head in. 'Can I come in?'

Charity looked up from writing yet another something in her notebook. 'It's your house now.'

'Through no fault of mine,' AnnaLise said, not bothering to sit down. 'Listen, I've been thinking. We know that a call came in to Debbie Dobyns' cell early Thanksgiving morning from this house, correct?'

'Correct.'

'Is there any reason why it couldn't have been made by Debbie herself? You could check the GPS on her phone, or—'

Charity pushed back in the chair, making it squeal like a metallic pig. 'Ms Dobyns called . . . herself?'

'Yes. Think about it.' AnnaLise put her palms on the desk and leaned forward. 'She conks Hart, maybe in self-defense. She's still in the master suite with his body, trying to figure out what to do.'

'And Ms Dobyns stays there for what must have been another five, even six hours? Why?'

'First of all, assuming our Debbie's not a stone-cold killer, she's trying to calm down, think things through.' Something else suddenly occurred to AnnaLise. 'Or, and maybe more likely, she'd been drugged. Hart gave her the wine with the Rohypnol, making—'

Charity frowned. 'And just how would you know we found that?'

'You asked Nicole if Chef Debbie had mentioned roofies. You can't honestly think that this stuff doesn't get around, even among relative strangers. This may be a big house, but Dickens' death is the six-hundred-pound gorilla in the bedroom.'

A resigned sigh. 'Continue.'

'Anyway, Debbie realizes she's been drugged and – outraged – slugs Hart with the champagne bottle.'

'And then passes out.' It wasn't a question – Charity seemed to be seriously considering the possibility.

'And wakes up hours later, remembering – or not, depending on a roofie's power – what happened. Either way, she'd want out.'

'And to remove any evidence of her ever being there.'

AnnaLise sensed something. 'Like fingerprints?'

Charity hesitated, and then nodded. 'The glass with the sediment only had one set of fingerprints on it, and according to the Las Vegas police they're not hers.'

AnnaLise looked at her own fingertips, still smudged with ink. 'Are you saying they're mine?'

'Not surprising, seeing as you told us about carrying it in. For what it's worth, there were no usable prints on the other glass. Or the bottle.'

AnnaLise shook her head. 'But there should have been Nicole's and mine, at least. And Hart's for that matter. He tasted the wine in the first place.'

'Does seem odd now, doesn't it?'

'Somebody wiped down the bottle and one glass, but not the other? Why?'

'Time will tell, as it generally does.'

AnnaLise barely heard Charity's observation. 'So, we have Debbie in the master bedroom, waking up after being drugged and finding herself with Dickens' body. She cleans up, but misses . . . Wait, that unwiped glass was on the stairs to Hart's library. In fact, the top step. With the trauma and the Rohypnol, Debbie certainly could have forgotten to check up there.'

The police officer cocked her head. 'Except I've just told you that her fingerprints aren't on the glass.' Then a level gaze. 'Sure you haven't . . . forgotten that *you* carried it up there?'

For a panicked moment, AnnaLise wondered. But then, no. She was sure she'd left both glasses on Hart's dresser. What happened to them after that was anybody's guess.

'I'm sure. And as to the call I supposedly made to Chef Debbie's cellphone, is it possible she called from the phone in Hart's bedroom? She'd have had to turn her ringer off, so it didn't—'

But Charity was raising her hand up and toward AnnaLise like a school-crossing guard to an oncoming car. 'Only there is no telephone in that bedroom. We checked.'

Step back and start over. 'So Debbie used another extension. Maybe here in Dickens' office or . . . yes, the kitchen. There's an old wall phone. I remember because Mama slammed the refrigerator door so hard she made the receiver fall off it. Having worked in there, Debbie would certainly have seen the thing.'

'And used it to make the call,' Charity took up. 'She wouldn't even have needed to talk, just stay on the line long enough that it would appear that a terse conversation took place and she was fired.'

'What do you think?' AnnaLise asked.

The officer cracked the first smile AnnaLise had seen from her in some time. 'I think that it's certainly worth telling the county detectives tomorrow.'

AnnaLise resisted pumping her fist in victory. 'Thank you.'

'Don't thank anybody,' Charity said. 'All we're doing as the Sutherton town police is maintaining the crime scene. And collecting information to provide the county with when they get here.'

'Still, I appreciate you're being comprehensive. Did you say the sheriff's department will be here tomorrow?' AnnaLise pursed her lips, thinking. 'Which is . . . Saturday? I'm losing track of time in all this.'

'I wish your guests were,' Charity said, putting away her notepad and rising. 'I've been asked no less than ten times how soon they all can leave.'

She tamped her pen into a narrow pocket on the sleeve of her uniform. 'All of a sudden, I'm getting the impression these people would gladly let you fry if it meant they could get back to their dental practice or brokerage by Monday. And maybe as heirs.'

Dental practice/brokerage heirs. 'You're talking about my – perhaps – half-brothers, Eddie Boccaccio and Tyler Puckett?'

'And their mothers, who we've also spoken to, along with everybody else. Apparently the "boys" aren't doing particularly well financially.'

AnnaLise wasn't surprised that the police had interviewed Rose and Lucinda, but she did find it interesting that Charity included the women amongst those willing to let AnnaLise 'fry.'

A mother/son team, with the mother diposing of the bag in the lake? Rose, at least, had to be a longshot despite admitting she managed to 'hoist herself out' of the wheelchair on occasion. *And* she'd admitted to being in Dickens' room the night of the murder to snag the marijuana, albeit well before the crime was committed. And as for Lucinda . . . 'I heard that the market has been unkind to Tyler. What with all the ups and downs—'

'He's had more downs than ups, from what we've been able to find out, his clients even more so.'

'You've been looking into Tyler?' AnnaLise asked. 'And Eddie, too?'

'The junkie dentist? Of course.' The officer lifted her uniform jacket.

AnnaLise sensed that Charity, as forthcoming as she'd been, had nevertheless reached her limit. 'Any word from Chuck?' AnnaLise asked, trailing behind her and into the foyer.

'Not surprisingly, our chief called in practically the moment he got off that plane in Ireland,' Charity said, shrugging into her jacket. 'His mother's the one who booked their flights, so they stopped in Rome, Paris and London.'

'Wow. They visited each of those cities?'

'More like each of those airports, from what I gather. The time on the ground was barely long enough to pass through security and high-tail it to the next flight.'

'Yet, Mrs Greystone will always have bragging rights,' AnnaLise said. 'After all, how many people in Sutherton can say they've visited Rome, Paris, London and Dublin?'

'Not to mention all in less than twenty-four hours,' Charity acknowledged. 'Anyway, once the chief picked up his messages and realized what was going on here, we had to do some heavy talking to keep him from flying directly home.'

'Or indirectly, if Mrs Greystone had anything to say about it.' AnnaLise was making light of the situation, but there was a part of her that desperately wanted the police chief back in Sutherton. Though having Chuck Greystone and Roy Smoaks in the same county, much less the same town or even room, admittedly might not be the best idea. 'So you convinced him to stay, I hope?'

'We did. Told him we were already doing everything the way he would.' Charity opened the front door. 'Thoroughly and professionally.'

'Again, thanks for that,' said AnnaLise.

'And again, none necessary.' Charity stepped out onto the porch.

'You'll be back tomorrow?'

'We will, with the county. Fearon is pulling another long shift here tonight.'

'Poor guy.'

'Hey, he volunteered. Seems the man can't get enough of Mama's cooking.'

AnnaLise smiled and was about to close the door when Charity stopped her. 'One word of advice?'

'Any I can get.'

'Not everybody here is your friend, and many stand to gain something with Dickens Hart gone. Some would benefit even more if you were gone as well.'

Charity flipped on her parade hat, then straightened and tugged it down onto her forehead, as though she were about to brave a windstorm.

AnnaLise said, 'Thanks, Charity. But from our conversation just now, I'm not quite as worried about being hauled off to jail.' Operative word: quite.

Charity Pitchford smiled once more, but this time grimly, and glanced around as if for eavesdroppers. 'AnnaLise, when I said "gone," I meant one way,' she pointed an index finger to the police logo on the crown of her hat, 'or . . . another.'

The officer drew the same index finger across her own throat from ear to ear.

TWENTY-NINE

AnnaLise Griggs shut the door, shuddering more than the solid wood did thudding into its frame.

All right, settle down. And make at least a quick, mental list of who might consider acting against you in Charity's 'another way.'

The obvious people who would benefit most with Dickens Hart dead and AnnaLise out of the estate picture were Eddie Boccaccio, Tyler Puckett and, by extension, their mothers. Neither man, according to Charity, was doing well financially.

The charming Tyler's problems had to do with the market. Prickly Eddie's? Apparently Daisy was spot on about the drug habit, and that, in AnnaLise's journalistic experience, always translated into a need for money as well.

Interesting that Rose, the sixties' stoner, had begotten a son who was addicted—

'*Mangia!*' The shouted word, followed by laughter, interrupted AnnaLise's thoughts.

She trailed the sound to the stoner herself in the kitchen with Phyllis Balisteri, the latter doubled over in hilarious reaction to something.

'Everybody OK in here?' AnnaLise asked.

'Sure, sure. We're just fine.' Phyllis was trying to catch her breath. 'Rose was just telling me stories about her family.'

'From the name Boccaccio, also Italian, I assume?' AnnaLise snitched an olive from a tray of antipasto Rose was arranging at the table.

'Is the Pope Catholic?' Rose asked, sending both two older women into paroxysms again.

AnnaLise smiled, hoping the hilarity was from people of Italian heritage sharing nostalgia, not cannabis, especially given the police presence in the person of Officer Fearon. Though he was apparently so in love with Mama's cooking that he was willing to forego sleep.

That might encourage his just winking at a little of the wacky-terbaccky as well.

'AnnieLeez, don't you go ruining your dinner now,' Mama said. 'Rose is teaching me to make that antipasto *and* her macaroni.'

'Macaroni?' AnnaLise repeated. 'Like the elbow kind?'

'No, no,' Rose said. 'My own mother called all pasta macaroni. We're making penne with homemade sauce.' She nodded to a huge kettle bubbling on the stove top.

'It smells fabulous,' AnnaLise said, going over for a closer inspection.

Phyllis looked on approvingly. 'There's meatballs and pork and sausage and . . . What did you call those rolls, Rose?'

'*Bracciole* – kind of Italian *rouladen*. We were saying that both our families came over in the nineteen thirties, so what we consider "Italian food," is as dated in Italy as . . . well, whatever people were eating here in the U.S. in the thirties.'

Phyllis gave Rose a look. 'Well, isn't *that* . . . depressing,' sending the two off again.

AnnaLise didn't get it. 'What's so funny about—'

'The nineteen thirties. You know, The Great Depression?' They both opened their palms to her in a 'get it?' gesture.

'Oh, right. And funny, too.' Like a stick in somebody else's eye was funny. 'Um, have you seen Daisy?' AnnaLise actually hoped to talk to Boozer Bacchus, but figured if she found one, odds were she'd find the other.

'Daisy took the younger generation downtown,' Phyllis said.

'Downtown' consisted of three blocks, centered on Sutherton's Main Street.

'I hope with Coy or Charity's permission.'

Phyllis's chin dipped toward her chest. 'Don't know.'

Given AnnaLise's trips to the inn and Bradenham, she didn't have grounds to scold. 'That's OK. Who went?'

'That Tyler, Eddie and Lacey,' Phyllis said. 'Oh, and our Nicole, too.'

AnnaLise asked, 'You two didn't want to go?'

'The only important thing on Main Street is Mama Philomena's,' Phyllis said, 'and we're not open. Besides, Rose and I are having a fine time in this lovely kitchen.' She ran her right hand almost sensually along the granite countertop.

'You're a lucky woman, AnnaLise,' Rose said. 'A lot of people would kill for a house like this.'

Phyllis' eyes bugged out. 'Rose Boccaccio, you didn't really just say that, now, did you?'

'Say what?' Realizing, Rose clapped a hand over her mouth and the two dissolved into giggles again.

Not seeing a way to improve on the situation, AnnaLise went through the back hall and out the rear door of the house. Reaching the driveway, she rubbed her arms against the cold, but didn't go back to don one of the slickers she and Joy had returned inside the door.

Yet that's exactly what she believed Chef Debbie had done early on Thanksgiving morning – pulled on one of the slickers for her walk through the clump of trees to the end of the pier. There she'd dumped the overnight bag before returning to the house where she would have hung the disguise/raincoat back on its hook and made the call – to herself – from the kitchen phone before driving to the Sutherton Inn.

But . . . why did Debbie feel the need to get rid of the bag in the first place? Had she seen AnnaLise sneaking out of the bedroom after all? Or did Debbie know that something on – or in – it could link her to the crime? Like Dickens' DNA . . . The bloody champagne bottle had been left on the slipper chair, where the bag had been. Blood certainly could have smudged it as the killer wiped and dropped the murder weapon.

As AnnaLise walked onto the driveway, an exterior door cracked open on the second floor of the garage and Boozer Bacchus stepped out between two webbed-and-aluminum lawn chairs on the tiny balcony. 'Can I help you, AnnaLise?'

'Actually, yes. I was wondering if you knew where Chef Debbie's car was parked on Wednesday night.'

'I do,' Bacchus said, not bothering to pull the door closed behind him. 'I asked her to put it about where you're standing, so she wouldn't get blocked in by the arriving guests.'

'Of course,' AnnaLise said, 'because you thought she wouldn't be staying overnight.'

Bacchus leaned forward, his arms braced on the railing. He was wearing short sleeves, exposing tattooed arms that didn't seem to be feeling the now swirling, chilly air. 'I have to tell you, I never liked to ask about sleeping arrangements when it came to the lieutenant's women.'

AnnaLise jumped on that. 'So, Debbie *was* one of Dickens—'

'Now, I don't know that for sure, I have to say. Definitely his type, though, even these recent years.'

'"Recent years," but not days?' AnnaLise backed closer to the house so it could act a wind break. 'Had something changed?

'Well, like all of us, he was getting older, for one thing.'

'I thought a man could keep it up—' She raised her hand, hoping the flush in her cheeks could be blamed on an ambient, phantom guest of wind as she saw Boozer try to hide a grin. 'I don't mean that literally. Let's say, instead, that an older man can continue a full sex life. I mean, look at . . .'

She'd been about to say, 'you,' but given the circumstances, thought better of it. '. . . Hugh Hefner, Dickens' idol.'

'That's true. But then things had come along to make even the boss reconsider his wicked ways.'

'What things?'

'Well, you, for instance.'

'Sorry, but I don't see how that can be true. Dickens believed Bobby Bradenham was his son for decades and, by all accounts, that didn't stop him from hounding around.'

'True enough. But you were different, somehow – maybe being female. And there was your mama, Lorraine, too. I think he always felt bad about . . . that part of his life.'

Because Dickens' only real friend was in love with Lorraine 'Daisy' Kuchenbacher Griggs, even back then?

Perhaps. But AnnaLise could tell there was something else. 'Was Dickens ill, Boozer? Rose said she found marijuana in his nightstand earlier that evening.'

'Now why was that woman nosing around in—' Bacchus started angrily, but then seemed to realize it didn't matter anymore. He rubbed his chin. 'I got him it to try when chemo made him so sick. The boss had prostate cancer.'

A neighbor of AnnaLise's in Wisconsin had been diagnosed with it. She could recall him saying, 'If you're male, and you're going to get cancer, this is a good one to get.'

Still, AnnaLise shivered. 'But that's very curable, isn't it?'

Boozer nodded his head once, and then kept it down. 'It was when they first found it, some years ago. The boss' own daddy died of the same way back, so your daddy was checked "early and often," like they say today.'

'And treated?'

'He was, but, well, Mr Hart was a proud man and he didn't want
. . . um . . .'

'Erectile dysfunction?' AnnaLise guessed, echoing the commercials on television. 'But there's medicine for that.' As put forth by
those same commercials.

Bacchus nodded. 'There wasn't, so much, when he was originally
diagnosed, so he chose a more conservative path and thought he
was cured.'

'But Dickens wasn't.'

'No. Started with him having pain sitting. In the lower back.'
Bacchus seemed near tears.

'That was his cancer?' AnnaLise asked gently. She was remembering Dickens' discomfort while seated at his desk as they'd first
discussed this weekend. And the red cushion on the chair at the
head of the dining table.

'It had metastasised, the doctors told him, to his bones and spine.
He'd done his best to hide it this weekend, what with pain pills and
standing up more than sitting down.'

The pain pills would have been the prescription drugs Charity
said had been found in Dickens' system. Along with alcohol. 'He
was drinking wine,' AnnaLise said. 'Couldn't the combination of
alcohol and his pain meds have—'

Boozer rocked forward, both hands on the railing in front of him.
'It's an argument I plain tired of having with him, AnnaLise. The fact
was your daddy didn't care, so long as the hurting stopped for a while.'

This time AnnaLise didn't flinch at the word 'daddy.' 'Was he
undergoing any kind of treatment?'

'Not in the last couple of months, since he first got the idea for
this weekend in his head. Said he didn't want to feel sick as a dog
with everybody here. But he hadn't given up, by no means. No, he
just wanted to . . . well, get his affairs in order.'

And Dickens Hart had certainly succeeded in that, his last night
on earth: former lovers arrayed chronologically in his home, from
cougar Rose Boccaccio to aspiring graphic artist Lucinda Puckett,
AnnaLise's own mother Daisy to underage Sugar Capri and, finally
and perhaps fatally, chef Debbie Dobyns.

'I warned him it was a bad idea.' Bacchus was shaking his head.
'And, it turns out, more deadly than his cancer.'

The loyal soldier turned and went back through the door, closing
it this time.

THIRTY

The sounds of a car approaching reached AnnaLise as she stood thinking about what Bacchus had said. It was likely Daisy returning from squiring the 'younger generation' around Main Street. Instead of circling to the front to greet them, AnnaLise went in the other direction, to the rear of the house.

She didn't feel like talking to anybody right then.

Picking up one of the blankets Joy and she had left outside the door, AnnaLise wrapped it around her shoulders and threaded her way through the trees to the pier.

At its end, the crystal clear water of earlier now looked murky gray to her as the clouds had lowered. A 'brumal' sky, she thought. The word had been on the 5 January page of the Word a Day calendar one of her co-workers had gifted her for their holiday exchange. The perfect present for somebody like AnnaLise, who loved words nearly as much as she did people.

Sometimes even more so.

Brumal means 'wintery.' It would snow by morning. AnnaLise, a child of the High Country, knew that as surely as she did that her mothers loved her. And that Boozer loved Daisy.

A gust of wind blew the blanket off her shoulder and AnnaLise caught it, a metaphor for the theory she was also trying to hold onto.

But maybe she had it all wrong.

Dickens Hart knew he had cancer – a reoccurrence of the prostate variety that had already spread to his bones. AnnaLise hadn't asked Bacchus what the prognosis had been, but it must have been dire enough that 'the boss' was putting his affairs in order.

Hart's being ill shouldn't have been surprising to his daughter. Rose had even suggested it as a possible explanation for the pot in Dickens' nightstand. What better trigger to make a man reconsider life than the specter of his own death?

But . . . Dickens had prostate cancer. Taking into account that and the fact it had metastasized so painfully to his spine, would he have invited Debbie Dobyns to the master suite for a – possibly last – fling in the sack?

AnnaLise was by no means an expert – or even an intermediate – on men's sexual psyches, but it didn't make sense to her. Bacchus, though, hadn't ruled out the possibility. Maybe there were other things Dickens and Debbie could have 'done'? Maybe . . .

'Aren't you cold out here?' a man's voice said.

AnnaLise turned to see Eddie Boccaccio stepping on to the pier. She felt no desire to exchange pleasantries or ask how the excursion had gone. She wanted only to get rid of him. 'Your mother's in the kitchen with Mama.'

'Making sauce, from what I've heard and smelled,' he said, refusing to take the hint and instead walking toward AnnaLise. 'Your lake's beautiful.'

'The lake is cold,' she said flatly, not even looking at him. 'And it'll only get colder. Sutherton is not the most pleasant place to spend a winter.'

'Skiers seem to think otherwise,' Eddie said, seeming a bit surprised and now standing next to her. 'They certainly pay big money to hit Sutherton's slopes.'

'That's because they're here to party. They don't have to go to work. They don't have to make a living. They get snowed in, they sit and drink. Or strap on skis and go downhill.' Much like her attitude.

'I'm sorry,' Eddie said. 'Did I say something to offend you?'

AnnaLise knew that she should be careful. After all, she was standing on the lake end of a long pier with one of the guests who would benefit from her being 'gone,' as Charity had put it. But AnnaLise simply didn't care. She was just plain pissed at the world. 'So, potential-half-brother Eddie. What exactly are you abusing?'

He flinched like she'd punched him. 'What—'

'You're not fooling anybody,' AnnaLise said. 'Even Daisy noticed your eyes. And the police have made—'

'The police?' Eddie grabbed her at both elbows.

AnnaLise shook him off, teetering a bit on the not-quite-even planks. 'Of course the police. If you're hooked, you probably need money. Think, motive?'

'A motive for . . . are you saying they think *I* killed Hart?'

'Not such a cause for celebration when it's you they're sizing up for handcuffs, is it?'

Eddie now pantomimed warding her off with his palms. 'Listen, I don't need this.'

'Apparently you do. As does our handsome, potential half-brother, Tyler.'

'Tyler?'

'People repeat what somebody just said to them to buy time, did you know that?' AnnaLise said. 'I'm a police reporter, or have been, and it's the first thing I noticed about liars.'

'Liars? Why, you—'

AnnaLise pushed past him.

'Wait.'

She kept walking.

'AnnaLise. Please?'

Safely off the pier now, she did stop. Beyond her, the house lights were coming on and the place would look festive, if you didn't know better.

Eddie drew alongside, glancing at her and then away, seeming to be weighing something. 'OK.'

'OK, what?'

'I take a few pills. I have back problems and take Percocet. Sometimes . . . too many.'

Tote up another one for Daisy. 'I can understand that. Given you're a dentist, you can prescribe it for yourself. Or for patients that don't exist?'

'I've never done that. But even if I could have, it doesn't mean I need money so much that I killed Dickens Hart in the faint hope I'd get his.'

AnnaLise started walking again, circling around the knot of trees so as not to be caught alone there with him. 'Somebody did.'

'Sure,' Eddie said, falling in step with her. 'This chef—'

'Have you had your back checked?' AnnaLise asked.

'Checked . . . what do you mean?'

'I mean, did a doctor tell you why your back hurts?'

'Not specifically. Just said I must have pulled something.'

'He or she prescribed Percocet because you probably pulled something?'

'You know how it is.' Eddie seemed to search for something plausible. 'Professional courtesy?'

'So, another dentist . . .?'

'No. No, it's a family practice guy. He just . . . well, I take care of him and his family's mouths for free and he—'

'Takes care of you. Got it.' Reaching the patio, AnnaLise dropped her blanket on a chair.

Eddie touched her arm. 'I admit that I may be addicted to pain-killers, but I didn't write illegal prescriptions. The police can look all they want. They won't find anything.'

AnnaLise looked at his hand until he dropped it. 'Good for you. But I'd suggest you have that back checked.'

'Why?'

'Could be cancer. Runs in the family, 'case you didn't know.'

'There you are,' said Daisy as AnnaLise entered the Lake Room. 'People were looking for you.'

'I was down at the pier. But how did your tour go?'

Daisy touched her daughter's cheek. 'You're freezing. How long were you—?'

'Too long, apparently.' AnnaLise reached the bar, its counter bare. 'We out of wine?'

'I don't think Hart's Head will be "out" for centuries. Nicole is getting some from the wine cellar. Really now, AnnaLise. Are you all right?'

The younger woman turned, not sure why her eyes were welling with tears. 'Oh, God, Daisy. I thought I had it all figured out, but now . . . I'm so confused.'

Her mother pulled AnnaLise to the couch and sat her down. 'I was going to ask, "About what?" but it's pretty obvious.'

AnnaLise passed the back of her hand quickly, even roughly, across her eyes. 'Did Boozer tell you that Dickens had cancer?'

Daisy hesitated, and then nodded. 'Yes.'

'Do the police know?' If so, it would explain why Charity had said that the prescription drugs in Dickens' system were "accounted for."'

'I'm not sure,' Daisy said, confusion crawling across her own features. 'Why?'

'Because if Dickens was dying it could change everything.'

'AnnaLise, I'm not crazy, but I still don't understand what you mean.'

'Look, maybe I'm the one who's crazy.' AnnaLise was rubbing her hands against each other. 'In fact, it's hard to believe I'm even thinking this.'

The mother took her daughter's hands, holding them still. 'What is it that you're thinking?'

AnnaLise whispered, 'How well do you know Boozer?'

'Boozer? Why, I've known him for years. No, more like decades.'

'But how *well* do you know him? For example, do you know he's in love with you?'

Daisy blushed. 'Oh, don't be silly, AnnaLise. Just because we spent a night togeth—'

'No, Daisy. I mean it. He's in love with you. And I think he must have been since the White Tail days.'

Her mother seemed almost stricken and sat back. 'Did he tell you that?'

'No.'

'Then how—'

'It's obvious. As clear to me as that it's going to snow tonight.'

Daisy didn't bother to glance out the window. 'Does that bother you?'

'That Boozer loves you? No. I'm just afraid . . .'

'Please, spit out. You're scaring me.'

AnnaLise looked over her shoulder to make sure nobody else was within earshot, then scooched forward, their knees nearly touching now. 'Daisy, could Boozer kill somebody?'

'Of course not!' Daisy jumped up. 'How could you possibly say that? Why would you ever say that?'

'He loves you,' AnnaLise said, standing, too. 'And he loved Dickens, who had cancer that was causing him suffering.'

'And you're suggesting what? A mercy killing?' Daisy demanded. 'With a champagne—'

'Boozer's witnessing his own father dying a slow, terrible death and he's told me it's tearing him apart. He also said his dad used to be a veterinarian.'

A lot of blinking. 'Well, yes. But what's that got to do with anything?'

AnnaLise looked over her shoulder again before saying, 'Euthanasia. Boozer said his father advised people on when they should put their farm animals – even pets – out of their misery.'

'Out of *whose* misery? The pets or the owners?'

It was only then that AnnaLise remembered Timothy Griggs' lingering death. 'I'm sorry, Daisy. I forgot about Daddy.'

'This isn't about your father – or at least *that* father. I just can't believe you're accusing a kind man like Boozer—'

'That's just it, Daisy. He is kind. He could have done it to save Dickens further pain.'

But Daisy was swiveling her head back and forth, back and forth. 'No. No, no. That just doesn't make sense. Even if Boozer believed he was sparing Dickens, why do it that way? And during this weekend with a house full of . . . gold-diggers?'

'Maybe for *just* that reason,' said AnnaLise.

'In the hope that someone else would be blamed?' Daisy's voice squeaked at its upper register. 'Absolutely impossible, AnnaLise. Boozer would never do that – especially since suspicion could fall on you more than anybody else. He would never put my daughter in that—'

'The man loves you, Daisy. Which is why this weekend was *exactly* the time for him to . . . forgive me, but kill two birds with one stone.'

Daisy looked dangerously close to killing her own baby bird with what might be close at hand. 'AnnaLise Griggs, make yourself clear this second.'

Her daughter took a deep breath. 'Maybe Boozer thought that by sparing Dickens from his suffering this weekend, he'd also protect my inheritance from those very gold-diggers you mentioned.'

THIRTY-ONE

'So, I noticed your mother wasn't talking to you at dinner just now.' Despite – or, maybe because of – the outside temperature, Joy Tamarack fired up a cigarette.

She and AnnaLise had repaired to their usual nest on the patio after dropping a plate of food off with on-duty officer Gary Fearon.

Now AnnaLise hunched closer to the space heater. 'I may have made a tactical error. Or just an error, period.'

'Give.'

'I suggested to Daisy that the new man in her life may have killed the old man in her life.'

Joy gasped. 'Boozer killed Hart?'

'Possibly.'

'What happened to your old theory about our Debbie? Weren't you going to the police with *that* one?'

'I did.' Before elaborating, AnnaLise got up and pulled her chair even closer to the heater. 'Charity seemed quite interested, in fact. She also told me that the fingerprints had been wiped off the champagne bottle and the glass in Hart's room that still held wine.'

'What about the other one, the one with the stuff in it?'

'Turns out the stuff was, indeed, Rohypnol. And the only fingerprints on the glass were mine.'

The corners of Joy's mouth tilted down like a cartoon character's. 'Well, that's not good.'

'Agreed. But I was reassured that they're still also considering Eddie and Tyler and their mothers as possible suspects. Both men have money problems – Eddie because he's a druggie, as much as he denies it. And Tyler is a stockbroker.'

'Tyler's a stockbroker?'

'*That's* the part that stops you?' AnnaLise said, remembering Joy had been coming down from her own brush with illegal substances when they'd discussed the two men's professions during Thanksgiving dinner.

'Of course.' Joy took a long drag on her cigarette. 'Everybody should have known Eddie was sky high.'

'Speaking of which, should you be smoking next to the space heater?' asked AnnaLise. 'The tank is filled with propane gas. We could be blown from here to the mountain top.'

'Honestly?' Yet, Joy didn't put the thing out. 'Back to Tyler. Was he convicted of insider trading or something?'

'Not that Charity told me. Just that he gave some bad advice, resulting in both him and his clients losing a lot of money.'

'And probably losing the clients as well. What else?'

'From Charity? Nada.'

'Well, good. That mean's Debbie's still on the table as a suspect.'

'I think so far as they know. But it's something I found out later that makes me think maybe it wasn't Debbie.'

'Damn, I take an afternoon nap and the world around me switches poles. Spill it.'

'Dickens Hart had prostate cancer.'

'I thought it must have come back.' Joy's cigarette glowed orange in the dark.

'You knew?'

'Of course I did. I was his wife, remember?' Another dangerously deep drag. 'Actually, his *ex*-wife by then. Hart was diagnosed just after we divorced. I told him it was divine retribution for getting his dicky sticky in Sugar.'

Thanks *ever* so much for sharing. 'That would have been, what? Nineteen ninety-six?'

'Thereabouts. It's a long time to be in remission.'

'Assuming he was that entire time. Boozer told me they didn't find it until Dickens' back started hurting.'

Even Joy flinched. 'The cancer went to his spine?'

'Yes. He'd had treatment, hence the pot that Rose found in his nightstand, but—'

'Wait. Rose stole Hart's medical marijuana?'

'I'm afraid so. Though Boozer said Dickens wasn't—'

'And she shared it with me.' Joy was smiling. 'What a cool old broad.'

AnnaLise shook her head. 'If you say so.'

'OK, I understand that Hart's cancer had returned. But why does that let Debbie off the hook and put Boozer on it?'

'Because I can't imagine Dickens inviting Debbie to his room if he was dying of prostate cancer.'

'Why not?'

'Well, because . . . I mean, isn't the prostate in his—'

'Dicky? No. Besides, if Hart's joystick fell off, he'd pick the thing up, duct-tape it back on, and start all over again.'

'Joy, please?'

'Sorry. Forgot we were talking about your father, not just my unfaithful scumball of an ex-husband. But my point is that Hart didn't have the recommended surgery when he was diagnosed in the first place.'

'Boozer said he was afraid of erectile dysfunction.'

'That and incontinence, both of which can be addressed a little better now.' She tapped her cigarette on the arm of the chair and a glowing clump of ash fell downward. 'Dead, however, can't be fixed. Ever.'

AnnaLise sighed. 'Quite true. So are you telling me that I just hurt Daisy for no reason?'

'I'm saying that Hart let nothing slow him down, sexually, so I wouldn't be so quick to rule out Debbie. But back to what you said about Boozer Bacchus maybe killing Hart: why in the world would the loyal retainer do that? Boozer's one of the few people here that Hart didn't fu—'

AnnaLise didn't let her finish. 'A kind of mercy killing, maybe? One that would also save my fortune?'

Joy seemed to mull that over. 'But it wouldn't, so far as I can see. Patrick said Eddie and Tyler still have time to prove their paternity. Or Hart's of them, I guess.'

'Boozer didn't know that?'

'Maybe not. But it seems like a pretty major thing to overlook. Besides, if "mercy" was Boozer's motive, why now?'

'That's exactly what Daisy asked me,' said AnnaLise.

'And your answer?'

'Only that he needed to do it before things proceeded further.'

'Lame,' Joy said. 'And it doesn't address my point. Boozer could have killed Hart a couple of weeks ago, before any of the "potential heirs," as Patrick put it, were even contacted, much less actually here.'

'Dickens' prognosis had worsened? Or Boozer needed time to plan once Dickens told him about this weekend?'

'And how does Chef Debbie fit in? If she didn't kill Hart, somebody sure tried to make it look that way. If you hadn't gone into Dickens' room that night she'd have been the clear prime suspect.'

AnnaLise sat up straight. 'Maybe it was Boozer who called Debbie from the house.'

'As a woman?'

'All he'd have to say is "you're fired" in a falsetto.'

'Maybe, or . . .'

AnnaLise felt Joy's gaze, even in the dark. 'What?'

'Boozer could have had a woman do it.'

'What woman?' AnnaLise demanded. 'There's nobody who Boozer—'

As AnnaLise realized who Joy had in mind, the snow began to fall in silent, clotted handfuls.

THIRTY-TWO

'**D**aisy?' AnnaLise whispered hoarsely.

Joy didn't answer.

'My mother would never have had anything to do with Dickens' – or anybody else's – death.' AnnaLise felt herself struggle to get the words out.

'I'm not suggesting she did,' Joy said.

'That's exactly what you suggested.'

'What I meant was the telephone call. Listen to me, AnnaLise. It's clear that Boozer and Daisy have something going on, which is great. Hell, they've known each other nearly all their adult lives. What would Daisy have done if Boozer had told her what'd happened?'

'That he'd crushed his boss' skull with a champagne bottle?'

'A boss who Daisy couldn't care much for in the first place, given their history.'

'Their "history" being me?'

'Obviously. But let's assume your mother didn't despise my smarmy ex-husband for knocking her up. We *do* know she cares about Boozer. If he brained Hart to spare the great man pain, especially as part of a misguided effort to protect you, isn't it possible Daisy would agree to help Boozer cover up the killing, even if she didn't fully approve? Smoaks said he thought a woman dumped something – and we're thinking the overnight bag – into the lake. Could it have been Daisy?'

A gust of wind blew some of the falling snow toward their feet. AnnaLise put a hand to her forehead, realizing she was shaking only when skin drummed against skin. 'Daisy, aside from being my mother, is one of the kindest people I've ever known. She might want to help a man she loved, given there was nothing she could do at that point to save Dickens, but I just don't see her helping Boozer in any plan to pin it on Debbie.'

'Could Daisy have done so during one of her – I think we're calling them . . . "spells"?'

AnnaLise's heart plummeted. 'Daisy's possible dementia made her forget it's bad form to be an accessory to murder and frame an innocent person?'

'Accessory after the fact, at worst, but you know what I mean. Your mother doesn't always think as clearly as she used to.'

AnnaLise stood. 'Sorry, I can't talk about this anymore.'

Joy got up, too, letting the now stub of her cigarette fall from her fingers. The dying orange glow sizzled when it hit the snow before going out. 'No, I'm the one who's sorry. Just trying to work through your theory number two – or is it three? Anyway, I didn't mean to upset you.'

'I know you didn't,' AnnaLise said. 'I guess . . . well, I guess I know now how Daisy felt when I accused somebody *she* loves.'

'Your mother may care about Boozer, but not the way you love Daisy. And, again, I truly apologize.'

AnnaLise gave her a hug. 'All forgiven.'

'Can we just agree to still suspect Debbie for the time being?' Joy offered. 'It would make everything *so* much tidier.'

'Agreed,' AnnaLise said, before reaching and pulling open the door to the Lake Room. 'And I'm grateful we can expand the list to include a few spares like Eddie, Tyler and—'

'Do I hear my name?' Tyler Puckett was standing at the bar and turned, drink in hand, as they crossed the threshold from the patio. 'What happened to you two lovely ladies?'

'It's snowing,' AnnaLise said, using her blanket to try to mop up the mess she was making on the floor. The mess she'd continue to make with her mouth was unfixable.

'So I noticed. Was this forecast?' Tyler seemed more concerned about the weather than anything AnnaLise might be saying about him.

'We're in the High Country during late November,' Joy said, brushing herself off before joining Tyler at the bar to empty a wine bottle into the same glass that had held the Scotch. 'Forecasts don't help much. It can be blizzarding on one side of the mountain and not on the other.'

'Hope this doesn't keep us from leaving on Sunday,' Tyler said, bringing his drink along to look out the unboarded window. 'Our flight is at nine a.m. out of Charlotte.'

Joy actually uttered the 'harrumph' sound. 'That will make for an early – no, a very early – morning. You're two-and-a-half hours from the airport, even on dry pavement.'

'Tyler, have you been cleared to leave?' AnnaLise asked.

He paused with the glass halfway to his lips. 'Cleared?'

'As in, by the police.'

'Oh, your down-home, husband-and-wife tag team?' Tyler, grinning, brought his drink all the way to his mouth for a hearty swig. 'No, but I'm sure even a podunk county sheriff's department will be able to straighten things out once they get here and arrest that missing chef.'

AnnaLise swallowed his insult to her homeland. 'Debbie Dobyns?'

'An eminently doable piece like that in jail – what a waste.'

'Christ.' Joy rolled her eyes as she took a first hit of wine. 'Maybe he *is* Hart's bastard kid.'

Just another grin. 'Only time – and modern means of testing – will tell.'

'As far as Debbie is concerned,' AnnaLise said, 'she may be the current prime suspect, but we all know that I'm next, with you and Eddie right behind me. It's anybody's guess when the sheriff's department will let any of us fly this gilded cage.'

Tyler frowned and the freckles on his nose seemed to congeal. 'Why would I – or Eddie, for that matter – be suspects? We barely knew the man.'

'And yet you both hoped to inherit tens of millions from him,' Joy said, getting into the spirit of the moment. 'That kind of swag would come in pretty handy, I'll wager.'

Definitely no grin now. 'What are you implying?'

'The police know about your recent stock dealings,' said AnnaLise. 'And that they cost your clients quite a chunk of money.'

Tyler's face beneath the freckles grew pale. 'Everybody knows it's been a bad year for the market.'

'Not really,' Joy said. 'In fact, my portfolios – and lots belonging to others – rebounded nicely. Some temporary ups and downs, of course, but nothing like what your clients seem to have experienced.' She took a measured sip from her wine. 'Might even be downright criminal.'

AnnaLise threw Joy a look that said, *You're making this up as you go*, and, simultaneously, *Well done!*

'Those charges were dropped,' Tyler said. 'And I did nothing wrong.'

'Then you have nothing to worry about from either our "husband-and-wife" tag team or the probably equally inept sheriff's department.'

'Listen,' Tyler said. 'I'm sorry if I insulted your "High Country,"
but—'

'Is AnnaLise . . .? Oh, there you are.' Lacey Capri was at the
hallway door. She held up AnnaLise's iPad. 'I'm afraid your battery
died.'

'I'll run up and get the charger,' AnnaLise said. 'Just a sec.'

'Criminally' leaving the young Lacey to referee Joy and Tyler,
AnnaLise took the stairs two steps at a time, grateful to be away
from any confrontation, even one that might prove advancing.

Once inside her room, though, she had no idea where the afore-
mentioned charger might be.

The valets Hart had hired for Wednesday – could that have been
only forty-eight hours ago? – had unpacked the arriving guests'
luggage. Opening drawers, AnnaLise pushed aside the clothes she'd
brought for the stay. Nothing.

The iPad itself had been on top of the desk before she'd lent it
to Lacey, but there was no charger there either. And no telltale cords
trailed from any outlets she could see, except the one for her
cellphone.

AnnaLise briefly examined the phone charger, wondering if it
could be used for her iPad, too. Probably not. 'Damned essential
technology.'

She moved to the room's closet, thinking she might have packed
the charger in a side pocket of her navy suitcase. Which, if memory
served, the valet had hoisted onto the highest—

Lost in thought and reaching for the door's handle, AnnaLise
was unprepared for the heavy, paneled slab of wood to be flung
outward with such velocity it slammed the back of her skull into
the bedroom wall.

THIRTY-THREE

*W*hat the hell . . . had just . . . happened?

Stunned and on the floor with her back against the
wall, AnnaLise gathered her thoughts before she struggled to her feet, kicking the offending door back toward its frame.

As it struck and half-rebounded, there was a timid knock

from the hallway outside, then a creak as a voice said, 'AnnaLise?'

Lacey Capri's face appeared. 'I'm sorry, but did you find—' The blue eyes now focused with concern on AnnaLise's. 'Are you OK?'

The reporter took her hand away from a rapidly bulging lump on the back of her head and checked her fingers and palm for any blood. Nope. 'I'm fine, but someone must have been in my closet. Did you see anything in the hallway?'

'Nobody, I only just came up the stairs,' Lacey said, eyes now wide and a little scared. 'Are you sure you're not hurt?'

The reporter realized she was spooking the girl and raised both hands. 'I'm sure, truly. Just got a bump on the head and I'm a little . . . well, shocked.'

'What was somebody doing in your closet?' Seemingly reassured, Lacey's question had a note of outrage in it.

AnnaLise shook her head, as much to clear it as to answer. 'The door flew out and knocked me against the wall but whoever was behind it was gone by the time I pushed the thing out of my face and looked around. As for why he or she came in here, I don't have the faintest idea.' AnnaLise swung the closet door wide open.

'Anything taken?' Lacey asked.

'Taken, no.' AnnaLise stared down at an object lying crumpled on top of her neatly arranged shoes.

'Oh, what a cute little . . .' Before AnnaLise could react, Lacey reached in and retrieved it.

'No!' AnnaLise reflexively grabbed the revoltingly familiar floral bag away from the girl. Then immediately thought, *Damn.*

Damn, damn, damn.

'I'm sorry,' Lacey said, her nose reddening as tears began welling over.

'It's not you,' the journalist said a little too sharply as she dropped the bag on the floor. Then she softened her voice and pointed down. 'It's just . . . that.'

Lacey took a step back. 'Is there something inside?' She shuddered. 'A spider? Or a snake. Ohmigod, I hope it's not a snake. I *hate* them!'

AnnaLise shook her head. 'I don't know if there's anything in it. But I'm afraid something could be *on* it.' She looked at Lacey. 'This is the bag I saw in Dickens Hart's room.'

Three quick blinks, residual tears trickling down from the nose-side corners of the teenager's eyes. 'I don't understand.'

AnnaLise sighed. 'I was in Dickens' room before he was killed and, well, that thing,' she pointed again, 'was on his chair when I left. Only the bag was gone when his body was found the next morning.'

Lacey's eyes grew wider than her earlier smile. 'You think it belongs to the killer?'

'I don't know.'

'But where did you find—' Then the girl's expression hardened. 'Wait a second. Is that why you were in *our* closet last night? Looking for this thing?'

Embarrassed, AnnaLise said, 'Well, I—'

'Because later, thinking about what you said, I didn't see why you'd be turning down our bed.' Lacey struck a proud pose. 'It wasn't turned down any other night, and in mysteries that's the first clue the detective looks for: something out of place.'

'And I was out of place,' AnnaLise admitted. 'If it's any comfort, my plan was to search everybody's room. You just happened to be the one who caught me.'

Lacey blinked, this time just once. 'And did you?'

'Did I . . .?'

'Search everybody's room for that bag?'

'Uh, no,' AnnaLise admitted. 'In fact, your room was the first and only place I looked.'

'Well, that's not very comprehensive of you,' Lacey said like a disapproving chief inspector in a middle-school play. Then her face changed. 'But if you didn't keep searching, how did you find it?'

'I didn't. Whoever attacked me must have stashed it here.'

'Interesting.' The girl was evidently warming to her mock investigation. 'So it wasn't there when—' Lacey's hand flew to her mouth. 'Ohmigod, that's what you meant by something *on* the bag. Fingerprints!'

And maybe – worse – blood, thought AnnaLise. The bag had felt damp to her touch when she'd grabbed it away from the teenager.

'This is *so* like in the mystery novels,' Lacey was saying, her eyes now like saucers. 'I touched the bag, so now my fingerprints will be on the thing.'

'Mine, too. But at least we have each other to explain why.'

Lacey slumped her shoulders, but seemed to lighten up, too. 'That's true, isn't it?' Another glance down. 'So, do you think it's OK for us to look inside while it's still here?' She took a hesitant step forward.

AnnaLise stopped her. 'Uh-unh. The two of us have probably done enough damage.'

'Well, OK. But we should call the police. You were assaulted.'

And have the bump to prove it, thankfully. Even so, AnnaLise didn't relish handing Coy and Charity yet another piece of evidence against her in the form of the floral bag. Especially given where it had apparently been hidden. 'It's nearly ten.'

Lacey looked the most surprised AnnaLise had seen her to date. 'And that's late here?'

Outside, snow was piling up on the balcony above the French door's sill. 'In this kind of weather, yes.'

Lacey cocked her head. 'But Officer Fearon is right downstairs. We can report the attack on you and give *him* the bag. Want me to get him?'

'Please,' AnnaLise said. The girl was right, of course, and there was no use putting it off.

The teenager started for the hall door.

'But first, Lacey?'

'Yes?'

'Bring Mr Hoag up here, OK?'

'Lawyer before cop. Good idea.'

The upstairs hallway had seemed large when AnnaLise had arrived Wednesday afternoon, but with the entire assemblage of guests crammed elbow-to-elbow in it, the space now seemed awfully tight.

'Are you sure you weren't badly hurt?' Patrick Hoag whispered to AnnaLise. They were standing just inside her bedroom with Lacey Capri, while Gary Fearon, hovering over the floral bag, pulled on latex gloves.

'Yes, and thank you for being here. You're the closest thing I have to legal counsel right now.'

Hoag opened his mouth, but AnnaLise didn't give him a chance to comment or, more likely, object. 'I know, I know. You can't represent me, Patrick. But you're an officer of the court, so I figured it couldn't hurt to have you around when Lacey brought in Officer Fearon. I just didn't expect,' she scanned the crowd, 'that everybody else would come with you.'

That included both of AnnaLise's mothers, who had immediately rushed down to the kitchen, one – Daisy – returning with a bag of whole kernel corn from the freezer to soothe the bump on her daughter's head and the other – Mama – a bag of frozen green beans. AnnaLise had finally been forced to banish both them and their cryogenic veggies to the hallway.

'Everybody was in the Lake Room,' Lacey said apologetically. 'Word traveled kind of fast.'

'Welcome to Sutherton,' AnnaLise heard Joy say from somewhere in the mob.

Fearon was lowering the small bag into a larger, clear plastic one, carefully making sure the handle and straps went in as well.

Straps? 'Is that a backpack?' AnnaLise asked, squinting. The second shoulder strap must have been hidden underneath the bag as it lay on Hart's chair, but she'd been right that it would fit a change of clothes and a toothbrush. Definitely *not* a bottle-cum-murder-weapon, which explained why the killer hadn't thought to stuff the champagne bottle inside the bag and dispose of both as Joy had suggested.

'Looks like it.'

'Do you see any blood?'

Fearon glanced up reflexively. 'Not on preliminary visual examination. You have reason to expect there would be?'

AnnaLise nodded. 'The champagne bottle that killed Dickens was found on the chair where that sat the night before. I thought if Dickens' blood had gotten on the bag, it would explain why the killer dumped the thing.'

'In the *heiress*' closet.' The stage whisper sounded like Lucinda's voice. 'What a coincidence.'

'Shut your mouth, you hear?' Mama's also disembodied voice growled.

AnnaLise feared things might come to blows in the peanut gallery, but Officer Fearon just stood up calmly. 'I've spoken with Coy and he wants me to secure this in the master bedroom until they and the county arrive tomorrow morning. The snow's bad and getting worse. Some accidents on the mountain roads need responding to.'

'Tomorrow?' Lacey asked anxiously. 'Did you tell them we touched it? AnnaLise *and* me?'

'I did, little lady. Don't you worry.'

Lacey beamed and nodded before wading back through the crowd.

AnnaLise, for her part, was feeling considerably less cheery. 'Can you tell if anything is in that thing, Gary?'

'Not without pawing through it,' Fearon said. 'Can I ask what you were hoping for, AnnaLise?'

'A luggage tag with Debbie Dobyns' name on it?' asked Tyler Puckett, head just inside the doorway. He and Eddie Boccaccio laughed.

'Steady girl,' AnnaLise's pseudo-lawyer whispered. 'Don't let the bastards grind you down.'

She smiled grimly. 'The way things are going, if they do find identification on that thing my name'll probably be on it.'

'You wear flowered backpacks?'

'Not past seventh grade, though Daisy probably still has them all squirrelled away somewhere.'

Hoag threw her a worried look. 'Please tell me this isn't one of them.'

'Don't worry, Patrick. It's not.'

The attorney let out the breath he must have been holding.

After Hoag re-oxygenated, AnnaLise asked, 'How bad is this?'

'Honestly? I don't know. Theoretically, despite your version of events, it's possible you knocked yourself on the head.'

AnnaLise started to protest, but Hoag waved her down. 'I'm just saying it would have been a whole lot better for the bag to be found in a dumpster somewhere between Sutherton and the Atlanta airport.'

'As in, jettisoned by Debbie?'

'Exactly. It's tough to envision how she could have put it in your closet at any time, much less assault you just a few minutes ago.'

AnnaLise had been watching Fearon with the evidence bag, but now she turned to Hoag. 'Which means, obviously, that our killer is still somewhere here in this house.'

THIRTY-FOUR

'Hart's fountain is frozen.'

AnnaLise, sitting cross-legged on her bed, rubbed her arms to reduce the goose pimples. 'Could you close the balcony door, please? It's already freezing in here.'

Joy Tamarack turned, snowflakes flecking her hair. 'You don't want to see this? It's really pretty cool. The water nymphs look like something out of a sci-fi movie and the circle drive could host a hockey game.'

'I'll pass. Close, please?'

Joy complied and climbed up next to AnnaLise, filching a cookie from the plate on the comforter.

Before taking a bite, Joy asked, 'Toll House Chocolate Chip?'

'Mama made them fresh for me.' AnnaLise gingerly touched her goose egg and decided she needed another cookie. 'Since I got hurt.'

'Mmmm.' A crumb squatted on Joy's lower lip. 'Imagine the spread she'd put out for a funeral.'

AnnaLise gaped at her supposed friend. 'That's a horrible thing to say.'

'I'm just talking special events. You know, baptisms, weddings, anniversaries, whatever.'

'And your first thought in that line goes to funerals?'

'I didn't say yours, in particular, though I do think you have to face the fact somebody wants you out of the way.'

'Dead?' AnnaLise pointed at the crumb.

Joy salvaged it. 'Or in prison. So long as you're sentenced for Hart's murder, it would serve the same purpose.'

Why didn't Joy's elaboration make AnnaLise feel better? 'Listen, thanks for agreeing to this sleep-over. I really don't want to be alone tonight.'

'Understood. Not sure why you wouldn't let me bring the snubbie, but so long as the gig includes chocolate and red wine, I'm here for you.' She lifted her glass.

'Spoken like a staunch supporter.' They clinked glasses in an undedicated toast and AnnaLise plumped two pillows behind her before taking a sip of her own wine. 'So, what do you think?'

'I think you caught somebody in the process of planting the bag in your closet. You said you felt blood on it?'

AnnaLise shook her head. 'No, just dampness. I wasn't thinking straight – obviously any blood from Wednesday night would certainly be dry by now. Especially on a nylon backpack.'

Joy's face grew thoughtful. 'So, it was washed?'

'Or thrown into the lake and retrieved. But by whom?'

'Oooow, let me think. Oh, I know: the murderer. Duh.' Joy snatched another cookie. 'And the reason, if you're going to ask that next, is to pin the crime on you.'

AnnaLise rubbed her forehead. 'OK, maybe a recap will help clarify this mess for me. On Wednesday night, Dickens Hart went to his suite at eleven-fifteen only to be killed sometime after that.

Whoever did it took the floral bag away with them, presumably because leaving it there would somehow implicate them.'

'We'd hoped that person was Debbie, but she obviously doesn't have the bag, and you – as the saying goes – have been left holding it.'

'Amen to that,' AnnaLise said. 'Debbie also says I'm the one who called to tell her she was fired.'

'You need to call that lawyer.'

The consensus opinion, seemingly. 'You think it's that bad?'

'It's been that bad for a while. Now it's knee-high to dire and nigh on catastrophic. If we weren't like best buds, even *I'd* think you did it.'

'Thanks,' said AnnaLise, going for deadpan. 'But there's a witness. Roy Smoaks saw a woman toss that bag into the lake. Would I do that only to fish it out and plant the thing in my own room?'

'Smoaks saw somebody toss something into the water.' Joy took her third cookie. 'And, pray tell, was that before or after he, undoubtedly drunk, shot out Hart's window?'

'After.'

'My point is that Smoaks is not exactly poised on a stack of Bibles, much less a witness stand.'

'Well then, if he's not a credible witness, we'll make him a suspect,' AnnaLise said. 'When Coy and Charity get here, I'll have Boozer give them the bullet. They can match it to the rifle Smoaks was using.'

'Didn't you say it hit the fireplace?'

'Yes.' AnnaLise had reached for another cookie herself but stopped mid-air. 'Why?'

Joy shrugged. 'You're a police reporter. Yet I, a fitness trainer, have to tell you that a slug suffering that kind of damage is pretty much useless for matching to anything?'

'A fitness trainer who *packs*,' AnnaLise reminded her, but dropped her cookie hand back into her lap. 'Besides, the gun is likely Bobby's and I wouldn't want to implicate him.'

Joy gave her a disbelieving look. 'Girl, you are way beyond worrying about other people. "Implicate" Bobby and Smoaks. Hell, implicate me if you have to.'

'I wouldn't do that.' AnnaLise looked at her friend. 'I mean, unless you actually did it.'

'If wishes were horses, Hart would have been trampled years

ago. But no, I had nothing to do with this. I'm just saying you can benefit from all the reasonable doubt you can muster.'

Reasonable doubt. Like in a trial. A murder trial. 'OK, breathe.'

'Huh?' Joy asked.

'Not you, me. I'm trying to control my breathing. Find serenity and maybe . . . um, stabilize my core.'

'Hey, I'm all for mind-body fitness crap, but if you want flat abs, lay off the cookies. If you want inner peace let's go through your timeline to see who we should throw to the wolves.'

'Oh, yeah, good idea,' AnnaLise said, one hand going reflexively to the bump on the back of her head. Calm down and focus. She climbed off the bed to get paper and a pen from the desk, then settled back down on the comforter. 'So we know Dickens went to bed at eleven-fifteen.'

'And everybody else pretty much immediately thereafter.'

'They all trooped upstairs?'

'That's my memory.'

'I was already in bed,' AnnaLise said, 'when I heard the group moving, so that matches up. And you said you were getting a nightcap and came to your room about . . . eleven-thirty?'

'Uh-unh.' Joy shook her head. 'I was right on the heels of the group. Where did you get eleven-thirty? It didn't take me fifteen minutes to pour even a jumbo glass of wine.'

AnnaLise sat up straighter. 'Well, somebody went by my hallway door, I'm sure of it. And Shirley had come upstairs with me earlier, so she was already in her room.'

'Maybe she went back downstairs for something?'

'I don't think so,' AnnaLise said. 'Nicole was in the kitchen or foyer until almost midnight when Sal picked her up. She would have seen anybody who came down.'

'I went out like a light,' Joy said, 'so I'm not going to be much help with your timeline from this point onward.'

'Well, the footsteps came down the hallway past my room and a door opened and closed. I guess I just assumed it was you.'

'Nobody would be wandering to find a bathroom, obviously, since each room has its own en suite.'

'True.' AnnaLise realized she was worrying her lip again and forced herself to give the poor body part a break. 'Maybe a booty call, as our dear Rose would say?'

'Hell-on-wheels, I like that woman,' Joy said with a grin. 'But again, there are only two suites past this room of yours. It wasn't me, and Shirley's too mature for casual sex.'

'Tell it to my mother,' AnnaLise muttered under her breath. 'Maybe somebody went to the corridor closet to get an extra blanket or something?'

'No linens in there, at least in my time. Besides, did you hear them come back with their "blanket or something"?'

'No. That's why I assumed it was you.'

'Again, Einstein, it wasn't.' Joy had been examining the cookies – probably deciding which merited her next selection – but now she turned toward AnnaLise. 'Despite my giving you permission to implicate me.'

'I know, and continuing thanks for that. But then who was it, and where did they go?'

Joy was already pushing herself off the bed. 'I can't answer the "who," but if he or she didn't join me in my room or Shirley in hers, maybe they hid in yet another closet.'

'But Dickens' bedroom is downstairs. Why come up here at all?'

'Like you said, Nicole had a clear view of the halls on the main floor. Maybe whoever it was came out of Hart's bedroom and, catching sight of Nicole, panicked and huddled on the steps. Once there, there was nowhere to go but—'

'Up. I follow you. Not sure I believe it, but I got it.'

'Let's go take a look-see.' Joy, bounding like a cat, was already at the bedroom door.

'For what? The killer can't possibly still be there.' Unless, AnnaLise thought, he or she was playing musical closets.

Joy shook her head. 'But maybe they left signs. You know, what a trial judge calls "evidence"?'

That caught AnnaLise's attention as she moved the depleted plate of cookies to her nightstand. 'Well, maybe—'

'Great. I'll get my snubbie.'

'You just want an excuse to carry your gun.' The journalist had started to follow, but stopped in her tracks. 'I'd feel safer without it.'

'In that case,' Joy said, opening the door. 'After you.'

'It's past midnight,' AnnaLise whispered as she stepped out into the hallway. 'Keep your voice down.'

Ignoring her, Joy led the way along the corridor – bypassing her own suite and, blessedly, the snubbie – before unceremoniously throwing open the hall closet door. 'Well, I see nothing has changed since my time here, except the boxes of crap are packed in even tighter. God knows what could be—'

But AnnaLise's eyes had narrowed. 'Boxes?' She lifted the flap of the closest one. 'Joy, this is a carton of books.'

'Yeah?' She yawned, seeming already tired of the game if she couldn't play it armed. 'So what? Hart always had a million of 'em.'

'But—' AnnaLise exhaled as thoroughly as she could, to slip sideways into the walk-in clost between its wall and the stack. Contorting her way through the maze of boxes to the adjoining perpendicular wall, she saw her goal: a doorframe, mostly hidden behind yet another highrise of cartons and, again, just far enough from the wall for her to slip through and crack open the frame's door carefully to peer into the room. 'This leads to Dickens' library.'

'Really?' Joy herself shimmied and slalomed along the maze behind her friend.

AnnaLise swung the door wider to reveal Hart's library in all its cushy glory, the reading chair illuminated by snow-softened exterior lights. 'Makes sense. It would be so much easier for movers to use the elevator and then get books and furniture in this way, rather than up those narrow stairs in the bedroom from Dickens master suite. And the huge—'

But Joy Tamarack, apparently not thinking about the convenience of workmen, stepped out into the room and, fists on hips, looked around. 'Why, that little *bitch*.'

THIRTY-FIVE

'So, you think Sugar Capri knew about that upstairs entrance we found to Dickens' library?'

They were back on AnnaLise's bed, both sitting cross-legged but whispering like two seventh-graders in study hall.

'She must have known,' said Joy. 'How else could Sugar have snuck into our marital bedroom without anybody ever seeing her? And believe me, I asked. The only way that I even tipped to it was finding a scrunchy under one of Hart's pillows.'

'A scrunchy?'

'Yeah, the fabric-covered elastic bands for your hair?'

'Oh, sure. Mama was always trying to make me pull my hair back in one.' AnnaLise absently put a hand to the back of her head, then started from the still-tender lump there. 'Of course.'

Joy said, 'What?'

'The flowered bag. It's not just a backpack, but a backpack *purse*. That's why the thing's so small, with the handle in addition to the straps.'

'OK. But . . . so?'

'So I bet this one belongs to Sugar.'

Joy looked doubtful. 'I'd be thrilled to have her added to our list of suspects, only your point feels like something of a leap.'

'No, focus. You've seen Sugar's wardrobe. Babydoll dresses and plaid miniskirts, knee-highs and berets. All nineties fashions, and I'd also bet they didn't come from a vintage clothing store but the woman's very own closet. Why not a backpack purse from the same fashion era?'

Now Joy's features turned thoughtful. 'The thing does look like the nineties threw up on it.'

AnnaLise was thinking of her conversations with both Sugar and Lacey. 'Sugar said that Dickens bought her clothes way back then, and I got the impression that money is tight now for the two-person Capri family. Lacey said she hadn't been enrolled in a traditional school because they'd been moving a lot.'

'So they're poor. That doesn't mean Sugar killed Hart. I mean, why would she?'

'Don't know,' AnnaLise admitted. 'Sugar herself told me that she hoped to get back with Dickens. Romantically, that is. Can't you imagine her carefully packing his gifts to her in order to wear them for him when she arrived here?'

'Sadly,' Joy said, looking none too pleased, 'I can. And as pathetic as the picture of the current-day Sugar sneaking into his room *Auld Lang Syne*, why would she then kill the aging goose that still might not only lay her, but the golden egg?'

Joy did have a way with words. 'Because . . . granted, a reach, but he turned her down?'

'So hell actually *has* frozen over.'

AnnaLise flopped a hand toward her window, where the snow was howling by horizontally. 'You be the judge.'

'Cute,' said Joy. 'But I *told* you. Even if Hart's dick—'

'Joy. Please?'

'I *do* seem to make you keep saying that to me.'

'Because you keep painting word pictures that I will *never* be able to get out of my head.'

'And you think that image of Sweet Sugar sneaking into my ex's room wearing nothing but thigh-high knee socks and a cute little beret is pleasant for *me*?'

AnnaLise drew in a deep breath, then exhaled, saying, 'I didn't realize that it still stung, but of course it should. You just always seem so strong that I don't—'

'Oh, it doesn't sting, girl.' Joy was stretching both arms over her head. 'Barely registers, in fact. I just wanted to see how righteous indignation feels.' Lifting the top sheet, she slipped between it and the fitted one beneath. 'I must say it's not bad. I can see why you enjoy it.'

'Thank you.' AnnaLise was trying to maintain her patience.

'You're welcome. Now, you were saying?'

'I was saying,' AnnaLise said through clenched teeth, 'that your ex-husband *slash* my father, Dickens Hart, was ill and in pain. His pride might have kept him from telling Sugar *why* he was rejecting her. But if the woman was desperate, she could have—'

'Beaned him with the champagne bottle?' Joy wasn't swayed. 'Seems a little drastic for a "Not tonight, dear."'

With a sigh, AnnaLise collapsed onto her back, forearm under her head. 'Maybe we're making too many assumptions.'

'We?' Joy plumped a pillow of her own and pulled up the blanket.

'Yes, *we*. Each of us has been assuming that the floral bag belonged to the killer.'

'Why else would it have gone missing?' Joy asked. 'And subsequently turned up in your room? And how does Roy Smoaks' slicker-clad "broad" figure in?'

AnnaLise could hear sleep creeping into her friend's voice. 'Good questions. I've got to think about better answers.'

'You do that.' Joy re-settled herself. 'I'm going to get a little shuteye.' Seconds later, she was snoring softly.

But AnnaLise lay awake, staring at the ceiling. At about four a.m., she sat bolt upright, though apparently without disturbing her still-snoring bedmate. Hart's secret closet entrance, the figure in a slicker on the pier the next morning, the assault on AnnaLise and the reappearance of that floral bag – damp, but with no blood visible on it. Suddenly everything made sense.

And then, as equal parts of relief and sorrow spread through her body, the daughter with two live mothers and two dead fathers began to cry softly, so as not to cause her good friend to even stir.

THIRTY-SIX

AnnaLise jolted out of a dream she couldn't remember. The sun was shining brightly and Joy was gone. Not surprising, either, since the nightstand clock showed eleven-twenty a.m. AnnaLise could hear snatches of conversation wafting up from downstairs.

'. . . to go, Mom?' She heard Lacey Capri call out. 'The limo's here.'

'Right with you.' Sugar's voice, much closer.

AnnaLise jumped out of bed and, after grabbing a robe, opened the door just in time to see Sugar bounding down the stairs shouldering a duffel bag. 'What's going on?'

Politely, Sugar stopped halfway down. 'The sheriff's here.' She nodded toward a deputy standing by the front door in the massive vaulted foyer below. 'They've given us all permission to go home. Thank you for . . . well, just everything.'

A chill went up AnnaLise's spine. If the sheriff was letting the rest go, that meant they'd closed in on their prime suspect. As she thought that, the deputy looked up and, seeing AnnaLise, said something into the radio on the epaulet of his uniform shirt.

AnnaLise realized it had become now or never time. 'But aren't you forgetting something?'

'I don't think so,' said the woman, looking around. 'Oh! Do you mean your iPad? Lacey didn't want to disturb you, so she left it on our dresser.' A proud smile. 'With a thank you note, of course.'

In the hallway below, the deputy had been joined by Sutherton officers Coy Pitchford and Gary Fearon. All three uniformed men were now looking up at AnnaLise.

'Lacey has lovely manners, but I meant your pretty backpack purse, Sugar. I'm sure Officer Fearon will give you some kind of receipt so you can reclaim it later.'

Sugar's eyes bugged out. 'It's not mine,' she said, beginning to unsteadily descend the remaining steps one at a time, leading with her left foot.

'Oh, I'm betting it is,' AnnaLise called down. 'You haven't had a lot of resources to buy new things over the years. I'm surprised you didn't ask Dickens for money. He certainly owed you at least that.'

'I don't know what you're talking about.' Sugar was nearing the bottom of the stairs.

'Of course you do,' AnnaLise said, following the elder Capri, but slowly. 'Dickens Hart sexually assaulted you when you were just fifteen.'

'I lied to him about my age, and the sex was consensual, like I told you,' Sugar said, as the front door cracked open and Lacey entered, probably having taken her own luggage to the waiting car.

But AnnaLise couldn't let the girl's presence stop her. 'It doesn't matter what you told Dickens, Sugar. You weren't yet of an age *to* consent. Though I have to give you points for resourcefulness, if not smarts. And you *do* have an affinity for hiding in closets, it seems. Or was it Dickens who suggested you sneak into his room though the hall walk-in upstairs?'

AnnaLise could see from Coy's eyes that she now had his attention. 'That storage area connects to the library on the upper floor of Dickens' master suite. I'm sure that Officer Pitchford would have noticed if there hadn't been so many boxes piled up, blocking the door.'

She nodded at Coy. 'I missed it too, when I was snooping around the night Dickens was killed. From either door, it seemed to be a storeroom packed chock-full. No indication, even, that a second entrance existed. But last night, Joy and I noticed those boxes were just far enough from the door for a small-framed person to slip through and make their way to the other door.'

'Joy was there?' Sugar's eyes were wide.

'Yup. It was she who realized you'd used the closet access years ago to sneak into her husband's suite – well, theirs, really – without his staff seeing you. You wanted to surprise him on Wednesday night with a bottle of champagne. *His* champagne, of course, since you couldn't have afforded Dom Perignon.'

AnnaLise looked at Lacey, who had begun sniffling. 'Did you catch a chill? The lake water is cold this time of year. I didn't understand, at first, how the floral bag fit into all this. Then you, Lacey—'

'Leave her out of this!' Sugar dumped her duffel bag on the floor and, still at the bottom step, turned to confront AnnaLise.

'You let my mother alone!' Lacey screamed from below. 'She had nothing to do with it. It was all me, AnnaLise. I killed your super-rich bastard of a father.'

The sheriff's deputy and Coy Pitchford allowed themselves two seconds of astonished staring at AnnaLise and Sugar on the stairs before moving toward Lacey.

'She's lying!' Sugar said, jumping down with both feet from the last step and running to pull her daughter into her arms. 'I did it. I went to Hart's room with the champagne bottle, hoping that maybe . . . maybe if he and I got together again, Lacey and I wouldn't have to live on the streets anymore. I just thought—'

'No.' Tears streaming down her face, the daughter put a finger on her mother's lips. 'It was *my* turn to take care of us. And I would have been OK, because I brought the roofies along.'

'That's what didn't make sense,' AnnaLise said. 'The roofies were for Dickens?'

'For him? No.' Lacey's blue eyes were startled behind her tears. 'They were for *me*, of course. I put one in the empty wine glass on the dresser and added just enough wine from the other so I could choke it down. I went into the bathroom to shower and change into the nightie and when I came out I heard the old lech at the door, so I grabbed the glass and hid upstairs until *he* went into the bathroom. Then I chugged the rest and went down and climbed into his bed. I figured that by the time he came out and . . . did me, I'd be so totally out of it I wouldn't even notice, much less remember what he'd done.'

Lacey met her mother's eyes. 'That's what roofies do, right? Women don't even remember? So once it was over I'd be fine, but we'd *have* him. Because I'm so obviously underage, he'd have to give us whatever we wanted this time. Take care of us both for the rest of our lives.' Her hands were balled up now and she pounded on her mother's own slight shoulders. 'Why couldn't you just *let* me? Why did you have to bust in on everything and *hit* him?'

Sugar pushed her daughter's lush hair away from her face. 'I'm your mother, honey. It's my job to take care of us. You're just a baby.' Her voice cracked. 'My baby.'

Then Sugar Capri began to croon something that sounded like a lullaby as mother and daughter, clutching each other, sank to their knees on the marble tile floor.

THIRTY-SEVEN

Eddie Boccaccio raised his glass. 'To the Last Supper.'

'Amen,' said AnnaLise Griggs.

It was finally Sunday night, and most of the disparate people Dickens Hart had assembled for his affairs-in-order weekend were sitting around the dining room table one final time before going their equally disparate ways. Sugar and Lacey Capri were in police custody, of course, their seats taken by Boozer Bacchus and Nicole Goldstein.

AnnaLise, for the first time, sat at the head of Hart's table. She set down her glass. 'I'm sorry you had to miss your flights today. Were you all able to reschedule?'

'The airlines took pity on us,' said Eddie's mom, Rose. 'We leave tomorrow night, now that the sheriff's department has wrapped everything up.'

'And we're tomorrow afternoon?' asked Lucinda Puckett, looking at her son Tyler. He nodded back.

'Well, that's good,' AnnaLise said, feeling weary to the bone. 'Because you sure can't stay here anymore.'

Eddie gave what sounded like a genuine laugh. 'Our paternity tests have still to come back.'

AnnaLise's turn to nod. 'And, when you get those results, let me know. But for now, I think everybody will be happy to be parted from each other.'

'Hear, hear,' said Phyllis Balisteri, raising her own wine glass. The woman didn't drink, so she put it right back down again, but her call-out seemed as genuine as Eddie's laugh. 'Only, AnnieLeez, would you mind going over the whole thing one more time? For us slow learners?'

AnnaLise sighed. She just wanted to put the entire weekend behind her. But then, she wasn't a restaurateur who considered floaters good for business.

Joy Tamarack raised her hand like a second-grader volunteering an answer to her teacher's question to the class. 'Allow me?'

'Please.'

Her friend smiled. 'Usually AnnaLise communicates that as "Joy. *Please?*"' There was giggling all around at her spot-on impersonation.

Then Joy continued: 'Sugar Capri wangled an invitation this weekend, thinking she might rekindle her romance – if you can call it that – with Hart. Apparently she and Lacey had been living hand-to-mouth for years.'

'We know how that can be,' Rose said, but looking at AnnaLise rather than her son, Eddie.

Nicole seemed puzzled. 'But then how did Lacey get involved? She seemed like a nice girl. And really smart.'

'She was – is – both,' AnnaLise said, the reporter in her not being able to let Joy continue the story solo. 'Which is why Lacey decided she wasn't going to let her mom waste the rest of a lifetime with Dickens, whom Lacey saw as an "old lech." Instead, the daughter would sacrifice herself for their financial security, but just the once.'

Shirley Hart asked, 'So Lacey thought that if she could seduce Dickens, they'd be able to blackmail him?'

'Exactly.' AnnaLise glanced at Joy.

Hart's ex-wife shrugged. 'Speaking from experience, he *was* a fairly easy target, blackmail-wise.'

But Nicole still projected confusion. 'So where did the roofies come in?'

'Basically,' Joy said, 'the kid was anesthetizing herself.'

'That is just so sad.' Nicole was shaking her head.

Back to Joy. 'While Dickens was in the bathroom, Lacey drank the wine she'd doctored, then slipped into bed, wearing one of Sugar's naughty negligees. He comes out to find her there and, according to even the still-sentient Lacey, seems horrified.

'Unfortunately,' Joy went on, 'Sugar was up to her old tricks. She came through the book storage room and into the upstairs library. Mama Bear got far enough down the steps to see Hart standing over her nearly naked fifteen-year-old daughter and just reacted.'

'Had Sugar brought the champagne with her?' Shirley asked.

'Yes,' AnnaLise explained. 'You'll remember that Dickens was serving Dom Perignon as people arrived and, recognizing the label, Sugar pilfered a bottle, thinking it would make for a special reunion.'

Phyllis shook her head. 'But what about the flowered bag? Whose was that?'

'Sugar's, as I suspected,' AnnaLise directed a significant look toward Joy, 'but Lacey brought it with her to carry the roofies and her mother's negligee.'

Daisy nodded. 'So, it was Lacey who came in when you were upstairs?'

AnnaLise was pleased that her mother was following the storyline closely. 'Yes. As you'll recall, Lacey didn't watch *When Harry Met Sally* in the media room Wednesday night.'

'That's right,' Tyler said. 'I remember thinking I wasn't surprised she skipped it, given her age.'

'But, back to the act itself,' Patrick Hoag redirected. 'Sugar has just hit Dickens with the bottle, mistakenly thinking that he's about to rape her daughter. What did they do then to implicate the chef?'

'Surviving on the streets takes guts and smarts,' AnnaLise said, thinking the lawyer sounded like he was fact-finding for the defense. Or maybe, God forbid, a book contract. 'Sugar probably went into cover-up mode. She got Lacey, who was shocked yet conscious, out from under Hart, who had fallen on her. Then she wiped off the bottle and Hart's wine glass, as well as the bowl of mine, which is the only part of that glass Lacey had touched. That left my prints on its stem, though Sugar had no way of knowing they were mine. In fact, she may have assumed it was Debbie Dobyns' glass, given the Las Vegas phone number Sugar would have seen on Hart's dresser.'

'But if Lacey wasn't trying to trick anybody into *drinking* the roofies,' Nicole asked, 'why not just pop a pill and wash it down with Mr Hart's wine rather than use your glass at all?'

'Apparently she thought the residue in the glass might come in handy for later blackmail.'

'Smart kid,' Eddie said.

'But still just a kid. In fact, she didn't dissolve the roofie in Dickens' full glass of wine because she didn't like the taste of alcohol and knew she couldn't choke it all down.'

'At least the girl isn't a drinker,' Phyllis said. 'But what about that telephone call to the chef lady?'

AnnaLise looked to her friend. 'Joy?'

The fitness trainer coughed a little on her own wine, but recovered nicely and took over the narrative. 'Sugar grabbed the paper with the phone number from Hart's dresser, probably recognizing the area code as one for Vegas and therefore Debbie Dobyns'. Maybe Sugar was jealous, or maybe she already knew what her improvised plan required her to do.'

'Which was . . . what?' asked Lucinda Puckett.

'Use the number to call Debbie from the house phone here, pretending to be AnnaLise, since she obviously couldn't pass as Dickens.'

'Sugar did a fair imitation of her daughter Lacey for me,' AnnaLise contributed, 'and, apparently, an equally fine one of me for Debbie. Though I doubt the chef, having only just met me would have questioned the identity of the caller anyway.'

'What exactly did you – or Sugar – tell Debbie?' Nicole asked eagerly.

AnnaLise was starting to think it was the college student planning a book, instead of Patrick Hoag. 'Just that she was no longer needed and that I would pay her to get – and stay – as far away from Dickens as possible, and as quickly as possible.'

'Smart.' Hoag was nodding. 'Given the theme of this weekend, Debbie would think AnnaLise was protecting her inheritance from yet another person she believed to have financial designs on her father.'

Joy continued. 'Debbie was angry at the assumption, but she did as she was told. As for Sugar, her aim was to implicate the chef and slow the investigation so she and Lacey could just evaporate.'

'Speaking of Lacey,' Shirley Hart said, 'what was *she* doing all this time?'

'Not much, probably. By then she had to be feeling the effects of the Rohypnol, so I'm sure Sugar waited until Sal picked up Nicole, then snuck her daughter upstairs.'

'Tell them about the bag, AnnaLise,' Daisy prompted.

Her daughter obliged. 'When Lacey woke up the next morning, she found a note from her mother saying Sugar and the others had gone hiking. Piecing together what had happened the night before, Lacey examined the flowered backpack and saw blood on it from the champagne bottle when it was dropped on Hart's slipper chair.

'The girl had read enough detective fiction and seen enough TV to fear that just rinsing the thing in their bathroom sink with hand soap or shampoo wouldn't wash away all the traces of Hart's blood. Not only that, Lacey thought the blood in their sink trap itself could implicate them.'

'It does on television,' Rose said. 'So she decided to hide the bag in your room?'

'No,' said AnnaLise. 'Lacey took advantage of everybody being gone and went to the pier and threw the bag in the lake after weighting it down with sand from the beach.'

Phyllis pursed her lips. 'That was good thinking.'

'Yes, but Lacey didn't close the bag completely, so some of the ballast washed out.'

Now it was Lucinda who looked perplexed. 'But how do you know all this? Did Lacey tell the police everything you've just told us?'

'Most of it,' AnnaLise said. 'And Roy Smoaks – umm, a former police chief here – saw her from across the lake.'

'That far away?' Daisy asked, her nose wrinkling in disbelief.

'He had binoculars,' AnnaLise replied, 'but even so, he couldn't see her face. Just a small figure in an oversized slicker she'd pulled on as a disguise of sorts.'

Phyllis chimed in again. 'No surprise to me, Roy Smoaks spying on young women.'

'He also shot out the Lake Room window,' AnnaLise said. 'But that was just pure spite, not part of the story, as things turn out.'

'So get on with it, then,' Phyllis said, suddenly impatient, as if she'd just now realized her restaurant had been without her for days. 'A busted window is nothing around these parts, leastways in comparison to murder.'

'It was Thanksgiving morning when Lacey disposed of the bag,' AnnaLise said. 'By the time I got around to searching their room that evening—'

'Wait a minute,' Eddie interrupted. 'You searched the Capris' room?'

'AnnaLise intended to search everybody's,' Phyllis said, looking proud.

Eddie the Pill-popper didn't look pleased. 'But you—'

'Not to worry,' AnnaLise said, reaching out to pat his hand. 'My attention was diverted and I never got around to the other guests' rooms. Which doesn't mean that everyone else shouldn't keep their own houses in order.'

'Point taken,' said Eddie.

'Fine, fine,' Daisy said to him. 'You're not going to abuse prescription drugs anymore. Now, can we get on with my daughter's story?'

'So,' AnnaLise said, resisting the urge to laugh at her mother's new-found forthrightness, 'the floral bag was already in the lake when Lacey interrupted my search. Doubly good for them, since not only had there been the blood to consider, but word had already gotten around that I'd seen the thing on Hart's bedroom chair.'

'But then, how did it end up in *your* room?' Rose sounded testy. 'And who popped out of your closet?'

'When Lacey told Sugar not only about the bag, but that she suspected I was looking for it in their room, Sugar got worried.' AnnaLise turned to Joy. 'Remember on Friday, when you and I were on the patio with Patrick and I was freaking out about being arrested?'

'Which time?'

AnnaLise ignored her. 'Anyway, I thought I heard the side door. Turns out Sugar had sent Lacey to make sure the bag was either safely gone or to hide it better.'

'That must be why Lacey was sniffling this morning at breakfast,' Daisy said. 'What kind of mother sends her daughter into a freezing cold lake?'

AnnaLise didn't bother with the 'you don't get colds from being cold' battle she'd always fought with her own mother, but continued. 'Anyways—'

Now Lucinda interrupted. 'That gaudy thing was still there?'

'The sand had only partially been washed out, as I said. The bag began to rise and one of the straps got caught on the pier piling. Figuring any evidence was long gone, Lacey managed to pluck it out and wipe it off before stuffing the thing under her coat to bring back to the house. I was with Sugar when she came in, but all I saw was Lacey's head around the corner as she told her mother she was "back from her walk" and intent on taking a hot bath.'

'Sounds like a signal,' Daisy said. 'Between the two of them, I mean. But, as Rose keeps asking, why put it in your room?'

'By then, I'm thinking that Debbie and I were clearly neck-and-neck for chief suspect. The bag being discovered in my room probably seemed like the final nail in my coffin. By the time the police sorted it out – *if* they sorted it out – mother and daughter would have been long gone.'

Daisy visibly shivered, but it was Tyler who asked the next question. 'So it was Sugar you surprised? But if you'll recall it was Lacey who sent you to look for the iPad charger in the first place. Wouldn't she know her mother was there?'

'They wanted me to find the bag, but with Lacey as witness, so I'd be forced to turn it in. Only problem was that Sugar was delayed because she had trouble getting the thing to stay on the high closet shelf, given how short she is. Well, that most of us are.' She glanced around the table.

'And?' Phyllis prompted.

'*And* Lacey practically collided in the hallway with her mother after Sugar knocked me down. Realizing what had happened, Lacey came in to do damage control.'

Phyllis, seeming placated, muttered, 'The younger really *was* wilier than the older.'

'Smarter, certainly,' AnnaLise said. 'Once inside my bedroom, Lacey even managed to pick up the bag, so any of her own prints she might have missed throughout all this would be accounted for.'

'But what about Sugar's fingerprints?' Nicole asked, frowning. 'She's the one who couldn't get the bag on the shelf.'

'Let me, let me,' Joy said, waving her hand. 'Remember the thigh-high knee socks Sugar wore with the short skirt to go hiking?'

'I don't think any red-blooded American male ever would forget them,' Eddie Boccaccio said. 'But please don't tell me she wore them as gloves while planting the bag.'

'Well, it turns out she did, yes.' Joy shot eye-daggers at the man for stepping on her line. 'It explains why Sugar botched the job. The woman had socks on her hands.'

'It's all so horribly sad.' Nicole slid back her chair and stood to clear the table. 'A modern O'Henry's *The Gift of the Magi*. By Sugar and Lacey each trying to save the other, they . . .'

'. . . destroyed everything,' AnnaLise finished softly for the college student. 'Including Dickens Hart.'

Rose Boccaccio was the last to leave the next day. AnnaLise was by the mansion's door, having already said goodbye to all the other guests.

Rose rolled up in her wheelchair and dropped a plastic sandwich bag containing a dried, leafy substance in AnnaLise's hand.

She looked down at it. 'Don't tell me you're giving up weed.'

'Hell, no. I'm just not quite old or stupid enough to try carrying marijuana onto a plane.'

AnnaLise smiled and tossed the bag into the foyer's decorative waste basket. 'It was genuinely good meeting you.'

'Same here.' The older woman hesitated.

'Is something wrong?' As much as AnnaLise liked Rose, the new owner of Hart's Head had been being very honest the night before at dinner. She wanted all these people gone.

Now.

Rose stammered a little. 'I'm afraid I have a confession.'

'You snagged something else besides pot?'

'No.' She shook her head and looked up at AnnaLise. 'I heard the elevator that night.'

'The night of Dickens' . . . death?' Sugar may not have been protecting herself, but she'd certainly thought she was protecting her daughter. Homicide, certainly, but murder? Though who knew how the district attorney or jury would see it?

'Yes,' Rose said. 'I was having a little late-night smoke and, as you know, my room was closest to the elevator. I thought I heard something and rolled out into the hallway, and there were Sugar and Lacey. No way was the girl getting off that elevator under her own power. I couldn't be much help physically, but I did,' she tapped her armrests, 'let Sugar use my wheelchair to get Lacey to their room.'

'Did Sugar tell you what happened?'

'She did.' Rose took AnnaLise's hand. 'I apologize that suspicion had to fall on you. I just felt so sorry for the two of them. I . . . well, I'd been there. On my own, like Sugar, with a child to protect. And needing to anesthetize myself, as Lacey did, against my only option at the time. Once the two of them were safely away, I'd have gone to the police. There was never any intention on their side or mine to let you take the punishment for this.'

AnnaLise remembered how Rose had looked at her and not her son, Eddie, during the 'hand-to-mouth' exchange at the 'Last Supper.' 'It's OK, Rose. And I do appreciate your telling me now.' She leaned down and kissed the woman's musk-scented cheek.

'It's the least I could do,' Rose said, rolling over the threshold and out onto the porch before executing a one-eighty in her chair. 'We have to stick together, you know?'

'Because we're family?' AnnaLise asked, wondering what Bobby Bradenham would have to say about that sentiment after weathering the visit by Grandpa Smoaks.

'Because we're women.' Rose grinned. 'And don't worry, dear. My Eddie's not your half-brother.'

'But you told me you weren't sure.'

'Ach, I was being melodramatic. Fact is Dickens couldn't get up his nerve, much less his *kielbasa* that night.'

'But his diary said—'

'Dickie probably remembered his sexual "debut" as he chose to. Who am I to crush a young man's wet dreams?'

With that and a wave, discreet cougar Rose Boccaccio rolled down the ramp and off into her proverbial sunset.